Desert
Star

BOOK YOUR PLACE ON OUR WEBSITE AND MAKE THE ARABESQUE ROMANCE CONNECTION!

We've created a customized website just for our very special Arabesque readers, where you can get the inside scoop on everything that's going on with Arabesque romance novels.

When you come online, you'll have the exciting opportunity to:

• View covers of upcoming books

• Learn about our future publishing schedule (listed by publication month and author)

• Find out when your favorite authors will be visiting a city near you

• Search for and order backlist books

• Check out author bios and background information

• Send e-mail to your favorite authors

• Join us in weekly chats with authors, readers and other guests

• Get writing guidelines

• AND MUCH MORE!

Visit our website at
http://www.arabesquebooks.com

Desert Star

KIM CARRINGTON

BET Publications, LLC
http://www.bet.com
http://www.arabesquebooks.com

ARABESQUE BOOKS are published by

BET Publications, LLC
c/o BET BOOKS
One BET Plaza
1900 W Place NE
Washington, DC 20018-1211

All Kensington Titles, Imprints, and Distributed Lines are available at special quantity discounts for bulk purchases for sales promotions, premiums, fund-raising, and educational or institutional use. Special book excerpts or customized printings can also be created to fit specific needs. For details, write or phone the office of the Kensington special sales manager: Kensington Publishing Corp., 850 Third Avenue, New York, NY 10022, attn: Special Sales Department. Phone: 1-800-221-2647.

BET Books is a trademark of Black Entertainment Television, Inc. ARABESQUE, the ARABESQUE logo, and the BET BOOKS logo are trademarks and registered trademarks.

First Printing: December 2005

10 9 8 7 6 5 4 3 2 1

Printed in the United States of America

Acknowledgments

For the past three years my life as a published author has been very sweet, and I thank my God for each and every blessing he has bestowed upon me.

To Linda Gill, Demetria Lucas, and Guy Chapman, thanks to all of you for your hard work and the dedication you gave to my novels. You're an unbeatable team!

Words will never be enough to express how I feel about my sister, Karen Adams. I really appreciate the work you did organizing my book signings in Atlanta and doing all the publicity work. Thank you for teaching me how to love myself, bringing out the best in me, and accepting Kim, no matter what. I love you.

I am so grateful to Malaika Wilcher and Jackie Hyche, for all the enthusiasm they showed at my book signings in Jacksonville, Florida. You guys really created an atmosphere of excitement and got the ball rolling and sales jumping. Thank you.

Where on earth would our students be without teachers like Mrs. Connie Korte, from the DePaul School—West Beaches? Thank you for proofreading and editing the manuscript for *Desert Star*, and getting it ready for my editor. You are truly a phenomenal teacher and friend.

I would also like to thank Susan Miller, the reservation agent at America West Airlines. Your expertise gave *A Special Place* and *Desert Star* more authenticity when my characters traveled.

Without the love and support of my family none of this would be possible. Thank you, James, Nia, and Marc, for putting up with all the times I literally lived at the computer desk so that I would make my deadline. I love you all the more than words can express.

Chapter 1

Jill stood looking out the window of her apartment admiring the breathtaking view of the Colorado mountains. The sun was rising and casting a golden glow over everything its rays touched. It was a view she had come to adore, but had never taken for granted. Jill smiled to herself, taking another long sip of her coffee and leaning against the wall. Her life had come full-circle in the last year. Never in her wildest dreams had she thought she would be living out West and preparing for her own wedding. She had found all the happiness she had secretly been longing for in Durango.

At first, she thought she would miss the hustle and excitement of New York, but knew she had much more to gain by leaving it all behind and following her heart. She had a new, extended family—Bebe and Sharon were like sisters to her, and Tony and Eric like brothers. After working so closely with Bebe Simmons on the grand opening of her fiancé Kyle Robert's spa and ranch, A Special Place, Jill had become quite fond of her. Now, the two women were more like sisters. Tony and Eric, Kyle's brothers, who were co-owners of the property, were warm, kind, and funny. Jill had accepted them into her heart as family long before Kyle had popped the big question. Although Jill thought of Eric's wife, Sharon, as a spoiled and pampered housewife, she was family too as far as Jill was concerned. She enjoyed her future sister-in-law's company and tried to look past her faults. She still marveled at how it had all come together.

Even with all these new relatives, Jill wondered if she would be able to manage being even farther away from her family. New York had been only a short plane flight to Pittsburgh. Now she truly had to fly cross-country to visit her parents, Rob and Maddie Alexander, and her sister, Barbara, whom everyone called Barbie. Though it was tough, Jill had been able to manage it so far, mostly because she made it a point to go home almost every time she and Bebe went back East on business. Jill definitely missed her family and was happy that her mother and sister would be in Durango to help with the final details of the wedding in the next few weeks.

All the preparations for the wedding were made and, aside from having her Vera Wang dress altered, Jill was ready for the big day. Initially, she had wanted the event to be small and intimate, but she had already received over four hundred of the five hundred invitations she and Kyle had sent out.

After her soon-to-be in-laws had handed her their guest list, she realized that it would be anything but small. The Roberts's guest list alone came to 250 people, and Jill was surprised that she had a little over that number as well. But weddings were supposed to be a time to bring families and friends together, and everyone would have a chance to celebrate the love two people shared. Jill wanted her union to be a celebration of the perfect love she and Kyle shared, so she didn't mind that the wedding was to be a big event.

Jill's heart warmed, and she smiled as she thought of the man she would marry soon. Her relationship with Kyle was more of a fairy tale than anything else. That was all she could compare it to. Her finger circled the rim of the warm cup as she thought about him, and how he had become her soul mate. Kyle was the stuff her dreams were made of. Though she hadn't allowed herself to admit it at first, she knew the moment she laid eyes on him that there was a connection. It was as Darlene, her ex-next door neighbor had said: her life had become perfect without her even trying. She had fought falling in love, but in the end love did have its way with her. Now that she was in a place as close to paradise as she could find, Jill was happy that love had found its way into her heart.

The phone rang, breaking her thoughts of Kyle. She glanced at the clock as she walked toward the phone. Seeing that it was 8:30 a.m., she knew immediately who it was. Jill set her coffee on the table and picked up the cordless phone.

"Good morning, Bebe," she said, happy her friend and business partner had called.

"Jill, did I wake you?" Bebe asked anxiously.

"No, I was already awake. Is everything all right?"

"No, everything is a mess. I need to talk to you. Will you be in the office early today?"

"I will be if you need me. Bebe, what's going on?" Sensing the sound of alarm in Bebe's voice, Jill sat down at the table and prepared for some bad news.

"Jill, do you remember what I did with the contract on the McMartin account?" Bebe asked frantically. Jill smiled as Bebe continued hurriedly, "I have been up all night and I can't find it anywhere. I remember signing it, but after that I don't know what I did with it."

"Bebe, calm down."

"I can't calm down. That contract was supposed to be in the mail today. Jill, I've been looking all night, and I can't find it anywhere. I drove back to the office twice to look for it, and it's nowhere to be found," Bebe said in a frustrated voice.

"Bebe, you gave the contract to me, remember?"

"I did?"

"You gave it to me last night as we were leaving the office. I offered to put it in the mail since I had to drive past the post office on my way home," Jill reminded her.

"Oh, Jill, I forgot all about that. I did give the envelope to you last night as you got into your car. I can't believe I did that," Bebe said as she let out a sigh of relief.

Jill snickered at her friend's absentminded behavior. "Do you still need to go to work early today?"

"Are you kidding? I think I'm going to lie down for a little bit and get some rest. I am so tired and worn out from searching for the contract. I'll be in before noon though."

"That's the beauty of being your own boss, you can pretty much come and go as you please."

"Yes, and I love it. What do you have planned?"

"I think I'm going to stop by Kyle's before I go into the office."

"How is the redecorating coming along?"

"It's coming along well. I can't wait till you see what I'm doing with the living room," Jill said excitedly, as she thought of her decorating project.

"I hope you're not going with your mom's suggestion of the rose-printed curtains."

Jill laughed. "No, but I am trying to give it a more feminine touch. I'm giving the bedroom a few of my own personal touches, but I'm leaving his office alone."

"I'm sure Kyle is thankful for that," Bebe joked.

"Hey, my baby loves what I'm doing to the place. Besides, he wants me to make the place comfortable for me too."

"Okay, I better go before we're on the phone for an hour with your stories about Kyle. I'll see you later."

"See you later, Bebe."

Jill rose from the table and went to take a quick shower. She dressed in a pair of jeans and a long-sleeved, tailored white blouse. *This, too, is the beauty of being your own boss, making up your* own *dress code*; she thought as she smiled to herself. Of course, she had to dress to impress when she and Bebe had to meet with clients, but Jill did enjoy being able to dress causally when she went to her own office. She brushed her hair, letting it fall loose to her shoulders. Then she grabbed her purse, keys, and briefcase and headed out the door.

The drive from her place to Kyle's was only twenty minutes, but the real reason she was in such a rush was that she wanted to try and catch Kyle before he left for the ranch. If she didn't catch him before he left for the day, she wouldn't see him until lunch. She thought of calling him on her cell phone, but didn't want to make him wait for her just so that she could say good morning to him. She would rather not inconvenience him since he had to go to work also.

As she backed her car out of its parking spot, she turned on the radio and put on her sunglasses. Jill reached the entrance of her apartment complex and turned in the direction of A Special Place.

Though she wasn't speeding, she drove with a sense

of urgency as she realized that she hadn't spoken to Kyle since early yesterday evening. Since the ranch's grand opening, he and his brothers had been even busier than ever. Still, she had an insatiable need to be held and kissed by him several times a day. She felt like she was crazy in love with this man, but it was okay because he was just as crazily in love with her, and Jill knew it. She looked down at the speedometer. She was ten miles an hour over the speed limit so she lightened her foot's pressure on the gas pedal.

"Kyle, you had better still be at home. I need you," sne whispered to herself.

Pulling up in front of the cabin, she parked her Mercedes and got out. Jill walked up to the cabin and let herself in with her key. "Kyle!" she called out, but there was no answer. Jill dropped her keys on the coffee table in disappointment. She went upstairs to get the fabric samples she had chosen for the curtains in the living room and the master bedroom. She walked into Kyle's bedroom and got the samples off the dresser. Hearing a noise suddenly she froze in place. Jill strained her ears trying to detect where the faint sound had come from. After several seconds of silence, she gathered that it must have come from the horses outside.

She grabbed the samples and went back downstairs. Just as she reached the bottom step she heard the same noise again. Softly she walked to the kitchen. Jill listened intently as she walked toward the counter. Looking out the window, she could see several horses in the back of the house, but Patches was not there.

Jill assumed that Kyle had ridden his favorite horse to the ranch, and decided to leave. Just as she turned around, she jumped, startled to see Kyle standing right behind her with a big, silly grin on his face.

She slapped his arm playfully as she began to laugh. "Don't do that, you scared me half to death," she said, trying to stop her heart from racing.

Kyle wrapped his strong arms around Jill's waist and kissed her good morning. Jill returned his kiss, happy that she had not missed him, and grateful to be in his loving arms again. It had been a year since she had met him, and since then they had become so close that she already believed they were one. Jill gently caressed the nape of his neck, and couldn't imagine a day, no, not even a minute without the love of her life. Kyle represented everything that was wonderful and perfect in her world, and she would not let go of that joy for anything in the world.

Kyle's kisses became more intense as he began to slip his hand under Jill's shirt. Slowly he backed up, heading toward the living room. With her lips still locked on his in passion, Jill followed him onto the sofa.

"Kyle, we are both going to be late for work," Jill objected halfheartedly, even as she assisted him in undressing her.

"Well, it's a good thing that we work for ourselves." He continued on his quest to please not only himself, but the woman of his dreams as well.

Moments later, Jill found herself experiencing the exquisite lovemaking that she had come to appreciate and expect.

Kyle kissed her beautiful brown skin from head to toe, only stopping briefly to gently lick the areas that made her pant with pleasure. After his tongue finished tantalizing her body with its touch, Kyle positioned himself above her and she opened her legs to take him in.

They had made love countless times in the year they had been together, but Jill still found herself arching her back to accommodate the massive size of his manhood. Kyle was a masterful and patient lover, but in his need for her, his thrusts became more forceful. Jill wrapped her arms around his back and she held him tightly to her as she breathed deeply. She matched the rhythm of his movements and soon they exploded in ecstasy together.

Kyle lay on top of her as he tried to catch his breath, and Jill continued to softly caress his strong, muscular back, which was now moist with sweat. *God, I love this man,* she thought. She looked at him, then kissed his cheek. Sheer, unadulterated contentment was the only way she could explain how she'd felt ever since she moved back to Durango to be with Kyle.

Though they had used protection this time, she couldn't wait until after the wedding when they wouldn't. Jill wanted to have his child so badly. Secretly, she prayed for a little boy who would look exactly like his father. But she didn't want to stop there; she hoped they would have at least four children, two girls and two boys. With this thought in mind she smiled and kissed the man of her dreams several more times.

"Hey, hey, what's come over you?" he asked, noticing the serene smile that graced her face, and the intense emotion in her eyes.

"I never thought I would be so in love with someone," she said softly.

Kyle kissed her lips. "I did but I was just waiting for my dreams to come in the form of you," he said, kissing each of her eyelids before he rolled off her and stood. Holding Jill's hand, he helped her off the sofa, embracing her naked body again. Kyle looked deep into Jill's eyes and could see something stirring inside her. "Is there something you want to talk to me about?"

"No," Jill answered in a low voice as she glanced at the floor.

Kyle gently placed a finger under her chin, forcing her to look at him. "Jill, I know you, and I know when something is on your mind. Don't shut me out. Let me know what's bothering you, maybe I can help."

"I want to marry you, Kyle."

Kyle chuckled and then said, "Well, you're in luck because I'll be all yours in two months." When Jill didn't smile, he knew there was a serious issue on her mind. "Jill, what's going on?" Kyle asked with a concerned look on his face.

"I want you, Kyle, I want all of you. I want to have your baby, and I feel like I'll just burst if we aren't together forever." Jill's words tumbled from her lips. She felt a little foolish letting her emotions get the best of her, but she didn't know how to control them.

Kyle smiled at her, thankful that the intense love he felt for her wasn't one-sided. He knew that Jill loved him and wanted to marry him, but only he knew just how much she meant to him. He was happy to now know that she too knew they were soul mates.

"Baby, let me tell you something. I am going to stay with you and love you until I draw my last breath. I love you and want you to have my children," he said as he kissed her. Jill smiled, assured that Kyle felt the same way she did. "I was thinking we would have about six or eight kids, you know, enough to handle my business and yours when we get old."

Jill laughed loudly as she pushed Kyle away. "Wait a minute, I was thinking maybe four kids."

"Four is not enough, baby. That's only enough for the ranch and you're going to need help too," Kyle teased.

"I think four is plenty," Jill shot back playfully.

"Okay, but I'm putting in my order first. You get whatever is left, because I need at least four."

Jill shook her head at Kyle's teasing and picked up her clothes. As she headed for the stairs, she said, "I'm going to take a shower, Kyle. I'll be sure to leave you some hot water."

"I'm not counting on it," he chided. "Hey, what do you want for breakfast?"

"Surprise me," she answered, continuing up the stairs.

Inside the master bedroom, Jill carefully laid her still-clean outfit across the bed, before she went to the bathroom to take a shower. She stepped inside the stall and let the warm water massage her back, then quickly washed herself. When she finished, she dried off and sat at the vanity Kyle had installed just for her. All of her personal toiletries and makeup were on the table. She began to apply lotion to her arms and legs; then she moisturized her face and applied her makeup. Jill pulled her hair into a quick ponytail, and when she was finished pampering herself she went back into the bedroom and dressed.

As she walked into the kitchen, she could see Kyle had put on a robe and was ready to serve her breakfast. He was a fabulous cook. Jill inhaled deeply and saw that he had made them a hearty breakfast of eggs, bacon, toast, and grits, with a glass of orange juice sitting next to each plate.

Softly with the back of her fingers, she rubbed his cheek and then whispered, "Thank you," as she sat down.

"You're welcome, love," he replied as he sat across from her.

"Kyle, you're going to be sorry one day for spoiling me so much," Jill said after they'd blessed their meal.

She began eating the delicious breakfast Kyle had made for her, and chatted about what she and Bebe had planned for the day.

Kyle sat quietly, eating his meal and patiently waiting for Jill to notice the little red box that sat right in front of her. Finally, after several minutes, she took a drink of her juice. It was then that she noticed the jewelry box. Jill looked down in shock, and then up as her eyes met Kyle's.

"Is this for me?" she said, smiling.

"Yes, it is, but I was beginning to wonder if you were ever going to notice it."

"Honey, what's this for?" she said, wiping her hands on her napkin before touching the box and the card that came with it.

"Open the card and you'll see," he said with a smug look on his face.

Jill did as she was told. She couldn't imagine what the occasion was. Her birthday had already passed. Kyle had thrown her a huge party at Jillian's, and had flown in her family for the occasion. That night, he gave her a pair of two-carat, pear-shaped, diamond and sapphire earrings. Unable to guess the reason for this gift, she opened the card and read.

Jill's face softened as she read the anniversary card. Kyle was celebrating the fact that they had known each other for one year. He was right; it was a year ago today that they had met. She didn't know how she had let the date slip her mind except that she was so busy with work, redecorating, and wedding plans.

"Oh, Kyle, I love you, baby," she said as she returned the card to its envelope.

"I love you too," he said, noting that they told each other "I love you" so many times a day that he couldn't keep track. It didn't matter, he wanted Jill to know love and feel love, and be content with *his* love. So far, it was working.

Jill picked up the jewelry box and opened it. Her eyes widened as they fell on a beautiful heart-shaped diamond necklace.

Kyle stood and walked around to where Jill sat. "Do you like it?"

"Kyle, you know I do," Jill answered honestly.

He took the necklace from her hand and undid the clasp. Carefully, he placed the necklace around her neck and fastened it. The beautiful heart fell just above her cleavage, and sparkled with her every breath.

Jill stood to allow Kyle a better look at the jewelry he had given her. He kissed the heart as it lay against her chest, and then he kissed her lips and whispered, "I'll never leave you, Jill."

"I'll never leave you either. Kyle, you are so thoughtful. I have to make this up to you. Our anniversary completely slipped my mind." She kissed him again until he released her from his embrace.

"Aahhh, and I know just how you can make it up to me too, but I'll collect on that later." He winked and gave her a sly smile. "Right now I better go take my shower. If I'm any later than I already am, Eric and Tony will think they have the day off or something."

"I better get going too. Bebe is probably already at work. She said she would be there by noon," Jill said as she cleaned the table.

With a final kiss good-bye, Kyle said, "See you later, babe," patted Jill's backside, and ran out of the kitchen.

Jill smiled and walked into the living room. She picked up her purse and keys, along with the fabric sample she wanted to show Bebe, and left the cabin. She got into her car and headed in the direction of their office, which was in downtown Durango.

As she drove, her hand gently played with the beautiful necklace Kyle had just given her. A slight smile came to her lips as she recalled his thoughtfulness. He had remembered the exact day they had met and celebrated it by not only giving her a present and making her breakfast, but also by making exquisite love to her. She had known for some time that he was the only man for her, but it seemed that Kyle had the ability to reinvent himself, giving her something new to learn about him. Today, she learned that he had a great romantic memory and she was surprised at herself that their anniversary had slipped her mind.

Jill drove in to the rear of her office building and parked next to Bebe's car. She grabbed her things and went inside.

Their company, Desert Star, wasn't as lavish or expansive as the public relations firm Jill had worked for in New York, but Jill and Bebe had put their own special touches on the place. Each woman had her own personal office. There was also a conference room for meeting with clients and a reception area for Monica, the secretary they'd hired. They had decorated the place with Native American and Spanish themes, which they both loved, and hung pictures and placed artwork tastefully around the office. Each room was painted a different hue of light brown, with curtains in burgundy and brown to match. At Jill's insistence, she and Bebe each had a huge mahogany desk in their offices. And finally, Jill had the same size office as her old boss Phil Harmon's. She smiled at the thought that she owned this business as she set her purse on the desk next to the computer.

"Jill, is that you?" she heard Bebe call from down the hall.

"Yes, it's me, I'm in my office."

She smiled at the sight of her business partner entering her office. Despite her lack of sleep the previous night, Bebe didn't look as tired as Jill imagined she would. Bebe was also dressed casually since they had no clients to see. She wore a pair of sexy, tight-fitting Seven jeans that she had dressed up by adding a beautiful salmon-colored, bell-sleeved shirt that had a V-neck but tied loosely in a bow at the neck.

Seeing the radiant glow on Jill's face, Bebe smirked. "I'm going to take a guess and say you just left Kyle." Without giving Jill a chance to reply, she took a seat in the huge leather chair in front of Jill's desk. She crossed her legs and added, "You always look like the cat that swallowed the canary when you see him first thing in the morning."

Jill leaned against the front of her desk and looked at Bebe. She was right; pleasure was written all over her face, and there was no use trying to hide it. Anyone who knew her knew that Kyle kept a smile of complete joy and utter contentment on her face, especially after he made love to her. Jill blushed slightly at her thoughts, knowing that Bebe could see right through her and knew what she was thinking.

Her fingers found their way to her neck as she gently toyed with her newly acquired piece of jewelry. She held it out, saying, "See what my man gave me?"

"Oh, Jill, it's beautiful," Bebe said. She leaned forward to get a better look at the necklace. "He sure has excellent taste. What's the special occasion?"

"Bebe, you won't believe it, today is our one-year anniversary. I can't believe that I completely forgot about it."

"But your baby didn't. Jill, you're so blessed." As Bebe finished, her voiced cracked a little, and Jill could tell that her friend wanted in on some of the romantic love she was receiving.

Kyle's youngest brother, Tony, had wasted no time or energy in letting Bebe know that he wanted to take their relationship to the next level. He had known Bebe ever since they were children, and had loved her from the moment he'd laid eyes on her. Even though they had expressed their love to each other verbally and physically, Bebe was still reluctant to give in to Tony's marriage proposal.

"Bebe, you know that this same kind of love is waiting for you," Jill said, approaching the sensitive subject tenderly.

"I know. I just don't want to do anything I'll regret. Tony is becoming impatient with me. Last night we had an argument over my not wanting to get married. Jill, I do want to spend the rest of my life with him, but I just don't want to ruin what we have now. I don't want to ruin our friendship," Bebe said hopelessly.

"Bebe, if you know you love him, if you know you want him, you better make a move or you just might lose him," Jill finished, looking at Bebe sympathetically. Not wanting to push Bebe to tears, she quickly changed the subject. "I'm going to get started on the Billingsly account. I'm going to call the company and have them overnight all the information they want included in their promotional package."

Bebe wiped her eyes gently, not wanting to smudge her mascara. "I have several letters to type and get in the mail today and only a few phone calls to make, but I should be ready by lunchtime. What did you have in mind for lunch?"

"It's up to you, Bebe."

"Why don't we go to A Special Place, and have lunch at the Ranch House with the guys? Maybe a hug and a kiss from Tony will be all I need to make it through the rest of the day," she joked.

Jill smiled at Bebe's desire to see Tony, and secretly began plotting how to make her friend see what she already knew: they belonged together.

"That sounds great. I'll be ready about noon. Oh, take a look at the fabric samples for the curtains I'm planning to order for Kyle's cabin," Jill said, as she handed the swatches to Bebe.

"I like both of these, but which one did you choose?"

"I chose the cream one. I like the texture and the color goes well with the carpet."

"I think you're right," Bebe said as she stood. She handed the samples back to Jill, told her she would see her later, and walked back to her own office.

As she worked, her mind drifted back to Bebe. She wanted desperately to help her friend but was uncertain as to how to go about it. Tonight she would talk to Kyle about the situation. She knew that he wanted to see his own brother as happily in love as he was. Jill was certain that Kyle would be able to give her some valuable input.

Before she knew it, there was a light knock on her office door. Jill looked up to see Monica standing in the doorway.

"Good afternoon, Ms. Alexander," the younger woman said timidly.

Jill glanced at her clock and saw that Monica was right, it was already 12:30 p.m. "I must have really been in the zone, I didn't realize it was so late," Jill said as she stretched. "By the way, you have to stop calling me Ms. Alexander. Please, call me Jill." She stood from her desk and grabbed her purse.

Monica smiled politely and handed Jill the day's mail. "I'll try to remember, Ms. . . . I mean Jill."

"Would you like to join Bebe and me for lunch? We're going to the Ranch House."

Monica's face lit up at the prospect of going to the beautiful resort that was the talk of the town, with her bosses, but the smile faded. "I'm afraid I can't. I'm meeting my boyfriend in town for lunch."

"Well, maybe another time then. Perhaps he would like to come out to the ranch too."

"Thanks . . . Jill," Monica said hesitantly. Addressing her boss in such an informal way made her feel uncomfortable, but it was what Jill wanted. Monica turned and walked back down the hall to her desk.

Jill got the distinct impression that she intimidated Monica and had hoped inviting the girl to lunch would make her feel more comfortable.

Another knock on the door broke Jill's train of thought. It was Bebe, who had her purse on her shoulder and was ready to go.

"Hey, Jill, you ready?" she asked.

"I sure am," Jill replied as she followed Bebe out of the office.

It was incredibly hot outside, and Jill and Bebe quickly made their way to Jill's car. Jill quickly started the engine and turned on the air conditioner. Bebe fanned herself with her hand, as she waited for cold air to blow out of the vents.

"Is that better?" Jill joked, watching her friend fan herself furiously.

"Much better," Bebe replied without shame.

Jill laughed as she pulled off and headed in the direction of the resort. As she drove, the women chatted about everything imaginable, but most importantly, they talked about Jill's wedding.

Chapter 2

As they pulled into the main entrance of A Special Place, Jill noticed that there wasn't a parking space to be had. The resort was a very popular spot for locals and visitors alike. Even those not staying there came for the use of the wonderful facilities. The place was always busy with horseback riders or people using the spa. Jillian's, the upscale restaurant Kyle had named after Jill, was booked to capacity every night, and the Ranch House was always bustling as well. Though A Special Place catered to an exclusive clientele used to the finer things in life, there was something there for everyone.

Jill found a spot in the employee parking lot. She and Bebe got out and hurried to the Ranch House. Though the lunch crowd had thinned out, she was happy to see that Kyle, Tony, and Eric were still there. Jill and Bebe joined them.

Before sitting, Jill stood behind Kyle and caressed his muscular back. He tilted his head backward and she kissed his lips. She derived as much pleasure from touching him as he did from being touched. She stopped and slid into the seat next to him and helped herself to one of his fries.

"Baby, I never come in here and find you eating anything healthy," she said as she ate another fry.

"I know, but I eat so well at home. I bet any amount of money that you make me eat a salad tonight," he said as he took another bite of his burger.

"Hello, Bebe."

"Hey, Kyle," she replied. Though she had kissed Tony hello and sat contentedly next to him holding his hand, Jill could tell that something was wrong.

"How is work going for you two?" Eric asked as a yawn escaped from him.

"So far so good, but you sound exhausted, Eric," Jill said.

"Yes, Ally had us up all night."

"I can't believe that your little angel would create any disturbance such as that," Bebe teased.

Sharon and Eric Roberts had named their newborn baby girl Alehandra Jewelita, and Tony had quickly given her the nickname of Ally. Jill sat and listened as Eric talked about his daughter, and found herself hoping one day to be giving birth to a beautiful baby for Kyle.

"Well, hello, ladies. I was beginning to wonder when you'd get here," Grace, the waitress, said, interrupting Jill's pleasant thoughts.

"Hi, Grace," Jill and Bebe said in unison.

"What can I get you for lunch?"

"I have a wedding dress to get into, so I'll have the usual," Jill answered.

"And I don't, so I'll have the special," Bebe said jokingly.

After Grace walked away, Tony slumped down in his

chair and said to Bebe, "You could fit into a wedding dress right now if you really wanted to."

"Tony, I don't want to discuss this right now," she said abruptly.

Tony began to reply, but before he could he felt a hand on his shoulder. He looked up and saw a woman standing next to him. As his eyes fell on the petite Hispanic beauty, Tony sat up in his seat. A broad smile replaced the frown as he realized who stood before him.

"Rosy, I can't believe it's you!" he said excitedly. Tony quickly stood and gave the woman a hug, as did Kyle and Eric. Eric pulled another chair to the table and offered it to Rosy and she joined them, sitting close to Tony.

Though Bebe said hello to Rosy also, she wasn't as thrilled to see her as the men were. Jill observed her friend awhile longer, trying to figure out why Bebe wasn't as happy to see the old family friend. She made a mental note to ask Bebe about the matter later, and then turned her attention back to the beautiful woman who had joined them.

Jill could tell that without her stilettos, Rosy was a short woman, probably standing only five feet tall. But the high heels not only gave the woman the appearance of height but also made her legs appear even more shapely and sexy. Rosy wore a beautiful cinnamon-colored minidress that had a halter back. The color of the dress showcased her warm, caramel-colored skin, giving her a glow that oozed sensuality.

Kyle introduced Jill to Rosy as his fiancée and the two women shook hands. Rosita Hernandez was the daughter of Miguel Hernandez, an old family friend. Like the Robertses, Miguel's family owned some valuable real estate in Durango, but not nearly as much as Kyle's family.

Kyle filled Rosy in on the details of their upcoming nuptials and asked if she would be in town for the ceremony. When she said yes, Kyle told her that he wanted her to make it a point to come to the wedding. He also told her that she had been included in the invitation that had been sent to her parents.

Rosy's full head of long thick curls bounced as she spoke with thick, full, glossy lips. Jill quickly realized that the woman had a taste for the good life. Though the Hernandez family had been sent an invitation, Rosy told them she had been spending much of her time traveling abroad and had only recently returned to Durango. Jill looked at the woman's well-manicured hands and saw a huge diamond and ruby ring on her finger and matching earrings on her ears. Rosy picked up the menu and decided what to have for lunch.

When Grace returned to deliver their orders, Jill noticed that Grace's greeting to Rosy was just about as warm as Bebe's, which intrigued Jill even more. There was more to Rosy Hernandez than what met the eye, and Jill was determined to find out what it was.

Rosy ordered a chef's salad and an iced tea, and Grace quickly left the table. Rosy flung her hair over her shoulder, and Jill caught the scent of her perfume. She wore Shalimar, which was one of Jill's favorites.

As the group sat eating and catching up on what had been going on with Rosy, Jill could see that she had an eye for Tony. Most of her conversation was directed toward him, and Jill was certain that Rosy's breasts brushing up against Tony's arm more than once was no accident.

"So, Tony, tell me, are you still as great a dancer as I remember?" Rosy asked in a thick accent.

Tony's smile broadened. "I'm every bit as good as you remember, probably even better." He leaned back in his chair and smiled, revealing perfect sexy, white teeth.

Rosy grabbed his hand, which was resting on his thigh, and held it tightly. "I would like to think you would take me dancing at Roland's while I am in town," she said, baiting him with a voice that oozed honey.

Jill's eyes darted over to Bebe, who ate in silence. She seemed unaffected by the fact that Rosy was making an obvious play for Tony. Though she wanted desperately to pull Bebe aside, Jill had to remind herself that now wasn't the time for such conversation. When they were back in the car, she would ask her friend all about this Rosy Hernandez.

Grace returned with Rosy's salad. She wedged herself between the two, forcing Rosy to release Tony's hand, and then set the plate as well as a drink in front of Rosy.

"Thank you, Grace," Rosy called out after her as Grace walked away.

"You're welcome," Grace replied flatly without turning around.

Jill glanced at Bebe's plate and saw that she was finished with her meal. She wanted to make an excuse for them to depart, but feared leaving Tony with Rosy. Though Bebe showed none of Jill's concern, Jill thought she had better look out for her friend's best interest, since Bebe obviously wasn't in the frame of mind to do it herself.

"Rosy, how long do you plan to be in town?" Kyle asked.

"At least for the next three months. Don't worry, Kyle, I won't be leaving before the wedding. I will make sure I am there front and center. I still can't believe that Little Kyle is tying the knot." She looked up at Kyle through long, sooty eyelashes. "Of course I will be at your wedding. I will have to see it with my own eyes that the handsome Kyle Roberts is off the market," Rosy finished.

Kyle glanced over at Jill and saw that she wasn't amused, which made his own smile fade as he sat up in his chair.

"Jill, I think we had better get back to the office," Bebe said, sensing the tension. "We still have a little work to finish."

Jill looked at her friend in astonishment. For the life of her, Jill couldn't imagine what Bebe was thinking. Rosy wasn't making it a secret that she wanted Tony, and Bebe was making it easy for the woman to make a play for him.

"I guess we'll see you guys later," Bebe said as she stood, urging Jill to follow her lead.

With a quick kiss on Kyle's lips, Jill did the same, and then said, "It was very nice meeting you, Rosy." She extended her hand to shake Rosy's.

Rosy took her time putting her fork down, and then took her napkin to wipe her mouth and hands; then she shook Jill's waiting hand.

"It was a pleasure to meet you too, Ms. Alexander," Rosy said.

Though the dig Rosy had just delivered to Jill went right over the men's heads, Jill knew just what Rosy was doing. It was a carefully stated, yet deliberately delivered statement to remind Jill that she wasn't Mrs. Kyle Roberts yet.

With an arched brow, Jill slowly turned her head until her eyes met Kyle's. As Rosy released her hand, she said with an air of challenge, "For now, you can call me Jill, but soon, I will only want to be called *Mrs.* Roberts." Jill pushed her chair under the table, and said good-bye to everyone. As she turned to leave, she saw the first real smile on Bebe's face since they had started eating lunch.

Jill left the Ranch House with quick deliberate steps. Bebe followed Jill's fast gait out the door and to the car. Inside Jill's car, Bebe allowed her laughter to thunderously erupt. Jill didn't join her.

Though the temperature was over ninety degrees outside, that wasn't the reason her blood was boiling. She turned on the AC and ran her hands over the top of her head.

"Jill, I can't believe that you let that little hoochie get the best of you," Bebe said, still laughing.

Jill finally laughed too, only because she had never heard Bebe use the word *hoochie* before. The word sounded funny coming from her usually proper friend, but Bebe was right; Rosy was definitely a hoochie.

Jill started driving in the direction of Desert Star. "I can't believe she didn't get under your skin. Bebe, she wants Tony and in a big way." She sucked her teeth in disgust.

"Why should I worry over Rosita Hernandez? She's not Tony's type. She is as she always will be, a family friend. But if I had it my way, I would run her out of Durango on a rail."

"I've only just met her and I already want to run her out of town on a rail. Bebe, didn't her blatant flirting with Tony bother you at all?" Jill said seriously.

"No, Rosy is only as powerful as I let her be, and I choose not to give her any power. Tony loves me and I love him."

"Well, you better start showing him that love."

"What do you mean?"

"Bebe, you didn't even kiss him good-bye when we left. In fact, you two parted on a bad note. You were just about to argue when Rosy showed up. Then you left him with a woman who had just put a smile on his face and wants to get something going with him, and I don't mean just friendship."

"Tony won't let anything go that far with Rosy," Bebe said confidently.

"'Oh, Tony, I hope you are as great a dancer as I remember. Please, Tony, please, take me dancing while I'm in town,'" Jill teased, trying to speak with Rosy's thick accent.

Unable to hold it in any longer, Bebe burst into laughter again at Jill's silliness. Jill pretended to fling her hair over her shoulders and purse her lips together into a sensuous pout like Rosy's and Bebe laughed even harder.

Jill continued to make light of the situation as they pulled up in front of Desert Star. Inside, they found Monica already back from lunch and hard at work.

"I guess you two had a great time at lunch," Monica said, handing Jill and Bebe the messages they had received while they were out.

"Yes, but you didn't miss anything special. Bebe and I are just a little silly right now," Jill told her.

Bebe glanced through her messages briefly. "Jill, I am going to my office. I want to try to get out of here before six o'clock tonight."

"That sounds great. I was hoping to get home at a decent time too." Jill checked her watch as she went to her office.

She finished reading her messages and saw that she and Bebe would probably be going to Florida to meet with a client in the next week. She sat back in her chair and wondered how she could work in a quick visit with her family. They were coming to see her soon and she knew this visit could only be for a day, but it would still be good to see them even for that brief amount of time.

Jill made a call regarding another account, and then began working on the Fitz and O'Neal assignment. Fitz and O'Neal Boating and Accessories had hired Desert Star to bring more business in. This was a big account, and one that had been given to them by Joan Singletary, her ex-boss's wife, who was quite influential in the New York social circles. Jill didn't know why Joan felt comfortable giving her business when her own husband, Matt, had a huge and successful public relations firm, but Jill was thankful.

She got busy drawing up new contracts for Fitz and O'Neal, and putting a file together for them. Jill buzzed Monica and had her type up all the necessary standard papers for a new client. Next she went to Bebe's office and told her that Fitz and O'Neal wanted them to come to Jacksonville to meet with them.

"How soon?" Bebe asked.

"Well, I still have to give them a call, but I wanted to see if you had any time preferences."

She shook her head. "Not really, I don't have anything planned."

"I'll call and set up the meeting." Jill started to leave, but there was one more question she needed to ask. "Bebe, I know this is a sensitive subject, but are you in love with Tony?"

Bebe avoided eye contact with Jill, choosing to look out the window instead. She knew that the subject would come up, especially after the Rosy incident. She and Jill had made fun of the situation in the car, but now the issue was serious, and Bebe knew that Jill wanted a straight and honest answer.

"I know that you love him, but are you *in* love with him?"

Finally, Bebe turned to face her friend, "Of course I love him and I am in love with him, too. Jill, you know better than anyone just how much I love Tony Roberts. He is my best friend. I can't imagine life without him, yet I can't imagine being his wife either."

"Why, Bebe? He loves you and is totally committed to you. You two are perfect together. You see that, don't you?"

Bebe sighed heavily. "Yes, I see it, but I am still afraid that we'll no longer like each other if we were to marry. I stand to lose a lot if a marriage didn't work out. I would lose him and the only family I've ever known by taking things to the next level. I'm afraid, Jill," she finished, tears welling in her eyes at her hopeless situation.

Jill, sensing that she had pushed her friend hard enough for one day, stood and walked behind Bebe's desk to give her a hug. "Bebe, don't be afraid. The only thing that will happen is that you will gain all the love, happiness, and joy you so richly deserve. I'm going to help you, no matter what it takes, girlfriend."

Bebe managed to smile through her tears and return Jill's hug. "Thanks, Jill," she said as she grabbed a tissue and dried her eyes carefully so as not to smudge her mascara.

"I better get back to my office and get some of this work done or I'll be sitting at work all night by myself," Jill said, giving Bebe a final pat on the back.

Back in her office, Jill called Fitz and O'Neal and made arrangements to visit them. Then she buzzed Monica and told her of the travel dates, so that she could make all the necessary arrangements.

As Jill worked, her mind kept drifting back to Bebe. It hurt her heart to see her friend in such a miserable state. Even if Bebe didn't see Rosy as a threat, Jill knew that if a man were pushed past his breaking point—which Tony was certainly nearing—he could be tempted by another woman. She knew Tony was in love with Bebe and he knew Bebe was in love with him, but it wasn't enough. He wanted to make Bebe his wife. He wanted to start a family with her.

Somehow, Jill had to make her friend see that marriage to Tony would be the best thing for her. And Bebe had told him more times than Jill could count it was only a matter of time before Tony stopped asking and started looking elsewhere. She had to make Bebe realize that there was nothing to fear, not with a love that was as strong and as passionate as theirs.

Jill stopped what she was doing and leaned back in her chair. All sorts of ideas were running through her mind as to how to help Bebe. Finally, she closed the door to her office and picked up the phone. Quickly she dialed Kyle's cell phone number.

"Hello?" he answered.

"Hey, baby, what are you doing?"

"Well, I was working, but I can take five for you. Are you missing me?"

"You know I'm always missing you, but I have a problem, Kyle."

"What's wrong?" Kyle said as he closed the gate to the corral.

"I'm worried about Bebe. Honey, you know how much Tony loves her."

"Yes, I do, but we can't control their relationship. Jill, when Bebe is ready, she'll come around to Tony's way of thinking."

"By that time it might be too late. I saw the way Rosy was looking at him. She wants your brother, and I don't mean just as a friend." Jill rolled her eyes at Kyle's laughter, then continued to talk. "Kyle, I don't see what's so funny. Rosy practically asked him for a date in front of all of us."

Kyle stopped laughing to reply. "I know, Jill, and I have some bad news. Tony is taking Rosy to Roland's tonight."

"Tonight! Who else is going?"

He chuckled at Jill's naivete. "No one, they're going by themselves."

"Shouldn't someone be with them, you know, sort of as a chaperone?"

Kyle chuckled at Jill's outburst. "Jill, we are talking about two grown people. I don't think Tony would appreciate anyone tagging along as a chaperone."

"But, Kyle, Rosy is just trying to get her hooks into him. You know that as well as I do."

"Yes, I do, babe, but this is something Bebe and Tony have to work out for themselves," he said, emphasizing the last two words.

Jill sighed heavily, thinking of a solution. "I still think we owe it to Bebe to at least try to show her what she is missing. We need to give her a little push Kyle, because if she loses Tony she will never find a love like his again. Just imagine if our relationship had disintegrated, we wouldn't be where we are right now."

Against his better judgment, he gave in. It was hard for him to deny Jill anything. "What do you think we should do to help them?"

"I don't have all the answers, but if Tony is going to take Rosy out tonight, he is already feeling the need of another woman's attention. Maybe we should have a party at the cabin and invite them. I get the feeling Tony would bring Rosy."

"Jill, this might blow up in your face. I don't think

Bebe knows that Tony and Rosy are going out tonight," Kyle warned.

"No, Kyle, she doesn't. Bebe always assumes that Tony is her date no matter what we do. If Tony arrives at the party with Rosy, that might put things in perspective for Bebe. Maybe she will see that she has far too much to lose by not joining her life with his."

"You are such a romantic," he growled.

"Oh yeah?" she asked, raising a questioning eyebrow.

"Yeah, can I show you that I am just as romantic as you are tonight?"

Jill's face broke into a silly grin. "I think that can be arranged, Mr. Roberts. I have to go home after work to get a few things, but then I'll be right over and I'll be all yours."

"I like the sound of that, but don't eat because I'll have dinner waiting when you arrive, baby."

Jill smiled contently as she whispered, "Bye, honey."

She hung up the phone and tried to busy herself with work, but it was all in vain. Jill's mind was filled with thoughts of what Kyle had in store for her. Then her thoughts turned to Bebe and Tony. Rosy Hernandez would not be part of the Roberts family if she could help it. There was no way she could entertain the thought of someone else taking Bebe's place as her sister-in-law. Jill hoped that her plan would work, and prayed it didn't blow up in her face as Kyle had warned.

At the end of the long workday Jill, Bebe, and Monica left the building. They turned on the security alarm and locked the doors. Saying their goodbyes, they each got into their cars and headed home.

Jill felt miserable about not telling Bebe of Tony's plans for the evening, but she had a plan of her own and hoped it finally would bring the two lovers together.

Chapter 3

Jill opened the door to Kyle's cabin and was met with the delicious aroma of the meal he was preparing. She had told him a year ago that he would spoil her by taking care of her so well, and her prediction had come true. He did spoil her immensely by not only making her dreams come true, but also by far exceeding them. Never did she imagine living out West, preparing to marry a man who was intelligent, fun loving, and had a great sense of humor. Kyle was the most passionate and powerful lover a woman could desire, and he was no stranger to hard work. After a long day, he could still come home and be happy pampering and cooking for her. Jill knew that being in the kitchen was also a form of relaxation for Kyle, and since he was the better cook, she didn't mind.

She set her things on the floor next to the sofa and tiptoed into the kitchen. Jill walked quietly behind Kyle, who was preparing a salad over the sink. Slowly she wrapped her arms around his waist and let her body excite him with its warmth. A smile of deep pleasure came across her face as she caressed his tight abdomen, enjoying the taut muscles she found there.

"You keep that up and I'm sure to ruin dinner," he said in a low voice.

"If I weren't starving it would almost be worth it."

Kyle turned around and gave her a kiss and returned her warm hug. His hands were still wet as he rubbed her back, but Jill didn't seem to mind. She was home now, and she was with her man. Kyle nuzzled her neck for a moment, and then he gently rubbed his face against her cheek, kissing it before he loosened his hold on her.

"How was the rest of your day?" he asked.

Jill stepped away. She took a raw carrot off the counter and began chewing on it. Sitting at the kitchen table, she began telling Kyle what was on her mind.

"Well, honey, it looks like Bebe and I will be going to Florida. The client wants to meet with us in person. Monica should have everything ready for us tomorrow."

"When are you leaving?"

"By the end of the week," Jill said in a voice that was a mixture of sadness and hopefulness.

Kyle smiled at her nonverbal way of asking him to join her. Jill hated pulling him away from his work to accompany her on hers, but she also couldn't stand to be apart from him for days at a time either.

He bent over and kissed her forehead. "I can make it, baby."

A smile lit up Jill's face. "Kyle, thank you. I'll make sure you have a wonderful time."

"I bet you will," he said, turning to give her a playful wink. "Hey, are you going to try to swing by Pittsburgh and visit the family?"

"I was thinking about it, but I didn't know how much time you could take off. If we're able to spend a day there that would be nice.

"How long do you think we'll be gone altogether?"

"About four days. Is that okay?"

"Uh-huh. I just want to make sure I know how long to let Eric and Tony know that I will be gone. They'll be fine without me."

Jill finished her carrot and stood to help Kyle finish preparing dinner. He was preparing steak, baked potatoes, salad, and dinner rolls he'd made from scratch. For dessert, he'd baked a blueberry cobbler. Jill began cutting the tomatoes for the salad, and Kyle noticed that she seemed preoccupied.

"Jill, are you still thinking about Bebe?"

Jill smiled at his knowing. He truly was her soul mate, being able to read her mind so well.

"Yeah." She released a deep sigh. "She has no idea that Tony and Rosy are going on a date tonight."

"I wouldn't call it a date," Kyle said nonchalantly. His meal was done, and he began piling food on their plates and set them on the table.

"I don't know what else to call it," Jill said as she poured them each a glass of iced tea. "They are going out *alone* to Roland's."

"Babe, they are just old friends, nothing more," Kyle said, trying to alleviate some of the worry that was now forming in Jill's mind.

They sat down to dinner and Kyle blessed the meal. Jill cut into the succulent, tender meat and put it into her mouth. The steak was seasoned to perfection, and Jill once again remembered how fortunate she was with everything that surrounded her life, especially Kyle.

With this thought, the conversation returned back to Bebe and Tony. "Kyle, you have to admit that Bebe does love your brother."

"Of course, babe, I don't deny that. In fact, I think they will be the next to marry after us," he said as he continued to eat.

"Then be honest with me, Kyle, do you truly not see Rosy as not wanting anything more than a friendly relationship from Tony?" She watched Kyle's face intently, looking for any sign of hidden feelings.

Kyle looked up at her sheepishly, knowing that he knew full well that Rosy Hernandez wanted something more from his brother. "Jill, I just believe that love will have its way with them, just like it did with us. If Bebe and Tony are supposed to be together there is nothing anyone can do about it. Besides, Rosy isn't the type of woman Tony would marry."

Jill took another bite of her salad as she pondered what Kyle had just told her. "You're right, but we had a little help getting together."

"Yes, we did, but that was different, Jill. You and I were meant to be. Bebe and your old job just gave us a little shove in the right direction, because we were heading there anyway," he finished, raising his hand to her lips and taking notice of the beautiful diamond engagement ring that he'd put on her finger. "I think it's time we go off the subject of Tony and Bebe, since we have better things to do," Kyle said, raising his eyebrows. Still holding Jill's hand, he rose from the table and led her through the living room and up the stairs.

Jill could feel her heart beating faster with each step she took. Kyle had made love to her many times, but each time she found herself filled with deep anticipation. As they walked into the bedroom, Kyle turned around and began kissing Jill. She could still feel the warmth and tenderness of his full lips after they left hers in search of other tender places on her body to touch.

Kyle began to undress her, and as he uncovered new patches of flesh he planted more moist kisses. When her clothes had all been removed, he continued to press his lips against hers, holding her body tightly as he guided them toward the bed. Once there, he laid Jill back onto the huge king-sized bed, cradling her body as if she were the most delicate creature on earth. Though Kyle was still fully clothed, he climbed on top of her and began kissing her again.

He slid his tongue inside her mouth as his hand fondled her nipple. Jill felt as though she had no control over her body as her legs wrapped around his. Kyle slid a hand between her legs and touched her in a way that made her beg him to take her. Her arms caressed his back, and feeling such desire for him, she wanted to rip his shirt off.

"Baby, I can't take it anymore. *Please* make love to me—now." She forced the words out between pants.

He always made sure that he drove Jill to the brink of sexual insanity before he gave her what she needed. Kyle was out of his clothes, had slipped on a condom in seconds, and was inside Jill in even less time. Her legs wrapped around his again as their bodies began a rhythmic dance. She was in much need of him and couldn't wait to satisfy his own need more completely.

Jill felt total pleasure as Kyle finally entered her. She stuck her tongue inside his mouth, enjoying the wet silkiness she found there. Kyle let his hands slowly rub up and down Jill's perfect body. He felt her taut abdomen, and then he allowed his hands to find their favorite place to rest. He held her voluptuous backside as his own passion began to mount. Kyle's thrusts became more powerful and Jill found herself arching her back as she tore at the sheets in order to accommodate their explosive passion. She cried out in pleasure as Kyle satisfied their hunger. Finally, they lay quietly still wrapped in each other's embrace. Aside from the gentle hum of the ceiling fan, the only other noise in the room was their heavy breathing.

It was still early, but Jill just wanted to lay there and be held by the man that represented her world. After his breathing had slowed down, Kyle slid to the other side of the bed. It was as if he had read Jill's mind, as he turned on his side and pulled her body close to his, wrapping her lovely figure in his arms.

Jill smiled as she looked into the eyes of the big, strong, rugged cowboy. She turned to face him more completely and began gently playing with the soft curls on his head. She lay there saying nothing, but peacefully enjoying his closeness.

"Please don't ever leave me." Though she said it quietly, the words were out before she even gave them any thought.

Kyle's brow furrowed. "Where did that come from?"

Though she tried to hold it back, a tear escaped and rolled down her cheek. "I just love you so much, Kyle. My life with you is just so perfect that I feel like something is going to happen to mess it up."

Kyle pulled her even closer and kissed the tear away. "Baby, I'll never leave you. I'm afraid that after we are married you're going to wonder what you've gotten yourself into, and try to run away from me," he teased.

"The only direction I'd run is into you."

"I love you, babe, and I'll never ever leave you," he promised. Still holding each other in their arms, they fell asleep.

Jill stretched in bed and realized that Kyle was gone. Though it was still light outside, she looked at the clock and saw that it was seven p.m. Since it wasn't too late, she decided to call Bebe.

"Hey, Bebe, what's going on?"

"Nothing, Jill, I just came in from the grocery store. I tried to call Tony to see if he wanted to come over for dinner, but there's no answer at his place."

It bothered Jill greatly not to come clean with her friend, but she just couldn't stand to break Bebe's heart. "Well, I needed to ask you something. Next week when we leave for Florida, I was planning on going to Pittsburgh. I just wanted to make sure that you wanted to go before I tell Monica to finish the travel arrangements."

"Of course I want to go. I love visiting your family. I think your mother would have a fit if I didn't come to see her."

Jill laughed knowing that Bebe was right, but she was still concerned about Bebe leaving Tony alone with that man-hungry Rosy Hernandez around.

"I just wanted to make sure that I wasn't messing up anything you had planned. Kyle will be coming with us, since we are only going to be gone for four days."

"That's great. I just wish that Tony could come too," Bebe said hopefully.

Unable to take the pressure of keeping such a big secret away from her friend any longer, Jill cut the conversation short. "Bebe, I have to go. I took a nap and I hardly got anything done tonight. I'll see you tomorrow at work."

"Bye, Jill," Bebe replied, just as she heard Jill hang up the phone.

Jill got out of bed. She could hear the television going and pots and pans clanging in the kitchen, and wondered if Kyle had taken a nap with her at all. She walked into the bathroom and started running the shower. She stepped in and washed herself mechanically since her thoughts were still on Bebe.

It seemed that no one felt as if there was anything to worry about except her. She knew what danger Rosy presented. Kyle was right, and she agreed; Rosy wasn't the kind of woman Tony would marry, but she was the kind of woman that could destroy a romantic relationship. Bebe deserved Tony, and she decided she would make sure her friend got him.

Jill finished her shower and dried off. She quickly completed her nightly routine of facial and body moisturizers, and then slipped into a short pajama set that had matching slippers. She quickly brushed her hair before heading downstairs.

She found Kyle on the sofa watching television in the living room. She curled up next to him and he couldn't resist caressing her extremely long, soft, sexy legs.

A smile came across his face as he said, "I am the luckiest man alive."

"Since you're so lucky, I want to run something past you."

"What is it, babe?" he asked.

"Well, I was thinking that maybe we should have a party."

"A party—for what?"

"For Rosy."

"For Rosy! Jill, you don't even like the woman," Kyle said loudly.

"No, I don't like her, but hear me out, baby. I think that if we had a welcoming party for Rosy, maybe Bebe would get to see Tony interact with her in a very social environment. Kyle, this might be the little push in the right direction they both need," Jill finished and waited to hear what Kyle thought of her plan.

After a moment of silence, Kyle said, "If you think this will help them, then let's do it."

Jill leaped into his lap and covered his face with kisses. "You won't be sorry, baby," she said.

Kyle began to laugh and said, "I already am not sorry." He returned her kisses, and then asked if she wanted some dessert.

"Kyle, I think I'm still worn out from earlier," she answered.

"No, baby, I made you blueberry cobbler for dessert, remember?"

"Oh yeah, I'd love a piece and cover mine with whipped cream," she said as she pulled her legs off his lap.

Kyle stood shaking his head and said, "You're insatiable."

"No, I'm not, you are," Jill shot back, laughing.

"Only for you, baby," he said as he went into the kitchen.

Moments later, Kyle returned with a big dish of blueberry cobbler smothered with whipped cream, and one spoon. He sat next to Jill, and she put her legs across his lap again. Kyle took the spoon and dug into the mouthwatering dessert, feeding Jill the first scoop of the blueberry cobbler. Her eyes closed in ecstasy as she enjoyed the sumptuous treat. Kyle pulled the spoon out of her mouth slowly, and Jill opened her eyes to see him smiling at her.

"Is it good, baby?" he asked.

"It's better than good, it's delicious. I think you should make blueberry cobbler for the party."

Kyle ate some of his dessert. "When are you planning to do this?"

"I was thinking that maybe we should have it this

Friday. Bebe and I are going to Florida next week and I want to stop and see my family in Pittsburgh.

Kyle gave Jill another spoonful as he said, "Baby, what's the rush? Rosy will be here for a while, she said so herself. Why can't we have the party when we come back?"

"Kyle, I don't think it's a good idea to wait any longer than we have to. Rosy might not be the kind of woman Tony would marry, but she sure is the kind that would mess up what he has going on with Bebe. I would feel better if I at least tried to help before we went away."

"You two have been as close as sisters since the day you met."

"You're right, and I don't want to see Bebe unhappy. You understand, don't you, honey?"

"Yes, I do. So tell me, what do you want me to prepare for the party?" he asked.

Jill began to play with Kyle's hair as she said, "I think we should keep it fun and simple, so why don't we fire up the grill?"

"That's okay with me. I'll do some ribs, potato salad, corn, and rolls."

"Oh, and don't forget the blueberry cobbler," Jill reminded him as she stuck her finger in the remaining whipped cream.

She licked her finger slowly as Kyle watched. He set the empty dish on the coffee table and took off Jill's slippers, and then he began massaging her feet. Jill laid her head back on the sofa and closed her eyes, enjoying the warmth of Kyle's strong hands on her tired toes. She still felt as though she were dreaming, and would soon awaken and find that he, as well as the whole place, was just a fantasy.

She was just about to fall asleep when Kyle said, "Hey, babe, let's go upstairs to bed."

Jill was incredibly tired, and started walking upstairs with Kyle close behind. She went into the bathroom and brushed her teeth, then crawled into bed and pulled the sheet over her. Kyle went into the bathroom next, and when he emerged he was completely naked. He climbed into bed next to Jill and turned out the lights. Jill rested her head in the crook of his arm, and he cuddled her until they both feel asleep.

Morning found Jill and Kyle in a hustle to get to work. Kyle was the first to leave the house. He kissed her good-bye with a promise to meet her at the Ranch House for lunch.

After Jill ate a bowl of cereal, she too rushed out the door to work. Though she had no one to report to, she still maintained the high work ethics she had established at Iguana, her former employer in New York. When she arrived at Desert Star, she was greeted by Monica, who was anxious to know all the details needed to make the travel arrangements for Jill and Bebe. After Jill told Monica what was needed, she quickly went to her own office to go through her mail, and then she went to Bebe's office.

Jill gently knocked on the door, and Bebe looked up from her computer. "Hi, Jill," Bebe said in a tired voice.

Jill entered the office and took a seat. "Is everything all right?"

"No, everything is not all right. I told you that I wanted to invite Tony over for dinner last night, but I couldn't reach him. I even tried his cell phone, but he didn't answer it. Jill, I tried calling him until midnight and he still wasn't home. Did he come over and visit Kyle last night?"

Jill, unable to maintain eye contact, said, "No, Bebe, he didn't come to the cabin last night."

"Well, I'm worried maybe something happened to him."

"Why don't you try to call him on his cell phone now since he should be at work?" Jill offered. As Bebe picked up her phone to try Jill's suggestion, Jill said, "I'll be in my office. Let me know if you reach him."

She walked quickly back down the hall and into the conference room. Closing the door behind her, she dialed Kyle's cell phone.

"Hello?"

"Honey, it's me," Jill said nervously.

"Jill, is everything all right?"

"I'm afraid not. Bebe is really worried about Tony. She has been trying to get in touch with him all night and hasn't been able to."

"That would be because Tony didn't come home. He and Rosy got in late and he stayed at her place. I think you are right, we better do something, and fast."

"I have to go, Bebe will be looking for me soon, and I don't want her to find me hiding to use the phone. Bye, honey," she whispered and hung up the phone.

Jill walked back to her office and was about to sit down when Bebe entered.

"I finally got a hold of Tony. You'll never believe where he was last night."

"Where?" Jill asked casually trying to conceal her nervousness.

"He went to Roland's and got home really late. I wonder why he went to Roland's on a Wednesday. You know as well as I do how he hates my going there because he thinks it's just a pickup joint. Jill, do you think he went there for that reason?"

Jill didn't want to answer Bebe, but she tried to take a neutral stance in answering her, and said, "Bebe, Tony loves you, you just have to show him that same love back." Then she quickly went on to the matter of business that concerned their upcoming trip to Pennsylvania and Florida. She told Bebe that Monica was making all the arrangements, and that they would be leaving Saturday evening.

Though Bebe was glad that everything was being taken care of, Jill was just happy that Bebe had nothing more to say on the matter of Tony. Bebe thanked Jill for the information, and returned back to her own office to finish working. It was hard for Jill to concentrate, but she managed to get some work done before lunch.

At noon, Jill met Kyle and Tony and Bebe, who'd left earlier to talk to Tony, at the Ranch House. When Jill arrived at the table, Tony and Bebe were sitting next to each other, but his usual silly playfulness was missing. Jill also noticed that Bebe wasn't her normal self either. Jill took her seat next to Kyle, and Grace took their orders and left the solemn group.

Kyle tried to bring the table to life. "Bebe, did Jill get a chance to tell you about the little party we are planning tomorrow?"

"No, she didn't. Why are you having a party? I mean, we have to leave town on Saturday. Won't you guys be exhausted?"

"I think we'll be fine," Jill said as she took a sip of Kyle's lemonade. "We're not planning anything elaborate, but we wanted a chance to unwind with friends and family before we left town, and to give everyone a chance to say hello to Rosy," Jill explained.

Bebe was stunned that Jill was having a party for Rosy. She knew that Jill felt the same way about Rosy as she did, and imagined that the idea to have the party must have come from Kyle.

"I pretty much did all the inviting already, and we're expecting sixteen people," Kyle said.

"I'll be there," Tony told them, thankful for a chance to lighten his mood with his family.

"Me too, and let me know if there is anything I can do to help," Bebe said.

"I sure will," Jill said, smiling as if she had landed a big contract.

Grace returned with their food, and they all began to eat and converse. Though Bebe and Tony were finally speaking to each other, there was still an air of discomfort surrounding them. Jill hoped that by tomorrow evening all the negative emotions would be replaced by feelings of genuine love.

When they were finished with lunch, everyone returned to work. The rest of the workday flew by, and Jill, Bebe, and Monica left the office. After a quick stop at her own apartment, Jill drove straight to the cabin. With the wedding approaching fast, she began to feel more at home at the cabin, and less comfortable at her own place. Soon, Kyle's home would be her home too.

At the cabin, she found Kyle cleaning and preparing for the party. Kyle prided himself on making friends feel like family and wanted the cabin to look as welcoming as possible.

Jill quickly changed her clothes and began working with Kyle to ready the place. She smiled as they worked side by side, knowing in her heart that this was how it would always be. She loved him more than she ever thought she could love a man. Together, they made one complete soul—she was half of him, and he her. She found herself staring at the man who would soon be her husband and decided to kiss him long and passionately. As she held her man in her arms, she said a silent prayer that Bebe would find the same completeness, the same joy that she had found.

Chapter 4

Monica was a wonderful addition to the little firm. She had made all the arrangements for their business trip, which included airline, hotel, and car rental, not to mention setting up the meetings with the client and having the contracts and all necessary paperwork in order. She wasn't Lois, Jill's assistant at her old job but she was hardworking and tried to be as efficient and helpful as possible.

At Iguana, it was as if Jill could do the work of two people with Lois's help. In a few weeks she would see all of her dear friends from Iguana, and the thought warmed her heart. Iguana was like family to her as well, and she probably would never have left if she hadn't met Kyle. Of course she would have struck out on her own, but she would have done that in New York. Now she was where she was supposed to be, and content with the weekend calls she received from Lois and Diane, another former co-worker.

With everything set for their trip, Jill and Bebe decided to work half a day so Jill could get home to help Kyle with the preparations for their guests.

"Jill, are you sure you don't want me to come over and help you guys?" Bebe asked.

"Thanks, Bebe, but I think we'll be fine," Jill said as she turned out the lights to her office and closed the door.

"Okay, I'll be over about six o'clock."

"That will be great," Jill said as the two women made their way down the hall with their briefcases and purses in tow.

"Good night, Monica, see you at the party," Jill said.

"See you later, Jill," Monica replied, still feeling a little uneasy addressing Jill so informally, but thrilled to have been invited to the party.

Jill and Bebe said good-bye and each got into her car and headed home. As she drove, Jill felt a mixture of excitement and nervousness in the pit of her stomach. She felt good trying to do something wonderful for her friend, but thinking that things could turn out badly made her pulse race.

Her gut instinct told her that Rosy would be as flirtatious as possible regardless if Bebe was on Tony's arm or not. Jill hoped that her friend wouldn't put up with Rosy tonight. Given the fact that Tony had partied the previous night with Rosy, Jill wondered if he would be arriving with Bebe to the party. She felt her heart skip a beat as she realized that things could go terribly wrong. It was too late to call the party off. She could only hope for the best and prepare for the worst.

She put her car in the garage next to Kyle's Navigator, so that there would be plenty of room for their guests to park in front of the cabin. Jill left her suitcase in the car, but grabbed her briefcase and purse and then went inside. As soon as she opened the door, she was greeted with the aroma of barbecued ribs. The place looked incredible, and music played quietly. Jill knew that the low volume of the music wouldn't last for long once the party started. Tony would be the first one to pump up the volume.

Jill set her things down at the bottom of the stairs and went in search of Kyle. She found him outside on the deck covering his ribs in his signature barbecue sauce. He looked up and saw Jill walking toward him, stopping what he was doing to greet her.

"Hello, beautiful," he said as he slid his arms around her tiny waist.

"Hello, handsome," she said softly and began covering his lips with soft, moist, kisses. "I missed you, honey."

"I bet not half as much as I missed you," he managed to say as Jill continued to smother him with one delicious kiss after another. With her arms resting gently on his shoulders, she played in his soft, curly hair, as was her habit.

"I'm going to take a shower and get dressed for the party. Is there anything I can do to help before I go upstairs?" she asked as she made her tongue quickly brush his upper lip.

"N-no," Kyle stammered. "But would you like me to join you?"

Jill smiled, realizing she had gotten the desired response and said, "If you join me we will be late for our guests."

"Well, they will just have to wait," Kyle said, as he returned Jill's passionate kisses.

"I will make it worth the wait tonight, I promise," she whispered and then gently nibbled on his ear.

"Jill, I wish you wouldn't tease me so much," Kyle said as he kissed her cheek one last time before releasing his hold on her. She smiled as she turned to walk away and Kyle lovingly gave her backside a quick swat as she left.

Once inside, Jill gathered her things and went upstairs to the bedroom. She undressed and took a shower. When she was done she set her hair in hot curlers and then went to the walk-in closet and found a beautiful blue, chiffon sundress, which had a V-shaped neckline. Jill slid the dress on, and was pleased to see how it showed off the heart-shaped necklace Kyle had given her as an anniversary gift. She put on a pair of small sapphire and diamond earrings. She walked back to the bathroom and applied a little makeup before taking out the curlers from her hair. She brushed the curls and let them fall loosely to her shoulders.

Jill put on a pair on matching blue sandals with a kitten heel and went downstairs to help Kyle. When she went outside to the patio she saw that Eric, Sharon, and Ally had arrived, and a few moments later, Monica and her boyfriend, Orlando, came. Monica's personality seemed more relaxed than when she was at the office. She chatted easily with Jill about how beautiful she thought the cabin was, and then complimented Jill on her dress. Jill was happy to see another side of the usually uptight office secretary, and hoped that now that the ice was broken, the change in Monica would continue at the office.

Jill looked up to see Bebe coming through the door. She was alone and Jill was anxious to find out if she had spoken to Tony. Excusing herself from the other guests, she walked over to speak to her friend.

"Bebe, I'm so glad you're here," Jill said as she hugged her.

"You look wonderful."

"Thanks, so do you," Jill replied as she admired Bebe's outfit. On her shapely figure, Bebe wore a sexy white halter top that tied into a bow at the waist. Her skirt was pale blue and fell just above the knee with a ruffled hem. Like Jill, she wore a pair of white kitten sandals that gave her calves a curvaceous lift.

Bebe had definitely dressed to capture Tony's attention, and Jill could only pray that that would happen. But lingering in the back of her mind was the knowledge that he had been spending time with Rosy, who was obviously no newcomer to obtaining and holding a man's attention.

Jill saw Bebe's eyes darting around the room and knew immediately who she was looking for. "Bebe, he's not here yet," Jill whispered so no one else would hear her.

A look of disappointment clouded Bebe's face, which Jill knew was due mostly to the fact that Bebe hadn't heard from him and she was anxious to see Tony. Jill gently rubbed her shoulder but added nothing else.

Jill noticed Kyle going out the front door to greet more guests that were arriving. She and Bebe followed him outside. As they caught up to him, they saw that some of Kyle's close friends from the ranch had arrived. A big smile appeared on his face as he greeted the men. Kyle shook Emilio's and Juan's hands as they approached him. Both men had brought girlfriends, women Jill and Bebe had never met, yet they extended warm welcomes to them.

The group was about to enter the cabin when Bebe saw Tony's car coming. Kyle and Jill turned to see what she was looking at, and waited to greet him also. The three walked down the steps and toward the car, but as they approached, they saw that Rosy Hernandez was with him.

Tony pulled up in front of the cabin and parked his

car. Then he got out and walked around to the pas-
senger's side and assisted Rosy out of the vehicle. He
opened the door for her and held out his hand. Rosy
slid her manicured fingers into Tony's rugged palm
and then swiveled her body around in order to step
out of the car. Slowly she let one leg touch the ground
and then the other before scooting her bottom to the
edge of the seat. This simple action made her skirt rise
higher upon her thighs, and Tony glanced down and
caught an eyefull of what she wanted to offer him.

In a clumsy attempt, Tony averted his eyes, looking
around as Rosy continued to try to captivate him. Momentarily, he looked at Bebe and just as quickly he
looked away.

Bebe stood frozen in place as she looked at Rosy
from head to toe. With her curly hair falling over her
shoulders, Rosy held on to Tony's hand tightly. She
was wearing a sexy floral-print halter dress that showcased her cleavage and showed plenty of thigh. Rosy
continued to smile at everyone, before letting her vic-
torious gaze finally rest on Bebe.

Tony was aware of the stare he now received from
Bebe. She had a look on her face that was a mixture
of jealousy and bewilderment. He knew how she
must be feeling right now, and lowered his gaze in
order not to see the pain on her face. Quickly recovering, Tony began walking into the cabin with Rosy.

Kyle followed behind his brother and Rosy, while
Jill walked into the cabin beside Bebe. Jill wanted desperately to console Bebe, knowing the humiliation she
probably felt. She didn't know how to comfort Bebe
without bringing more attention to the situation, so
she decided to leave the problem alone for now.

Once inside, Jill and Kyle began placing the food on
the table so their guests could serve themselves from

the buffet. When she was finished assisting Kyle, Jill looked around the room for Bebe. She didn't see Bebe in the living room so she quickly ran upstairs to see if she was there. Moments later she returned downstairs and continued her search. Jill pushed back the screen of the sliding glass door and walked outside to the backyard, where she found Bebe standing at the far end of the property near the trees.

Bebe was leaning against a tree and tears rolled effortlessly down her cheeks. Jill gave her a hug, and Bebe let out a pain-filled sigh.

"Oh, Jill, you were right and I did lose Tony," Bebe said, sobbing.

"Bebe, don't say that. I refuse to believe that Tony is in love with Rosy after only one date."

"Jill, he's never even looked at another woman, and now he is spending time with her."

Jill released Bebe from her arms and said, "Bebe, Tony loves you, he has and always will love you." Jill gently wiped the tears from Bebe's cheek, only to be met by another flood of fresh ones. "Rosy is just giving you a run for your money. She is beautiful, exotic, and a big flirt, but she is not the kind of woman Tony would make his wife. Besides, can you really visualize him telling his parents that *she's* going to be his wife?"

The last comment made Bebe laugh since she knew that though the Robertses were friends with Rosy's parents, she really wasn't the kind of woman that would fit into their family. She wiped her tears away again and said, "Jill, when he arrived, he acted as if I weren't even there. He didn't even say hello to me. I was invisible to him."

"Bebe, maybe he was really ashamed of how he was making you feel. Tony knows you love him, and I know he loves you."

"Tell me what you know, Jill."

Jill smiled as she remembered how Barbie had tenderly made her realize her need for love, and coaxed her into accepting Kyle's love. Bebe had gently pushed her into Kyle's arms as well. Now it was her turn to show another woman that there was nothing to be afraid of when two people were meant for each other.

"Bebe, I know this because I see how Tony's face lights up every time you enter the room. He makes excuses just to be near you. If you don't know this, then let me tell you—Bebe, you're that man's lifeblood. Tony Roberts would be lost without you, and he knows it."

Bebe leaned her back against the tree and let her mind rediscover every aspect of her life with Tony. He had been by her side when she graduated from high school and college, and had been her prom date too. After sitting in the hospital for hours, she had been the first person he saw when he had awakened from his knee surgery. She recalled spending every Christmas with him at his parents' house ever since she could remember, and every Thanksgiving too.

Perhaps she had taken her relationship with Tony for granted. Maybe she needed a wake-up call before it really was too late.

Bebe couldn't stand the thought of living her life without Tony. She was comfortable with their relationship just the way it was, but she knew he had a right to want more. Tony deserved more from a woman and she wanted to be the one to give it to him. Bebe knew in her heart that she wanted the same thing as Tony, and she knew that in order to take the next step she had to put her fears aside.

A smile formed on Bebe's face as she thought about what Jill had said and pointed out the obvious. She wanted Tony; no, she needed Tony in her life. He was her man, her soul mate, and she would not let Rosy Hernandez ruin that.

Jill could see the misery in her friend's eyes being replaced with determination. Bebe patted her cheeks dry, and then said, "I guess I better go get my man." She began to walk in the direction of the cabin; then Jill stopped her.

"Bebe, I have a little confession to make," Jill said. The two women stood facing each other and Jill stammered as she continued. "I—I sort of planned on Tony and Rosy coming to the party together."

"Do you mean you asked Tony to be her date?" Bebe asked, confused.

"No, I would never do that," Jill answered honestly. "I knew that Tony had taken Rosy to Roland's the other night. You couldn't get a hold of him because he stayed at Rosie's that night," Jill finished softly. Unable to look Bebe in the eye, she lowered her head.

"Jill, you knew all this and didn't tell me?" Bebe said hotly. For the first time since they had met, she felt as though Jill couldn't be trusted.

"Bebe, I wanted to tell you but I didn't know how. I didn't want to hurt you."

"What do you think you're doing now? You even got him a date for your party."

"You're wrong, Bebe, I just wanted to show you what you were blind to. I wanted you to see that you could lose Tony, if not to Rosy, then to someone else. He loves you and I want to do whatever it takes to see you two together."

Bebe dropped her head, realizing that Jill would never do anything intentionally to hurt her. She said, "Jill, I'm so sorry. I shouldn't be mad at you. Actually,

I am not mad at you. I am mad at Tony and he is going to pay." Bebe began walking toward the cabin again.

As Bebe approached the deck, she stopped walking. As she turned to face Jill, sadness filled her face again. "Jill, do you think he slept with her?"

"I don't know, Bebe. If I did I would tell you. I only know how much he loves you and know that since it's not over between you two, I don't think he would completely ruin things by sleeping with Rosy."

Bebe smiled as she turned and walked through the sliding glass door with Jill close behind her. Inside, the music was blaring and just about everyone was dancing and eating. Several guys were playing pool, drinking cold beer, and bragging about their playing expertise.

Bebe could see Monica and her boyfriend, Orlando, sitting on the sofa. They shared a plate of food and Orlando lovingly placed an olive in Monica's mouth. Bebe couldn't help thinking that she and Tony should be doing the same thing, as her gaze fell on Tony dancing with Rosy.

Rosy danced provocatively with Tony and he was smiling and obviously having a good time. Jill, who had been standing in close proximity to Bebe, saw the determined look in her eyes. She wasn't certain what Bebe had planned, but hoped that it wouldn't cause a commotion.

Bebe poured herself a glass of sangria and sipped it slowly, letting her hips sway back and forth slowly as she began dancing in place. Her sensuous moves caught Tony's eye several times, as he tried futilely to keep his attention on Rosy. He knew she wanted to dance with someone as well, and secretly wondered whom she would choose. Setting her glass down on the table, Bebe walked over to a cowboy who was new to the ranch. He was invited to the party as were all the ranch hands, but he didn't know the weave of relationships.

Bebe stood very close to him and continued to dance as she said in a soft voice, "Hey, cowboy, would you like to dance?'

The man's face broke into a huge grin as he stood to oblige Bebe's offer. He was not as tall as Tony, nor as handsome, but he would work in carrying out her plan. Bebe led the man to the center of the floor and they began to dance. She could feel Tony's eyes on her even though she wasn't looking at him. Bebe and the new ranch hand danced closely. With his chest against her back she began to dance in a sexy way. Bebe caressed her thighs with her hands as the man held her hips gently. He began to grind on her backside and then Bebe turned to face him. She continued to dance as she wrapped her arms around his neck. She focused her attention on him as she smiled into his eyes. Bebe was completely unaware that Tony stood angrily behind them until she heard him speak.

"Bebe, can I see you outside!" Tony's voice boomed louder than the music.

Not waiting for an answer, Tony turned and walked away. With all eyes on her, Bebe excused herself and followed Tony out the door.

Jill looked anxiously at Kyle. She had never seen Tony so mad before. She knew that Tony cared about Bebe; she just hoped that they hadn't pushed things beyond repair. Jill began to consider her own role in this whole mess. She still felt badly about not telling Bebe the truth when she first knew it, but she couldn't think about that now. She walked over to Kyle and he put his arms around her.

"Babe, I've never seen Tony that mad," he said somberly.

"What do you think he'll do?"

"I don't know. I know that there is no other woman for him except Bebe. I just don't know why they think they have to prove something to each other," Kyle said, and planted a kiss on Jill's forehead. He released Jill and said in a loud voice, "The party is not over, but the show is. Come on, everybody, there's plenty to eat and let's keep dancing."

Orlando walked over to Jill and asked her to dance. Jill smiled and started dancing with the young man. Kyle offered Monica his hand and they joined Jill and Orlando on the floor. When the song was over, Jill and Monica went to get something to drink, leaving Orlando and Kyle alone for a moment. Jill chatted with Monica for a while and saw that the woman didn't seem as nervous and uptight about being around her boss. Jill was happy that Monica had relaxed completely and was calling her by her first name.

Glancing up at the clock, Jill saw that an hour had passed and Tony and Bebe had not returned. She excused herself from Monica's company and went outside to see if everything was okay. Jill could not see Bebe and Tony and noticed that his car was gone. She went back inside. The party was in full swing again, and the new ranch hand had a new dance partner, Rosy.

A few hours later Jill and Kyle stood on the porch of the cabin waving good-bye to the last of their guests. Both were tired yet aware that Tony and Bebe had never returned to the party. They walked back inside and Jill flopped her tired body on the sofa and Kyle joined her.

"What do you think happened to Bebe and Tony?" she asked.

"I don't know," he said. He pulled her legs across his lap. He then took off her shoes and began to massage her feet. "I think everything is okay though."

"What makes you think that? Tony was so mad when they left."

"Because Bebe would have called you by now if everything wasn't okay."

Jill looked down sadly and Kyle noticed and asked, "Hey, babe, what's wrong?"

"I told Bebe about my plan to make her jealous. I also told her that I knew where Tony was Wednesday night. Kyle, she was pretty mad at me, too."

Kyle shook his head and then said, "I told you this might blow up in your face. Was she still mad at you when she left?"

"Not really, we cleared the air before we came inside from talking, but she is still a little hurt. I'm going to call her and see if she is all right," Jill said as she reached for the phone.

Jill quickly dialed Bebe's cell phone number, and after several rings she hung up. Then she called her at home and got the answering machine.

Jill decided to leave a message and said, "Hi, Bebe, it's me, Jill. I was just calling to make sure that you're okay. Give me a call no matter what time you get in. Remember, Bebe, we have a flight to catch tomorrow afternoon. I love you, bye.

"We better get started on cleaning this place," Jill said as she pulled her legs from Kyle's lap. She slid on her shoes and stood up as Kyle watched her.

"Jill, I hope you aren't blaming yourself for this mess. Though you had a hand in it, you didn't create this mess," he said as he stood.

"I guess I do feel a little guilty. Bebe is my friend and I should have been honest with her." She picked up several empty glasses and began taking them into the kitchen.

"Tony and Bebe only have themselves to blame. If they would stop playing games with each other, things would never have gotten so bad," he said as they continued to clean.

Jill did not respond to Kyle's analysis of the situation, but she felt as though he was right in his assumption. Still, she did feel partly to blame for the way things had turned out.

It took the couple over an hour to get the place in decent shape. When they were finished Jill was exhausted, and wanted only to take a shower and go to bed. She began walking up the stairs to the bedroom, and knew that she had to finish packing before she could start to even consider going to sleep. In the suitcase in the car was all of the clothing she planned to take on the business trip. She only needed a few personal items, which she could throw into her carry-on bag. Jill quickly packed what she needed, since she was worried that she would forget something. Kyle had come upstairs too and went into the bathroom. He began taking a shower and Jill joined him.

Every time she disrobed in front of Kyle it was a sensual experience, and every place he touched her body made her feel loved. But tonight they were both too tired. Kyle lathered up a loofah and began bathing Jill. She smiled warmly as her scrubbed her body gently. When he was finished washing her, she did the same to him. Their conversation was minimal, but their silent pleasure spoke volumes. It was if they had known each other for more than a lifetime, and knew just what each other desired.

When they finished showering they got out of the tub and began drying off. Jill started putting a rich moisturizer on her skin, and Kyle watched in appreciation of the exquisite female figure that moved in front of him. He had seen her nude many times, but still she was able to capture his attention and hold it for as long as she pleased.

Taking the moisturizer from her, Kyle poured some into the palm of his hand, and began putting it on her back. Jill delighted in every stroke of his huge, strong fingers. She turned and kissed him and then did the same for him. When she finished her nightly ritual she left the bathroom. Once in the bedroom, Jill slipped into a black negligee and climbed into bed. She pulled the comforter over her body and rested her head on a pillow. She could hear Kyle in the bathroom brushing his teeth and hoped he would come to bed soon.

Kyle finished what he was doing and entered the bedroom. He stood in the doorway, and though the room was dimly lit, he could see that Jill was fast asleep. He smiled and turned out the light. Then he climbed into bed and cuddled the amazing woman who made all his dreams come true. Brushing the loose tendrils of hair from her face, he kissed her cheek.

"Thank you for being mine," he whispered into her ear. Then he fell asleep still holding tightly on to Jill.

Chapter 5

As morning light peeked through the curtains, Jill gave her body a gentle stretch. She was still nestled in Kyle's arms and she didn't want to wake him. She looked up at the man who was soon to be her husband, and could only find love, passion, and admiration for him. Kyle was everything she wanted and needed in a man wrapped up into one neat package. He knew how to take charge, yet was never overbearing. He could push her to her sexual peak, yet reinvent their lovemaking so it seemed as if it was her first time.

Next to her lay a man who had so many magnificent talents. Kyle managed a ranch and had graduated from college with a degree in architecture. The home he had built was beautiful, and Jill always felt as though she never had to worry about a thing when she was with him. His sense of humor enchanted her, and his sense of compassion left her in admiration of him.

All of this is mine, she thought as she viewed Kyle's handsome face. She planted a tender kiss on his massive chest, and then she crept out of bed.

Jill quickly put on a robe and went downstairs. Today

she wanted to make breakfast for her man. Though she knew Kyle loved to cook, she wanted to surprise him with a meal for a change. Western omelets, toast, and grits were his favorites, so Jill quickly started preparing them. She put on a pot of coffee and then set the table.

She was almost finished with breakfast when she looked up and saw Kyle leaning against the doorway with a big smile on his face. Though he had on a robe, it was open and exposed his beautiful, muscular chest. Jill's eyes dropped farther to the narrow waist. His white briefs only accentuated the rich chocolate color of his skin. Jill felt her heart skip a beat as she realized she was staring. Immediately she stopped what she was doing and walked over to Kyle. He opened his robe and took her inside.

"You did all this for me, baby?" he said as he nibbled her juicy lips.

"Yes, I did," Jill replied. "I wanted to take care of you today," she told him as she wrapped her arms around his waist.

She placed her hands firmly on his back, and her fingers massaged the soft, warm skin they came in contact with. The couple stood kissing for a while before Jill said, "We better stop because your eggs are getting cold."

"Forget about the eggs, I'd rather have you," he said as he continued to kiss Jill.

Jill laughed as she pulled away. "Come on, I'm trying to impress you with my own culinary skills," she said as she took his hand and led him to the table.

Kyle followed her to the table and sat down. "Oh, babe, everything looks great," he said as he observed the food and saw that Jill had made all of his breakfast favorites. "You're going to make someone a wonderful wife."

Jill playfully pulled his ear and then said, "I'll make *you* a wonderful wife, Mr. Roberts."

Kyle laughed as he pulled her into his lap and kissed her again. He kept her there as he ate and shared his meal with her. "Jill, you're a wonderful cook."

"Well, I'm not as good as you, but I manage."

"You do better than manage," Kyle replied as he held a piece of the omelet to Jill's lips with the fork.

Jill took the food that he offered and as she finished chewing she said, "Honey, I know we are supposed to meet Bebe at the Ranch House to leave for the airport at noon, but would you mind if we start a little earlier?"

"You still haven't heard from her, huh?"

"No, and I'm just a little anxious to see what's going on."

"No, I don't mind leaving early. We can leave as soon as we're dressed."

"Thanks, honey," Jill said as she kissed his neck.

"No problem, babe," Kyle replied as he continued to eat.

Jill stood up and said, "I'm going to go get dressed." She massaged Kyle's shoulders briefly before heading up the stairs.

Jill quickly did her makeup and pulled her hair back into a sleek twist. Then she put on a pale blue, silk pantsuit, which fit her shapely, slender body perfectly. Jill put on her jewelry, which consisted only of the pieces Kyle had bought her. She slipped into a pair of matching heels and grabbed her tote and then went back downstairs and found Kyle tidying up the kitchen. He had finished, and after admiring his beautiful fiancée, went upstairs to get ready for their trip.

When he returned, the couple left the cabin and put everything they were taking on the trip into Kyle's vehicle. They drove to A Special Place and

Kyle pulled into the employee lot. He looked at Jill from the corner of his eye and could see that she was searching for any sign of Bebe or Tony. Finally, she spotted Bebe's car and Kyle noticed a sense of relief come over her.

Kyle cut the engine off and turned to face Jill. He started to speak, then paused, unsure how Jill would take his advice.

"What's wrong?" Jill asked as she noticed the hesitation in his actions.

"Jill, what if things did go badly for Tony and Bebe, how are you going to handle it?" he asked slowly.

The relief that once filled Jill's face had disappeared as she contemplated the idea that things could have gone terribly wrong for the couple.

"I don't know what I'll do. I should have left things alone, but I couldn't stand to see Bebe lose Tony." Jill took a deep breath and leaned her head back. She massaged her temple and said, "I'm acting just like my mother. I always wanted her to stop meddling in my love life and now I've gone and messed up someone else's."

"Jill, you don't know if you've messed up anything at all. I just want you to be prepared if things didn't turn out the way you had hoped they would. No matter what, Bebe will know that you were only trying to help."

"By throwing a party for a woman who has the hots for her man? I don't think Bebe will see me as doing her any favors, Kyle," Jill said.

"We're not getting any answers out here. Come on, let's go inside," Kyle said as he raised her hand to his lips and kissed it.

They got out of the vehicle and started walking holding hands, but Kyle felt as though he had to run to keep up with Jill's fast pace.

He stopped and pulled her to him and said, "Jill, I know you're concerned about Bebe, but you have to remember that this isn't completely your fault."

"I keep trying to tell myself that, but I have a feeling that something terrible has happened, and if that's true, Kyle, then she has every right to blame me," Jill said quietly.

"Babe, why would you say that? Bebe is smart enough to know not to blame you alone. She and Tony have more to do with this mess than you do."

"Then why didn't she call me?" Jill replied in nervous agitation.

"Calm down, nothing bad has happened," Kyle told her as he gently stroked her cheek with the back of his fingers. He kissed her lips tenderly and said, "I think that if something bad happened you would have heard about it by now. Come on, let's go to the Ranch House and see what's up."

Still holding hands, they continued walking toward the restaurant. Kyle opened the door for her and Jill walked in. Her eyes glanced quickly around the room until she found Bebe and Tony in a booth. They sat side by side, and Jill could see that Bebe was even smiling. Jill let out a sigh of relief as she and Kyle made their way over to their table.

"Good morning, Jill," Bebe said with a genuine smile on her face.

"Hey, Bebe, how is everything?" Jill asked, as she studied their faces for any sign of animosity, but she found none.

"I'm fine," Bebe said as she picked up her glass of orange juice with her left hand.

Tony sat quietly for a moment, which was totally out of character for him. He had a smug smile on his face that made Jill even more concerned.

"Tony, are you okay?" Jill asked cautiously.

"I'm the finest I've ever been," he answered.

The table was quiet, and Bebe picked up a knife to cut her French toast. It was then that Jill saw it. Her mouth fell open as she gasped in surprise.

"Oh, Bebe, I can't believe it!" Jill said as she grabbed Bebe's hand.

There on Bebe's ring finger sat a huge, princess-cut, diamond engagement ring. Jill's face was filled with excitement and happiness for her friend. She quickly got up and went to hug and congratulate Bebe and Tony, as did Kyle.

"No wonder you didn't call me," Jill said.

"I couldn't, this man kept me very busy all night long," Bebe told her with a quick wink.

"I feel terrible, Bebe. You two just got engaged and you have to be separated by a business trip," Jill told her.

"Not so, sis. I am going along too," Tony said. Before Kyle had a chance to protest he continued, "I worked it out with Eric, and he said he could handle things without us for a few days."

Not having the heart to separate the newly engaged couple, Kyle said nothing. He knew all too well how it felt to be without the woman of his dreams, even for a day. It would almost be like a family vacation, and he knew that Jill and Bebe would want to talk about weddings all the way to Florida and back.

The hungry foursome ate a huge breakfast and continued to talk about work. Jill and Bebe made sure that they had everything they needed for the business trip, and Kyle and Tony made mental notes of items they needed to discuss with Eric, so he knew just what needed to be done while he was away.

After breakfast Kyle said to Tony, "Let's go talk to

Eric and make sure he knows what needs to be done while we're away." Before standing he kissed Jill on the cheek and promised to return shortly.

They watched in silence as Tony gave Bebe a long kiss good-bye. He held her face tenderly in his hands as his lips pressed lovingly against hers. Jill's heart filled with joy, and the emotion was expressed on her face as she watched the couple. As Kyle looked on, he knew he had made the right decision letting Tony come along. The lovers had just recognized what others had seen in them all along: that they were meant for one another.

Tony finally released Bebe's lips from his and said, "I'll be back for some more of that," with a mischievous grin on his face.

The two brothers left the Ranch House in search of Eric, and Jill and Bebe continued to talk. Jill was filled with questions and wanted desperately to hear more about the previous night, but since it was imperative for them to be ready for their client, the conversation remained on the job.

When Kyle and Tony returned, they all piled into Orlando's truck. He was their ride to the airport, and would pick them up when they returned. Monica had wanted to see them off as well, but with all the luggage there wasn't enough room for her too.

Once at the airport, they quickly got out of the truck and went to curbside check-in. On the plane it was just as Kyle had imagined. Jill and Bebe talked excitedly about Bebe's engagement and the events of the previous night. Bebe's night was nothing like the horrible thoughts Jill had imagined. Bebe explained that after they had left the party she and Tony drove to his cabin, where they continued to argue.

"Jill, I knew Tony loved me, but I didn't know that

he loved me that much. I mean, he just held me and cried. I have never seen him cry before, and all the while he was telling me that he needed me in his life, and that he wanted me as his wife. Tony said it hurt him to see another man enjoying my body. I had to remind him that we were only dancing."

"I'm so glad things turned out this way," Jill said softly.

"I am too. I tried so hard to make every part of my life fit perfectly, but I guess life is not supposed to make sense. I love Tony so much that it hurts when I'm not with him, but I guess that's the price you pay for ecstasy."

"Ecstasy?" Jill asked with a raised eyebrow.

"Ecstasy. Jill, we made love all night, and for the first time I felt like we really did belong together. I felt like my body would only accept him and no one else would ever do."

"What about your thoughts of ruining your friendship with him?"

"The way he made me feel last night let me know that marriage to him could only enhance our love. The only thing I'm worried about is telling his parents."

"Bebe, this is probably the moment they have been waiting for. They have know you since you were little, so you're already family," Jill said tenderly.

After their commuter flight they boarded another plane that would take them straight into Pennsylvania. It was early evening when the plane finally landed. They exited at Greater Pittsburgh International Airport and went to baggage claim to get their luggage.

When they had finished collecting their bags they headed outside where they found Jill's father and her sister, Barbie waiting for them. They exchanged hugs and said hello before putting all the suitcases into

Barbie's van and into her father's car. Though the air still held the heat of the day, Jill looked at the sky and knew the stars would soon be out.

During the forty-five-minute drive, lively conversation took place in both vehicles. While Jill and Kyle rode in her father's car, they told him how life in Durango was coming along.

Bebe and Tony rode in Barbie's van and she was thrilled to hear Bebe's news that she and Tony were engaged.

The sky was completely dark except for a few stars by the time they arrived at Jill's parents' house. The women went inside and the men unloaded some of the suitcases. It wasn't necessary to bring them all in, since they were only staying overnight, then leaving by tomorrow afternoon.

As Jill, Barbie, and Bebe walked into the house they were immediately greeted by Jill's mother, and the delicious aroma of her father's home cooking. Kyle reminded her of her dad. It seemed the men in her life loved to cook, and did so better than the women.

"Well, hello, ladies," Jill's mother, Maddie Alexander, announced as the group came through the door. She hugged and kissed them, and was thrilled to see her soon-to-be-married daughter. Jill's father, Rob, and Kyle entered the house as well, and Maddie was surprised to see Tony with them. She hugged the brothers warmly, and then said, "See, Rob, I told you we need to keep this big house. You never know when your children and their friends will come to stay," she said, laughing.

"Actually, Mom, we'll all be family soon," Jill told them.

"What do you mean, sweetheart?"

"I'm getting married too, Mom," Bebe said, smiling brightly.

"Oh, I have two daughters getting married now. God is truly blessing me," Maddie said jubilantly. She threw her arms around Bebe again and hugged her lovingly. Then she and Barbie looked at Bebe's impressive engagement ring.

Rob looked at the ring too, and then said, "Wow, that's a beautiful ring. You girls know how to pick them." He then gave Bebe a hug and said, "Congratulations, Bebe. And if that young man gives you any trouble just let me know."

Over the past year, Jill's family had become her family too. They had adopted her as one of them during their visit to Durango, for the grand opening of A Special Place. Bebe loved Jill's family as well, and quickly felt comfortable calling her parents Mom and Dad.

Maddie and Rob showed their guests where they were going to sleep. The fact that Jill and Bebe were engaged didn't matter; Maddie was very old-fashioned and had the women sleep in one room and the men sleep in another. Jill knew this and kissed her mother as she went to put her things in her old room.

When they were finished putting their luggage in their rooms, Rob called everyone into the dining room for dinner. At the long, elegantly set table, the family sat down and Rob said grace over the meal. He had cooked a huge dinner, which consisted of a honey-baked ham, macaroni and cheese, greens, yams, and corn bread. The hungry group began to eat, and the conversation flowed freely.

"Barbie, where are the kids?" Jill asked.

"They are with my next-door neighbor. They're anxious to see you—especially Ricky—but I told them they could come see you tomorrow. Besides, I knew Mom and Dad would have a houseful."

"Bebe, have you and Tony set a date for your wedding?" Maddie asked.

Bebe laughed and said, "Oh no, we've only been engaged for a day."

"Well, just let me know if you want me to do anything," Maddie told her.

"I think Jill will be collaborating with Bebe on wedding ideas," Kyle said.

"I hope you're right, big brother, because I can't wait to make Bebe Mrs. Antonio Roberts," Tony said. As he spoke his eyes never left Bebe's. Everyone at the table could tell by looking at Tony that he was hopelessly in love with his woman.

Rob reached over and patted Tony on the back, as the family made excited conversation over the upcoming weddings. Jill glanced at her mother, who was in her glory with having two weddings to plan for. Maddie asked about Eric and Sharon, and was told by Kyle that someone had to stay behind to handle things at the resort.

"How is the baby?" Maddie asked.

"Ally is doing fine," Kyle replied as he retrieved his wallet from his pocket and handed Maddie a picture of her.

"She's a beautiful little girl, Mom, and she looks a lot like her father," Jill said.

"That must make Eric very proud," Rob commented as he took the picture from his wife. He smiled admiringly at the picture of the child and then handed it back to Kyle.

"It sure does, but I think they will try for a boy next year," Tony added.

"No doubt you two will be giving us grandchildren

in a year or two as well," Maddie said, hoping to
plant a seed in Jill's and Bebe's heads to consider re-
producing as soon as they were married.

Jill stared at her mother in disbelief, but Bebe
replied with blissful honesty, "I must admit that I
can't wait to have a family, but I want to spend some
time enjoying married life with just the two of us
before we make any additions."

"I can understand that. Just don't make me wait too
long to see grandkids from you. I'm not getting any
younger, you know?"

Bebe patted Maddie's hand and then said, "I promise I won't."

Though Jill remained quiet on the subject, she
was happy that Bebe had extinguished her mother's
baby talk for the time being.

Maddie looked at Bebe. She had known her for a
little over a year, and in that time she had gone from
being a complete stranger to a family member. Barbie
was comfortable adopting Jill's new, extended family
as her own as well. Jill knew that Bebe, Barbie, and her
mother conversed on the phone regularly, and she
was happy that all the relationships were so cohesive
and loving.

After dinner the men retired to the living room,
where Rob offered Kyle and Tony one of his fine
Cuban cigars. Then he turned on the television so
they could watch the baseball game.

In the kitchen Jill, Bebe, Barbie, and Maddie began
cleaning the dinner dishes. All four women worked
together smoothly, as they discussed what had been
going in each other's lives since the last time they saw
one another. As they spoke, Jill could see that the look
of loneliness that once filled her mother's face was
absent. Maddie had so much to focus on that she

didn't have time to miss Jill so much. Now she not only had Barbie's family to concentrate on, but Jill and Kyle, as well as Bebe and Tony, too.

Maddie and Rob had also made several trips to Durango over the past year, as well as Jill returning home a few times. Neither of her parents had a forlorn look when she left anymore, since they knew both they would see her again soon. Jill knew this was due to the fact that she kept the promise she had made to herself, and that was to come home as often as she could—even if it was only for an overnight visit.

When the women were finished cleaning, Maddie poured each of them a glass of iced tea, and they went outside on the patio to relax and talk.

While Maddie was chatting with Bebe, Barbie used the opportunity to talk on a personal level with Jill.

"So tell me, sis, how are things going with your cowboy?"

"They're great, Barbie."

"No, you're not getting off that easily. I want to know all about the sheer pleasure and romance I know you're experiencing. Come on, Jill, you can't hold out on me," Barbie said, almost begging for details.

"Oh, you want details," Jill said with a coy smile. "Barbie, I didn't know being in love could enhance the pleasure you get out of having sex by one hundred percent. Kyle is the only one who does for me what no other was able to when we're in bed."

"So we should hear the pitter-patter of little feet soon after the wedding?"

"You sound just like Mom, Barbie," Jill said as she rolled her eyes and shook her head. "Of course we want children one day, but right now I'm still nurturing Desert Star, and Kyle is very busy on the ranch. We're still using protection, but I must admit that I'd love to have Kyle's baby." She looked up through her lashes bashfully.

Barbie smiled at her sister's enthusiasm over being in love. She imagined that Jill and Kyle would plan on having children soon after they married, and Barbie was anxious for Jill to make her an aunt as well.

"I'll be right back, I need a refill on my iced tea," Jill said as she stood.

"Oh, would you bring me another glass, too?" Maddie asked as she lifted her glass for Jill to take.

"Sure," Jill answered as she took the glass from her mother.

Jill entered the house and noticed that Kyle and Tony were sitting alone. She didn't bother them as they talked, but made her way quietly into the kitchen. As she prepared to pour more tea, she could hear the men talking.

"So tell me, baby brother, how did you get Bebe to finally say yes to marring you?" Kyle asked.

"Kyle, man, I thought I was going to lose it when I saw her dancing with Eddie."

"I know, and I thought you were mad enough to give him a severe beat-down, or at least fire him."

"No, I didn't fire him, but word got out that if he ever went around Bebe again, I would."

"Yeah, I wonder how that rumor got started," Kyle said, laughing.

"I think Eric started it, but it's true. Kyle, Bebe is the only woman who continuously blows my mind. I sleep, eat, and dream her, man, and when I got her alone at my place, I made the kind of love to her that let her know that she really can't afford to lose me either."

"I heard that," Kyle replied.

"Kyle, you have to know that I've always loved Bebe."

"Everyone has known that you've wanted her since you were ten years old."

"Yeah, well, I couldn't lose her, and without giving you all the details, I popped the question before she fell asleep."

"You did?" Kyle asked.

"I had to. I couldn't fall asleep after making love to her until I knew she was mine," Tony admitted honestly.

"When did you have time to buy the rock?"

"I've had it for a while. I was just waiting for the perfect time to give it to her."

"Maybe if you hadn't waited so long you could have saved us all from the headache we suffered yesterday," Kyle told Tony.

"You might be right, but I thought Bebe still wasn't ready for me."

"Well, she wasn't about to let Rosy get her hooks into you."

"I think Bebe knows that Rosy isn't my type. She just didn't like her hanging on to me, and my not being available for her," Tony said.

Jill finished what she was doing and was about to tiptoe back to the patio, when she ran into her father as he came out of the bathroom.

"Oops, I almost made you spill your drinks. I'm sorry, sweetheart," Rob said.

Tony and Kyle, who had been unaware of Jill's presence, turned to see her smiling as she continued on her way outside. She was pleased to hear the passionate way Tony voiced his love for Bebe. She knew in her heart that Bebe was as deeply loved by one of the Roberts boys as she was.

When she returned to her seat, she handed a glass of tea to her mother, then began to converse with her sister. They talked about her wedding and when

Barbie and her mother would be in Durango to help
with the preparations. Then the two sisters turned
their attention to their mother and Bebe. Maddie was
filled with questions about Bebe's plans, and though
she really didn't have any yet, she delighted Maddie
with marital talk.

It was getting late and they were all very tired, so
they went inside the house, where they found the men
watching the baseball game. Barbie kissed her father
and mother good-bye. She waved farewell to the rest
of the family and then left for her own home. Jill and
Bebe were exhausted. They each kissed their man, as
well as Maddie and Rob, good night before heading
up to Jill's old bedroom.

They took turns in the bathroom and then quickly
dressed for bed. As they both got into bed, Jill could
see a smile playing across Bebe's lips.

"What are you smiling about?" Jill asked as she
turned out the light.

"I was just thinking about how perfect my life has
become over the last twenty-four hours. I wasn't even
expecting all of this amazing fulfillment and here I
am right in the middle of it," Bebe said. She lay on
her belly with her eyes closed, and rested her head as
she squeezed the pillow. Given the time difference in
Pittsburgh, Jill knew at any minute Bebe would be
asleep, and so would she.

Jill turned from looking at her friend to the window
and saw twinkling stars in the darkened sky. With a
silvery moon illuminating the room, she was quickly
reminded of the time she had spent there over a
year ago. She was so lonely back then, but she fought
hard to ignore it. Now God had blessed her in so many
ways that as she fell asleep she thanked him for each
and every one of them.

* * *

The next morning Jill awoke hearing many voices downstairs. She rolled over to see Bebe's bed empty and already made. Jill got up and took a shower and dressed, and then she went downstairs. In the living room were all of Barbie's kids. Jill's nephew, Ricky Jr. was the first to run up to Jill and give her a big hug. Lacey was next, followed by James, to welcome their aunt. She sat on the sofa next to her brother-in-law, Rick, and gave him a hug as well.

Jill chatted and played with the children for a while before going into the kitchen. There she found everyone sitting down to breakfast. She imagined that her father had to get up pretty early in order to prepare breakfast for them all. Barbie's kids had eaten at their grandparents' as well, so Jill was happy that everyone pitched in to help. She took over for her mother, who was still making pancakes and bacon.

After breakfast, Tony, Kyle, Rob, and Rick all went out to the patio. Jill smiled at the sight and was so happy that all of them really liked each other. Briefly her mind thought of a huge family vacation, and hoped that she could organize something for next year.

It was getting close to noon, and they had to be at the airport for their flight. Rob and Barbie were taking them. The family said their good-byes and then they were off. Once at the airport, Jill hugged and kissed her father and sister again, as did the rest of the group.

"Kyle and Tony, you guys take good care of my girls," Rob said sternly as he shook their hands.

"You can count on it Dad," Kyle replied.

"Same here, sir," Tony agreed. "It was good seeing you again. You take care of yourself."

"I sure will. See you later," Rob told him.

They made their way to the curbside check-in and then through the airport to their gate. The feelings of warmth and love still filled Jill's heart. They were feelings that she had had ever since she had accepted Kyle's proposal. Everything in her life was so happy and complete, yet she couldn't help fearing that something terrible was going to happen, that something devastating was going to take her man away forever. She reached for his hand and squeezed it tightly. Kyle looked down into her eyes. He had seen that look of quiet fear in her eyes before. He pulled her close, knowing she would find comfort and security in his embrace, and in the warmth of his body.

After an hour's delay they finally boarded the plane. The couples sat across from each other. Jill could see that Tony was holding Bebe's hand. Occasionally he planted a kiss on it, but he never let it go. Bebe rested her head on his shoulder and it seemed to Jill that she had never looked as content as she did now that she was Tony's.

The flight attendant came by and offered them something to drink. They all asked for a soda and refused the light snack since they had eaten a hearty breakfast. After a brief layover in Atlanta, they arrived in Florida. They exited the plane and collected their luggage. Afterward, the group of travelers made their way outside. The weather was hot and humid, which made all of them wish they had dressed for the warmer climes. Kyle hailed a cab and told the driver to take them to the Sea Turtle Inn in Neptune Beach.

Chapter 6

After a forty-five-minute drive, the cab finally pulled into the driveway of the Sea Turtle Inn. It was beautiful and quaint and sat right on the beach. Jill could hardly wait until she had time after work to slip into the salty ocean. Each couple checked into their room and got settled. They had all promised to meet at 7:00 p.m. for dinner.

Once in their room, Jill opened the window, which overlooked the Atlantic Ocean, and was immediately greeted by a breeze that carried in the salt air. Tomorrow she and Bebe had a full day of meeting with Fitz and O'Neal, but tonight she wanted nothing more than to satisfy her need for Kyle.

As if reading her thoughts, Kyle was suddenly behind her wrapping his strong arms around her. Jill smiled as she felt his hand slip under her blouse to cup her breast.

"I thought spending the night at my parents' house would make you miss me," she said as she turned around to kiss him.

"That's your parents' home, so sleeping together was out of the question. But you're right, I did miss you very much," Kyle said as he continued to kiss Jill. He started to undress her and she assisted him. Her body ached to have his, and she couldn't hide her eagerness.

Jill climbed in bed, pulling Kyle on top of her. She seductively and sensuously licked his lips, which took him from zero to sixty in under six seconds. His hand disappeared between her thighs, and he found that she was ready for him as well.

"You know I want you, so let's do this," Jill whispered in his ear. Unable to keep her lips off him, she planted warm wet kisses on his lips and neck.

Her words along with her actions made Kyle anxious to satisfy her needs as well as his own. Kyle carefully put a condom over his hardened member. Spreading her legs apart widely, he pressed himself inside her. Jill elongated her body as she threw her head back. Her body was receiving exactly what it needed, which was a good dose of loving. She wrapped her legs around Kyle's and joined in the rhythmic motion of his body. Her hands caressed his back, which was already coated with a thin film of perspiration. Her face was also wet, which gave evidence to the power of their lovemaking.

She was thankful that Kyle wasn't a minute man, because her need would take a while. He never left her hanging; in fact, he always met her needs before his own, or at the same time. Only after Kyle had successfully made Jill cry his name several times did he allowed himself the pleasure of releasing inside her body.

When they were finished, their bodies lay entwined and exhausted. They lay quietly trying to catch their breath, enjoying each other's warmth and touch. Twenty minutes had passed, but they were comfortable just being held by each other.

When Kyle raised his head, he looked deep into Jill's eyes. Stroking her hair he said, "Babe, I get the feeling that sometimes you think that I am going to leave you. Am I right?"

"I can't help it. Everything is just so perfect. It's almost too perfect, Kyle. Life is ever changing, and if that is true, and my life is already perfect, what else am I to expect?"

"More perfection, Jill. You can't live your life wondering when the rug is going to be pulled from under you."

"I know, but of everything I have, losing you would be the one thing I couldn't bear."

"Jill, I'm young and healthy. Nothing's going to happen to me. And why are we putting my neck on the chopping block? Why can't something else tragic happen besides my death?" Kyle said as he rolled over.

"Like I said, I couldn't stand to lose you." Jill's voice cracked as she spoke.

Kyle pulled her into his arms again and said reassuringly, "Baby, we are going to grow very old and very gray together. The time will come when you can't stand me and will want me out of the house."

"Never," Jill said softly.

Kyle raised her hand and kissed its palm, then fell asleep.

Standing at the window, Jill looked out over the Atlantic Ocean. The sun shone brightly in the sky and the ocean's waves danced restlessly. She glanced back over her shoulder to see Kyle still sleeping peacefully. Jill couldn't help but smile at all the perfection God had placed in her life. She returned her gaze to the powerful ocean, and said a silent prayer asking God to keep her surrounded in the rich blessings in which she found herself.

Jill went into the bathroom and quickly took a shower and dressed in a shapely, white sundress. She did her makeup and hair, and then, giving Kyle a gentle kiss on the cheek, left the room.

As Jill walked through the hotel, she took notice of the tropical theme. Past the main lobby and down two short flights of stairs, she passed several ballrooms. Rattan ceiling fans and paintings with beach themes gave the place the ambiance of an island paradise. Comfortable sofas lined the walls, which were painted in soft colors that complemented each other.

At the end of the hall she arrived at Plantain's Restaurant. Though she would wait for Kyle to have breakfast, she wanted to find out what else the hotel had to offer. As she glanced over the posted menu, she saw that the restaurant served what they called a Floribbean menu. Immediately Jill saw crab-crusted grouper and sesame-seared tuna, and hoped that Kyle would want to have dinner here. She imagined he would, since she saw that Plantain's offered several of his favorites as well.

She was lost in thought, and jumped as she felt someone's arms circle her waist. Jill exhaled quickly in relief as she realized that it was Kyle who was now kissing her cheek.

"Good morning, beautiful," he said, continuing to hold her and planting another kiss on her lips.

"You scared me," she whispered.

"Well, that's what you get for sneaking out on me."

"I didn't sneak out on you, baby," she said as she turned to face him. "I just wanted you to get as much rest as you needed, because I plan on wearing you out today."

"Jill, you're insatiable," Kyle told her playfully.

"No, Kyle, I meant that after breakfast we should go shopping and check out Jacksonville. Maybe Bebe and Tony would like to come with us."

"Maybe, but I doubt it. Since those two have gotten engaged they seem to want to be alone most of the time."

"Well, if they don't want to come with us, we'll just make today our own," Jill said as she embraced Kyle.

"Actually, I prefer that," Kyle replied. He looked deep into the eyes of the woman he intended to marry and wished she would be content to spend the day in bed with him. But he knew Jill better than that. Today, she would probably shop until his legs ached, and after dinner she and Bebe would meet and make sure they were prepared for their meeting tomorrow.

Kyle turned and looked at the menu posted on the wall behind Jill. As he read, a smile began to form on his face just as Jill had anticipated.

"Oh, babe, did you see this?" he asked, now releasing Jill from his arms. "The Jamaican-spiced short ribs sound great, and so does the jumbo Mayport shrimp. I haven't had shrimp in a while. We have to eat here before we leave," he finished excitedly.

"I was thinking the same thing."

"Hi, guys," Bebe said. She and Tony approached smiling and holding hands. Jill smiled too. She had not seen her soon-to-be sister-in-law so happy since the day they met. Sure, Bebe was a fun person to be around, but Jill noticed that all the underlying tension that once held Bebe's mind and heart captive had now disappeared.

"We didn't think we would see you two today," Kyle said to Tony with a teasing look of surprise on his face.

"If I had it my way you wouldn't, but Bebe wants to get out and do some sightseeing," Tony said.

"Great," Jill said. "But I'm a little hungry. Let's get something to eat first. There are already some people eating out on the veranda. We could eat out there," she suggested.

Everyone turned to look outside and saw that the veranda was inviting, with a view of the magnificent Atlantic Ocean. The group agreed to have breakfast there, and walked outside where they were greeted by a hostess. She seated them at a table that was closest to the water. Moments later a waitress arrived to take their orders.

Though Kyle and Tony ordered coffee, Jill and Bebe opted for fresh-squeezed orange juice. The group feasted on omelets, grits, toast, and fresh fruit, and when they were finished, they paid their bill and left the hotel.

The clerk at the registration desk had told Jill about the wonderful shops that were within walking distance of the hotel. They all decided to try the local merchants, in hopes of finding beautiful, one-of-a-kind items.

They walked down First Street, and Bebe and Jill were thrilled to find the many beautiful boutiques that lined the street. Jill considered herself shopping for her honeymoon, and bought several island-styled dresses in bright, tropical colors. Bebe did as well, and then the two women found a shop that had the sexiest bathing suits Jill had ever seen.

Kyle and Tony accompanied them into the shop, and Kyle noticed that Jill only picked up one-piece bathing suits to try on. He was shocked that such a beautiful woman wouldn't want to show off her magnificent figure. He knew Jill was self-conscious about the scar on her abdomen, but he had hoped she had come to accept the minor imperfection.

Kyle looked around the store until he found two swimsuits he wanted Jill to try on for him. One was a white bikini, with a fuchsia flower serving as a front closure. A delicate flower was also attached to each side of the panties of the bikini. He also chose a black and gold halter-top bikini. The cutout heart on the right side of the suit would show up as a tan line once the suit was removed. Kyle smiled as he walked over to Jill with his choices in hand.

"Hey, honey, why don't you try these on for me?" he whispered, low and sexy.

Jill looked at the suits and then at him before saying in a hushed voice, "Kyle, you know I can't wear anything that shows my abdomen."

"Why not? You're beautiful, Jill."

"I just don't want people looking at me and cringing at that ugly scar. I won't wear that, Kyle," she said defiantly and walked away.

"Baby, would you at least try them on for me? I want to see my beautiful woman showing off what she's got. Just once, baby, and only for my eyes," Kyle whispered pleadingly.

"Okay, I'll try it on for you, but you'd better be standing close to the fitting room door, because I'm not coming out," she said and reluctantly took the bathing suits from him.

Inside the dressing room, Jill tried on the white suit first. She had to admit, the bikini did look fantastic on her. The slight smile on her face faded as she looked at her scar. She tried on the suits not for herself, but to please Kyle. She opened the door to the dressing room slightly, and as promised, Kyle was standing there.

He peeked in and studied her figure from head to toe. He smiled appreciatively and then said, "Girl, you don't realize just how much you have it going on. I love it on you, Jill. You look fantastic. Will you try the black and gold one on for me now?"

"Yes, I will," she said, trying to resist the smile that was appearing on her lips.

Kyle closed the door and Jill slipped out of the suit. He had a way of making her feel so womanly and beautiful. His words made her believe that not another creature existed that could match her. She put on the next suit and found herself in awe at her appearance. She let her hands rest sassily on her hips as she posed in front of the mirror. A smile of self-acceptance formed on her lips, and her eyes paid no attention to the minor imperfection. Since she had gotten the scar, she had not put on any garment that would reveal her problem. But now, at Kyle's urging, she stood looking in the mirror and was completely enchanted with her own reflection.

There was a knock at the dressing room door and Jill turned to let Kyle in. Her smile quickly faded when she realized that it was the store clerk, asking if the suits fit. The door was opened wide, and Jill could see Tony looking at her.

Before she could cover herself Tony said, "Wow, sis, you look great." He walked closer to get a better look and then said, "You mean my brother is going to let his woman go on the beach looking that hot?" With a boyish grin, his eyes twinkled as he saw that Jill was smiling too.

"This suit was you brother's idea. I wanted to get something more conservative," Jill said.

"Well, you really should take his advice. With you wearing that suit his eyes won't roam for a second."

"That is one of our best-selling bikinis," the sales-clerk said, smiling at how well Jill wore the suit.

Just then, Kyle returned with Bebe. In his hands, he had a pair of flip-flops that matched each suit. His face grew serious, but a gleam of appreciation filled his eyes as he saw Jill standing in the doorway. She looked up shyly at him only to see the look of admiration and love in his eyes.

"Well, Kyle, what do you think?" she asked slowly.

"I think you're an amazing beauty, baby. Are you going to get this suit?"

"I think I'm going to get both of them."

"Well then, you might be interested in this," he said as he walked toward her.

Kyle set the shoes down, but in his hand he still held a chain. It was long and gold and Jill couldn't imagine it being a necklace. As he began wrapping his arms around her waist, Jill realized what it was. The belly chain Kyle had fastened around her waist now rested sexily on her hips. It matched her black and gold suit perfectly and had little seashells dangling from the ends.

Jill looked in the mirror and saw for the first time just what Kyle was seeing. She did look hot. For the first time in years she was able to say she looked hot in a bikini, and she owed it all to Kyle.

"Thank you," she said softly as she caressed his cheek

Jill closed the dressing room door and turned to admire her reflection in the mirror one last time before removing the suit. She quickly dressed and went to the register where Kyle paid for her items. Bebe and Tony were waiting outside for them and the group continued shopping.

They stopped in a few more stores before they

headed back to the hotel to freshen up. As they walked out along the water's edge, they took off their shoes and enjoyed the feel of the sand between their toes. Jill's mind raced with excitement over their plans to honeymoon in Jamaica. She squeezed Kyle's hand in a silent thank-you. She now completely accepted her body. The scar that had held her captive, no longer did.

Tony's words had only given her added confidence. He looked at her in the bikini and didn't even notice the scar. Perhaps it didn't look as bad as she imagined, she thought.

Stopping briefly in their rooms to freshen up, the group decided to head back out. It was almost five o'clock, and they were anxious to see more of what the beachside city had to offer. The clerk at the swimsuit shop had told them about Joe's Crab Shack, and they decided to try the place. Since the restaurant was too far to walk they drove the rental car to the eatery.

The drive to the restaurant was straight down Third Street, and then two blocks left on Beach Boulevard. Kyle parked the car and the group crossed the street. As they walked up the ramps to the entrance, Jill could smell the fabulous aroma of perfectly seasoned food coming from inside. The exterior, as well as the interior, was decorated in a nautical theme. The restaurant sat right on the beach and was a lively, festive place. A large, handmade whale was hanging from the ceiling.

Though the décor was quite different, Joe's Crab Shack reminded Jill of the Ranch House. The music was loud and everyone seemed to be enjoying themselves. Even the people who worked there seemed to enjoy working as they smiled with the same energy that the place had. Jill imagined that some of the people where regulars, and probably came here every weekend.

The hostess greeted them warmly as she asked their seating request. They decided to eat outside again, because it had been a long time since anyone had been to the beach.

Once they were seated, a waitress came and took their drink orders and handed them menus. She left and returned quickly, and then asked if they wanted to start with an appetizer.

Kyle ordered the awesome appetizer platter, and Tony ordered the crab balls.

"Aren't you ladies going to order an appetizer?" Tony asked.

"I thought I'd share with you," Bebe told him.

"As hungry as I am, I think you'd better get your own food. I'm not sharing," he said, trying to be serious.

"Tony, you're not going to share with me?" Bebe said. She placed her hand gently on his thigh and then kissed his cheek softly.

"Thanks, miss, that will be all for now," he said to the waitress. Then he turned to Bebe, who had a big smile on her face. "You know you have me just where you want me," he said, leaning toward her and planting a kiss on her lips.

"Hey, knock it off. This is a family restaurant," Kyle said jokingly.

Jill sat quietly and just smiled at her friends. The thought occurred to her that she had to stop referring to them as friends. Very soon the people who sat at this table would all be family, her family. She listened as they laughed and talked. They all truly enjoyed each other's company. Jill was so happy for Bebe and Tony, and knew she was blessed to be coming into a big, loving family herself. She regretted that Eric and Sharon weren't with them.

Jill's concentration was broken when the waitress returned shortly with the appetizers. She took the orders for their entrées and then left.

"Kyle, when are you and Tony going to charter a boat?" Jill asked as she began to eat.

"I don't think it will be too hard to get a boat tomorrow morning. I know it will be short notice, but Tony and I are going to leave early to go to the Mayport docks. The registration clerk at the hotel gave us several boats that do charters."

"Yeah, she even gave us the captains' names. Man, I can't wait to go. I haven't been deep-sea fishing in a while," Tony added.

"I can't believe they get to go play while we work," Bebe said, trying to sound irritated.

"Somebody has to work, Bebe. It might as well be you and Jill, since Tony and I are really on vacation," Kyle said. Tony lifted his bottle of Corona and toasted his brother.

Jill laughed and said, "Okay, just remember those words when I get in tomorrow after the meetings and I'm too tired to—"

"Don't worry, baby, I won't let you get that overworked," Kyle said as he fed her a piece of broiled shrimp.

The waitress returned and set their plates in front of them. Kyle and Tony had both ordered the sirloin and shrimp combos. Bebe had decided on the blackened chicken breast. Jill, who was determined not to gain a pound before the wedding, had the coconut shrimp salad.

The group began eating, talking, and enjoying each other's company. As they ate, a train whistle blew and ceiling lights began to flash. The waiters and waitresses lined up and formed a train through the restaurant, joined by many of the patrons. Tony, who was always up for a good time, grabbed Bebe's hand and joined in on the fun. Kyle smiled and did the same with Jill. It seemed like the entire place was one giant party, and for that moment, they were all friends.

Chapter 7

Jill reached over, wanting to hold Kyle, but soon discovered that she was alone in bed. She noticed that he had left her a note on the pillow and she read it.

I know Desert Star is going to wow them in the meeting today. Have fun and knock them dead. I'll see you later, baby.

All my love,
  Kyle

It was a short yet sweet note, and Jill was happy he had been considerate enough to leave it. She then picked up the phone and dialed Bebe's room.

"Hello," Bebe answered, still sounding half asleep.

"Hey, Bebe, it's me."

"Jill, it isn't even seven o'clock yet. What's up?" Bebe asked.

"Nothing important. Is Tony gone too?"

"Yeah, he left about an hour ago."

"I didn't know they were leaving so early. Kyle left me a note, but I wish I had seen him off."

"I wish we could have gone fishing with them, but we're here to do a job. I have everything ready on my end."

"Good, so do I. Monica did a good job in helping prepare everything and making all the travel arrangements."

"Yes, she did. I think she's a keeper. Well, we have to be at Fitz and O'Neal at nine a.m., so we might as well start getting ready. Do you want to meet downstairs for a quick breakfast?"

"I think we'd better. There's no telling how long the meetings will last, and I don't want my belly growling during the conference."

"I booked the Plantation North conference room, and my Power Point presentation is ready," Bebe informed Jill.

"Well, it looks like we're all set then. I'll meet you on the veranda in an hour." Jill said good-bye to Bebe and hung up the phone.

Jill took a shower and dressed in a smart salmon-colored business suit, with a cream-colored blouse. She did her makeup in the soft tones that were appropriate for a business meeting. She brushed her hair and then pulled it back into a sleek knot that rested almost at the nape of her neck. As a finishing touch, she added her small, gold hoop earrings and her watch.

Jill slipped into cream-colored shoes that matched her blouse, grabbed her purse and briefcase, and headed out the door to meet Bebe.

When she arrived at the veranda, Bebe was already waiting for her. She was dressed in a khaki-colored skirt suit and had pulled her hair back into a bun as well. She looked very businesslike and had kept her makeup and jewelry to a minimum.

"I think we're both dressed for success," Bebe said as Jill approached the table and sat down.

"Yes, we're dressed in colors that make you think of the sea," Jill said, laughing.

"Yeah, but we look good. I ordered some scrambled eggs, toast, fruit, and orange juice and coffee for both of us."

"Everything looks great," Jill said as she looked down at her plate and picked up her fork. "Thanks, Bebe."

"No thanks necessary, I only did the ordering. I couldn't cook a breakfast like this even if I wanted to," Bebe admitted as she continued to eat.

"You can't cook?" Jill said, stunned.

"Nope."

"Well, I can't lay bragging rights to anything. Kyle cooks way better than I do. What are we going to do when we're married?" Jill said, laughing.

"Count on Kyle to feed us." Bebe shook her head pathetically.

"We should practice cooking together."

"Why? We would only end up with something no one would want to eat."

"No, we'll follow a really good cookbook. I'll get my mom to send one."

"That sounds like a good idea. At least you have Kyle. Tony and I would starve if we weren't at your place."

The two women finished their meal and paid their bill. Moments later they were on their way to Fitz and O'Neal Boating and Accessories. The boating facility was located just before the Intercoastal Bridge on Atlantic Boulevard, and was a ten-minute drive away.

It would be good for Jill and Bebe to land this account. Though Desert Star was doing very well, most

of their accounts had come by way of recommenda-
tion of Joan Singletary. It would be nice, Jill thought,
for their firm to land some major contracts on their
own. Fitz and O'Neal were big, and had clients all
along the eastern seaboard. To nail this deal would
be of significance for Jill and Bebe's firm.

Jill pulled into the parking lot and they went inside.
Bebe, who had gotten used to projecting a positive
image in the world of public relations, told the receptionist whom they were there to see. As Jill observed
how Bebe had grown personally and professionally
over the past year, she was pleased to see that she had
stepped into the role of business owner and public relations executive, with the grace and poise of a well-
seasoned veteran.

The receptionist stood and led the women to the
conference room, where Mr. Harold Fitz and Mr.
Thomas O'Neal, along with several of the top executives, were waiting. The gentlemen quickly stood and
shook hands with the women, before everyone took
a seat at the table.

After everyone had introduced themselves, the
group took Jill and Bebe on a personal tour of the facility. Mr. Fitz spoke proudly as he showed off the fac-
tory, which he, along with Mr. O'Neal, had built over
the past thirty years.

When they were finished, the group got into their
vehicles and headed back to the Sea Turtle Inn,
where Bebe's promotional presentation was to be
given. They parked their cars and entered the inn.
The business associates conversed with Jill and Bebe
on the hopes of boosting the sales of the company.
Bebe walked confidently feeling sure she could deliver
what the boating executives were looking for.

Once inside the Plantation North conference room,

the businessmen took their seats and waited anxiously for the presentation to begin. Jill dimmed the lights as Bebe stood at the front of the room and prepared to begin.

"I have put together a presentation I want to show you. I know you wanted to see something that would boost sales, so let's take a look at what we've come up with so far," Bebe said as she started the Power Point presentation.

In the dimly lit room Bebe couldn't see the faces of the men who sat listening to her. She narrated key points on the screen, and her voice was filled with enthusiasm. Twenty minutes later she had finished. Bebe's energetic smile faded as she turned on the lights.

Bebe looked around the table at a bunch of unimpressed faces. Jill began handing each of them a packet of papers that outlined the goal of the publicity campaign.

"I don't see how increasing our demographic advertising area alone will increase our sales. People in the Midwest aren't going to want to come all the way to Florida to buy a boat or boating accessories," Mr. O'Neal said flatly.

"If you don't mind my saying so, this campaign is a little flat. I didn't come away with a feeling of excitement over our products," said one of the executives.

The group of businessmen continued to go over the packet Jill had given them, but without a hint of excitement.

"I'm afraid I'm not pleased either with what you're showing me," Mr. Fitz said in a disappointed voice. He stood, a clear signal for the rest of the board to follow suit.

"Mr. Fitz, please give us another day to come up with

something else. I think we have a better understanding of what you want and the direction you want your company to take," Bebe said quickly.

"Yes," Jill added. "Later today we'll come back to your business and show you the rest of our campaign. Of course we will have to do a lot of revamping, but Desert Star came here to wow you, and we're going to do just that," she finished on a positive note.

Jill could see that Mr. Fitz was giving what she had said careful consideration. He looked at Mr. O'Neal, who gave him a nod, and then he said, "Okay, our afternoon meeting is still on. I'll see you ladies at four o'clock, and I hope you have something to show me that will create some waves in the world of boating."

He continued to walk toward Jill. He shook her and Bebe's hand again and then left the room. The others filed out as well, leaving Jill and Bebe to come to terms with their first major failure.

"Oh, Jill, it looks like we blew it," Bebe said solemnly.

"No, we haven't. Now we have a better idea of what this customer wants and only five hours to give it to him," Jill said.

"I don't think we have enough time."

"Not for negative thinking, we don't. Come on, Bebe, we can do this."

Equipped with laptops, pens, paper, cell phones, and coffee, the team set out to design a campaign that would make waves in the world of boating for Fitz and O'Neal. Within the hour they had deliveries arriving from Copymax, John Casablanca Models, and room service. They worked nonstop and by 3:30 were prepared to land the deal they wanted.

Jill and Bebe arrived at four o'clock at Fitz and O'Neal. They were quickly ushered into the conference room where everyone from the meeting that morning was already seated. Bebe glanced around the room and saw the same unimpressed faces. Her confidence had been shaken earlier, but now she knew she had what it took to win them over. Once again she started the conference as Jill handed out the packets of information covering the new approach to the campaign.

"Gentlemen, take a moment to look around. Here, as well as at your office, I noticed that you are lacking one important element, women. With all due respect, women enjoy boating as much as men do, and I don't see you capitalizing on that aspect. As a matter fact, our fiancés are out boating right now, and we really wanted to join them. In the short time since our earlier meeting, we did meet with them briefly. Please take a moment to look at the new ad campaign we have developed."

Jill dimmed the lights and turned on the television. With the help of Tony and Kyle and a Sony Handycam, Jill had created a DVD of Kyle and Tony boating and deep-sea fishing with two models, and then a shot of all of them outside the Fitz and O'Neal building. Jill had called Kyle and told him of the situation. He and Tony were only too happy to help, since it really didn't present a problem.

Kyle had the captain pull back into the dock to pick up the models Jill and Bebe had hired, and Jill text-messaged Kyle with a small script for each of them. Then she paid one of the employees from the hotel who had just finished his shift to go and pick up the finished DVD.

Jill and Bebe previewed the DVD and were happy with its outcome. Now, as they looked around the room, they could see approving smiles on the faces of the men who had been ready to cancel the deal. The clip ended and Bebe turned up the lighting and pushed the television back against the wall. Jill moved toward the front of the room. An air of assuredness surrounded her as she smiled easily.

"Well, gentlemen, what did you think this time?" Jill asked.

"Ms. Alexander, we want you to develop this into a full campaign," Mr. Fitz said exuberantly. He stood and shook Jill's and Bebe's hands and then said, "Thank you. It's obvious that you worked very hard," as he gave them a quick wink and then left the room.

"Send over your contracts and I'll have our legal department take a look at them. If everything is in order, you should have them signed and on your desk by the end of the week," Mr. O'Neal told them. "Oh, and we'll see about getting a couple of female executives on board. My wife's been after me to do that for years, but I'm beginning to see what she means," he said, laughing.

The rest of the group followed out of the room shaking Jill's and Bebe's hands in congratulations. After the last person exited the room, Jill collapsed into a chair. She was worn out.

Bebe came and sat down beside her. "You look like I feel," she said. Though she had a faint smile on her lips she was every bit as tired as Jill. Bebe leaned forward and rested her elbows on her knees and her chin in her palms. "How do you manage to stay so positive and so self-assured during times like this?"

"I always seem to do better under pressure," Jill answered, smiling. "But I think the excitement of having Kyle and Tony with us didn't keep us as sharp creatively as we could have been."

"I know. We just have to make sure that never happens again."

"We won't land every deal, but the reason we don't shouldn't be that we didn't give it our best."

"An important lesson. I'm starving. Where are we going to eat tonight?" Bebe asked.

"I thought we could eat here at Plantain's," Jill said.

"That sounds good. Why don't we pack everything up and go change into some more comfortable clothes?"

"Sounds good."

They collected all their belongings and headed for their rooms. Once inside, Jill began to change her clothes. After she was undressed, she let her fingers trace the beautiful belly chain Kyle had bought for her. She decided to keep it on and also put on the white bikini. She dressed in a pair of shorts and a sleeveless top. She brushed out her hair and decided to let it fall loose around her shoulders. Jill changed her gold, hoop earrings for a pair of larger ones and then slipped on a pair of sandals.

She heard someone at the door and was surprised to see Kyle enter. Though she was happy to see him, she refrained from hugging him. Smelling like salt air and fish, Kyle was in desperate need of a bath.

"How did things go?" he asked.

"We got the contract," Jill told him excitedly. "Baby, thank you so much for all that you did for me today. I have to find a way to make it up to you."

"A hug will do," Kyle said, smiling and walking toward her.

"Oh no, Kyle. You really smell like a fisherman. A hug will have to wait until after you have showered."

"I'm just teasing, babe. Where are we going to eat tonight?" he asked as he began to strip off his clothes.

"Bebe and I decided that we wanted to eat at Plantain's. Is that okay with you?"

"It's fine with me. I'm going to clean up and then I'll meet you there," he said as he went to take a shower.

"Honey, why don't you put your swim trunks on under your clothes? I think I want to go down to the beach after dinner," she yelled out to him.

Kyle stuck his head out of the bathroom door and replied with a smile, "I'll be sure to do just that." Then he disappeared back into the bathroom.

As planned, Jill met Bebe at Plantain's. She was alone, but said that Tony would be joining them as soon as he cleaned up.

"That's what Kyle is doing right now," she said, laughing, and took a seat at the table. "I feel so bad that they were fishing all day and didn't get to bring back what they caught. To add to that, we interrupted their boating trip."

"I know. I feel pretty bad about that too. We'll just have to make it up to them. They really were great to help us out on such short notice," Bebe said, sipping her drink.

"Well, I don't see what they could complain about. You did find two of the most beautiful models to work with them," Jill said in mock irritation.

"They both came highly recommended from the agency. Since they had some acting experience, I thought we'd better go with them. They proved invaluable in helping Tony and Kyle with the impromptu taping, don't you think?"

"I couldn't agree more. You did an excellent job, Bebe."

"No, we did an excellent job."

The restaurant was filled with the delicious aroma of house specialties being cooked and served. Though they were sitting inside, the music from the live band filtered in. The atmosphere was serene and beautiful, but made Jill homesick.

When Kyle and Tony arrived, the group ordered. They started with Caribbean conch fritters, and Ahi tuna tempura roll, which was filled with Jamaican vegetables and black bean mango vinaigrette. Since there would be no more driving today, the entire table ordered Corona beer with lime. After they had finished the appetizers, the waitress bought their entrées to the table. Jill and Bebe had both ordered the oven-roasted salmon, while Kyle ordered the black angus filet mignon, and Tony had crab-crusted grouper.

They all ate heartily, as Jill and Bebe had only nibbled as they worked on their second presentation for Fitz and O'Neal. Though Kyle and Tony had no fish to show for their hard work, they were just as hungry.

The waitress returned to clear the table and take their dessert orders. Each couple opted to share a slice of delicious key lime pie. Sharing a fork as well, Kyle fed Jill as the group finished their meal and swapped stories of the day's events. Kyle reached into his pocket and produced a packet of pictures that he and Tony had taken while on the chartered boat. Jill and Bebe were impressed with what the guys had done and seen while fishing, and agreed to go with them on a trip soon.

"Maybe next time we need to make plans so that Eric and Sharon can come with us," Jill said.

"They want to plan a family vacation after the wedding," Kyle told them as he handed the waitress his credit card.

He had generously tipped her, and she stammered, "Oh, thank you, sir." With a big smile and wide eyes, she quickly went to process his card.

Kyle smiled and winked as the waitress left. As he turned around, he was met with the adoring gaze of his fiancée.

"Your day has been filled with beautiful women, but don't forget who you have to go home with," Jill said.

"I could never do that," he replied as he kissed Jill's lips.

It was a beautiful evening in Neptune Beach, Jill noticed as they all went outside. Though the sun was beginning to set, the weather was still hot and humid. Bebe and Tony decided to sit poolside while Jill and Kyle walked the short distance toward the beach.

As they approached the water they began to undress. Kyle could hardly take his eyes off Jill. He noticed that she was wearing the white bikini and the belly chain, which hung seductively around her hips. He took her hand and kissed it as they walked into the ocean.

Jill playfully jumped on Kyle's back and he ran deeper into the water. The waves were mild and as he went deeper into the ocean, Jill realized what Kyle was up to. In one quick motion, Kyle spun around as he released his grip on her legs. Jill flew off his back, and butt first, went completely under. She stood up laughing and splashed water on him.

The couple laughed and played like a couple of kids. Then Kyle pulled Jill to him and held her tightly. Ringlets of wet curls framed her face as she looked at him with beckoning, almond-shaped eyes that he loved. She was everything a man could ever dream of having as his wife. He leaned toward her and kissed her lips, which were still salty from the sea water, but he only managed to find the sweetness in them.

As always when he held her like this, Jill was conscious of nothing else. The only thing that mattered was her oneness with him. Time was suspended indefinitely as she allowed him to continue to hold and kiss her.

"Let's go back and join Tony and Bebe for a while at the pool, before we go back to our room," he said when he finally released her lips from his.

Hand in hand they left the ocean and walked back to the hotel's pool. As they approached, they could see the couple sharing a chaise longue and blissfully watching the last of the day's sun disappear.

Jill and Kyle sat and talked with Bebe and Tony for a short while before they made their excuses to return to their room. Tony could only smile as he said good night to his brother. They had an early flight in the morning and all needed to be well rested for it.

Once back inside their hotel room, Jill and Kyle stripped out of their wet swim clothes and went into the bathroom. Jill started the shower adjusted the water to a nice warm temperature, hoping to chase away the chill that made her body tremble. She stepped inside the tub and began to rinse the salt water out of her hair.

"Let me do that," Kyle said as he joined her.

"Okay," Jill said as she handed him the shampoo and conditioner.

Kyle took both bottles from her and set the bottle of conditioner down on the edge of the tub. Pouring a generous amount of shampoo into his hands, he began to wash her hair. His hands worked until Jill's head was covered with bubbles. He loved the feel of her hair as it slid filled with lather through his fingers. After he had washed her hair twice and rinsed out the soap, he then used the condition. The rich smell of coconut filled the air, as he continued to caress her long tresses.

After he rinsed the conditioner out as well, he

took a washcloth and began bathing Jill. Whenever they did shower together, it was something that Jill enjoyed immensely. She loved how he washed each part of her body slowly and deliberately. Kyle seemed to derive pleasure just from touching her, and she was always happy to oblige him.

"Now it's my turn," she said softly.

Kyle sat down on the edge of the tub and Jill moved in between his thighs. She poured some of the shampoo into her hands and began working it into a good lather. Jill cleaned his hair and massaged his scalp.

Kyle watched hypnotically as her breasts bounced and swayed in front of him. He cupped one beautiful breast in his hand and then took it into his mouth. Jill inhaled sharply, as her nipple enjoyed his tongue's attention. When he finished, he looked up to see pleasure dancing across her face.

She quickly conditioned and rinsed his hair and then took another washcloth and began to lather it. With the same deliberate motions he had used to bathe her, she began to cleanse him. Kyle moaned deeply as his own body expressed pleasure from what Jill was doing to him. She took his hard member into her soapy hands and continued bathing him. Her strokes were firm and long and within a few minutes Kyle was pouring out his love, both verbally as well as physically.

Chapter 8

When their commuter plane finally arrived at La Plata County Airport in Durango, it was 3:00 p.m. The weather was just as hot as it had been in Florida, but not as humid. The group was exhausted from their trip, and after retrieving their luggage, was happy to see Eric waiting for them outside.

"Oh, man, it's good to see you," Kyle was the first to say as he grabbed his brother's hand in a strong shake and gave him a hug with the other. "Is everything okay at the ranch?"

"Everything is fine, man. I told you I could handle things while you were gone. I'm not Tony," Eric said and snickered as he grabbed his brother in a bear hug.

"Hey, hey, I had work to do in Florida. I can't be in two places at once," Tony said in playful animosity.

Eric gave Jill and Bebe a warm welcome-home hug and then assisted the women with their luggage. Inside the vehicle, Eric updated his brothers on the events that had taken place at the ranch and informed Bebe about the status of the resort.

As she listened to Eric, Jill couldn't help but wonder how long Bebe could keep working full-time at both jobs. Bebe still managed A Special Place. She had been with the project since its conception, and it was her first baby. Though she was doing exceptionally well at both jobs, it left very little time for relaxation.

Now Bebe had given birth to two new babies: Desert Star, and the role of being Tony's fiancée. Maybe juggling all three wouldn't present a problem for Bebe, Jill thought, but when the couple decided to have kids it probably would. Jill knew from seeing how difficult it was for Barbie to manage family life and going to school that it was no easy feat. But Bebe was smart, efficient, and patient, just like Barbie. When Jill saw the similarities between the two women, she realized that Bebe would undoubtedly have no problem maintaining her fast-paced life.

Eric dropped Jill and Kyle off first. He pulled up in front of the cabin and helped them with their luggage.

"Welcome back, man," Eric said as he finished putting the last suitcase on the porch.

"Thanks, Eric, you really did a good job while we were gone," Kyle told him.

"I think you'd better reserve that comment until you have a chance to check out things for yourself," Eric said as he winked at Jill.

"But you said that there were no problems," Kyle said as his brows furrowed. Finally, it dawned on him that Eric was just teasing him. He smiled halfheartedly at his brother's humor. "I'll see you later, man," he said as he turned to enter the cabin.

"Oh, by the way, Mom and Dad will be here this week," Eric informed Kyle and Jill.

"Is something important going on?" Kyle asked.

Eric dug his hands deeper inside his blue jean pockets and shrugged his shoulders. "I guess Dad just wants to check on things, but Mom wants to meet with

Jill for some reason. They'll be here tomorrow," he said. With a wave of his hand he got into the truck and drove off.

Jill and Kyle entered the cabin and set their luggage at the foot of the staircase. Then Jill walked into the kitchen and poured two glasses of ice-cold lemonade. She returned to the living room and sat on the sofa next to Kyle as she handed him a glass.

Kyle was talking to her, but her mind was a million miles away. Eric had said that her future mother-in-law was coming to see her, and for the life of her, she couldn't figure out why. In the past year since their engagement, Jill had only seen Mrs. Roberts a couple of times. She was always so busy with her charitable work and accompanying her husband on his many business trips that Jill really didn't get a chance to know her. Now she sat wondering what she wanted to talk to her about.

"Jill, what's on your mind?" Kyle asked, realizing that Jill hadn't paid any attention to what he had been saying.

She contemplated momentarily not telling him exactly what she was thinking, but decided she should be completely honest since she needed honest answers.

"Kyle, do you realize just how much time your mother and I have spent together since the time we met?" she asked, looking into his eyes.

"I know exactly how much, very little. And I know exactly what you're thinking. You're wondering, why does she want to see you now? Jill, maybe she just wants to get to know her future daughter-in-law."

"I was thinking that too, but I just feel a little uneasy about her coming to visit me now. Don't get me wrong, I think your mother is very sweet, but she doesn't strike me as the type of woman who stops by her daughter-in-law's house to have a cup of tea and chat. I mean, I can't see us making plans to go shopping together either," Jill finished in an almost breathless manner.

She looked up to see an amused smile on Kyle's face. He sat there grinning, but said nothing.

"You would find this funny. You don't have the same problem as I do. You and my family get along great," she said in an irritated voice.

The smile left Kyle's face as he turned to Jill and said, "Jill, that's not fair. Your family is always home and available when we go to see them. And when they come out here, of course I make time for them because I enjoy them. Babe, anyone who is important to you is important to me. I hope that you feel the same way about my family."

"I do, Kyle, and I think you already know that. I just don't think I really fit into your mother's world. She is so classy, and so perfect. She keeps a smile on your dad's face twenty-four-seven."

"Uh-huh, and how would you know that? You're not around her long enough to know that, remember?" Kyle said teasingly.

"I know that because I've seen the way they look at each other. They each represent half of a perfect love, which is their marriage. There is no place on this earth your mother would rather be than right by your father's side. Kyle, she's a lot to live up to," Jill finished softly.

It dawned on Kyle what was going on in Jill's mind. She was feeling insecure, and to that he said, "Jill, you're right, my mother is perfect." Jill let out a sigh, but Kyle continued, "She is a perfect match for my father. They have made for themselves a good life, a very wealthy life. You probably won't find my mom baking cookies for her grandchildren, but she will make sure they attend every cultural event from here to New York."

He leaned back on the sofa and wrapped Jill in his arms. Kyle looked at her face and saw that he hadn't completely erased all the doubt she had.

"Kyle, I just want her to like me. I know I'm no slouch, but I'm not a Regina Roberts, either. I can't compete with perfection."

"Jill, you already are perfection. What my parents have going on in their lives works perfectly for them, but it wouldn't work for us. I don't jet-set across the country landing huge real estate deals. I'm a ranch hand."

"Yeah, but you own the ranch and the resort," Jill retorted playfully.

Kyle laughed, and then said, "Okay, so I own the ranch, but what I'm getting at is that I love my life. I love what I do and I love you. In my eyes, everything I have is perfect, especially you. I'm happy in our world, baby. We both have careers that we love, family and friends that we care about, and a beautiful home. Is it enough for you?" he asked as he let his hand trace the bridge of her nose before kissing her lips gently.

"Yes, it's more than enough for me," Jill said, smiling, and kissed Kyle in return.

"I'm going to take our luggage upstairs. Why don't you go and freshen up and then I'll make us dinner?"

"You want some help?"

"No, it won't take me long," Kyle said.

They both stood and went upstairs. Jill was anxious to take a shower, and went to the bathroom and prepared to do that.

Kyle returned downstairs and began making them

a quick yet sumptuous meal. In no time at all he had made them a dinner that consisted of spaghetti, garlic bread, and a salad. From his extensive wine refrigerator, he retrieved a bottle of red Bordeaux. Placing two wineglasses on the table, he poured the garnet-colored liquid.

He finished setting the table and filled their plates. To add to the romantic ambiance of the room, Kyle turned on some music, and mild jazz filled the air. He lit vanilla-scented candles, which were Jill's favorite, and dimmed the lights.

As Jill walked into the kitchen, her face broke into a huge smile of appreciation. She walked over to Kyle and lovingly placed her arms around his neck. She began kissing him warmly and passionately on the lips before she whispered, "Thank you," in his ear.

"Thank you for what? I have to eat too."

"Thank you for knowing more ways than one to make love to me. I feel like you have been bringing me to the heights of passion all day long. Every time you touch me or even look at me I feel so loved. It's in the way you talk to me and take care of me, Kyle. I hope I do the same thing to you."

"Woman, you should know by now just what you do to me," he said as he pulled Jill closer toward him. "I find myself on constant guard not to give in to my primal, male urges."

Jill giggled at his description of himself and then said, "I hope we always feel this way about each other. Please don't ever leave me."

Kyle looked deep into her eyes, and saw urgency there. Jill looked to him as though she could sense impending doom. Doom with no name, nor evidence as to when or where it would come, but was destined to arrive. He kissed her cheeks trying to reassure her of his presence. He knew in his heart that he would never leave her, but also knew she wasn't so sure.

"Jill, I would never leave you on my own accord, and I would move mountains to get back to you if we were separated—know this, baby."

She smiled and kissed him one last time and said, "I do. Hey, we'd better eat. Everything looks delicious."

Kyle released her from his embrace and the couple sat down to their evening meal. It had been a long and exhausting day, and they were both happy to be home and with each other. As they ate, they talked about their plans for the rest of the week. Kyle would be able to settle back into the daily routine of his work, but Jill had doubts that her week would be the same.

The next day, Jill worked in her office for hours, and Bebe and Monica had both noticed her quiet mood. Though they each had tried to strike a conversation with Jill, she remained tight-lipped as to what was on her mind. Jill only talked about issues concerning work, and nothing more.

Bebe stood in the doorway of Jill's office and said, "Jill, Monica, and I are ready for lunch. Are you ready to go?"

"No, Bebe, I'm not going to be able to go to lunch with you today. I have a lot of work I want to finish. I'm going home early and I want to complete as much as possible before I go," Jill said as she stood and walked over to the cabinet.

With determined steps, Bebe walked inside the office and sat down. "Okay, Jill, what's up?" she asked, determined to get an answer.

"Nothing's up, Bebe, I just have some things that I have to work out."

"Okay, since you won't tell me, let me guess—some things like Regina Roberts," Bebe said flatly, yet with a smile on her face.

Jill turned around to see Bebe's face. A small grin formed on her own face as she realized there was no use in hiding what was going on from her.

"Yes, it's Regina Roberts—our future mother-in-law. Bebe, did you know that she was coming today?"

"I only found out yesterday. I called you last night but you didn't answer your phone. I guess Kyle had you tied up."

"Something like that." Jill grinned and looked up sheepishly. "I'm just shocked that she wants to see me."

"You're not alone, she wants to see me too."

"And you're not nervous?"

"No, why would I be?" Bebe asked quizzically.

"Because she never comes out just for a visit. Now, since we are engaged to her sons, she wants to come see us. I just can't imagine what she's going to say."

"Jill, the soon-to-be senior Mrs. Roberts is very sweet. Once you get to know her you'll really like her."

"I do like her, I just don't feel comfortable around her. She's just so beautiful and perfect."

"Well, she didn't get that way overnight, she had to grow into herself. If we're lucky we'll get to do that, too," Bebe said as she stood to leave. "Are you sure you don't want to come have lunch with us?" she asked a final time.

"Yeah, I'll see you later. Hey, when are you going to see her?"

"At lunch," Bebe said with a smile.

Jill took in a big gulp of air and held it for a moment. Bebe laughed and waved good-bye.

Having finished what she had to do at the office, Jill headed for her own apartment. When she arrived, she retrieved a ton of mail from her mailbox.

She unlocked her door and stepped inside, quickly dropping everything on the sofa. She thumbed through the letters and opened all the important ones.

There was a letter from her mother, and she kicked off her shoes and sat down on the sofa to enjoy it. As she read her mother's tender words, she couldn't help but wish she were there. Right now, she really could use the strong, encouraging words of her mom, and a second later, she picked up the phone and dialed her number.

"Hello."

"Hi, Mom, it's me, Jill," she said softly into the receiver.

"Hello, sweetheart. You say your name like I don't know your voice," Maddie said lovingly.

"I got your letter today. I can hardly wait to see you," Jill said in a quiet, heartfelt tone.

"I can hardly wait to see you either," Maddie said, loving hearing the words from Jill. "What are you doing home in the middle of the day? Is everything all right?" she asked with concern.

"Everything is fine, Mom. I just needed to hear your voice."

"I'm always here for you, Jill, but I know something is bothering you. Why don't you tell me what it is?"

Knowing in her heart that she desperately wanted to share her problem with her mother, Jill gave in and said, "Kyle's mother and father are here in Durango."

"Isn't that a good thing?" Maddie said cautiously.

"Yes, Mom, it is, but she wants to visit with me today," Jill said in a forlorn voice.

"Well, maybe she just wants to get to know you better, Jill."

"I've been here for a whole year, Mom, and she's

come out only a handful of times. She has never asked to meet with me. It is getting so close to the wedding, I just feel like something terrible is going to happen," Jill blurted out. "Kyle's mother is not like you. I don't know how to approach her."

To this statement, Jill heard her mother's laughter. "Mom, what's so funny."

"Jill, my Jill, you have never had any trouble holding your own in any arena. You are a force to be reckoned with in your own right, sweetheart. Given the line of work you're in, you move in the same circles as Regina Roberts does. How else can you explain your presence in her life? You are preparing to marry her son, and from what I gather about Regina, family is very important to her. I am sure she knows how important you are to Kyle, and would never do anything to upset that."

"I knew you would know just how to calm my fears. Thanks, Mom," Jill said as a faint smile came across her lips.

"Don't mention it, sweetheart. I love you."

"I love you, too," Jill said.

Maddie went on to say how much she had enjoyed the visit from Jill, Kyle, Bebe, and Tony, and Jill told her mother about the business trip before the phone call ended.

With the loving support of her mother, Jill felt ready to take on the world, or at least, Regina Roberts. She got up and headed for her bedroom, and began looking for an outfit appropriate to wear for a meeting with one's future mother-in-law.

Having chosen several outfits to wear, she left the closet and stood in front of the full-length mirror that hung from the door. Jill held each dress up in front of her as she examined her appearance, and quickly

discarded the entire bunch in a heap on her bed. She
went back to the closet and returned to the mirror
with a second group of dresses to consider wearing.
The color red is out, since it obviously represents power,
she thought. The dresses with a low neckline were
quickly tossed, and since she didn't want to come off
looking too sexy, the formfitting dresses were discarded as well.

For a third time, Jill hopelessly entered the closet.
She was about to surrender and go out on a quick
shopping trip, when she spotted a tan dress between
several of her business suits. Jill removed the dress
from the hanger and walked back to the mirror. The
dress was sleeveless and fell just above the knees. It
had a V-shaped neckline, but didn't plunge too deeply.
She smiled at her reflection and was thankful she had
found something decent to wear.

Jill quickly took a shower and dressed. She pulled
her hair back into a sleek knot and then applied a little
makeup. Jill opted to keep her jewelry simple. Aside
from her engagement ring, she wore only the diamond
earrings Kyle had given her. She sprayed on some perfume and slipped into a pair of medium-heeled tan
shoes. Again she studied her reflection in the mirror,
and liking what she saw, she smiled at herself.

It was two o'clock, and she was supposed to meet
Regina at Jillian's. Jill grabbed her purse and left
her apartment. She got into her car, and as she drove
off, she couldn't help wondering how Bebe's meeting with Regina had gone. The thought of calling
Bebe on her cell phone had crossed Jill's mind, but
she was afraid she would be interrupting so she didn't
bother.

As she pulled into the rotunda of the resort, a valet
quickly took the car from Jill, and she went inside. The

atmosphere inside Jillian's was mellow. It was not quite time for the dinner crowd, but there were a few people inside. Jill declined the hostess's offer to seat her as her eyes fell on Regina.

Regina was sitting alone at a table near the window, and Jill began walking toward her. She could feel a thin film of perspiration forming on her forehead, and could only hope her deodorant would hold up. Her throat felt dry and her hands felt clammy, and Jill hoped Regina would not notice. Jill tried to replay the words of confidence her mother had planted in her head. "You can hold your own in any arena," she had said, but this was the most difficult and challenging job she had ever taken on—that of daughter-in-law.

As Jill approached, Regina looked up. The older woman's smile was genuine, and Jill bent to plant a kiss on her cheek.

"Oh, Jill, I'm so glad that you agreed to meet with me. I know how busy you are," Regina said sincerely.

"I'm happy to see you, too," Jill said, hoping that Regina didn't notice her voice crack as she spoke.

"I know it is rare that we get to see each other, darling, but I am hoping to change all that. You've been living in Durango for a year and we've only seen each other a few times."

Jill shifted uncomfortably in her chair as Regina spoke. There was a purpose for their meeting, and Jill wasn't sure if it was good or bad. Just then, the waiter came and asked if Jill would like something from the bar.

"Yes, please, I'd like a Chambord and soda with lime." Though she really could have used something a lot stronger, she didn't think it wise to request it now.

The waiter left and Regina continued, "Jill, I deeply regret not being here for my boys. Well, they aren't boys anymore, they are grown men. Eric is married and has given me a beautiful little granddaughter. Ally is still a baby, and I don't want to miss out on her growing up," she finished softly with regret in her voice. "My husband and I both agree that it's time to make Durango home base. We're not going to miss enjoying our family anymore, especially since it's growing by the second." Regina's smile was warm, yet filled with misgiving.

"Yes, she is an adorable child," Jill agreed, still unsure of how she felt about her in-laws coming to settle in Durango.

"I am very fond of Bebe. Actually, I couldn't love her any more if she were my own daughter. I'm thrilled that she and Tony are engaged."

"They *are* perfect together," Jill said, smiling.

"Yes, they are, which brings me to you," Regina said pointedly.

Jill felt every muscle in her body tighten. The waiter returned and set the glass of Chambord in front of her. Jill picked up the glass and quickly took a drink. She instantly regretted not ordering something a lot stronger.

"Jill, Kyle is my eldest son. He has been nothing but a blessing to his father and me. True to his birth order, he is a good example and a great leader to his brothers. Kyle has a loving and giving spirit, but for the longest time I had given up on him finding love. Then you came into his life."

Jill still didn't know what Regina was getting at, and she silently wished that she wouldn't prolong the torture and would get to the point. Fighting to be patient, she continued to listen to what Regina had to say.

"Though we don't know each other well, I see in you some of the same qualities I see in my son. You both have a strong sense of who you are and what you want. He loves you, Jill. Every time he talks to me about you he lights up. Kyle is the happiest he has ever been, and it's all because of you. You are so important to him, Jill, and that makes you incredibly important to me."

Jill's own smile was genuine as she said, "Oh, Mrs. Roberts, you don't know how good it feels to have your acceptance. I hope you know that I love your son very, very much."

"There's no doubt in my mind that you do. That's why I want you to have this," she said as she reached inside her purse.

Regina pulled out a navy blue, velvet box. The box was flat, of medium size, and looked to be a little worn. Regina's smile broadened as she handed the box across the table to Jill. Slowly Jill reached for it. She took it from Regina's hands and laid it on the table in front of her. Glancing briefly at Regina, Jill raised the hinged lid to reveal a stunning sapphire and diamond necklace. Her mouth fell open in silence as she looked inside the box. Set in gold, the gems cascaded to form a V-shaped design. The stones glittered and gleamed as they rested on the satin lining. It was obviously a piece of jewelry that had been in the family for years, and Jill took Regina's gift as a sign of love and acceptance.

"Oh, Mrs. Roberts, I couldn't possibly accept this. Though it's gorgeous, I know it's an heirloom. I couldn't possibly take this from you," Jill said as she closed the lid.

Laughing, Regina replied, "You're the first one to say that to me. The necklace is part of the four-piece set that once belonged to my mother-in-law. I was lucky, being that I was her only daughter-in-law, so she gave the complete set to me. I, on the other hand, have three daughters-in-law to consider. I gave Sharon the earrings and she quickly took them and thanked me. That one, she's a sweet girl but has always had a taste for the finer things in life. I can't say I blame her."

Jill laughed at Regina's comments knowing that she saw the same quality in Sharon herself, but she added nothing.

"I have known Bebe since she was a little girl and have always thought of her as my own anyway. I gave her the ring. I'm keeping the bracelet. I wanted you to have this piece and hope to come to know you as well as I know the rest of my girls."

Jill thought for a moment as she contemplated what Regina had said. She had called Sharon, Bebe, and herself "my girls." It felt good to be included in the group Regina considered her daughters. Jill looked at her mother-in-law's face.

She had come here today totally expecting to do battle with the dragon, and undoubtedly, one day she would have to. But that day was not today. Today she and her future mother-in-law were okay. The two women ordered something to eat and spent the rest of their time talking and getting to know each other. For now there was peace, but Jill knew that once they settled back in Durango, that might not always be the case.

Chapter 9

When Jill arrived at the cabin, Kyle was already there. He was playing pool by himself, but obviously enjoying the solitude. He stopped playing and laid the pool stick down when he saw Jill come through the door. As she entered, she could smell the scent of his fried chicken wafting through the air, and the sound of jazz playing softly.

To Jill, Kyle looked casual yet sexy as he walked toward her wearing a pair of dark denim jeans and a cocoa-colored jersey-knit T-shirt. The material clung close to him and made his thick, muscular chest irresistible to touch. He walked over and wrapped his arms around Jill. She could smell the fresh scent of his body and regretted not being home earlier to enjoy a bath with him.

"So, how did it go with my mother?" he asked as he studied her eyes.

"Oh, Kyle, she hates me," Jill said with downcast eyes and lips set in a modest pout.

Kyle released her from his embrace and stood in stunned silence. Jill kicked off her shoes and still carrying her purse flopped down on the sofa.

"What happened?" he said, trying to suppress the alarm in his voice.

"She wants you to marry someone who truly loves you," Jill said, looking away from Kyle.

"Jill, that's crazy. She knows how much we love each other, she told me herself," he said as his voice began to rise. Kyle sat down on the sofa beside her.

"She gave me this," Jill said as she pulled the navy blue, velvet box from her purse. "She gave each of her daughters-in-law a piece of the set. She also said she wants to get to know me better."

It only took Kyle a moment to recognize the box. It was part of the set his paternal grandmother had given to his mother. He studied the box a second longer as he pondered what Jill had said. Kyle began to smile when he realized that she was pulling his leg.

"Oh, I'm going to get you in a big way, lady," he said.

"I'm sorry, I just couldn't resist. You have to admit, you weren't sure just how my meeting with your mom was going to go either, did you?"

"No, I didn't, but I was sure that she didn't hate you."

Kyle shook his head and laughed and Jill began to laugh too. He looked up at her. In his eyes she could see all kinds of mischief brewing. Jill started to get up, but before she could Kyle grabbed her around the waist and pulled her back down onto the sofa. He got on top of her and began tickling her unmercifully. Jill laughed and begged him to stop and he did, but only to cover her lips with his kisses.

"That's an exquisite piece of jewelry, isn't it?" Kyle said as they both sat up.

"Yes, it is. She gave Sharon and Bebe a part of the set, and kept one piece for herself. Kyle, did you know that your parents are planning to move back to Durango?"

"No, I didn't, but it doesn't surprise me. You know they have a house here, and Mom has always loved Durango. I get the feeling that she misses being around her family."

"You're right. She said she doesn't want to miss Ally growing up, and she wants to spend more time with all of us," Jill said, trying to control the slight tremble in her voice.

"Jill, she's not the happy ax murderer here to do a number on you. Once you get to know her you'll fall in love with her."

Jill gave a faint smile in acceptance of what Kyle said, but he could tell that she wasn't completely comforted by his words.

"Mom is not intrusive like some mothers-in-law. If you don't believe me just ask Sharon."

"Kyle, Sharon has never had to deal with your mother living in the same city as her. She'll probably be all over her since Sharon has had her first grandbaby!" Jill finished, a little more forcefully than she had intended.

"Look, babe, between work, the wedding, and my mother's announcement that she plans to move back here, you're experiencing more stress than normal. Just try to relax a little and things will work out," he said as he massaged her shoulders.

Kyle stood and went into the kitchen. He checked the chicken and then returned to the living room carrying two glasses of red wine. He handed one to Jill before taking a seat next to her again.

"Dinner will be ready in a few minutes," he said.

Jill didn't reply, but leaned back and snuggled underneath Kyle's arm. Here with him she felt warm, safe, and protected. She could only pray he was right as far as his mother was concerned. Perhaps he was right, she thought. Regina did have two other daughters-in-law to contend with, not to mention a granddaughter. *Maybe she won't have time to find fault with me,* Jill thought.

She sat still nestled in the loving arms of her man as she took a sip of wine. Jill reflected on the meeting she had had earlier with Regina. It was a good meeting that was filled with love and acceptance. While there, Jill had actually found herself looking forward to her in-laws being around. More than anything she wanted to be part of the big, happy family life, and Kyle's family seemed to want that too.

Jill looked up at Kyle and then raised her hand to brush it softly against his cheek. He looked down into her soft brown eyes and was able to melt away any anxiety that rested in her soul.

"With all my heart I love you, honey. If you say everything is going to be all right, then that's what I'll believe without any doubt," she whispered quietly.

Kyle kissed her and then said, "I would never let anything harm you, Jill. I promise to love you and protect you with everything I've got." His words were rich and deep, and his tone was even, and Jill knew in her heart that he spoke the truth.

"Don't ever leave me," she uttered almost inaudibly.

Kyle took his arm from around her and stood up. He offered his hand to Jill and she stood as well. With their glasses of wine in hand, Kyle led her into the kitchen where she found he had prepared a sumptuous meal for her.

Jill began helping to fill their plates as Kyle refilled their wineglasses. They sat and ate crispy fried chicken, mashed potatoes, and green beans Kyle had prepared.

With the first bite of the tasty chicken Jill said, "Mmm, you cook almost as good as my father."

"If you had compared me to anyone else I would have been offended, but your father is awesome in the kitchen."

"He is, but hats off to you too, honey," Jill said as she raised her glass of wine to Kyle before taking another sip.

"Kyle, your mom always looks so well put together. Her hair looks like she just left the salon and her clothing is tailored and figure flattering. She's who I want to be when I grow up."

Kyle laughed and said, "I know she would love you to say those words to my dad. She says he is always complaining that she spends too much money on her hair and her clothing."

"Well, it's money well spent, because she's stunning."

"Yes, Regina Roberts is stunning. Back in her day she was a real beauty. Not that she isn't a beauty now, but in her younger years my father could barely concentrate on work for keeping an eye on my mother," Kyle said, chuckling as he reminisced.

"Are you saying that your father didn't trust your mother?" Jill asked, surprised.

"No, I'm not saying that at all. Mom was beautiful and men never failed to notice her. No matter what she wore or where she was, my mother would capture their attention without ever trying."

"That must have driven your father crazy," Jill said, shaking her head.

"It did, especially since Mom was always very friendly. She was very gracious and never wanted to hurt anyone's feelings. Still, Dad, knowing how a man could be, never wanted Mom out of his sight. When he started traveling he invited her to go along. Mom enjoyed going on trips, and when her boys were old enough to be left home alone, she started going all the time with Dad. I think the fact that he would spoil her rotten by letting her shop till her heart was content helped though."

"But it's obvious how much they love each other."

"Yes, it is. It's the same kind of love that you and I share."

"Are you trying to tell me that you're as madly in love with me as your father is with your mother?" Jill asked as she stuck a cherry tomato into her mouth.

"Yes, maybe even more so," Kyle replied as he looked deep into her eyes.

Jill smiled as they continued to eat. The couple enjoyed each other's company as they finished their meal. When they were done, Jill and Kyle cleaned the kitchen together.

Next, they went upstairs to the bedroom. Jill undressed and went to take a quick bath. Since Kyle had already taken a shower, he got in bed to wait for her.

As she bathed, Jill kept hoping that Kyle would surprise her by joining her, but he did not. After she was finished she dried off, and moisturized her skin with his favorite scented lotion, which smelled like coconut. She opted not to wear any nightclothes.

Jill walked into the dimly lit bedroom only to find Kyle fast asleep. Though she was disappointed, her lips curled into a faint smile as she climbed into bed with him. She pulled the comforter over them and snuggled close against his back. Enjoying the comfort she found holding his sleeping body, she fell asleep as well.

Over a quick breakfast of coffee, toast, and orange juice, the couple talked about their plans for the day and decided to meet each other at the Ranch House for lunch. That evening, Sharon and Eric planned to have a little get-together at their place to welcome Kyle's parents home. Tony and Bebe would be there as well. Jill and Kyle would meet at the cabin and ride to Eric's together.

After finishing their breakfast and making their plans for the day, they left the cabin and each headed to work.

When Jill arrived at the office, she was greeted by Monica, who was very excited. The young woman stood as Jill entered the reception area and gave her a huge, welcoming smile as she handed her the mail and messages.

"Monica, is there something you want to tell me?" Jill asked suspiciously.

"Yes, but I can't, Jill. I promised Bebe that I'd let her have the honors," Monica said, as if holding in the information was killing her.

Jill's eyes lingered on the secretary for a moment longer, before she asked, "Is Bebe in yet?"

"Yep, she's been here for about a half hour. She's in her office."

As Jill began to walk down the hall toward Bebe's office, she noticed that Monica was following her with a huge grin on her face. Jill smiled back but she continued to walk with Monica in tow.

"Good morning, Bebe," Jill said as she entered her partner's office.

"Jill, it's about time you showed up," Bebe said as she stood and walked around to the front of her desk. "Have a seat. I have some astronomically fantastic news to tell you."

"Astronomically fantastic, huh?" Jill said, now completely intrigued with whatever news Monica was holding and Bebe was about to produce.

"Jill, Desert Star has just been offered its first job overseas! If we get the contract, we'll be known internationally," Bebe said excitedly. Her eyes sparkled with excitement, as she bounced up, happily hugging Jill, and gave Monica a high five.

"You've got to be kidding!" Jill said in astonishment. Her eyes were wide with disbelief as she asked, "Who is the client?"

"It's a company in South America called Mulher Bela Swimwear. It means 'beautiful woman,' and their home office is in Rio de Janeiro, Brazil! Oh, Jill, I hope we nail this one," Bebe told her.

"Wow, I hope we do too. I guess we all better brush up on Portuguese," Jill said as she looked at Monica.

"All of us?" Monica asked quizzically.

"Yes, all of us. There's no way we could leave you behind on a job like this," Jill said, smiling.

"Yes, yes, I was hoping you would ask me to come along!" Monica said jubilantly as she began jumping up and down. Then, trying to contain her excitement, she gave Jill and Bebe a big hug and thanked them before going back to her own desk.

Bebe quickly gave Jill more details as to when they were expected in Rio. She explained that Mulher Bela Swimwear had heard about Desert Star by way of Mr. O'Neal, of the Fitz and O'Neal campaign they had just finished.

"Obviously they were quite impressed with Desert Star to have already recommended them to business acquaintances," Jill said with excitement.

"I believe so."

"Bebe, how did your meeting with Mrs. Roberts go?" Jill asked pointedly.

Bebe leaned back against her desk and faced Jill. She could see in her eyes all the restless suspicion that begged to be extinguished. Bebe could only hope that Jill would come to know and love Regina as she herself had.

"It went well, Jill, but you know, I have known Mom since I was a young girl, and she has always been like a mother to me," Bebe said, smiling warmly as she thought about the older woman.

"You feel comfortable calling her Mom?" Jill asked with unconcealed amazement in her voice.

Bebe smiled and said, "Yes, I do. Jill, I have always called her Mom. It is only during business or when she is entertaining that I don't. But given the fact that soon she really will be my mother by marriage, I guess I'll probably call her Mom all the time."

Jill's eyes lowered as she pondered Bebe's take on the situation. Bebe had no mother of her own and had know Regina most of her life. It stood to reason that she would accept Regina in the role of mother so quickly and easily. Just yesterday Regina had told Jill that she thought of Bebe as her own daughter. *Sometimes family is not always the one you are born into*, Jill thought.

In remembering what Regina had told her, Jill scanned Bebe's hands. She spotted the ring on her right hand. The ring was a beautiful emerald-cut sapphire with at least two carats in diamond baguettes, Jill guessed.

Bebe noticed what Jill was staring at, so she held her hand up for her to get a better look at the stunning piece of jewelry.

"She gave this to me," Bebe said proudly.

"Bebe, it's absolutely beautiful. Regina told me that she has always thought of you as her own daughter."

"I know she feels that way about me, but it's my understanding that you got a nice gift as well."

"Yes, I did. She gave me the necklace to the set."

"I guess it's her way of bringing the family together, showing her love and acceptance of her sons' mates, and a request."

"A request for what?"

"To be part of our lives," Bebe said simply.

Jill stood and smiled. She gave Bebe a kiss on the cheek and left her office with a promise to be ready to leave for the Ranch House by lunchtime.

As she walked down the hall, she couldn't help thinking how wise Bebe was. She had the innate ability to understand women and situations without any spoken words. Jill realized that Regina was doing exactly what Bebe had said, which was reaching out to all of them.

She had spent so much time accompanying her husband on business travel that her family was blossoming without her. Regina was wise in the fact that she knew it was time to return to her roots and enjoy her growing family.

When Jill entered her office, she sat down at her desk and picked up the phone. She dialed her parents' number and was thankful that her mother was the one to answer the call. Upon hearing her mother's voice, Jill instantly felt joy and happiness in her heart for having her own mother.

"Hi, Mom, it's me," Jill said warmly.

"Well, hello, sweetheart. How did lunch go with your Regina?"

"It went well. Actually, it went better than expected."

"I told you there was nothing to worry about."

"And you were right. She just wanted to tell me that

she and her husband planned on moving back into their house here in Durango."

"I think the whole family will be glad to hear that," Maddie said. She waited a few seconds for Jill to say something, but she was silent. "Jill, are you okay?" she asked softly.

"Yes, Mom, I am. Mrs. Roberts gave Sharon, Bebe, and me each a piece of jewelry, as she told us of her plans to move back here."

"And is that what's really bothering you?" Maddie asked, knowing there was more on Jill's mind.

"Mom, Bebe feels so comfortable calling Regina Mother. I know that they have known each other for a very long time, and she should feel comfortable calling her Mom. I just don't feel as comfortable doing the same."

"Is it because you don't know her well enough, because the feelings aren't there, or because you feel as though you would be disloyal to me?" Maddie asked matter-of-factly.

Once again Jill was silent. Her mother spoke as if she could see right through her. Jill had admitted to herself that she had never called any other woman Mother, not even her grandmother, whom she had called Nana. Would it hurt her own mother's feelings if she called another woman by the title that held immense love, honor, and respect? Did she not have those same feelings for Regina, even though they weren't as profoundly felt as they were for her mom? Jill silently admitted to herself that she did hold those same feelings in her heart for Regina, but on some level she knew that she could never hold her in the same regard as she did her own mother.

"Jill," Maddie finally said, interrupting Jill's train of thought. "You know you are and always will be my little girl. Sometimes a woman has to share herself and her heart with her husband's family, but that doesn't mean that she loves her own family any less. You're not betraying me by calling Regina Mother. In fact, I had expected that you would since she is your mother too."

"I love you, Mom, and you're my favorite," Jill said softly.

"I better be."

Jill told her mother about the exciting assignment Desert Star was hoping to land in Rio de Janeiro. Maddie was impressed and told Jill how proud she was of her accomplishments.

"I have a ton of work to do and none of it's going to get done with me on the phone," Jill said.

"Call me soon, sweetheart. I love you," Maddie said and then hung up the phone.

Between Kyle, Bebe, and her mother, all the anxiety and stress Jill had been feeling disappeared. Having put Regina's move back to Durango, as well as what to call her in perspective, Jill got busy with the ton of work she hoped to clear from her desk.

Jill had been working nonstop for several hours when a light tap on the door let her know that it was lunchtime. She raised her head to see Bebe and Monica standing in the doorway with purses in hand. Jill smiled and welcomed the break from work.

"Okay, you said you'd be ready for lunch," Bebe said playfully, obviously still walking on a cloud over the chance to work in Brazil.

Jill stood and stretched and then grabbed her purse. "I'm ready," she said as she walked out of her office to join them.

Jill was surprised that Monica, who never tagged along, had decided to come this time. She was happy that Monica was beginning to gel with them. Jill credited Rosy's party for Monica's acceptance of their friendship. The party had given Monica a chance to see herself and Bebe outside of the office, and not to view them only as her bosses.

Bebe drove quickly to A Special Place, and when they arrived she parked in the employee lot. The group exited the car and walked toward the Ranch House. The place was filled with most of the regulars, but a few new faces as well as guests filled the restaurant.

Tony, Sharon, and Eric were already seated at a table, and they made their way over to them. As Jill sat down next to Sharon, she noticed that she was wearing the earrings Regina had given her. Jill thought of the words Regina had used to describe Sharon, and a smile played on her lips.

"You seem awfully happy, Jill. What's up?" Sharon asked, smiling back.

"Just thinking of something that happened earlier," Jill said, and offered no further explanation. "Where's Ally?"

"She's with Mom. She wanted to give us a break so she said she would keep the baby for a couple hours," Sharon told them.

Bebe sat next to Tony and gave him a kiss as she greeted him. "Hello, handsome," she said.

"Hello, beautiful," he replied as he took her left hand in his and kissed her ring finger.

"Where's the rest of the group?" Grace said, as she approached the table.

"Kyle should be here any minute, but we can go ahead and start ordering," Eric said.

Grace took their orders and said a special hello to Monica, whom she had met at Rosy's party weeks earlier. She left to fill the drink orders and several minutes later returned with their beverages and asked if they were ready to order lunch, but Kyle had not arrived yet.

"I'm going to go and see what's keeping him," Eric said, as he glanced at his watch and saw that Kyle was twenty minutes late. "I thought he'd be the first one here, since he likes us back to work on time," Eric said, standing. He left the Ranch House as the rest of the group continued to converse.

Chapter 10

It was almost twenty minutes later, and the group had begun to eat lunch, when Eric arrived back at the Ranch House. Though his pace was fast, something in his step raised the hair on Jill's neck. He walked to the table and their eyes locked. The kind, relaxed expression that seemed to always grace his face was absent. Now his features appeared ragged and filled with despair.

He searched for the words to tell Jill the news gently, but he couldn't find any. His eyes darted pleadingly around the table looking for help, but no one could offer any. Tony, sensing his brother's urgency, took his arm from around Bebe and sat up in his chair. Eric had the whole table's attention.

"Kyle was involved in a bad accident," Eric started. Amidst sharp inhales of breath he continued, "He was obviously driving from the cabin to join us when a horse ran out in front of him. Kyle swerved to avoid hitting the animal and his vehicle ran off the road. It rolled over several times before coming to a rest at the bottom of a hill."

Jill stood and began to walk almost as if she were

a robot. Her mind was now on automatic pilot as she exited the Ranch House. The rest of the family watched and followed her, unsure of what she was about to do.

"Jill, where are you going?" Bebe asked.

"I have to find him, I have to be with him," she answered without making eye contact.

"Jill, Kyle was taken to Mercy Medical initially, but he's being airlifted to another hospital that has a level-one trauma center," Eric told her.

Upon hearing this, Jill lost control of her emotions. She began to cry and yell and Eric caught her in his arms.

"He promised, he promised he'd never leave me!" Jill screamed as she pounded on Eric's chest. "He's hurt bad, Eric. I know he's hurt bad. Why else would he need to go to a trauma center? Oh my God, what am I going to do?" she cried as she felt her body go limp.

Bebe whipped out her cell phone and made several calls. The first one was to Regina, who had anticipated having dinner at Eric and Monica's house this evening. Bebe had to tell her the news regarding Kyle; thus the dinner would be canceled.

Tony rushed off to get Eric's car, which was big enough for all of them, and Monica took Bebe's car back to the office to handle everything there.

When Tony arrived with the car, the group piled in and headed toward Kyle's cabin. Once there, Bebe went inside with Jill and gathered a few things she might need. Jill's mind could only focus on getting to the hospital as soon as possible, and her thoughts were only of being by Kyle's side.

Bebe was able to stay calm and focused. From years of working at the resort she knew each of the Roberts men had an insurance packet. Regina and Samuel were in and out of town so much when they were young that Regina kept an updated medical file on hand at the ranch. The file contained insurance papers, personal physician names and phone numbers, and next of kin contact information.

Since the boys had all grown into men, Regina had given the packets of medical records to them to keep. The status of Kyle's condition was not known, but given the terrible situation, Bebe thought it best to bring it along. When Jill went into the bathroom Bebe crept quietly into Kyle's office and retrieved the packet. He had always kept it in the bottom drawer of her desk. She opened the drawer and was instantly thankful he hadn't changed his filing system, and also, that she didn't have to worry Jill with such matters now, when she had so much on her mind.

Eric left to take his wife home and to prepare to go to the hospital. Even though Bebe had already informed his parents of Kyle's accident, he felt the need to see them and make sure they were okay. Eric drove quickly to the home of his parents. Inside, he sat down in the living room and spoke quietly with his mother. The two held hands and said a prayer filled with faith for the recovery of Kyle.

When Eric left, Regina called her husband to tell him the news. Though Eric had offered to drive her to the hospital, Regina decided to wait for her husband to come home. She told Eric that at a time like this she needed his father's strength to move forward. Eric left and returned to the cabin.

An hour later the group found themselves en route to the hospital. Through Bebe's phone calls they had learned that Kyle was in critical condition. He was brought into the hospital as a level-one trauma patient, since he was unconscious and not breathing on his own.

The news of Kyle's condition sent Jill further into her own little world. She said nothing but continued to stare out the window. Her mind couldn't conceive the idea of life without Kyle, yet he wasn't breathing on his own. His words continued to ring loudly in her mind to the point that they were almost screaming at her, "I'll never leave you, I'll never leave you." She shook her head as if to chase the words away. Bebe rested her hand on top of Jill's.

When they finally arrived at the hospital where Kyle had been taken via helicopter, they all got out of the car and went inside. They walked to the information desk to inquire as to where they needed to go.

"Excuse me," Eric said to the woman behind the desk. "I'm looking for my brother, Kyle Roberts. He was brought in via Life Flight today."

The woman looked Kyle's name up in the computer before she turned and told the group where to go.

"We need some information on your brother, so could one of you go to patient registration?" she asked in a tone that sounded almost apologetic.

"Sure, I'll handle that," Bebe said, thankful she had Kyle's medical file with her.

Bebe knew that the others were, like herself, anxious to see Kyle, and would only be infuriated having to fill out papers when Kyle was in such terrible condition. She was frustrated too by having to handle paperwork at a time like this, but hoped having all his information would make things go smoothly.

As Bebe left to take care of registering Kyle, Eric took Jill's hand and led her in the direction of the elevators. They took the elevator to the trauma unit and buzzed the nurses' station. A second later a voice came over the intercom. When Eric told the woman who they were looking for, she told him that she would be right out.

A nurse came out and ushered the family toward a small waiting room. There she informed them of Kyle's condition.

"Hi, I'm Molly Edwards," she said as she offered them a seat, but all preferred to stand. "As of right now, I know very little about your brother's condition." She could see the look of exasperation on each of their faces and quickly continued. "At present, your brother is in surgery. Mr. Roberts suffered a broken leg and arm. He also suffered some head trauma as well as a punctured lung."

Tears flowed down Jill's cheeks uncontrollably, and with each sob her body shook like a leaf in the wind. Eric grabbed her around the waist and lowered her to a chair fearing that she might faint.

Nurse Edwards looked at the sobbing woman and noticed the engagement ring on her hand. Her heart went out to Jill, whom Molly imagined feared losing her future husband. Molly sat next to Jill and put her arm around her shoulder.

"When will he be out of surgery?" Tony asked.

"It will be a while. There was a lot of internal bleeding, and the doctors have to get that under control first," Nurse Edwards said. She delivered the news with as much compassion as a seasoned professional, and then stood to leave. "I'll be sure to come and give you any updates as soon as I find out myself," she promised and left.

Bebe arrived after the nurse had left. She sat beside Jill and held her hand. As the minutes turned into hours, Eric inquired as to whether there was any new information about Kyle; there wasn't any. The group had been at the hospital for four hours and he was still in surgery. Kyle's parents had arrived and were given no more news than what was told earlier.

It was almost evening, and toward the end of Molly Edwards's twelve-hour shift, when she came out to talk to the family. They stood as they saw her approach and gathered around her.

"Kyle is out of surgery and will be taken to the recovery room. The doctors who worked on him will be up shortly to talk to you," Nurse Edwards said. She told them that she would let them know when Kyle arrived on the unit and when they would be able to see him.

Though Molly had explained that it would be a few more hours before Kyle would arrive, the family decided to wait. Understanding their concern, Molly turned and left.

A slight smile formed on Regina's face at hearing the news that Kyle was out of surgery. Jill looked at her and saw a deep inner beauty that resonated poise. Since she had arrived, Regina had been quiet and reserved. Though she was deeply concerned about her son, she didn't display it with tears, screams, and drama. She held her husband's hand and at times seemed to be saying silent prayers. Now she smiled as if part of her prayers had been answered, and she fully expected the rest of her prayers to be answered as well shortly.

Bebe went downstairs to the hospital's cafeteria and got coffee for everyone. Jill rejected her cup, and continued to stare at a blank wall. Her face was now void of emotion and she sat still and silent.

Regina stood and walked to where Jill was sitting. She took the empty seat next to her and placed her palm over Jill's. Jill turned to look into the eyes of the woman she was growing to love and accept as a friend as well as a mother. She saw in her eyes a quiet serenity.

"Jill, I know you weren't planning to go through the bad times so early in your relationship with Kyle, but, darling, he needs you to be strong for him as well as yourself," Regina said softly.

"Regina, I don't know if I can. I'm not ready to lose him. I just found him and he promised he'd never leave me. We have so much to do together and he isn't supposed to leave me, not now," Jill said as a fresh batch of tears began to flow.

"My darling, then you hold on to what gives you strength and let God know what you need. It is in His power to give each of us the power to do whatever needs to be done. Right now, you need the courage and strength to make it through this difficult time, but you have to know that between the two of you, not too much is going to happen that you can't handle."

The simple yet eloquent words Regina had spoken reached deep inside Jill's mind, where her own sense of strength and ability had tried to hide. But Regina had reminded Jill of all the things her own mother had taught her for years. The lessons of God's power and mercy had been instilled in her as a young child, and now she needed to demonstrate all that she had learned.

She gently wiped the remaining tears away with the back of her hand, before leaning over and kissing Regina's cheek tenderly.

"Thank you for reminding me of what I need to do," Jill told her.

"I knew all you needed was a little reminding," Regina said.

Moments later two doctors arrived to speak with the family. Dr. Wilson was the orthopedic surgeon who worked on Kyle. He told them that everything went well, but that Kyle would need physical therapy after his fractures had healed.

Dr. Johansen spoke next and his news was not as good. He told them that Kyle had quite a bit of swelling in his head, but he expected it to go down. The swelling appeared in the area of the brain that was responsible for sight. The doctor went on to explain that he wouldn't know anything more definitive until Kyle was conscious.

"When do you think he will be conscious?" Samuel asked.

"Right now, Kyle is in a drug-induced coma. He is hooked up to a respirator, which is breathing for him. His vital signs are good, but his body needs time to heal from the trauma it has been through. Tomorrow we will be running more tests on him and we will be able to tell you more then," Dr Johansen said.

After the doctors left, the group gathered together and tried to decide what to do. Nurse Edwards walked by and waved good-bye as she headed toward the elevator. Jill gave a slight wave back as she glanced at the clock on the wall. It was now midnight, and the relatives were deciding who would stay.

The business of running A Special Place and Desert Star had to be dealt with, so Bebe and Tony agreed that they should be the ones to go. But Eric was deeply concerned about Jill and thought she should go home.

"Jill, I promise to call with any news about Kyle," Eric said.

"That won't be necessary, Eric, because I'm not leaving this hospital without him."

"Jill, you need some rest and food. Tony can drop you off at the cabin and if anything happens, he can bring you back."

"Eric, I don't think you understand. Kyle needs

me and I am going to be here every moment that he is. So please don't ask me to leave again, because I'm not going to," Jill said firmly and went to sit down.

"Jill and I will stay. I don't think I can leave either," Regina said.

Knowing that once his wife set her mind she dug in her heels and couldn't be moved, Samuel hugged and kissed his wife and made her promise to eat something.

"I will," she told him. "And I'll try to get something in Jill as well," she promised him. Regina kissed her husband again, before he began to follow Tony to the elevator.

Bebe sat talking quietly to Jill for a second before she followed the two men, and then Eric sat next to Jill.

"Jill, you know I already love you like a sister, don't you?"

"Yes, Eric, I know. I love you too, but my place is with Kyle and I won't let him down."

"I understand, but once that big man is on his feet, I don't want him coming after me for not taking good care of you."

Jill smiled not only at the comment Eric had made, but at the same kind of faith he seemed to share with his mother. They both spoke as if they already knew the outcome of Kyle's situation, and Jill decided that that was what she had to do as well.

She leaned forward and kissed Eric on the cheek as she gently caressed his face with her hand. "Don't worry, I'll be sure to tell him that you took excellent care of me."

With that, Eric stood and left to join his family who were waiting at the elevator.

Jill turned and saw Regina looking at her approvingly.

The two women sat thinking the same thoughts and silently saying the same prayer, and very mindful that they were both cut from the same cloth. Each knew of the power and strength the other possessed. They were both incredibly capable women who were able to move mountains with their faith. Each had a deep sense of loyalty to her family, and even more so to the men they stood behind.

Jill and Regina sat talking and bonding for hours. Finally, a new nurse allowed the women to see Kyle. As she led them back into the trauma unit, she explained briefly what they could expect to see so that they wouldn't be alarmed when they walked into the room.

But no amount of preparedness could have gotten Jill ready to see her loved one in the hospital bed. Jill stopped at the doorway. She could see Kyle lying in bed. The room was dimly lit, and except for the rhythmic beep of the heart monitor and buzzing of the machines he was hooked up to, there wasn't any other noise.

Her feet stayed frozen in place as her mind prepared her for what she was about to see. Kyle, her Kyle, was so big and strong. It was hard for her to grasp that he was the one lying motionless in the bed.

Jill wanted to run crying and screaming about the injustice her life had just been dealt, but her heart helped her mind make sense of all the craziness she had to cope with. She moved forward slowly, until she reached the edge of his bed. Glancing down into the swollen face of the man she loved, Jill could see only what she wanted to see—the man she intended to marry. Slowly she took his hand in hers and instantly enjoyed the warmth she found there.

Jill leaned forward, kissed his cheek softly, and

then whispered in his ear, "I love you, baby, and when you decide to wake up, I'll be right here."

After giving Jill a few moments to be with Kyle alone, Regina moved closer to see her son. She ran her fingertips gently across his forehead before kissing him there. Then she too whispered a message in his ear.

"Hi, son, it's Mom. You get well and don't keep your beautiful future wife waiting, you hear?" Regina said with a smile in her voice.

They stood for a moment longer before the nurse told them it was time for them to go. Jill and Regina left the unit walking arm in arm. Together they had accomplished the devastating task of seeing Kyle in the trauma unit. It was a difficult thing for them to do, and each found solace in the other's company.

It was now almost 6:00 a.m., and Bebe was the first to return to the hospital. She arrived with breakfast for Jill and Regina, and at first Jill refused to eat. Regina took the sandwich and bit into it.

"Bebe, this is delicious. It doesn't taste like hospital food," Regina said.

"No, it's not. I got it from the deli across the street."

"Jill, please try mine," Regina said as she held the sandwich up for Jill to take a bite.

Jill took a bite, and agreed that the breakfast sandwich tasted great. Still, she didn't open her own bag, but did take several bites of Regina's sandwich when she offered it to her.

Regina and Jill told Bebe about their brief visit with Kyle. Bebe was anxious to see him too, but would not be able to since Kyle was having tests done. She could only stay for an hour since she had to get to Desert Star.

Bebe told Jill not to worry about work. She assured

her that she and Monica could handle everything and would keep her posted on everything that was going on. Bebe knew that Desert Star was on Jill's mind, and she did her best to let Jill know that as her business partner, she had nothing to worry about.

It was after Bebe had left that Dr. Johansen came to speak with Jill and Regina. The doctor came into the waiting room and sat next to Jill. She looked searchingly into his eyes trying to determine if there was any hit of urgency in his posture, facial expression, or voice, but she could detect none.

When Dr. Johansen spoke, his voice was even, yet held a tone of promise. He explained to the women that Kyle's tests all came back with good results, and that the swelling, which was what concerned him the most, had gone down considerably. He also told them that he would be taking him off the medication that induced his coma soon, and from there he would be weaning him off the ventilator.

Jill and Regina found encouragement in the doctor's news, and after he left they called the family to let them know what was said. On several more occasions Jill found herself saying prayers of gratitude. She felt as though God was gently guiding her to a place where she too had unshakeable faith.

It was a little past noon when they were allowed to see Kyle again. Visitation in the trauma unit was very limited, but even in knowing this, Jill refused to go home when Regina did. She stayed and waited for any news and every visit.

By evening Bebe had returned again, and this time with not only food, but also a change of clothing and toiletries for Jill. Jill went to the ladies' room to freshen up and returned to the waiting room when she was finished. Bebe had bought soup and sandwiches for

them to share, and she told Jill of the day's events at
Desert Star.

Later, the rest of the family returned to visit Kyle.
Taking turns, they were each allowed into his room
for a brief visit. When they were told that his condition was continuing to improve they were all happy,
but still anxious for him to awaken.

Over the next couple of days Jill remained at the hospital. Eric, as well as the rest of the family, understood the deep sense of love and devotion Jill had for
his brother, and didn't try to encourage her to leave
his side anymore.

Bebe returned every day to keep Jill company and
to see Kyle. She told Jill that everything was coming
along as planned at work, and that she and Monica
were working well together. Though things were
more difficult to handle without Jill's help, Bebe
didn't tell her that, preferring not to worry her friend
when she had so much on her mind with Kyle.

Kyle had been taken off the medication as well as
the ventilator and was doing increasingly well. His condition had improved so much that he was taken to the
step-down unit where he was expected to continue his
progress.

Jill had spoken to her mother several times and
Maddie had wanted to come to Colorado to be by Jill's
side. She knew her daughter needed her, but Jill refused her mother's offer and told Maddie that she
would be fine.

Still Jill never left the hospital. Visiting hours weren't
as strict as they had been on the trauma unit, and Jill
stayed in Kyle's room for hours at a time. She would
only leave his side to use the restroom, fearing that
he might wake up and she wouldn't be there.

She moistened his lips with glycerin swabs and

made sure he was comfortable. Jill remembered how much faith Regina had, and the thought reminded her to continue to pray that Kyle would make a full recovery.

Jill sat for hours at a time holding Kyle's hand and talking to him about the wedding. She even teased him about trying to find a way to get out of marrying her.

At Jill's request, Bebe brought several of Kyle's favorite books from the cabin. It was late evening and Jill had pulled a chair close to his bedside and began to read to him. As she read, she held his hand. Her voice was low, but she read as though he were awake and could hear every word she was saying.

Kyle's eyes slowly opened and he looked at Jill as she read. He noticed that she looked worn and tired, as if she hadn't had a good night's sleep in days. He looked around the room and realized that he was in a hospital, but he had no recollection as to why. He felt no sense of alarm, knowing Jill had obviously stayed with him. He gave her hand a gentle squeeze as she continued to read, and she squeezed back. A second later it dawned on her what he had done, and she looked up to see a faint smile on his still bruised face.

"Hi, babe," he managed to utter in a raspy voice.

"Hey yourself," she said to him as a single tear slid down her cheek. "I knew you wouldn't leave me." Jill stood and put the book on the edge of the bed as she leaned over and kissed him ever so sweetly.

The feeding tube that was still in place didn't stop him from talking. He was full of questions and needed answers.

"What happened to me?" he asked.

Jill pushed the button for the nurse and then began to explain to Kyle why he was in the hospital.

A few moments later the nurse arrived and examined Kyle. She was happy to see that her patient was awake and told Jill that she would have to leave the room while the doctors came to see him.

With another quick kiss on Kyle's lips, Jill left the room feeling the best she had felt since the day of his accident. She felt as though she had been holding her breath for almost two weeks, but now that God had answered her prayers, all the pain that had threatened to destroy her life was disappearing.

Jill went to the waiting room and began to make phone calls. First she called her mother, who had made it a point to call the hospital and get an update on Kyle's condition every day. Then she called all of his family and everyone promised to come to the hospital as quickly as they could.

Chapter 11

A week later Kyle was discharged from the hospital and, just as Dr. Wilson had told them after the surgery, he did need to have physical therapy. He had to have therapy twice a week, and until he could drive, Jill left work early on those days to take him. But after a few weeks Kyle didn't need the crutches and was able to drive himself.

When he arrived home he was happy to see Jill. He was surprised to find her in the kitchen cooking. She looked beautiful in her flowing, silk sundress that was a mocha-colored paisley print. He stood quietly observing her as she stood barefoot stirring a pot on the stove. The dress fell just above her knees and Kyle leaned against the wall admiring her shapely, lean legs. She bent over to check what she was cooking in the oven. With that one quick motion she was able to arouse his need for her, and he wanted to make his presence known.

Kyle walked up quietly behind her and placed a firm hand on either side of her hips, before pressing himself against her bottom. Startled, Jill jumped, before she realized who stood so close to her.

She smiled as she allowed herself to back into him, and said in a teasing voice, "Hank, I told you, you have to get out of here before Kyle gets home."

"Hank, huh? I guess I'll have to kill Hank," Kyle said as he spun Jill around and held her face in his hands. He continued to kiss her as she wrapped her arms around his neck.

"Don't kill him, he knows my heart belongs to you."

"Does he know that this belongs to me too?" Kyle asked as his hands slid down her back until they rested on her backside.

"Yes, he knows, and I know that too," Jill said. She was completely aware of the firm bulge in his pants that was requesting her attention, but she smiled as she slipped away.

"I guess that's your way of telling me not now."

"Yes, and maybe not until after we're married," Jill said as she looked up through her lashes.

A frown appeared on Kyle's face, but he had an idea as to why Jill wanted to stop having sex. Though she had been giving herself to him without reservation since they started seeing each other, Jill was still a traditional girl with traditional values. Even though she was almost thirty, he knew he had to ask her father for her hand in marriage.

Now she wanted to put sex on hold until they were husband and wife. Kyle smiled at the thought of making her his forever and, knowing that he could deny her nothing, he conceded to her wishes.

"I understand, babe, and I'm with you on this. I'm not saying that I like it, but I'll try to abide by your decision."

"Thank you, honey," she said as she began to set the table.

"Are you making spaghetti?" Kyle asked as he washed his hands.

"Yep, and I also made garlic bread and salad. I'm afraid that my sauce isn't as good as yours, but it will do."

"No, I bet it's better than mine. I love your cooking," he said as he sat down.

Jill made a plate for herself and him, and put the large bowl of salad on the table with a basket of the warm, crusty garlic bread. Then she poured each of them a glass of red wine before she sat down.

They held hands as Kyle said grace and then they began to eat. Kyle let out a satisfied moan as he ate his first forkful of Jill's spaghetti sauce.

"Oh, babe, this is delicious! What did you put in your sauce?" he asked sincerely.

Jill smiled with delight and said, "I have a few special, secret recipes too, Mr. Roberts, but if you must know, I added wine to the sauce."

"I've used wine before and it never turned out this good."

"That's because you didn't use the same kind of wine I used, and that, my dear, is the secret."

Kyle smiled, but didn't press Jill into revealing her secret. Then his smile faded as he said, "Jill, I'm so sorry that we had to postpone the wedding. I know how hard you worked on pulling everything together while you were working at Desert Star."

"We didn't have to push it back until the twelfth of never, so I'm fine with August eighth. Besides, that gives me extra time to gather my trousseau," Jill said as she seductively sucked a noodle into her mouth.

Kyle laughed as he asked, "Is there going to be any sexy lingerie in that trousseau?"

"Yes, sir, there will be. Lingerie that will make you glad you waited."

"I hope so," Kyle said as he shook his head trying to force the images of Jill wearing something very sheer from his mind.

After they finished eating dinner, they cleaned the kitchen together before relaxing in the living room. Kyle turned on the television and then sat at one end of the sofa and Jill sat at the other. She rested her feet in his lap and he massaged her toes.

She sat thinking of how good it felt being with him at home again. Since the accident, she had moved out of her apartment and had taken full-time residence at his home. It was soon to be her home too, and now even more so, she didn't want to be away from him ever again.

After a while, Jill said, "Take off your shirt and I'll rub your back."

She hopped off the sofa and went to get the massage oil. Kyle took off his shirt and lay down on the floor. When Jill returned, she sat down straddling his hips with her thighs. She poured the warm massage oil into her palms and then began to knead his back muscles with her delicate fingers.

"Tomorrow Bebe and I are going shopping after work," she said as she continued to rub his back.

"So I'll be on my own for dinner?"

"Yep, we're going to have dinner in town and she is going to help me with some of the reorganizing of the wedding plans."

"That's good, but I thought your mother was going to help out too."

"She is, she will be in town by the end of the month. She and your mom are supervising the decorating and they also are organizing the reception," Jill said nervously.

"What's wrong?" Kyle asked, sensing Jill's apprehension.

"I just want everything to be perfect. I hope our moms don't butt heads on anything."

"Babe, everything will be fine. Besides, our moms are the epitome of cooperation. I don't see Regina Roberts or Madeline Alexander arguing, since they both want this wedding to take place so badly," Kyle said.

Jill slid off his back and lay down on the floor beside him. Kyle turned to look at her as she lay on her side and rested her eyes on his adoring smile. She couldn't help returning the smile as she reached out and traced the sensuous outline of his lips. They were full and masculine and made her crave his kiss. Jill didn't wait for him, but moved close enough to steal one.

Kyle's eyes danced with anticipation, but he knew that he would be lucky if Jill even let him fondle her. Fondling could possibly lead to something more, and he knew she didn't want to make love until they were married.

Their wedding was almost two months away and he didn't know if he could hold out that long. But he would force himself to do it. It was what Jill wanted and it was important to her. But if she softened her resolve even the tiniest bit, he would be happy to take care of her needs, and in the process, satisfy his own.

Still lying on the floor, Kyle began to play in Jill's soft, curly hair. He wanted so much to undress her and just enjoy her body, but instead he decided to try to take his mind off sex.

"Did your mom still want to go with Paulina as the caterer?" he asked.

"No, she likes the idea of having the food prepared by Jillian's staff, and I agreed with her. Your mom was very impressed with Gentlemen of the Four Corners. They are an excellent band and I think Mom is going to go with them for the reception," Jill said, noticing that there was a smile of amusement playing on Kyle's face. "Why are you smiling like that?" she asked as she propped herself up on one elbow.

"You called my mother Mom. I didn't think you felt comfortable calling her that, or did you slip?"

"I didn't mean to refer to her as Mom, but it did feel right," Jill said as she thought back to the time when she and Regina had spent time alone at the hospital when Kyle was in the trauma unit.

Regina had stayed by her side and had given her the courage to face the devastation of Kyle's accident. She had even hand-fed Jill when she had refused to eat. She had always counted herself as a strong and resourceful woman, but Jill had never been so scared and felt so alone as she had in the hospital. It was Regina who reminded her that she was still that strong and powerful woman. Regina had gracefully shown Jill that God was quietly and continuously working to perform the miracle that they all desperately needed. Jill only needed to be still and let God do his work.

Jill smiled, knowing that it felt good and it felt right to call Regina Mom. Her own mother had said that in doing so it took nothing away from her, and Jill felt a closeness with Regina that was something akin to being her daughter. Both women had the innate desire to protect the family and to see it prosper and grow in love. Jill could see that she had more in common with Regina every day.

As she lay contemplating her new relationship with her mother-in-law, Kyle had drifted off to sleep. Jill lay quietly by his side hoping that for the rest of her life she would always find herself right here, right by his side and giving him all the love and support any woman could possibly give a man.

Kyle's stretch was cut short as he realized that he was not in bed, but had spent the night on the sofa. As his eyes focused, he could see that Jill was dressed for work and gathering her purse, briefcase, and keys.

Jill noticed that Kyle was awake and she walked over to the sofa. Sitting on the edge she rested her palms on his strong chest as she leaned over to kiss him good morning. His arms embraced her as she kissed him and he couldn't help but thank heaven that she was all his.

"I can't believe you didn't wake me to come to bed," he said groggily.

"I did and you stood up, but as soon as I turned my back you were asleep on the sofa. I didn't have the heart to wake you again, so I covered you up and let you sleep down here."

"That's not good, Mrs. Roberts. I don't ever want to sleep without you by my side," he said as he let each knuckle run across her blouse where her nipple could be.

Jill's breath caught in her throat as she looked deep into his eyes. It would have been so easy to give in to temptation and make time for a quickie, but she did not. Instead, she took his hand away from her breast and kissed it. "You are incredibly hard to resist, but I'm going to have to."

She stood and collected her things. Jill caressed Kyle's head before turning to leave. "I'll call you later, baby. I love you," she said, low and sexy.

"I love you too," he whispered back.

As the door closed behind her, Kyle found himself clutching the blanket in his fists. Before Jill came into his life he had done without sex for a long time, but now he acted like he had to have it every night. *Be patient, man, before you know it she'll be your wife—just hold on,* he thought.

Monica was thrilled to see Jill when she walked in the door. Though she had visited her boss at the hospital when Kyle was there, it was good to see her in business attire, looking good, and obviously feeling good.

"Welcome back, Jill," Monica said, as she stood and came from behind the desk.

"Thanks, Monica," Jill said as she hugged the woman.

"I really missed you."

"I missed you too, and thanks for coming to see Kyle and me at the hospital. I know it was hard on you picking up the slack around here and coming to visit us, but I appreciate it," Jill said sincerely.

"It was no problem at all. I'd do it again in a heartbeat."

"Is Bebe in yet?"

"Yes, she arrived just a little while before you did," Monica told Jill as she handed her the mail and messages.

"Thanks, Monica. See you in a bit," Jill said as she headed to her office.

Flipping through the mail Monica had just handed her, Jill entered her office. As she turned on the lights she noticed that someone had been working at her desk. Upon closer observation, she realized that all the files that she had left had been completed and filed. There was a note on her desk explaining what had been done, and where certain files had been placed, and it had been signed by Monica.

At first a sense of alarm went off in Jill's head. Though she trusted Monica to run the office, she wasn't quite sure if she knew what she was doing as far as managing clients, returning business calls, and handling her files.

Quickly Jill sat down in her chair and began going over some of the things Monica had taken care of. She was shocked to see that Monica had been working on the Mulher Bela Swimwear account, but what surprised her even more was that Monica had done pretty much what she would have done with the account. All the paperwork and contracts were in order and ready to be sent to the client, and all they needed was her signature.

Jill stood and walked out of her office and down the hall toward Bebe's. She stood in the doorway as Bebe finished a phone call. Bebe, noticing that Jill was standing there, signaled for her to enter and have a seat. Jill did.

A few moments later, Bebe ended her phone call and welcomed Jill back to work. Bebe stood and came from behind her desk to give Jill a quick hug and a kiss on the cheek. Then she leaned on the edge of her desk, making time to enjoy Jill's company.

"How does it feel to be back at work?" she asked, grinning.

"It feels wonderful, Bebe, but I have something on my mind," Jill said as she leaned back in the chair. She crossed her legs as a perplexed look came across her face.

"What's going on, Jill?"

"I noticed that Monica was working in my office and

that she did quite a bit of work on the Mulher Bela account."

"Yes, she did, Jill, but don't blame her, it's my fault. I told her to do as much as she could. I didn't want to worry you with business while you had so much on your mind with Kyle. I did get a little crazy around here, but Monica was a tremendous help on that account, while I worked on the Fitz and O'Neal account."

"Everything is okay," Jill said, waving her hand to dismiss Bebe's worries. "As a matter of fact, things are better than okay. You made a great decision having Monica take on more duties, and she did an excellent job. I was just thinking that maybe it's time we consider making her a junior partner. She's been here since we opened the place and she takes on all kinds of extra duties. What do you think?"

"I think you're right. When should we tell her?"

"You can have the honors later, but be sure to tell her that we have to find a replacement for her first. Right now I have to get busy with work," Jill said as she stood and prepared to leave.

"Wait, Jill, I have something I wanted to discuss with you," Bebe said quickly. "I just wanted to tell you that Tony and I are planning to have the wedding this weekend," she said, beaming.

"This weekend! Why so soon?"

"Well, we wanted to do it a few weeks ago, but then Kyle had his accident and we put everything on hold."

"But, Bebe, you don't have much time to get ready for a wedding."

"I don't need much time. I don't have any family except the one I'm marrying into. Regina is going to host the ceremony and reception at her estate. She has already taken care of the food, the photographer, and the band. It's going to be a very small ceremony, Jill, only about seventy-five guests, and I was hoping that you would be my maid of honor."

"Oh, Bebe, I'd be thrilled to," Jill said as she grabbed Bebe and almost squeezed the life out of her. When she released her Jill said, "Are you guys planning to go on a honeymoon?"

"Yes, we are, we are going to Hawaii," Bebe said, still beaming.

"That sounds wonderful," Jill said, as she remembered the trip she had given to Lois over a year ago. "I wish we could stand here and chat, but since we can't I want to hear all your plans at lunch."

"That sounds great. I'll be ready."

Jill made her way back to her office delighted that Bebe wasn't wasting time in getting married. She knew just how anxious Tony was to make her his wife, and probably wanted to do so before Bebe got cold feet.

Once in her office Jill began working at a fast pace. She made phone calls and signed contracts as she multi-tasked on the computer. All the while her mind kept drifting back to the wedding that would be taking place this weekend.

She had no doubt that Regina could throw an elegant event together in no time, but still she wanted the occasion to be as memorable as possible for Bebe. She made a quick call to Regina and offered her assistance. Regina thanked her for offering to help but assured her that she had everything under control.

Jill still wanted to do something special for Bebe and came up with the idea to throw her a bridal shower. Bebe still lived at the resort, and didn't have much to start a home with her new husband. Jill had been at Tony's cabin, and it was the typical bachelor pad.

He had all the basics, but nothing to start a life with his wife. The couple was in need of everything from the kitchen to the bathroom and every room in between, and immediately Jill knew that she was on the right track in giving Bebe a bridal shower.

Before she knew it, it was time for lunch and she was anxious to sit down with Bebe and hear more about her wedding plans. As she grabbed her purse, she buzzed Monica and told her that her presence was required at lunch. Monica was happy for the invitation and was standing at the door when Jill and Bebe arrived.

Jill drove and when they arrived at the Ranch House, they were surprised to find it almost empty during the lunch hour. They sat down and were greeted by Grace.

"Grace, where is everyone?" Jill asked.

"At the rodeo competition. It's just a little impromptu thing some of the guys put together a little while ago. What can I get you?" Grace asked.

The women ordered and Grace left. Then Bebe started telling Jill and Monica her plans. Jill could tell by the sparkle in Bebe's eyes that she was genuinely happy about becoming Mrs. Tony Roberts. She could remember not too long ago that their love was almost put in jeopardy by Rosy. Jill wondered if the woman was still in town, and if so, would she be at the wedding?

Grace brought the food and the women began to eat as Bebe talked. She told Grace about the wedding and she, too, hugged Bebe so hard that she could hardly breathe.

Bebe told them that she had already picked out a dress. It was a simple tea-length gown with silk sleeves that draped off her shoulders. She informed Jill and Monica that she wouldn't be in Friday, in order to get ready for the wedding. She also told them that she and Tony would be away on their honeymoon for a week.

Jill didn't tell Bebe about her plans for the bridal shower. She decided to make it a surprise and would enlist the help of Monica to get everything done before Friday. Jill planned on having the bridal shower at the cabin and wanted to ask Kyle to do the cooking, but he would probably be busy helping Eric plan a bachelor party for Tony. So she decided that she would ask Sharon to help her.

"Jill, I know the wedding is happening on such short notice, but I want to invite your mother. She is so good to me and I really want her and Barbie to come. Do you think they can make it?" Bebe asked.

"I'm sure that they'll do everything possible to make it here."

"Good, I'm going to give your parents and Barbie a call when we get back to the office."

When lunch was over the women returned to work and tried to get as much done as possible, since they would be short one person the following week.

Bebe stopped at Monica's desk and told her about her promotion, which would go into effect as soon as they hired another secretary to fill her position. Monica was surprised and the news made her very happy. Bebe also told her that Jill was pleased with the work she had done on the Mulher Bela account. After Bebe had finished talking with Monica, she went to Jill's office and thanked her for the words of praise as well as the raise.

It was then that Jill told Monica about the surprise bridal shower she was planning for Bebe. Monica was excited about Jill's plans and offered her assistance, which Jill immediately accepted. When Monica left her office, Jill called her mother.

Her phone call was short, but her mother told her that she had just gotten off the phone with Bebe and she and the entire family would be coming for the wedding. Jill asked if there was any way they could arrive on Wednesday, so that she and her sister could attend the bridal shower, which she hoped to host on Thursday. Maddie said that it wouldn't be a problem and that they would be there. Before they hung up, Jill told her mother that the shower was going to be a surprise, so that if she spoke with Bebe again she wouldn't mention it.

Jill ended the call telling her mother that she loved her and would be happy to see her soon. Then she finished her workday and was ready to go home.

Chapter 12

Maddie, Rob, and Barbie's family arrived at A Special Place late Wednesday afternoon. Jill was so happy to see her family and thankful that they were all able to make it to the wedding. Kyle and Tony had picked them up from the airport and had brought them directly to the resort. Maddie fondly remembered staying at the luxurious resort during the grand opening, and opted to stay there rather than at the cabin. Not only was Maddie happy to spend some additional time with Jill, but also with Bebe, of whom she had grown quite fond over the past year.

When her mother and sister entered the house, Jill's face lit up. Though she knew they were arriving today, she was still excited to finally see them. She crossed the room and greeted her family by hugging Maddie and Barbie warmly.

"Mom, I'm so happy you're here!" Jill said, unable to control the excitement in her voice.

"I'm happy to be here. Did we get here before Bebe?" Maddie asked.

"Yes, she should be arriving shortly. Barbie, how was your trip here?"

"It was great, sis. I just wish it wasn't going to be so short."

"Don't think of the negative, girls. Before you know it, we'll be back out here for Jill's wedding," Maddie reminded them with a hint of exhilaration in her voice.

"I know, but right now it's Bebe's turn and I am so happy that she and Tony are tying the knot," Jill said sincerely.

"I'm happy for her too. It feels like I have three girls instead of two," Maddie said truthfully.

"Why don't you guys go and mingle while I see how things are coming along in the kitchen? Sharon made some wonderful hors d'oeuveres, and I didn't even know she could cook," Jill said, making her mother and sister giggle.

The two women walked away and soon found many familiar faces in the room. After getting something to nibble on, they sat and talked with Grace as well as Regina Roberts.

Jill had worked hard in preparing a bridal shower for Bebe, and was quite surprised that Bebe hadn't caught on. Late Thursday afternoon guests had started to arrive. Jill didn't realize just how many friends Bebe had and knew she probably didn't either. The cabin was practically bulging with thirty women in attendance. Sharon was obviously an excellent cook, as the aroma of her meal wafted through the air, making everyone hungry.

As it neared four o'clock, Jill grew anxious for Bebe's arrival. Aside from helping to get the word out about the shower, Monica was supposed to bring Bebe to the shower. Knowing that Bebe would be suspicious seeing the cars upon arrival, Jill had told her that Kyle was having another barbecue.

At four o'clock on the button, Bebe and Monica

arrived. The lively conversation quieted as they heard
the two women approaching the door. As it opened and
Bebe entered, everyone in the room yelled, "Surprise!"

Bebe jumped at the outburst and blinked in amazement as she realized that the party was for her. She
smiled at Jill as she made her way to her friend. Bebe
hugged Jill fiercely as she whispered a quiet thank-you
in her ear. She couldn't stop the tears of joy that rolled
down her cheeks, and tried to wipe them away gently.

A fresh batch of tears escaped as her eyes fell upon
the faces of Maddie and Barbie.

"I can't believe you're here!" she said as she hugged
Maddie.

"Where else would I be when one of my girls is getting married?" Maddie said as she hugged Bebe back.

"I'm so excited for you, Bebe. Tony is a very lucky
man to land a sweetheart like you," Barbie said, as she
hugged Bebe also and offered heartfelt congratulations.

"Yes, he is." Bebe grinned as she stepped back and
looked around at all her guests.

The room was filled with many friends. Most of
them would become related to her by marriage or
were women she counted as family anyway. Grace
and several other women from the ranch were in attendance. Bebe had learned that family is not always
the one you are born into, and she knew she was
blessed to be included in this one.

Rosy Hernandez and her mother were invited and
sat toward the back of the room. Rosy, who looked
much like her mother, didn't appear as bubbly and
full of sex appeal as she normally did. Bebe thought
that Rosy would have preferred to be anywhere else
but here, and had probably been brought kicking and
screaming by her mother. Bebe imagined that Regina

had invited the longtime family friends since Jill really didn't like Rosy and may have considered her presence at the shower a problem.

As Bebe moved toward the sofa, she saw Regina. She had known the woman ever since she was a little girl. Regina had always treated Bebe with kindness and love. On many occasions she had told her that she thought of her as her own daughter, and Regina had always backed it up with her actions. Regina had been there when she graduated from high school and college, and then had offered her the job at A Special Place. When she was growing up, Bebe had gone on several family vacations with the Robertses and was always the object of Tony's attention.

Now they were getting married, and as she sat next to the woman who seemed more like a mother than a mother-in-law, she saw in Regina's eyes complete approval, acceptance, and love. Bebe knew that she had found her home and her family. In fact, she had always had them. It was only now that she realized how perfect her own life would be in marrying Tony.

"Hi, Mom," Bebe said as she sat next to Regina.

"Hello, darling," Regina said as she wrapped her arm around Bebe's shoulder and squeezed it. She kissed Bebe's cheek and smiled endearingly at the woman she had already accepted as family.

Knowing her son the way she did, Regina knew from the very day Tony set eyes on Bebe that he felt something stirring in his heart for her. Over the years she saw those feelings turn from the love of a dear friend to the love for a woman that he wanted to call his own, and Regina's heart was full of joy at having Bebe become an official member of the family.

Jill, Sharon, and Monica began serving drinks, and Sharon announced that the buffet was set up in the kitchen. The women laughed and talked as they ate and mingled out on the deck. Bebe smiled so much that her cheeks ached. After everyone was finished eating the wonderful meal, which consisted of fried chicken, potato salad, corn on the cob, and rolls, they congregated in the big living room as Bebe prepared to open her gifts.

Sharon had made hors d'oeuvres and everyone enjoyed them immensely. Jill was especially surprised that she could cook so well, since she knew that domestic tasks weren't her sister-in-law's strong suit. Sharon had even made Bebe's favorite dessert, key lime pie, and Bebe was pleased and very surprised.

Bebe opened gift after gift and got just about everything to make a beautiful home with Tony. She had received linens for the bed and bathrooms, as well as complete sets of pots and pans. For anything she might be missing she was given several gift cards.

Many of her guests had given her lingerie for her honeymoon, and Bebe blushed every time she opened a box to reveal a negligee from Fredrick's of Hollywood or Victoria's Secret in front of her soon to be mother-in-law. Regina, who only laughed at Bebe, said that she hoped the nighties would bring her more grandchildren. The comment seemed to lessen Bebe's embarrassment and she smiled.

Maddie looked around the room and saw Bebe sitting and talking to her soon-to-be mother-in-law. Bebe's face reflected all the closeness and comfort she found in Regina, and Maddie knew that Bebe, as well as Jill, had a real family in Colorado.

"Bebe seems truly happy," Maddie commented to Jill, who was now sitting between her and Barbie.

"Yes, she is," Jill said as she turned to look at Bebe. An expression of satisfaction was on Jill's face, and

Maddie noticed it. "I get the feeling you had something to do with that."

"In a way I did, Mom, but for a while I was afraid things might not turn out so well," Jill said with a sigh.

"Why do you say that?"

"Well, I wasn't trying to matchmake like you," Jill said, making Maddie chuckle. "But I did try to get things on the right track for Bebe and Tony."

"How?" Barbie asked.

"It's a long story," Jill began, and then lowered her voice and continued. "But suffice it to say that someone was going to cause trouble in their relationship, and I wasn't about to let that happen." Her eyes fell on Rosy and her mother, and Barbie followed her gaze inconspicuously.

Rosy still sat quietly next to her mother with all sexual charm going to waste, since no men were in attendance.

"That's good," Barbie said.

"Besides, Tony was ready to make Bebe his own, and I knew that in her heart, it's what Bebe wanted too. All I had to do was show her what she stood to lose."

When the last guest left at 7:30, Bebe was exhausted, but wouldn't leave the cabin until she helped Jill with the cleaning up. Maddie, Barbie, Monica, Sharon, and Regina helped as well, and in no time they had the cabin back in order.

"I wonder where Tony is," Bebe said as she grabbed an armful of gifts to put in Monica's car.

"I guess it's okay to tell you, he is at his bachelor party. Kyle is throwing him one right now at Roland's," Jill said.

"Uh, Roland's. I hope he isn't having too much fun," she said, laughing and rolling her eyes.

"I don't think you have to worry abut that. Eric

won't let things get out of hand," Sharon said with an air of assurance.

Sharon helped Jill, Bebe, and Monica to the car with the gifts. Bebe had received so much that Sharon had to put some of them in her truck. As they worked on getting all the gifts out of the living room, Maddie and Regina finished cleaning the kitchen.

Jill paused briefly in the doorway of the kitchen and watched as Regina worked alongside her mother. She wasn't surprised by her mother's actions, but she was stunned to see that Regina had rolled up her sleeves and gotten to work. Regina was the kind of woman who was never seen in public with a hair on her head out of place. She was always stylishly dressed and sporting a fresh manicure. Jill was shocked that Regina would risk chipping a nail while loading the dishwasher.

Jill smiled to herself as she continued cleaning when she realized that the wealthy woman even knew how to load a dishwasher. There once was a time when Regina had to keep up with and take care of three rambunctious boys, so Jill imagined that that time in her life had given her the skills she used now. With that thought Jill could only admire the kind of woman Regina was even more. She saw in her someone who wasn't afraid to take on any task at hand. At her husband's side at an important business dinner, or in the kitchen cleaning, Regina Roberts was all class.

When the women were finished, they stood outside on the porch of the cabin, and Bebe thanked each one of them for all that they had done for her.

"Darling, we're family, and this is what family does. We stick together and take care of each other," Regina said as she hugged Bebe good-bye.

Over Bebe's shoulder Regina winked at Jill and

Maddie, before releasing Bebe and walking down the steps. Having said her good-byes, Regina got into her Jaguar and drove off.

With a final farewell Bebe and Monica were the next to leave, followed by Sharon, who had to drop off the gifts at Tony's cabin before she went home as well.

"Well, I guess it's just us," Barbie said as she entwined her arms through her mother's and sister's.

"Yep, it's just us," Jill replied.

The rest of the evening was spent sitting in the living room talking to her mother and sister. They went over some of Jill's own wedding plans before talking about everything else under the sun.

"How is school coming along?" Jill asked Barbie.

"It's coming along fine, but it really took me a while to get back into the studying habit. But I don't want to talk about school, and before you ask, the kids and Rick are doing fine. Now, what I want to know is how is life out here? You look happy."

"Barbie, I am happy, and I'm thrilled to be getting married," Jill said, squealing with delight. Her face darkened as she added, "I was really afraid that I would lose Kyle when he had the car accident."

"I'm so sorry that we weren't with you when that happened," Maddie said.

"Oh, Mom, don't be. You can't fly out here every time I call."

"No, I can't, but that was a life-and-death situation, and I felt like I shouldn't have listened to you and should have come anyway."

Jill rubbed her mother's arm and said, "Regina was here, and she was almost as good as having you right beside me."

Maddie smiled back at Jill, knowing that she did have

family here too. She knew she didn't have to worry too much about her youngest daughter anymore.

After sitting and talking for a few hours Jill drove her sister and mother back to the resort. With hugs and kisses as they got out of the car Jill felt wonderful having her family in town. She drove home contentedly, but she knew she would be alone until Kyle got in from Tony's party.

It was only 11:00 p.m., and she wasn't surprised that Kyle still wasn't home. Though she hoped he was having a good time she, like Bebe, hoped he wasn't having too good of a time. She had been so busy with her own plans for Bebe's shower that she knew very little about what Kyle and Eric had planned. As she thought on the subject, she knew that Kyle probably didn't want to discuss the details of Tony's party with her anyway, knowing that too much information would only cause problems.

Jill kicked off her shoes and went into the kitchen and got the pitcher of ice water out of the refrigerator. She poured herself a tall glass and garnished it with a lemon wedge. Then she turned and headed upstairs.

She sipped the water before setting it down on the counter in the bathroom. Jill undressed and turned on the shower. As she stepped into the tub, she silently wished that Kyle was home. As she bathed, her thoughts returned to the bachelor party. She couldn't help wondering if there was a stripper there. Though the party was at Roland's Nightclub, there was a private party room there, and Jill imagined that that was where Kyle and Eric were hosting the party.

Suddenly it dawned on Jill that Rosy Hernandez probably would make it a point to go to Roland's tonight. She had noticed that Rosy hardly had two words to say all evening, and was one of the first people to leave as soon as the shower was over. Jill couldn't take into consideration Rosy's outfit, because the woman always dressed to tantalize. She wouldn't put it past the woman to try to snag Tony one last time before he got married.

Jill stepped out of the shower, and dried herself off and began to moisturize her skin before slipping into her nightclothes. She brushed her hair, turned out the lights, and left the bathroom.

Jill climbed into bed and fell asleep, hoping that Tony, as well as Kyle and Eric, had been a good boy.

Regina and Samuel Roberts's huge manicured backyard served as a beautiful location for Tony and Bebe's wedding. Rosebushes in pink and red decorated the area, and the weather was perfect. There wasn't a cloud to be seen in the pale blue sky. A gentle breeze swept across the grounds and blew the soft tendrils of hair that graced Bebe's face. Her hair was pulled back in a French knot with a decorative comb that shimmered with crystals adorning it.

Jill stood next to Bebe, and next to her, Sharon. Kyle was Tony's best man, and next to him stood Eric. Jill looked at Bebe and could see she was the happiest she had ever seen her. Bebe looked radiant as the minister read the wedding vows.

Kyle had confirmed her fears by telling Jill that Rosy had shown up at Roland's the other night. Although the bachelor party was held in the back room, Rosy had made an attempt to gain entrance. Rosy wasn't allowed in the back, but she did manage to see Tony.

Kyle told Jill that Tony gave Rosy a hug, kissed her on the cheek, wished her all the best, and then left to rejoin his friends. After that, Rosy left Roland's and that was the last they had seen of her until today.

Jill knew that Tony was made from the same fine stock as Kyle. Tony was the kind of man who believed in the foundation of love, honor, and marriage. He had always known that Bebe was the woman for him, and he didn't sway from the love he knew existed between the two of them.

As Jill looked on now, the sun shone as bright as the love that consumed Tony and Bebe. Slowly, yet cohesively, her own world was forming. This was not her new family, but an addition to one that she already had. With her own marriage to Kyle, Bebe, Tony, Sharon, and Eric would all be her family by marriage. The thought made Jill smile as she continued listening to the ceremony. She was happy for all that God had given her, and as everyone bowed their heads in prayer, she said one of gratitude of her own.

When she lifted her head, Jill glanced around to see Rosy. She sat with her parents, and once again looked as if she wished she could be anywhere else but here. Dressed in the same manner as she always was, totally hot, she listened inattentively as Tony and Bebe were married. Still, Jill hoped that Rosy would find happiness and contentment in her own life.

Bebe handed Jill her bouquet as she turned toward Tony and kissed her new husband. It was a long kiss, which was filled with all the passion Tony had seemed to be holding in for years. Cheers, applause, and whistles filled the air as Mr. and Mrs. Antonio Carl Roberts were introduced to the guests.

Immediately after the wedding ceremony, dinner was served. Regina had the event catered and everything tasted wonderful. Guests toasted the couple with champagne as music began to play. The band began

with the couple's wedding song, which was Pattie La-
belle's rendition of "If You Asked Me To."

Tony took Bebe in his arms as they performed
their first dance together as husband and wife. The
off-the-shoulder, satin and silk, tea-length wedding
dress flowed gently as Bebe glided across the floor in
her husband's arms. She looked up into her husband's face. Stars filled her eyes as she stared deeply
into the core of his soul. She knew her heart had
always had a home in his, and now as his wife she
found peace in the fact that Jill had been right; marrying Tony had enhanced their relationship and not
ruined it.

After a while, Samuel Roberts cut in on his son in
order to dance with his newest daughter-in-law, and
Regina danced with Tony. The rest of the wedding
party joined them on the floor and all wished for
many more beautiful, love-filled nights like this.

Long into the evening, the guests danced and
feasted on a sit-down dinner of prime rib and salmon.
Glasses of champagne were filled continuously at
each table and the wedding cake was devoured by all
during the joyous occasion.

With evening stars beginning to fill the sky, the
guests began to leave. As the wonderful evening drew
to a close, the newlyweds were seen continuously
holding each other's hand and relishing the sheer joy
of one another's touch.

Chapter 13

The week Bebe was away was a very busy one for Jill. She and Monica had been working nonstop on the Mulher Bela Swimwear account. Jill found out just how professional and skilled Monica was in handling the clients and the accounts. Given the situation, Monica had to take on more than her duties required, and she did it to the best of her ability and without complaining. Monica's professionalism far surpassed Jill's expectations.

Aside from the daily grind of work, Jill tried to work on her own upcoming wedding. It was times like this that she thought Bebe had the right idea. A quick and simple wedding would have left her life less hectic, but her parents would have been disappointed, not to mention herself. She had always dreamed of a big wedding and now she was having one. It just didn't seem like there was enough time to do all the planning.

Her mother had done a great deal of work as far as the wedding was concerned before she had gone back to Pittsburgh. Regina seemed to be continuously working on the wedding as well. Both women were completing a dream, which was to see all their children happily married. As Jill sat at the desk, she saw that her sister and her in-laws were all happily married, at least for now. She prayed that things would always stay that way for all of them. Life for Jill was exactly how she had hoped it would be.

Jill hoped that things would slow down after the wedding. With preparing for the wedding, Kyle's accident, and Bebe's nuptials, work was all Jill had time for. Kyle and his brothers worked together every day, but they had a dozen ranch hands to help them with the ranch. Jill sat staring at her computer screen thinking that if things didn't slow down for them, they might want to consider giving Monica more responsibilities before they hired another secretary. Desert Star was averaging a major new client every month, and was showing no sign of business slowing down. Jill decided that she would talk to Bebe about expanding their personnel pool.

It was twelve o'clock, and Jill and Monica had given up their hour-long lunch break all week. They simply packed their lunches and worked as they ate. By the end of the day both women were exhausted and dreaded taking any work home. Each knew that if she didn't, tomorrow would mean more work to catch up on.

Leaving the office, they said their good-byes and drove off. Though Jill was anxious to get home and see Kyle, she knew that by the time she arrived, ate dinner, and got some work done, he would be fast asleep.

Jill missed Kyle terribly. It seemed as though they hadn't gone out on a date since they had gotten engaged. Jill thought long and hard for a moment and then realized that she was right. The last time they had been out was in Jacksonville. Even then, Tony and Bebe were with them, and they were there on business.

When Jill arrived home Kyle had dinner waiting. Jill kicked off her shoes and set her briefcase and purse on the sofa. She walked into the kitchen and wrapped her tired arms around Kyle. He could see in her eyes that she was bone tired and probably not up to what he wanted to suggest. He too missed doing things with her, but tried to give Jill her space, remembering how dreadfully afraid she was that she wouldn't accomplish her professional goal.

Kyle planted a kiss on her forehead as she rested her head on his chest. It felt good to come home knowing someone was waiting there for her. They stood saying nothing to each other, but enjoying the warmth and pleasure each was receiving.

"I have an idea, babe," Kyle said as he continued to stroke her back.

"I hope it involves me, a blanket, and a pillow, because I am beat," Jill muttered.

"Not exactly." Kyle chuckled and continued, "But it does require me and you."

"What is it?" Jill asked as she looked up into Kyle's eyes.

"I was thinking that tonight we could go for a ride on Patches?"

Jill perked up a bit as she smiled and said, "We haven't gone riding in a long time."

"I know, and I was thinking that you could go and change and when you come down we can eat and then go."

Jill grinned and then tilted her head back to receive his kiss. "I won't take too long," she said.

As she left his embrace and walked through the living room, her eyes fell on her briefcase. She remembered all the paperwork she had to go over, but quickly decided being with Kyle was more important right now. Jill went up the stairs promising herself that when she returned she would get right to work.

When she came back downstairs Kyle had made a plate for each of them, and the couple ate quickly, anxious to go on the early evening ride. When they finished eating they went onto the porch and Kyle grabbed his hat from the hook. He let out a piercing whistle and seconds later Patches was in front of them. Jill greeted her favorite horse by rubbing her cheek against Patches, and then she climbed onto his back. Kyle climbed on behind Jill and Patches began to walk.

The air was still warm as the sun began to set. Jill could see a few stars trying to make their presence known early in the darkening evening sky. She let her body relax into Kyle's strong chest as Patches continued to walk gracefully over the terrain. Kyle held the horse's reins in one hand, and the other was instinctively wrapped around Jill's waist.

Jill closed her eyes and let her mind become free of all the issues that demanded her time away from Kyle. Right now, it was as it had been before, like nothing else mattered except the two of them and their need for each other.

Jill only opened her eyes when she felt the horse come to a stop. She looked around and saw that she was where Kyle had taken her the first time she had ridden Patches. He hopped down from the horse's back and held out his arms for Jill to climb into. She slid like butter into his waiting embrace, and the couple stood planting sweet kisses on each other for a moment.

Then they walked to the edge and looked down the mountainside where the resort was located. Jill stood in front of Kyle and his arms encircled her frame. As the sun continued to set, the moisture in the atmosphere gave way to colors that inspired and dazzled Jill's spirit. The sky was drenched in hues of purple and blues, and she missed having time to just sit back and enjoy the spectacular shows Mother Nature put on nightly. She remembered sitting in a chaise longue on the patio of her hotel room and watching twinkling stars dance before her.

Now more than ever, Jill realized that she wasn't Superwoman. She wanted to spend more time being a wife to Kyle when they were married. And she did want to have children, but if she continued to work like she did there would be no time to have sex in order to make a baby. She hoped they could find another reliable secretary for Desert Star, because she wanted Monica to become a junior partner fast.

"Did I tell you that Bebe and I decided to make Monica a junior partner?"

"What?"

"I think we need to make more time for each other. We haven't been to the movies or bowling, not to mention Roland's, in a long time. I want you to start taking me out on dates, Mr. Roberts, and I can't go if I'm spending every waking moment at the office."

"I'm available, but you aren't."

"I know, and all that's going to change," Jill said in a matter-of-fact voice.

"Babe, I understand that your time is tight. Starting a business is never easy and I know it is very demanding. I promised you I would be patient and would let you realize your dreams. I'm not going to renege on that now."

"No, you won't have to renege on your promise. I want to make Monica a junior partner because I realize what's important to me, and that is my life with you. I'm not giving up on Desert Star, but I know that it doesn't have to take up all of my time. Bebe is married now, and she will undoubtedly want to spend more time with Tony as well," Jill said, still inside Kyle's arms, but she turned around to face him.

"I think it's a great idea, especially if you're comfortable with Monica taking on more responsibility."

"Monica is a very capable secretary. She handled the Mulher Bela account to perfection while I was out, and all the while she kept up with her own duties. Desert Star is doing very well. We are averaging a major new client every month, not to mention the minor accounts we manage."

"When does all this go into effect?" Kyle asked with interest.

"As soon as we can find a replacement for Monica," Jill said.

She noticed the sky was getting darker and remembered that she still had some work to finish when she got home. Reluctantly, she released her arms from around Kyle's waist, and he did the same.

"Honey, I have to get back home. I have some work that I need to finish before I get in the office in the morning."

"I know, I saw your briefcase on the sofa. You only seem to bring it home when you have work to do," Kyle said, then whistled for Patches.

"Just imagine, soon all of our evenings will be free for us to enjoy each other."

"I can't wait," Kyle said.

Patches appeared and stood still so that the two riders could mount him. Though it was dark the horse began walking in the direction of his home. Jill had no worries and rested assured that Patches would get them to the cabin safe and sound.

Jill rested her back against Kyle's chest. Once again she closed her eyes and listened to the music nature provided. She could hear the crunch of fallen leaves under Patches's hooves and the sound of crickets rubbing their legs together. When she opened her eyes she was dazzled by the lights of the nearby fireflies. The little bugs seemed to be following them, illuminating the horse's path.

When they arrived at the cabin Kyle and Jill dismounted and Patches trotted off. The couple entered holding hands and with a kiss good night, Kyle headed up the stairs to bed, and Jill to the study to finish work.

The rest of the week seemed to drag on as Jill and Monica fought to keep up with all the work that needed to be done. It seemed that every time they thought they were ahead, something would happen to land them a few steps back. All of this was nothing new to Jill. She had had this kind of slump happen to her many times while working at Iguana. But now she was the boss, and incidents like this had an even more profound effect on her.

Though she and Monica were handling things well, she couldn't wait until Bebe returned. Perhaps, she thought, they should have hired an extra person a while ago. Their business had been growing by leaps and bounds since they opened their doors. Joan Singletary was still sending them business, but not as much as she once had been. Jill made a mental note to keep an eye on Desert Star's growth, and to hire additional help before she, Bebe, and Monica went under.

Jill was thrilled when Bebe and Tony arrived back in Durango after their honeymoon. She and Kyle were at the airport to pick them up and she couldn't wait to hear about their trip. As they waited outside for the newlyweds to arrive, Jill leaned against the car. Her hair was pulled back and she wore a pair of sunglasses to protect her eyes from the glistening sun. It was hot outside and the sky was void of clouds. Still, she loved the climate and couldn't think of another place she would rather be.

Kyle sat next to her waiting also. He was the first one to see the couple as they walked toward them. A broad smile came across his face as he stood and walked toward his brother and his new wife. Shaking his brother's hand as he hugged him, Kyle welcomed Tony home. Then he turned his attention to Bebe, who looked beautiful, relaxed, and completely in love.

Smiling warmly, Jill embraced Bebe and then helped her with her luggage. She welcomed Tony home as well; he looked like marriage was agreeing with him. Though Tony was always very attentive to Bebe's needs, and that was still evident, he now seemed more protective of her. Jill knew that she and Kyle shared the same kind of love and she was happy for what Bebe and Tony shared.

"I hope you took lots of pictures, because I want to know everything," Jill said excitely as she climbed into the SUV after Bebe.

"I did take a ton of pictures. Oh, Jill, I don't think I've ever been to a place as awe-inspiring as Hawaii. I want Tony to take me back there on our fifth wedding anniversary," Bebe said, smiling.

"I'll take you, Bebe, you, and Little Tony and Little

Bebe, and do we have time to get one more in before our fifth wedding anniversary?"

"Let's just work on one at a time, okay, cowboy?" Bebe said, laughing as she lovingly touched Tony's shoulder.

For the rest of the ride home Jill and Bebe caught up on over a week's worth of chitchat. It was obvious the two women had missed each other terribly, as did the two brothers. Jill caught a little of their conversation. She could hear Tony telling Kyle about Hawaii and married life, and Jill could see the pride in Kyle's eyes as he listened to his youngest brother talk.

Jill was thankful that it was Saturday and they had planned to spend the day with family at the cabin. To welcome Bebe and Tony back, she and Kyle were having a cookout, and had invited Sharon, Eric, and their parents to the cabin. After they dropped Bebe and Tony at their own cabin, Jill and Kyle went home to finish preparing for their guests.

Once home, the couple began cooking together. Kyle, who loved being the king of the grill, was outside on the patio. Jill was inside preparing all the side dishes except the corn, which Kyle put on the grill. She made sure that they had plenty on hand to drink and had set out dishes so that everyone could make their own plates.

An hour later Eric, Sharon, and Ally arrived. Jill held out her arms and Sharon handed the growing infant to her. Jill cuddled the little girl and went to sit down on the sofa with her. She marveled at how Ally reflected the features of both her mother and father. The baby had Eric's soft brown eyes and nose, but she had the rich copper skin color and delicate lips of her mother.

Sharon, who was happy to be baby-free for the

moment, grabbed a glass of lemonade and said, "I'm enjoying breast-feeding, but I can't wait to have a nice glass of wine." Then she went outside to join Eric and to say hello to Kyle.

As Jill continued holding Ally, she knew in her heart that she didn't want anything more than to have Kyle's child. As she studied Ally, she wondered if their baby would take on all of their best features, or would it reach back in the gene pool and arrive looking not too much like either of them? Jill found herself wishing she were expecting right now, and hoped one day to give Kyle a baby, too.

The front door opened, breaking Jill's fascination with Ally. She looked up to see that the senior Mr. and Mrs. Roberts were entering the cabin. Regina's face lit up as she saw her granddaughter in Jill's arms. She greeted Jill with a kiss on the cheek as she sat down beside her. Mr. Roberts kissed her cheek as well, but went outside to join the group that was forming there.

"I hope you had your fill of that little princess, because I'm ready to hold her," Regina said in a voice filled with love and excitement.

"No, I haven't had my fill, but I'll share her with you," Jill said as she handed Ally to her grandmother.

Jill continued to sit next to Regina and admired how the woman got such a kick out of her granddaughter. Each time Ally yawned or stretched, Regina marveled at her. She cuddled and cooed over the baby and didn't get the least bit upset when Ally drooled on her blouse. Jill smiled and was thankful that her in-laws had made the decision to move back to Durango. She knew that Regina wanted more grandchildren, and would be just as enchanted with any additional ones as she was with Ally.

The door opened again and this time it was the

newlyweds. Bebe and Tony should have been exhausted from their trip, but they seemed to be functioning off the natural high being just married provided. Whatever it was, Jill could only pray that she and Kyle would experience the same kind of bliss.

Kyle entered the living room and walked over to the sofa. He gave his mother a kiss on the cheek and then announced that dinner was ready. Sharon offered to take Ally so that Regina could eat, but she waved Sharon away.

"I'm a mother as well as a grandmother. I can eat and hold a baby," she told Sharon.

Inside the kitchen the family sat around the table as Samuel led the family in a prayer. He gave thanks not only for the food but for the family he and his wife had started. With the food blessed, the hungry clan began to eat, laugh, and talk in the comfortable family atmosphere. Jill looked around at her soon-to-be family. She knew this was where she was supposed to be and relished the day when she would be an official member.

The family feasted on ribs, smoked salmon, corn on the cob, potato salad, and Jill's homemade dinner rolls. Kyle had made his famous blueberry cobbler for dessert, and after dinner everyone congregated in the living room to watch Bebe and Tony's movie from their honeymoon.

Bebe popped a CD from her Sony Handycam and put it in the DVD player. Then she went to sit next to her husband, who wrapped his arms lovingly around her shoulders.

As the movie began to play it was obvious that the couple had had a wonderful time. Tony was obviously the director and didn't mind capturing his beautiful new wife on disc. He had recorded their arrival to the hotel as well as the beautiful room they stayed in. There was a segment of Bebe trying to hula dance, as well as them at a luau. There was a huge pig being roasted on a bonfire, and Bebe was laughing and talking with a couple of other women.

As the family watched the movie, Tony narrated and told them that the women were all opting not to eat any of the freshly cooked, still-headed swine, but that he and the other guys enjoyed eating the tasty animal. Jill agreed with Bebe, and knew she wouldn't have eaten any of the pig either.

Finally there was a shot of Tony trying to surf. Bebe did an excellent job of capturing his many attempts to catch a wave before he wiped out. The room filled with Bebe's voice as she yelled words of encouragement to Tony as he tried relentlessly. Her voice was loud as she became his personal cheerleader.

Jill glanced over to see a smile filled with happiness and contentment as Bebe held Tony's hand now and watched the movie. Bebe had been a radiant bride and still carried that glow. Jill noticed that Bebe seemed to possess an inner peace, which she attributed to her new role as Tony's wife.

When the movie ended Kyle turned on the lights and Tony was quick to stand and retrieve the DVD of his honeymoon.

"When will we get to see pictures and video of the wedding?" Sharon asked.

"I hope soon. I haven't heard anything from the photographer yet," Bebe answered. "Jill, is there anymore blueberry cobbler left?"

"Yes," Jill said, and stood to walk into the kitchen with Bebe close behind.

Bebe reached out and grabbed Jill's hand. She

had something on her mind and wanted to tell Jill in private.

Jill turned to face Bebe and said, "What's wrong?"

Her eyes studied Bebe's for a second and she could tell that Bebe needed to talk. As she stood waiting for Bebe to speak, Jill's mind raced with anticipation, and she hoped there wasn't trouble in paradise.

"Jill, do you know all that I have is because of you?"

"No, Bebe," Jill said, relieved that her fear was not on Bebe's agenda. "All that you have is because of you. You're smart and business-minded. You were a success when I met you."

"Not as big of a success as I am now. Now I am a business owner. And if it weren't for you, I wouldn't be married right now," Bebe said softly.

"Maybe not right now, but you would have married Tony eventually. I know as well as you do that another man doesn't walk the earth that makes you feel the way Tony does."

"You're right, but I know that I almost lost the best thing that ever happened to me."

"You mean Rosy?" Jill said, smiling and stifling a giggle.

"Yes, I mean Rosy—I mean all the Rosys of the world. I was pushing Tony away. I imagine that he would have given up eventually."

"No, he wouldn't have. The only thing Rosy Hernandez was able to do was get Tony to make you see that you two belong together. He would never have given up on you."

"Thanks, Jill. For always showing me the way to go," Bebe said as she hugged Jill.

"You're welcome," Jill said.

Then Jill went and prepared two bowls of blueberry cobbler and Bebe covered them with whipped cream. They headed back into the living room where the men were playing pool and Regina and Sharon were playing with Ally on the sofa.

Well into the evening the family continued to enjoy each other's company. Jill understood why Bebe was so grateful, but in her mind, all she had done was made Bebe see all that her life could be if she only gave in to love. As she looked around the room at her family, Jill shared in the same kind of gratitude Bebe expressed. She was thankful for all the love and happiness her heart could hold.

Chapter 14

With Bebe's return to work, Desert Star was in full swing again. The three coworkers made the most of their time by getting as much work done as they could before Jill's wedding. Everything on the Mulher Bela account was going smoothly, and Jill had let Monica handle most of the details on it since she was busy with the preparations for her wedding. Monica was doing a terrific job and Jill was happy having to only supervise.

Bebe had been settling into married life with ease, but she was just as anxious as Jill was about wanting to hire a replacement for Monica. Though the women had interviewed several people, none of them came with the same spirit of commitment that Monica had, nor did they have the skills she possessed. Jill wanted to hire someone soon because she didn't want to take time off for her wedding and leave Bebe and Monica scrambling to get everything done. It had been so hectic when Bebe was gone, and Jill imagined that Bebe had suffered the same way when she had been out during Kyle's accident. Jill could only pray that they would find someone, and soon.

With the wedding only two weeks away, Jill got butterflies every time she thought about getting married to Kyle. In her heart she knew it was what she wanted most of all, but her mind had a lot to say about it. She found herself in a constant battle trying to decide if her timing was wrong. Bebe did her best to try to alleviate Jill's fears, sensing that her getting cold feet had more to do with old fears than Desert Star, and she told her so during dinner at Jill's place Thursday night.

"Jill, everyone gets cold feet before their wedding, and you are no different," Bebe said as she helped herself to more salad.

"I just can't help thinking that the timing is all wrong, Bebe. You and Monica are practically running Desert Star by yourselves, and we haven't found someone to fill Monica's position so that she can be a full-time help to you while I'm out."

"We were fine the last time you were out. We will be okay this time as well. You know what I think?" Bebe said, and then took a sip of her sangria. "I think that you feel as though you are losing a grip on your dreams. Right now everything is happening so fast. Our company is growing, I've gotten married, you're getting married, we need another employee, but don't let all of this make you lose sight of what's important. Jill, Kyle is more important to you than all of that."

"He is important to me, Bebe, and being married to him is what I want more than anything. I just don't want to let go of Desert Star and see it slip into ruins. I want to be able to hold on to Kyle and make him happy. Still, I don't want to disappear in him either."

Jill picked up her own glass of sangria and took a long sip. She set the glass back down on the table and said, "I know I'm being silly."

"No, you're not. I felt the same way for years about

Tony. I knew I loved him but I didn't want to marry him. It wasn't until I ran the risk of losing him that I realized I couldn't live without him. There were many times in the few weeks we were engaged that I wanted to turn and run away, but I knew no matter how far I ran, my heart and soul would always belong to him."

"And now you're happy?" Jill asked. Already knowing the answer, she smiled at Bebe knowingly.

"Yes," Bebe said, returning the smile. "I am very happy. My only regret is not marrying him sooner."

As the women sat at the kitchen table eating and talking, Kyle entered the cabin through the front door. He could hear their voices and stopped to listen to their conversation.

"I really miss going out with Kyle," Jill said.

"Well, you'll have more time for that once we get the new person on board."

"I hope so, but I think we are already getting into a rut. All we seem to do is work. We never have time for romance. Bebe, I remember when Kyle took me to Mesa Verde. We had such a wonderful time. It was there, high upon a mountain, that we opened ourselves up to all the possibilities love between us could bring. He seemed to be making love to me just by looking at me, never mind how I felt each time he touched me. I just want to make sure that we haven't passed our high point in love and excitement."

"Jill, I know Kyle loves you and you are still as enthralling to him as the day he met you. The only thing standing in your way is too much work, and that goes for both of us. I want to be home when Tony arrives. We've only been married a couple weeks, but I miss him every moment we're apart. By the time I get home and get something to eat, it's time for me to finish the work I have to do."

"So work is interrupting your sex life?" Jill asked.

"Yeah, and the sooner we hire someone, the better off we will all be," Bebe said just as they heard the front door close.

Kyle walked through the living room trying to make as much noise as possible. He had heard more than he cared to, and now he wanted to make sure that he didn't hear any more. He walked into the kitchen and pretended to be surprised to see that Bebe was visiting them.

"Hey, babe," he said to Jill as he bent down and kissed her cheek.

"Welcome home," Jill replied

"Bebe, I didn't know that you were going to be here tonight, I could have told Tony to come over for dinner," Kyle told her.

"Did he go home already?"

"No, I think he and Eric are still at the ranch. They had a few more things they wanted to finish. What's for dinner?"

"Baked chicken," Jill told him.

"Smells great. I'm going to take a shower and then I'll eat," he said. Kyle walked over and kissed Bebe's cheek before leaving the kitchen.

Bebe helped Jill tidy up before she left. After a few more reassuring words to calm Jill's pre-wedding jitters, Bebe left and told Jill that she would see her tomorrow at work.

As Jill made a plate for Kyle and poured him a tall, cool glass of sangria, she thought about what Bebe had told her. Everything made sense, but she still felt as though she was being pulled in a thousand directions and failing at all her endeavors. She refilled her own glass feeling the need to relax her mood and hoping another glass of the fruit-filled drink would do just that.

As she waited for Kyle, Jill went over the contracts she had brought home from work. She rubbed her forehead as she tried to concentrate on what she was reading, but her mind was filled with wedding plans and employee hopefuls. Tomorrow they were interviewing several more people for Monica's spot, and Jill could only pray that one of them would fit the bill.

After a while she heard Kyle coming down the stairs. He looked and smelled delicious to her and she laid the papers she was holding down on the sofa as she stood up to greet him. Kyle took her into his arms and began kissing her. His lips began nibbling hers before his tongue entered her mouth. It was at that instant Jill's butterflies returned. She felt her legs go limp, but Kyle held her in his embrace. His tongue probed the inside of her mouth erotically as if it was trying to make love to her.

A tiny moan escaped Jill as she raised her hands to caress the nape of his neck. She inhaled deeply, and the scent of his cologne filled her lungs. Jill wanted to hold her breath indefinitely in an attempt to fill herself with him, but she released the air that filled her body a little at a time.

Slowly Kyle raised his head and made their lips part. He stood quietly for a moment looking deep into the soft brown eyes that he adored. Jill could tell that he was on a solo journey to the core of her soul. Though he said nothing, his eyes continued to speak volumes and he began kissing her again. This time he let his lips leave a trail of kisses from her moist lips down to her throat, and from there on to her earlobes.

Kyle took the soft flesh of her right ear between his

lips and tugged it gently before he let his tongue trace its outline. Then he made little circles deep inside it. So simple, yet so provocative was the action that Jill began to experience another way of having an orgasm.

To look at her, to touch her, was all he needed to inspire him to do whatever it took to make her happy. Jill was so caught up in the rapture of the newfound experience that she didn't quite hear the words Kyle whispered in her ear, but she thought he said, "You have no idea how I plan to keep a smile on your face."

Kyle continued to hold Jill tightly as her body tried to calm down from the experience. They stood there for a moment and Jill's mind was filled with memories. She thought of their first argument, and how they had made up in the barn. Kyle had held her in the same way that day in the stables.

And the way he had looked at her when he began to hold her. They were the same eyes that touched her soul on the mountain in Mesa Verde. She needed him to do all the things with her that he had done before. She didn't want to settle for anything less than what they had had before. She knew of the passion that only he could make her experience, and she wanted it back.

She thought about her request that they not make love again until they were married, and realized that that was probably very hard for Kyle to honor. Yet, he had not pressured her to give in to his needs. He respected her for what she wanted to bring to their marriage bed, but she now thought that her mood and pre-wedding jitters were brought on by her holding out.

"Honey, do you want to make love to me?" she asked him.

"No, I don't," Kyle replied softly.

Jill looked up into his eyes half expecting to see resentment there, but there was none.

"Why not?" she asked playfully, yet wanting to know the truth.

"Because I know you are not ready for that right now."

"Kyle, it's not only about me in this relationship. I apologize for cutting you off like that. We should have made the decision to hold off having sex together."

"Jill, every time I touch you I get satisfaction. I love making love to you, but I know that our giving sex a rest until we're married means a lot to you. I'm not a wild animal, I can wait for a while. But after we're married, don't expect me to keep the beast on a leash," he said with a little laugh.

Jill laughed too as she kissed him and took him by the hand. She led him into the kitchen saying, "Come on, let me heat up your dinner."

Jill settled into work at Desert Star and sat down in her chair. She opened her briefcase and was surprised to see a note from Kyle. She opened the envelope and began to read.

Hey, babe,
    I have a wonderful evening planned for us tonight. Don't make dinner when you get home because I have something special planned for us. Wear something casual, but sexy.

    I love you,
    Kyle

Jill's face lit up into a huge smile, knowing that this was just what she needed. She tucked the note into her purse and began to work. She felt good and was excited about interviewing the new candidates for the job they had available.

Jill concentrated on work and got all the contracts signed, then gave them to Monica to mail. She made a few business calls, before making sure she addressed the Desert Star's bookkeeping accounts. Their accountant had gone over their books and needed additional receipts from the company.

It was almost eleven o'clock and Jill and Bebe were ready to interview the last of the women who applied for the secretarial position at Desert Star. At eleven o'clock sharp the door opened and Sharon walked in. Both Bebe's and Jill's mouths fell open as they looked at their sister-in-law. Bebe had not looked at the name on the application, and was shocked that it was Sharon.

"Sharon, I didn't know that you applied for the secretarial position," Bebe said as she looked over the application.

"Of course I didn't," Sharon shot back as if insulted by the fact that anyone would think she needed to work outside the home. "I was hoping to persuade you all to join me for lunch in town today."

Though a sigh of relief accidentally escaped Bebe's lips, Jill quickly said, "I think it would be fun to go into town for lunch. Do you have a place in mind?"

"Yes, I wanted to try that new place everyone is talking about, Emilio's."

"I heard the food is great there, but we can't leave until we interview the last applicant for Monica's position," Jill said.

Just then the door opened and a woman entered.

"Hello, I'm Amelia Carson, I'm applying for the secretary position," she said.

Amelia was a short, wide woman who smiled easily and was well spoken. Bebe's eyes lit up at the thought that Amelia might be the one. She and Jill introduced themselves and took Amelia back to the conference room to interview her. After twenty minutes the three women emerged from the room. Amelia's face held the same bright smile she had worn when she entered the building. As she left, she shook Jill's and Bebe's hands and thanked them.

"We found someone!" Jill said triumphantly as she threw her hands up in the air.

"We did it!" Bebe said thankfully.

"How soon can she start?" Monica asked.

"She can start Monday. Amelia Carson is from Portugal. She has been in this country since she was a little girl, but goes home to visit every year. In fact, after we established her credentials, we talked about the Mulher Bela account. She has a twenty-year-old daughter that models for them."

"That wasn't what sold you guys on her, was it?" Sharon asked sarcastically.

"No, it wasn't. Amelia has a long list of glowing references and she has a ton of experience, not to mention her enthusiasm. That's what sold me on her," Jill said assuredly.

"Ditto," Bebe chimed in.

"Well, it seems we have a lot to celebrate. Now, can we please go to lunch?" Sharon said.

Even though Jill had seen another side of her sister-in-law-to-be, a side that was warm and showed compassion and familial loyalty, Sharon was still Sharon. She was still quite self-absorbed and acted as if the world revolved around her, and Jill accepted her quirky sister as she was.

The women gathered their purses and left to celebrate the hiring of the person who would give them all their lives back. They all got into Sharon's car, since she was the only one who knew how to get to Emilio's.

After a short drive Sharon pulled into a parking space near the entrance of the restaurant. The women got out of the car and went inside. They were immediately enchanted with not only the ambiance of the Spanish-styled restaurant, but more importantly, the aroma of the food they smelled.

They were ushered to a table by the hostess, who gave them menus. Jill saw right away what she wanted, and when the waitress came she ordered the paella Valenciana. Bebe and Sharon ordered the chicken Salteado, and Monica had a taste for empanada.

When the food arrived the women were greeted with Spanish cuisine that made their mouths water. They toasted their newfound employee with a glass of Chardonnay. Eating heartily, the women enjoyed being together. Though they were happy that Sharon had come to join them for lunch, they were more grateful that they could once again go out to eat, rather than enduring a working lunch hour.

"Why don't you guys come over to my place tonight? We could rent some movies and order pizza and just hang out," Sharon said.

"That sounds nice. I'll have to check and see if Tony has anything planned, but if he doesn't I'd love to come over," Bebe said as she continued to eat.

"You'll have to count me out," Jill said as she raised her wineglass to her lips. A sly smile curled upon her lips as she sipped the liquid.

"What do you have planned for tonight?" Bebe asked with playful suspicion.

"It's not what I have planned, but what my baby has planned for me. Kyle left a note in my briefcase telling me that he wants to go out tonight," Jill said with a promising grin on her face and continued to eat.

"Where are you guys going?" Sharon asked.

"I don't know," Jill said as she shrugged her shoulders. "But he told me to wear something casual, yet sexy."

"Well, I guess it's just us. Monica, you can come, can't you?" Sharon asked.

Monica stopped chewing and looked up from her plate in stunned silence. She had just assumed that Sharon's invitation didn't extend to her. Of the three sisters-in-law, Sharon was the most uppity, and she didn't think the woman would consider mingling with a lowly secretary.

"I'd love to come," Monica said, with eyes blinking in nervous surprise. She glanced at Jill, who winked at her, signifying that everything would be fine tonight.

The women finished eating lunch and then paid their bill. Afterward, they got back into Sharon's car and she dropped them off back at the office.

Once there they all got back to work and finished what needed to be done before the weekend. Monica planned on Monday being a busy day for her, since she had to train Amelia. She anticipated that the training would go fairly easily, since Jill and Bebe said Amelia already had a ton of experience.

Though Jill and Bebe were working hard as well, they did so happily, knowing that the end of their burning the candle at both ends was near. Jill was walking on a cloud knowing that she had a date with

Kyle that evening. She couldn't help wonder where
he was taking her, and she was thankful when the end
of the work day arrived.

As the three women left the office for the weekend,
they said their good-byes and Jill got into her car
and headed home.

When she arrived Kyle wasn't home. Since it was five
o'clock she knew he would probably arrive soon, so
she went upstairs to prepare for their date.

Jill kicked off her shoes and slid out of her clothes.
It felt good to dismiss the panty hose and she knew
whatever she chose to wear tonight, panty hose
wouldn't be part of the outfit. She went into the
bathroom and took a quick shower. When she was finished she dried off and applied her favorite pear-
scented moisturizer.

She applied her eye shadow, blush, and lipstick in
earth tones, before she decided on wearing a pair of
large hoop earrings. Since she had worn her hair
down at work, she changed her style and brushed her
hair, then pulled it into a ponytail high upon her
head. After a quick spritz of her signature cologne,
she checked her appearance once again in the mirror.
Liking what she saw, she left the bathroom.

Jill went inside the huge walk-in closet that she
shared with Kyle and tried to decide what to wear. Kyle
had told her to dress casual but sexy, and she tried to
adhere to his request, since she hadn't a clue as to
where they were going. She picked up one dress
after another, only to quickly discard it on the bed.
Everything she chose seemed to be too sexy, or not
sexy enough. Other than that, what she owned was
business clothes.

Finally, she came across a silk blouse with a plunging
neckline. It was almost formfitting and the shimmering

mauve color complemented Jill's skin tone. She slid the top on and then picked a pair of Seven jeans that always made Kyle want to hold her bottom. A pair of mauve-colored sandals with a kitten heel gave the outfit an added air of sexiness, and Jill felt she had achieved the look she wanted.

Jill was stuffing a few essentials into a tiny matching handbag when she heard a car horn. She walked to the window and looked down. She could see Kyle standing outside the Navigator, looking as handsome as ever. He stood outside the running vehicle and signaled for Jill to come.

She went downstairs, and when she opened the front door Kyle was standing there with flowers in his hand. He handed them to Jill as he kissed her on the cheek, and she accepted them and smiled easily.

"Is this what you miss, baby?" he whispered thickly in her ear.

"Yes," Jill answered softly.

"Well, hold on because this is just the beginning," he said as he took her hand and led her to the waiting SUV.

Kyle opened Jill's door for her and waited until she was seated safely inside before closing the door. She sat back in her seat and remembered how Kyle had charmed her the first time they had gone on a date alone. He certainly knew how to charm her. No, he hadn't started to take her for granted, she thought. The fault lay with her. She had to make time for him. Jill remembered what Dar, her neighbor from New York, had told her. Jill had to make her relationship with Kyle a priority, and that meant making time for dates like this.

She smiled as he got inside and started to drive off. At the moment, she knew there was no place she would rather be. Jill still didn't know where they were going, but it didn't matter, she was with Kyle, and that was really all that mattered. She reached over and held his free hand as he drove, and he smiled upon feeling her touch.

"How was work today?" he asked.

"Wonderful. Kyle, we hired a secretary to take Monica's place. Her name is Amelia Carson and she will be starting on Monday," Jill told him excitedly.

"That's great, but you didn't settle for just anyone because you were so anxious, did you?"

"No, of course not. Amelia has a lot of experience and a ton of excellent references. Bebe and I both interviewed her. Though we checked out her references before she arrived and everything panned out, we were even more impressed with her attitude. She's an older woman, but is enthusiastic and wants to be a team player."

"That's good, so you might be free next weekend?"

"That all depends, what did you have in mind, Mr. Roberts?" Jill asked.

Though she said the words in teasing seductiveness, her voice still shot through Kyle's body like hot oil. He looked at her as if he could make love to her right then and there. Instead he took in several deep breaths and focused his attention on the road ahead of him.

"I thought we might make weekends our time from now on."

"That sounds perfect to me, honey," Jill told him as she laid her head against the headrest and looked over at him through thick, sooty eyelashes.

There she goes again. I don't think she has any idea what she does to me, Kyle thought as he tried even harder to concentrate on driving.

"You haven't even asked me were we are going," he said, trying to take his mind off the beauty that continued to stare up at him.

"As long as I'm with you it doesn't matter where we're going."

Kyle chuckled and looked out the driver's-side window, before glancing over at Jill. She was managing to push all his buttons and he couldn't help but think she knew what she was doing.

"Oh, and by the way, the note and the flowers were a very nice touch," she added.

"Jill, you still don't know what you do to me, do you?"

"Am I making you want me?"

"Yes," Kyle answered, and his voice was now serious. "I never stop wanting you."

"Well, that's good because on our wedding night you'll see that I was worth the wait," Jill said, giggling.

"Woman, you are such a tease, and I'm the crazy one believing that you have no idea of what you are doing," Kyle said, smiling.

Chapter 15

It was just becoming dusk and the sky was turning different shades of orange from the remnants of the sun's rays. Now streaks of purples and blues began to give evidence of nightfall, and Jill loved the romantic aura nature was providing the evening.

"You didn't eat, did you?" Kyle asked.

"No, I didn't and I'm starving," Jill said as she rubbed her empty tummy.

"Good, I wanted to take you to a rib joint Tony has been raving about," Kyle said.

He drove on a little farther before turning into the parking lot of a restaurant called Rib Eyz's. The couple got out of the vehicle and went inside. The place wasn't as romantic as Jill had hoped, but the food smelled delicious.

They were seated and when the waitress came they ordered barbecue pork ribs and a mountain of fries. Though Jill ate a few fries, she also ordered a salad, since she still had a wedding dress to fit into. The couple enjoyed their meal laughing, talking, and holding hands.

"I know that's not all you're going to have," Kyle said as he noticed Jill adding a little dressing to her salad.

"No, it's not, but I do have to watch what I eat since I have to fit into a wedding dress in two weeks."

"Babe, you'll look fine, and I'd still marry you even if you were the size of a barn," Kyle said, trying to look sincere.

"Sure you would. I don't think you would have given me a second look if I didn't keep myself in shape," Jill shot back as she began to eat her salad.

"Yes, I would have. How could you think I could be so shallow?" Kyle said as he too began to eat. "I would have given you another look, but I doubt I would have chased you down," he said with his mouth full of food.

"Well, maybe you're not too shallow."

"I'm not at all. I just know what I like and what I want."

"I'll settle for that," Jill said. "Bebe looked so beautiful for her wedding. I just hope I look half as good as she did," she added as she stole a tiny rib from Kyle's plate.

Kyle noticed, but not wanting to make her self-conscious about her weight, he said nothing on that matter. Instead he said, "I told you, babe, I think you'll look beautiful no matter what."

"Thanks, Kyle. I am glad that Mom's helping me. I don't think I could pull this off without hers and your mother's support," Jill said as she sipped her drink.

"Don't worry, everything will fall into place."

When they were finished, they got back on the road and Kyle began to drive away. It was now dark and Jill realized that they weren't going in a direction she was familiar with.

"Where are we going?" she asked.

"I thought you said it didn't matter where we were going, as long as you were with me," he said, grinning, happy Jill had no idea where this date would lead.

But as she turned her head, she saw the huge red and white drive-in sign with the word ROCKET on the top of it. Jill could see that tonight's feature was *The Best Man*, one of her favorite movies.

Her mouth dropped open with surprise as she realized where Kyle was going. Jill hadn't been to a drive-in theater since she was a little girl in Pittsburgh. She remembered how much fun she and Barbie had when their parents would take them at least once a month. Under a blanket they would sit munching popcorn and sipping soda. Since they always had to plead with their father to take them to see the latest scary movie, they held each other and fought the urge to scream.

Once they would arrive at home, Jill and Barbie would decide to sleep together instead of in their separate beds, just in case the monster made a midnight visit to their house.

Tonight, if the romantic movie became more than she could stand, she had her beautiful black Adonis to hold on to. Jill squeezed Kyle's hand with delight as he drove up to the booth, and he was glad that he had put a genuine smile on her pretty face. Kyle paid and continued to drive on until he found a perfect parking place that would afford them an excellent view of the huge outdoor screen.

"I'm going to get us something to drink before the movie starts," he said as he started to get out of the vehicle.

"Bring back some popcorn, oh, and some red licorice too," Jill said excitedly.

"Okay, babe," Kyle said as he closed the door behind

him. "What happened to the wedding dress you want to get into?" he asked, smiling through the opened window.

"I'll be able to do get into it, but tonight is special," she said, smiling.

Kyle left and Jill settled back in her seat. She looked around and saw that the parking lot was filling up quickly. Undoubtedly, the drive-in would be filled with nothing but lovers, given the nature of the movie they were about to see. She was glad that Kyle had chosen to go to the drive-in this evening.

Upon his return, Kyle approached the car, carefully balancing their snacks on a tray. Jill reached over and opened his door and then leaned over to take the tray. Kyle got inside and then turned on the radio so they could listen to the movie. He tuned in to the drive-in station and settled back in his seat.

The movie began to play and Jill handed Kyle his Coke. She moved closer to him and snuggled under his arm, enjoying the movie and feeding Kyle popcorn. It was a quiet evening and Kyle watched Jill more than he watched the movie. She leaned contently against him as she ate and enjoyed the feature, and he gently stroked her hair and planted soft kisses on her temple.

When the movie finally ended, Kyle returned the tray to the concession stand and then they left. Jill had thought that their date had come to an end, but Kyle let her know that he still had one more surprise in store for her.

"It's almost eleven o'clock, what else is open?" Jill said, as she wondered where they could be going.

A second later she had the answer. Since Kyle had made it a point to steer clear of the Ranch House and

Jillian's, and they hadn't made plans to visit family, she guessed the next place they were going.

"We're going to Roland's, aren't we?" she said, smiling assuredly.

"Yes, but only if you're not too tired."

"It's been so long since we went out dancing, and I'd want to go even if I was tired," Jill said, sounding as if she had energy to burn.

Roland's was the place to be on a Friday night for the adult crowd. The parking lot was full, so Kyle had to park farther away than he wanted to. The couple got out and went into the club. The music was blaring and the people were dressed to impress, as well as to party.

Jill was ready to party too. She and Kyle made their way through the crowd to the bar, where they both ordered a drink. Standing at the bar since there wasn't a seat to be had, the couple enjoyed watching everyone on the packed dance floor.

The music had Jill swaying her hips, and before long she grabbed Kyle's hand.

"Dance with me. I love this song," she said as she led him away.

Jill and Kyle danced three fast songs and could barely catch their breath before a slow song began to play. As the floor became almost empty, she was reminded of the first time she and Kyle had danced together at Roland's.

As she slid into Kyle's arms, Keith Sweat's melodious voice filled the air. She had been so apprehensive the last time they had danced in public, but once she was in his arms all that mattered was him. Tony and Bebe, Sharon and Eric had been with them and she initially had been quite leery of Kyle. Now being held by him felt more than right, it felt perfect.

Kyle's hands rested low on Jill's hips, and hers gently around his shoulders as her head rested on his thick chest. She closed her eyes as she let her mind be filled with the music, and their bodies moved effortlessly in unison.

When the song ended Jill and Kyle reluctantly pulled their bodies apart. In an unspoken language they conveyed just how much they loved each other, and how much each of them needed to connect to the other.

Kyle led Jill to the rear of the club where he spotted an intimate table for two. The couple sat down and soon a waitress arrived. They ordered another drink and an appetizer to share, and then the woman left.

Jill looked around the club realizing that Roland's held a special place in her heart. It held fond memories. Serenity graced Jill's face as she continued to survey her surroundings. Kyle sat across the table from her and enjoyed watching her facial expression. When she looked at Kyle, Jill noticed the look of utter pleasure on his face.

"What are you thinking about?" she asked as she reached across the table and took his hand into her own.

"I'm just thinking that I must be the happiest man alive."

"Oh, why is that?" Jill asked coyly as she began stroking the hand she held.

"Because I have you. I've known since the day I laid eyes on you that I wanted you in my life. You made me work for your love and trust, but I'd do it all over, time and time again, just for the chance to be your man."

"Oh, Kyle, that's the sweetest thing you've ever said to me. But you have me, you know. Any extra brownie points are put in the bank for when you mess up," she said, raising a brow.

Just then the waitress returned with their order and set it down in front of them. Kyle paid her and she disappeared back into the sea of patrons.

They had ordered a platter of Buffalo wings, potato wedges, and artichoke hearts, and began then eating and enjoying each other's company. Kyle was happily enjoying the Buffalo wings, but Jill wanted him to try the artichokes.

"Here," she said, reaching across the table. She held in her fingers a piece of the vegetable and lovingly placed it inside Kyle's mouth. As he took the offered food from her, Kyle held on to her wrist, and sucked her delicate fingers for a second, before letting her go.

"Mmm, that tasted good," he said, licking his lips. "The artichoke is not bad either."

"No, but you are," Jill said, laughing but obviously enjoying Kyle's gesture.

The couple finished eating and after a few more dances left Roland's for the night, though they promised to return again soon.

During the drive home Jill relaxed in her seat and let her mind drift from one aspect of her upcoming nuptials to another. Her mother would arrive Monday, and Jill knew that with her help a ton of work would be lifted from her shoulders. Her mother's help, accompanied with the hiring of Amelia, would make her life more manageable.

Now more than ever she wanted to prepare for a life filled with living with and loving Kyle. Tonight had given her an idea of just how sweet their lives could be once things were in order. Jill laid her head back and let her thoughts wander to what she imagined life with Kyle would be like. Outside of their first disagreement, they had had no major arguments. They communicated well and worked on things together.

Jill had learned from her mother to let the man lead, but if he wasn't headed in the direction you wanted, well, there were ways to make him navigate toward your desired goal. Jill had watched for years as her father happily obliged her mother's requests.

Her father wasn't a hand puppet. There were times when he put his foot down and Maddie knew when it was a lost cause to protest or try to work her magic. But her mother, who was well versed in the ways of using feminine wiles, won more battles than she lost.

Jill looked over at Kyle, who was concentrating on driving. It was 2:00 a.m., and they both were thankful they were off tomorrow. She didn't have anything planned and hoped he didn't either. She wanted the whole day to belong to them.

Sensing Jill's eyes on him, Kyle turned and looked at her. "What's on your mind, babe?" he asked her.

"I was just wondering if you are going to be busy tomorrow."

"Yes, we both are. Remember, we're going to Sharon's house for a cookout?"

"Oh, I completely forgot about that. I had lunch with her today and she didn't mention it."

"I guess she didn't think to remind you since she gave you a note a week ago, and you tacked the note on the refrigerator to help you remember," Kyle said teasingly.

"I know, I remember now. I don't know how I let it slip my mind. I guess I've been so busy with work and the wedding that I just forgot about Sharon's cookout."

"If you're not up to going, we can cancel."

"No, I'm okay. I was just hoping to spend the day alone with you."

Kyle smiled knowing that he felt the same way that Jill did, and then he said, "Speaking of the wedding, how are things coming along on your end?"

"As you know, my dress is in, and I just have to go to the boutique and have it altered. Everything else is in place. Both of our mothers are pretty much handling everything else. And you, sir, had better have everything taken care of for our honeymoon," Jill said with playful sternness.

"Hey, I got my responsibilities covered. I'm surprised that you even have to ask me that, since I won't be getting any until we say 'I do,'" Kyle said in mock irritation.

"Just think, in two weeks I'm all yours."

"And I can't wait either," Kyle replied lustfully.

More than words ever could, the look of desire that filled Kyle's eyes made Jill blush. No one had ever unzipped her soul with their eyes and made her feel so sexually aware of her body, but Kyle did.

Jill felt an intense warmth come over her body and immediately credited it to Kyle's need for her. Her mind quickly flipped through the memories of all their hot lovemaking sessions. Her favorite memory was the first time in the barn at the ranch. It had been so spontaneous and passionate, and had left Jill's heart knowing that she belonged to him.

Now she sat next to the man who could make her melt with just a look. Jill glanced over at Kyle and wondered if she could hold out from having sex for another two weeks.

Kyle parked the SUV in the garage and the couple got out and walked toward the cabin. As they approached the steps and Kyle was about to unlock the door, Jill put her hand on his and stopped him.

"What's up, babe?" he asked as she turned his head to face her.

"Dance with me," Jill requested in a tiny voice.

"Right here?"

"Right now," Jill replied as she guided his arms around her waist.

"But there's no music," Kyle protested.

Smiling up at him, Jill said, "Yes, there is—listen." She wrapped her arms around his neck and began to sway her hips slowly to nature's nighttime melody.

Kyle held Jill gently as they danced with only silver sparkling stars illuminating the porch. The couple danced to the sounds of crickets, trees rustling in the wind, and the sensuous music held captive in their heads.

They stood dancing slowly for what seemed like an eternity before releasing each other. Kyle kissed Jill on the nose as he took her hand and led her toward the cabin door.

"Hey, what kind of kiss was that?" she asked.

"The kind that's not a prelude to having my way with you tonight," Kyle admitted reluctantly.

Jill giggled as she pressed the palm of her hand against Kyle's back and followed him into the cabin. She gathered her restraint against the idea of having his body pleasure hers. It had been a magical night, and as the couple walked hand in hand up to the bedroom they knew that they had what it took to make their love last a lifetime.

Kyle undressed Jill, and then she did the same to him. For a moment they stood and embraced as his tongue explored the deep recesses of her tempting mouth. Jill

could feel herself become weak with want of him, but
Kyle didn't take advantage of the prime moment.

Instead, he lifted her perfectly proportioned body
in his arms and then walked to the bed and deposited
her on its softness. Jill held the comforter open for
him to join her, and for the rest of the night they
found pleasure just holding each other. Before Jill fell
asleep she marveled at every well-etched muscle of
Kyle's body, and she enjoyed the warmth of his flesh.
His skin tone reminded her of a Hershey's Kiss, and
before she drifted off, she planted a kiss of her own
on his chest.

Chapter 16

Time was flying by and things were busy for Jill as she juggled preparations for her wedding and the growth of her business. Amelia was a perfect match for Desert Star, and had fallen into her position perfectly. The firm was continuing to grow. Monica now had her own office and was doing an excellent job on the Mulher Bela Swimwear account. Jill and Bebe continued to monitor her, but were busy handling their own workloads.

Maddie had arrived to help with wedding preparations, and with the help of Regina they had everything under control. Though things were going along smoothly, Jill's input was still needed, and everyone had to force her to take time off to manage preparations for the wedding.

She complied with reservation, fearing that things wouldn't get accomplished without her assistance. With Bebe's reassurance, Jill had relented and tended to her wedding.

The seamstress at Elaine's Bridal Boutique had been trying to schedule Jill to come in for a final fitting for the past week and now, with only two weeks to spare, Jill thought that she should attend to this urgent matter first. She called the shop and spoke to Elaine personally, and made an appointment with the seamstress for that afternoon.

Since she had almost three hours until her one o'clock appointment, Jill called her mother and Regina and made arrangements to sit down and finish their plans.

When Jill arrived at Jillian's, her mother and mother-in-law were seated and waving at her. Big, bright smiles adorned each woman's face, and Jill could tell they were both quite thrilled not only about the wedding, but that she had made time in her busy schedule to plan for it.

As she reached the table, Jill leaned down and kissed both women on the cheek before taking her own seat. It felt good to have both her mothers helping her, and she could feel the bond that was growing not just between the in-laws, but also between herself and her mother.

Momentarily her thoughts drifted back to when her mother's matchmaking had almost sabotaged their relationship. It was a trying time for Jill, since she wanted nothing to interfere with her dreams of owning her own public relations company. Now she truly had it all: a career, a family, and a wonderful man.

Jill's face glowed as that of a woman who is totally and blissfully in love. The look was not wasted as Maddie and Regina caught a glimpse of the content aura that framed Jill's face. They quickly smiled at each other before getting down to business.

"Jill, I'm so glad that Bebe encouraged you to take some time to finish the details of your wedding. Regina and I got a lot accomplished, but we still need your input," Maddie said factually, but filled with exhilaration.

"I know and I apologize, but Amelia is working out fine at Desert Star, and Monica is functioning in her new position nicely. I think that from now on I'll have time to take care of wedding matters. In fact, I have an appointment at Elaine's at one o'clock," Jill said happily.

"That's good, darling. We should go with you. I want to make sure the Vera Wang gown fits you perfectly," Regina told her.

Jill agreed to let them come. Though Jillian's didn't open to the public until 4:00 p.m., the staff was already there and brought the women croissants, fruit cups, and orange juice. They began to eat as they discussed everything from seating arrangements to which china pattern to use. They decided where the five-tiered cake would be placed as well as the champagne fountain. Jill felt butterflies in her stomach as she realized that in less than two weeks she would be getting married.

The three women stood and walked toward the kitchen of the huge, formal restaurant. Michael, the manager of Jillian's, met them at the door of the kitchen.

"Ms. Alexander, well, soon I'll have to call you Mrs. Roberts, won't I?" Michael said as he extended his hand to shake Jill's.

For a man he was on the short side, but was handsome enough to make up for what he lacked in height. With wavy, jet-black hair, and cocoa-brown skin, Michael Houston was quite handsome, but still unmarried.

"That's right, Michael, but I wish you would just call me Jill," she replied, trying to suppress the urge to blush.

Though Michael had been the manager of Jillian's since it opened, Jill had only seen the man once before. She could understand his reluctance to greet her so casually. Still, she wanted to maintain the sense of family and friendship that exuded from A Special Place, and preferred to be counted as one of them and not the boss's wife.

Regina told Michael why they were there, and he offered to accompany them. The group walked through the kitchen and into the storage room where the china and silver were kept. They had to look at every pattern and finally decided on the bone china, which was trimmed in gold. Then they chose gold flatware to match.

After Michael had checked to ensure that there was enough china and silver in the chosen pattern for each request, he informed the women that he would have it ready for the wedding.

With all their plans completed, the women got into Jill's car and drove into town for Jill's fitting. They had been at Jillian's for almost three hours and now they didn't have time to stop for lunch. The fruit and juice Jill had eaten earlier had not been enough to sustain her, so she hoped when they finished at Elaine's everyone would be ready to get a quick bite to eat.

"What are you thinking about, sweetheart?" Maddie asked, noticing the quizzical look on Jill's face.

"I was just thinking about Michael Houston. I wonder why he isn't married."

"Jill, you're about to get married. Now isn't the time to be thinking about other men," Maddie said, surprised.

"No, Mom, not for me," Jill said as Regina laughed.

"That's good to hear," Regina said, still laughing.

"I mean he just seems like a lonely guy. He has to be about forty-five years old, would you say?" Jill asked as she looked at Regina through the rearview mirror.

"I guess he would be about that age. Why?" Regina asked.

"Jill, I hope you aren't trying your hand at match-making," Maddie said in dismay.

Jill smiled as she thought of the person Michael would be perfect for. She said nothing but continued to drive as she glanced at her mother and then at Regina.

"Well, are you going to tell us who you are thinking about for Michael?" Regina asked as curiosity began to eat away at her patience.

"No, not yet. I have to get to know the other person better myself first, and then I'll tell you," Jill said as she parked the car.

It was now Maddie's turn to laugh at her daughter's use of her own old tactics, and at how easily it was to pique Regina's curiosity.

The women got out of the car and went inside the boutique. Elaine came from behind the counter as soon as she saw Jill. The slender woman smiled and greeted her most important patron of the year.

Jill's gown had been ordered from Vera Wang, and shipped to Elaine's for a final fitting. After Elaine had greeted them, she walked the women back to a fitting room and offered the mothers a seat. Jill stepped into a dressing room where her gown was waiting. She quickly undressed and slipped into the exquisite dress.

Vania, the seamstress, helped Jill dress. The beautiful summer gown was ivory in color, and was made of silk and organza. The sleeveless, V-necked gown seemed luminous as it sparkled from the Swarovski crystals that adorned the bodice. The full A-line skirt fell full at Jill's feet, and from the back, the dress plunged down to her waist with three rows of crystals draping across her back.

When Jill caught the first sight of herself in the mirror, she gasped at the beautiful woman who stared back at her. She couldn't believe her eyes as she continued to stare. Tears formed in her eyes and threatened to spill as it finally sank in that she was really getting married.

Over the years she had become an expert at hiding from love, and now love had found her. It had had its way with her, and in the end there really wasn't anything she could have done about it. Her destiny was to become Kyle's, and now she wished the eighth of August was today.

Vania opened the door to the dressing room and Jill walked into the fitting area. Maddie's hand quickly flew up to her mouth as she looked at her beautiful daughter. Regina gasped as she saw the beautiful bride-to-be coming toward her.

"You look stunning," Regina finally uttered. She walked over to Jill and kissed her cheek.

"Thank you, Mom," Jill said. She looked over at her own mother, who had managed to stand but not walk.

"Mom, what do you think?" Jill asked.

"I think you are the most amazing beauty I've ever seen," Maddie said.

Tears of joy fell down her cheek at seeing her youngest daughter in her wedding dress. This was the day Maddie had hoped and prayed for. She had used every trick in the book to get her daughter married, and now she was about to take that step.

Maddie finally walked toward Jill. When she reached

her she took her hand and said, "My sweetheart, you know how much I wanted this day to come, and now it is here. Jill, I just wanted to see you married so badly because I want you to have someone who loves you and would watch out for you. I wanted to see you with your own little family and not alone in the world. Of course you have me and your dad, but I want you to have more. Now you have Kyle, and I know beyond a shadow of a doubt that he loves you more than he loves his next breath. I'm just so happy for you, baby, and proud to be your mother."

Jill couldn't help but to join her mother and Regina as they cried openly. Vania handed them tissues and then waited quietly to begin working on the dress.

After the three women finished their outpouring of emotions, Vania began working expertly on the beautiful dress. Though Jill grew weary of standing as the seamstress tucked and pinned the silk and organza fabric, she stood and admired Vania's handiwork.

When Vania was finished, Jill, Maddie, and Regina were pleased with the outcome. Then Jill disappeared into the fitting room and changed back into her own clothes.

As she returned, Elaine was waiting for her. She had conferred with Vania, and the two women assured Jill that her dress would be ready before the end of the week.

Jill thanked the women, and then she, Maddie, and Regina left the shop. Getting back into the car, Jill glanced at her watch. Ordinarily she would be planning to go to lunch with Bebe and Monica, but there would be no lunch date with them today. Bebe had made her promise to stay away from the office until after the wedding, and Jill realized that it was the best thing to do. Though she was completely devoted to

Desert Star, she needed time to prepare for the biggest day of her life. No one could get fitted for her dress and decide on the seating arrangements for her, and Jill secretly thanked heaven for Bebe.

"While we're in town, why don't we stop somewhere and get a bite to eat?" Maddie suggested.

"That sounds great. I just noticed that it was lunchtime. Where do you want to stop?" Jill asked.

"I really don't have any idea. I don't know the restaurants around here," Maddie said.

"Well, what are you in the mood for?" Regina asked.

"I think I'm in the mood for pasta."

"I know of a great Italian restaurant not too far from here. It's called Antonia's and the food is delicious," Regina said.

"I know where it is," Jill said as she made a left-hand turn and continued on her way to the restaurant.

When they arrived, Jill parked and the three women got out of the vehicle and went inside Antonia's. It was a small restaurant, but Jill immediately knew why Regina liked it so. The place was elegant and classy, and Jill was positive the food matched the atmosphere. The group was quickly seated and their drink orders were taken.

They sat at a quiet table near the front window and chatted about the day's events. The waitress returned with their drinks and then took their food orders. After she left, the women began discussing the wedding again.

Jill was so happy to have her mother and mother-in-law helping, and with each item of preparation accomplished, she could feel her excitement growing.

The waitress returned and placed delicious-smelling plates of food in front of them. Jill had ordered herb chicken tortellini soup, and at the urging of Regina,

Maddie joined her and tried the fettuccini with portabella mushrooms, ham, and asparagus. The waitress had set a dish of hot, crusty Italian bread in the center of the table and when she left, the women began to eat.

With her first bite Maddie exclaimed, "Oh, Regina, this is delicious."

"I thought you would enjoy it. It's my favorite, and whenever I can talk Sam into bringing me here, I usually order the fettuccini," she said as she picked up her glass of red wine and took a sip.

"Jill, how is your soup?" Maddie asked.

"It's delicious," she replied as she picked up a small piece of the bread.

"I hope that's not all you're eating," Regina said worriedly.

"It is, but you have to remember that I have a wedding dress to fit into," Jill said, smiling.

"Ah yes, the wedding. Here's to the day we've both been waiting for, Maddie," Regina said as she raised her wineglass.

"Yes, the wedding we've been waiting and praying for," Maddie added as she and Regina toasted the union that would soon take place.

Jill laughed and continued to eat. At the end of their meal the waitress returned and offered them coffee and dessert. Though Jill declined, Maddie and Regina ordered tiramisu. When the dessert arrived, Jill couldn't keep her eyes off the tempting dish. As Maddie ate, Jill watched the fork leave and return to her mouth, carrying another bite of the coffee-flavored dessert. Finally, Jill picked up her fork and stole a tiny piece from her mother's plate. Regina and Maddie broke out in laughter, as they had both wondered when Jill would break.

Though their conversation was lively and the meal

was wonderful, both had ended too soon, like all good things.

After paying their bill and leaving a tip, the women left the restaurant and headed back to the resort. When they arrived, Jill pulled up in front of the building and let her mother and Regina out of the car.

As the doorman stepped out onto the curb to assist the women, Jill gave them each a quick kiss on the cheek and thanked them for all their help.

"Of course we want to be a part of this wonderful time in your life, sweetheart," Maddie said with heart-felt sincerity, and Jill knew she meant every word.

"It was my pleasure, darling," Regina said.

Jill smiled appreciatively, and could only hope things would remain the same between herself and her soon-to-be mother-in-law. Over the years she had heard all kinds of terrible mother-in-law tales, but for now, she was enjoying hers.

Having said her good-byes, Jill headed home. As she drove back down the long driveway, she looked around to see if she could see Kyle, but there was no sign of him or any of the ranch hands. For a moment she toyed with the idea of going to the Ranch House, but knew since lunch was over, he wouldn't be there either. She would be happy to see him at home tonight, and had plans to make him dinner.

The clock on the dashboard read 2:30 p.m., but she felt as tired as if she had just finished working fourteen hours at Desert Star on an assignment. She couldn't help wondering how things were going at work but knew not to go there.

When she arrived home, Jill took off her shoes and set her purse on the sofa. Then she went upstairs and washed her face and hands. She brushed her hair and pulled it up into a ponytail high upon her head, and then she changed into a comfortable, spaghetti-strapped sundress. It was pale blue and reminded her of the beautiful Colorado sky. It was also Kyle's favorite, and she wanted to look good for him when he came home.

When she was finished, Jill went back downstairs and began to cook dinner. She had decided to make baked chicken, macaroni and cheese, and broccoli, and for dessert she made a sweet potato pie. She knew she was not quite the cook Kyle was, but he made a big fuss over her meals and always asked for a second helping.

Jill smiled to herself as she prepared dinner for Kyle. She could hardly wait to see him this evening. She wanted to hear all about his day and tell him all about hers. As she continued to cook she realized that Desert Star had slipped her mind. She desperately wanted to know how things were going. Jill wiped her hands on a tea towel and picking up the phone, she quickly dialed the office.

"Desert Star Public Relations Group, how may I direct your call?" Amelia asked.

"Hi, Amelia, it's me, Jill."

"Hello, how are the wedding plans going?"

"Better than I expected. I still have a few more things to do but nothing I can't handle. Besides, Kyle's mother and mine are helping out a lot. How are things going there?"

"Things are fine, but it's not the same without you."

"Ahhh, thanks, Amelia. Is Bebe there?"

"Yes, she is. I'll transfer you to her office. See you soon, Jill."

"Bye, Amelia."

A second later Jill heard her best friend's voice on the other end.

"Hi, Bebe," Jill said, pleased to hear her voice.

"Jill, how is everything going?"

"More than fine, but what I want to know is—"

"I know, you want to know how things are going here, don't you?"

"Yes, I do," Jill admitted, laughing. "And you better be honest with me and tell me everything."

"Well, I must admit that we have been quite busy around here. There have been a few minor problems, but we're back on track."

"Do you need me to come in right now?" Jill asked with concern.

"No, Jill, I told you that we got everything back on track. Besides, you have a wedding to plan and I want all your knowledge and expertise to go into planning that. Desert Star will be here when you return. We won't run it into the ground before you get back," Bebe said, smiling.

"Bebe, I know you're completely capable of running the firm. I didn't mean to insinuate that you wouldn't be fine without me," Jill said apologetically.

"I know you didn't," Bebe replied, but she had made the comment to make sure Jill wouldn't get any ideas about coming into work, and her plan had worked. "So tell me, what did you, your mom, and Regina get accomplished?"

"Except for a few minor things, we're ready. I think I'm going to try and get Kyle to take me out this weekend, though."

"That sounds fun. Where?"

"I don't know yet, but I just feel the need to go on our last date as an unmarried couple before we tie the knot."

"You're such a romantic. Let me know if you need me to do anything else, Jill."

"You're doing plenty as my matron of honor."

"I just feel terrible that Barbie couldn't do it, but I know it would be hard for her living across the country."

"Believe me, she's happy that I have a friend like you, who is more like a sister to me, to stand in for her. Hey, I have to go before I burn my dinner."

"Bye, girl," Bebe said and hung up the phone.

Jill checked the stove and everything was fine. She began setting the table for two and retrieved a bottle of white wine from the wine cooler. With dinner almost finished and Kyle due any minute, she lit two candles and set them on the table. She heard the front door open and stepped into the doorway of the kitchen and leaned against the wall.

As Kyle closed the door behind him, his eyes fell on Jill. A smile expressing his delight formed on his lips as his eyes took their fill of her. Just being in her presence made all his senses come alive, and he couldn't wait to hold her.

Jill smiled too, as he walked closer toward her, and the moment she felt his arms around her waist made her extremely happy that she belonged to him. In exchange for a verbal greeting they kissed long and lovingly, but when their lips parted Jill was the first to speak.

"Welcome home, cowboy," she said in a gentle whisper as her lips barely brushed his earlobe.

This one simple gesture sent Kyle's mind racing and his body quivering with want of hers, but in return he only kissed her delicate neck passionately.

"I hope all my homecomings are like this," he said, as he planted one last moist kiss on her collarbone.

Jill took his hand and led him to the sofa. Kyle sat down and Jill sat comfortably on his lap. She loved being home to greet him when he arrived and hoped that since there was extra help at the office, she would be able to do this more often.

"How did things go on the ranch?" she asked as she gently stroked his temple.

"Things were fine, but not as fine as coming home to you," he said as his sexy brown eyes peered into Jill's.

Still stroking his temple, she leaned forward and kissed his cheek, and then said, "I hope you always feel this way."

"I will. That's one thing you'll never have to worry about. I wish that when I came home you were always already here."

"Well, if things go the way I hope they do at the office you just might get your wish."

Kyle looked at Jill quizzically and then said, "Jill, are you sure you really want to cut back at work? I know how much Desert Star means to you, and how you like to be on top of everything. I was just saying how I like coming home to you. I don't want you to think I'm trying to get you to quit your job."

"I understand, but I have figured out that I can have my career and be the housewife if I'm able to balance both. I decided not to work late or bring work home with me, but when I am at work I'm going to dedicate myself one hundred percent to my clients' needs. Besides, Monica and Amelia are working out beautifully, and Bebe is showing me that the place won't cave in just because I'm not there."

Kyle smiled as he realized that Jill had figured out a way to make her busy schedule work for her. "Dinner smells wonderful."

"Thank you and it should be just about done," she said as she stood up.

"I'm going to wash up and then I'll be right back down," Kyle said as he stood too.

Jill went into the kitchen and began making a plate for each of them. She filled two glasses of wine and sat down. Just then Kyle came into the kitchen and joined her at the table.

After saying grace, Kyle began to eat. Once again he made a big fuss over Jill's cooking, which was quite tasty. Candlelight illuminated the dinner table and they told each other about their day. It was something new and wonderful to Jill. Though she and Kyle had spent countless meals together, the idea of his coming home to her and having his meals ready made her feel more like his wife.

Momentarily her mind drifted back to only a few months earlier when she had almost lost him. Even now she had to fight back tears at the thought of going through life without the man of her dreams.

Now he sat across from her—her tall rugged cowboy with a heart of gold and the patience of Job. He was fun-loving and loved to make love, and he was all hers. As Kyle spoke, Jill reached across the table and rested her hand on his. She was thankful he was alive and that they belonged to each other.

Chapter 17

With morning sunlight filling the room, Jill stretched gently in Kyle's arms. As her eyes opened she could see that he was smiling at her. She smiled in return and glanced at the clock. It was after 11:00 a.m., and she wondered why Kyle was still home and not off to the ranch. She laid her head back down in the crook of his arm and then kissed his chest as she caressed it tenderly.

"Honey, you do realize that you're late for work?" she said in a sleepy voice.

"I'm not going in today. Yesterday really wore me out. Did you enjoy our last date as an unmarried couple?"

"Yes, it was wonderful."

"I thought you would enjoy it. I'm going to rest up for tonight. You aren't the only one having a party thrown in their honor tonight," Kyle said teasingly.

A slight smile formed on Jill's lips. "Yeah, but your party better not have any strippers there, and if there are you better not lay a hand on one," she said as she peeked up at Kyle's face for any sign of mischief.

"No, none of that for me. But I do want to know

about your party. I know Bebe is handling the food and Barbie the decorations, and that's okay, but I'm concerned with the entertainment and I know Monica is handling that."

"Bebe thought you might be listening to them the other night at her house."

"Well, I didn't mean to, but I couldn't help it. They were talking so loud and I had to wait for Tony. At any rate, they kept laughing and giggling and I just get the feeling that Monica wants to make sure you have a real good time before the wedding."

"I'm not going to touch a thing, I'm just going to look," Jill said playfully, and then started to get out of bed.

But before she could, Kyle grabbed her and pulled her back and then began tickling her unmercifully.

"And that's all you better do," Kyle said, trying to sound playful, yet a hint of seriousness filled his voice.

Jill laughed and wiggled but would not agree to his wishes until she was out of breath and couldn't take the tickling anymore.

"Okay, okay, I promise I won't do anything more than look," she uttered between gasps of breath.

Kyle stopped tickling her, and then he lay back on his pillow with a smug smile on his face, feeling as though he had won the battle.

When Jill caught her breath, she sat up and began getting out of the bed again. Her side ached from laughing so hard but she wasn't quite ready to give up. She glanced over her shoulder to see what Kyle was doing, and saw that though he watched her, his hands were clasped behind his head.

"And maybe one quick tap on the guy's tush!"

she yelled and laughed as she bolted toward the bathroom.

Kyle sprang to his feet and caught her just before she entered and squeezed her body against his. Jill giggled and tried to get away, but Kyle held her firmly in his arms.

"Jill, please stop teasing me," he said pleadingly. "I don't know why it's bothering me so much but I can't handle you oogling and pawing another man," he added, trying not to laugh at his own comment.

"Don't worry, babe, because the only man I want that way is you," Jill said as she stopped laughing and kissed his lips. "I'll only be a minute." She pulled away from his embrace.

Jill went into the bathroom and seconds later Kyle could hear the water running. Jill took a quick shower, did her hair, applied her makeup, and then returned to the bedroom. Kyle looked at her disapprovingly as she walked toward the closet.

"What's wrong, honey?"

"I thought we were going to spend the morning fooling around."

"Kyle, I thought we agreed not to have sex again until we're married," Jill said as she slipped into a black strapless bra and panty set.

"I didn't really agree, I just sort of went along with your suggestion."

Jill smiled and rolled her eyes as she put on a pair of white slacks and a black spaghetti-strap top, and then said, "Kyle, we'll be married in just a few days and then I'm all yours."

She walked over to him and kissed him good-bye.

"Where are you going?"

"Your mind is on one thing, isn't it?" she said, laughing. "I have to pick up Barbie from the airport."

"I didn't think her flight was due until this afternoon."

"It isn't, but I have to run an errand before going to pick her up," Jill said. "Everyone won't fit in my car, so can I take the Navigator?"

"Sure, the keys are under my hat."

As she turned to leave she looked over her shoulder and with a sexy wink good-bye, she was out the door.

Jill left the cabin and got into the vehicle and headed in the direction of town. She was thankful that Kyle hadn't pushed the issue wanting to go with her to pick up Barbie. She had only one stop to make, but it was in her opinion a very important errand.

Ever since she had decided that she wanted to wait until their wedding night before they had sex again, Jill's body had been craving Kyle's touch. Waiting had nothing to do with saving herself for that special night, but it did have a lot to do with passion. She wanted his body and her own to fill with love, lust, and want for each other.

Jill laid her head on the headrest and let her mind explore all the extreme pleasure her body would experience once she and Kyle made love again. Her daydream had her fantasizing about mornings that stretched into the afternoon with neither of them venturing far from the bed. With room service delivering a quick meal they would eat only to maintain their strength, and then commence making love over and over again.

She smiled and turned the AC on high as she continued to drive. She made a mental note of all the things she wanted to take with her and had a special tote she was putting all the things in. As she pulled up to the Meow, an exclusive lingerie shop, she parked and went inside.

There were a few other women shopping, and they raised their heads to see who had just entered the store. Given the kind of merchandise Meow sold, Jill imagined that most of the women were afraid someone they might know would come through the door. She smiled to herself as she began to look around.

The light scent of vanilla bean filled the air and, through the light chatter, Jill could hear Anita Baker sensuously sing "You're My Everything." Jill's thoughts immediately returned to Kyle. *God only knows how much I love that man,* she thought, and then set out on her quest to find the perfect naughty nighties to make Kyle weak in the knees.

By the time she was done, Jill had in her hand everything from nighties and body oils to candles and creams. She had enough of everything to last through their honeymoon and was sure she had what it took to keep a smile on Kyle's face and her own too.

Jill had spent an hour and a half in the store and didn't have time to stop for lunch. She put her packages in the car, making sure there would be enough room for Barbie's family and their luggage. Then she headed toward the airport.

Jill circled for twenty minutes before she spotted Barbie's clan. Excited, she waved as she pulled up to the curb and parked. Jill ran over and gave her sister and the kids a hug. Rick quickly put the luggage in the back as the women said hello. Moments later they were all in the car and headed to A Special Place.

When Ricky was finished asking Jill all kinds of questions about horses, Barbie started asking about the wedding. Jill assured her that everything was ready and that Lacy's dress was ready as well.

"I'm ready to do my part," Barbie said proudly.

Rick rolled his eyes in mock irritation and then said, "I hope this bachelorette party doesn't get out of control. I know how you two can get."

"Honey, you need to stop because what I planned for Jill is all good, clean fun," Barbie assured him.

"Well, I hope so because let's not forget that your mother will be there, and I'm glad too."

"He doesn't know Mom well, does he?" Jill whispered jokingly.

The drive to the resort was relaxing and Jill felt some of her tension melt away now having her sister by her side. As she drove, Barbie made a comment about how beautiful the sun-drenched mountains were. Jill looked out her window and remembered the first day they had dazzled her with their majesty.

As Jill pulled up into the rotunda of the resort the doorman came to assist them with their luggage. Jill accompanied her family to the registration desk and made sure they got a room that overlooked the breathtaking mountains. Then she called her parents' room to let them know that Barbie and Rick had arrived. Afterward she made sure the resort had an extra Jeep available for Barbie and Rick to use.

The registration clerk was able to put Barbie's family in the suite next to her parents. After the long flight the kids, as well as Barbie and Rick, were hungry, and Jill told them that she wanted them to come over to her place for lunch.

"Do you remember how to get to the cabin from here?" Jill asked them.

"Sure I do," Rick told her.

"Why don't you come over after you get settled into your room and see Mom? I'll have lunch waiting for you when you arrive."

"That sounds great, sis. We'll see you in a bit," Barbie said.

After planting a kiss on Barbie's cheek, Jill left the resort. She started the engine, but before she pulled off she called Kyle at home.

"Hello."

"Hi, honey, it's me," she said, loving the sound of his voice.

"Did your family make it in okay?"

"Yes, they did, but I wanted to have them over for lunch. Is that all right?"

"Sure, babe, I can't wait to see them. Do you want me to fix anything in particular?"

"My mind is in such a whirl that I don't know what I want to prepare, but would you mind getting started and I'll be there to help as soon as I can?"

"No problem. Listen, I know you are getting tense about the wedding, but don't let worry ruin the pleasure. This is supposed to be a beautiful time for both of us."

"I know, but I just want everything to be perfect and for us to be happy."

"I would be just as happy at the justice of the peace, so you know that whatever you do will make me happy."

"Me too, but would it make our parents happy?"

"I don't think so," Kyle said with a light chuckle. "But we're not doing this for them. This wedding is supposed to be tailor-made for us. You have to be having fun with it, Jill."

"I am, babe. I think what I am experiencing is nervous excitement."

"I guess that's okay."

"I'll be home soon," Jill said as she blew a kiss and closed the phone.

* * *

As she walked inside the cabin, Jill could see that Kyle was busy in the kitchen. He didn't hear her come in, so she ran upstairs and put her packages from Meow inside her special tote. Then she went back downstairs and joined him in the kitchen.

He worked over the sink cleaning vegetables to make a big salad, and Jill quietly walked up behind him. She slid her arms lovingly around his waist and pressed her body firmly against his back. Jill closed her eyes and rested her head as she continued to caress his thick chest with her fingertips. Kyle said nothing as he worked, but he enjoyed the woman's touch.

Finally he stopped what he was doing and dried his hands on a towel. Kyle turned and took Jill's face in his hands. He began to kiss her gently at first and then with more force. His tongue probed and explored her mouth and enjoyed the silky softness of her tongue.

Kyle's hands slid down to her waist and he pressed her hips toward him. Jill could feel how hard he had become and knew she had to find a way to calm him before her sister's family arrived. She took a step back and ended the kiss.

"Baby, I'm so sorry," she said apologetically.

"Jill, Jill—why do you start something you have no intention of finishing?"

"Because I want you so badly."

"Babe, you got me wanting you, too."

"Kyle, I promise, your honeymoon will be everything I'm saying it will be."

"I hope so," Kyle said, trying to shrug off his sexual frustration. He went to the fridge and took out an ice-cold beer. He popped the top and took a long drink.

It wasn't what he needed, but it would have to do for now.

Jill leaned against the counter smiling at Kyle. She wondered why men couldn't come down off a sexual high as quickly as women did, but she knew that now wasn't the time to ask such questions.

There was a knock on the door and she went to answer it. As she walked by, Kyle playfully swatted her backside, and Jill jumped as she rubbed the spot where his hand had landed.

As she opened the door Ricky, Lacy, and James ran inside. Her mom and dad had come with Rick and Barbie. Kyle came out of the kitchen to greet his in-laws and then ushered them into the kitchen for the lunch he had prepared.

Jill hadn't helped Kyle with the meal as she had planned, so she was thankful he was not only good but fast. As the hungry group ate, the last-minute details of the wedding were discussed. None of this pertained to the men, who were all happy to retire to the living room where they entertained themselves by watching the football game.

As the men watched sports, they joked about each others' favorite team. There was another knock on the door and Kyle went to see who it was.

"Hey, man, we thought we'd come by for a visit," Tony said as he entered the cabin. Bebe was close behind, and the idea to come for a visit had been hers since she knew that Barbie had arrived today.

Kyle looked outside and saw that Eric, Sharon, and Ally were coming in as well.

"Is Barbie here?" Sharon asked as she adjusted Ally on her hip.

"Yes, the women are all in the kitchen," Kyle told her.

As he welcomed Eric, the two men could hear the

loud shrills of joy coming from the kitchen. They could only shake their heads about the noise that came from the other room and threatened to drown out the football game.

Finally, when the game ended and the women had cemented the last details of their planning, they joined the men in the living room. Jill's dad and Eric were playing a game of pool, and Kyle had agreed to take Ricky and his dad horseback riding.

Jill looked around the cabin at her family and her heart was filled with more joy than any one woman had a right to have. This was her family and her life. She was more than pleased with the decisions she had made. She had done things in her own way and in her own time. Falling in love wasn't what she had originally come to Durango for, it was just an amazing added perk.

The following day was filled with shopping by the women. Jill took them into town and only regretted that there wasn't enough time for them to take in more of the sights. When they arrived at the Ranch House, Jill, Maddie, and Barbie were joined by Kyle, Rob, and Rick. Rick and Ricky had spent the day working on the ranch with Kyle and had thoroughly enjoyed the experience.

As the group sat down for lunch, Tony told Kyle that he would pick him up at 9:00 p.m. for the party. Kyle's bachelor party was being held in a private room at Roland's.

Bebe wasn't at lunch since she had so much she wanted to finish at work before the wedding. Though Jill had offered to come in and help her get caught up, Bebe wouldn't let her, insisting that Jill needed the time to prepare and be with her family.

The family laughed and talked for hours as they ate the Ranch House special, which was barbecue pork ribs, ranch fries, and coleslaw. Grace kept the iced tea coming and their plates full. It was almost 3:00 p.m. when Jill decided she had better get going if she wanted to arrive at Bebe's by six o'clock.

Kissing Kyle good-bye, she told him she would see him at home later on. He promised that after he finished taking Rick and Ricky around he would be home too. Jill knew how much fun Kyle was having with the guys. She imagined that she would probably miss him at home since he wasn't going out until much later and could afford to spend more time at the ranch.

She smiled as she saw Kyle's face light up as he spoke about being with Ricky. Though they had spoken about having kids and he wanted to get started right away, Jill was more reluctant. She wanted to continue to work and thought having a baby so soon wouldn't give her a chance to work even part-time at her own company.

Kyle had tried to reassure her that that was the beauty of owning your own company—that she could make the rules up as she went along. He had reminded her that she was the owner, not an employee. If she needed to take the baby in with her, work half a day, or not go in at all, it was totally up to her. Still, Jill was afraid of putting too much on her plate, being a newlywed too.

The only thing she knew for certain was that Kyle would be an excellent father. And with that she tried to put her fears to rest.

Jill said her good-byes and left the Ranch House. She went home and began preparing for the bridal shower. She ran the water to prepare a bath hoping that the hot water would ease her weary muscles as well as her tension-filled mind. She poured a handful of her fragrant bath salts into the running water and then slipped into the tub.

Jill lowered herself into the water, and its warmth began to take over her body. She rested her head and closed her eyes trying to free her mind of all its worries, but it was no use. Jill's mind was filled with concerns over the wedding, and she wondered if she had forgotten anyone or anything. She knew that Rick and Ricky were enjoying themselves and could only hope her parents were too.

She shifted in the tub as she tried to figure out what else could be troubling her so. As she continued to bathe, her mind drifted to Kyle and Ricky. Though she was sure that he was having a good time with Rick, she knew it was Ricky who was really making Kyle's day.

When Jill finished bathing, she stepped out of the tub and began drying herself off. She applied a rich moisturizer to her skin and then put hot curlers in her hair. As she waited for her hair to set, she did her makeup and selected an outfit appropriate for a bridal shower.

Jill then did her hair. She had chosen an ivory-colored, sleeveless dress and slid it on. She took the hot curlers out and wore her hair down but pinned it back on the sides with decorative, floral bobby pins. Then Jill decided to put on her pear-shaped diamond earrings and a tennis bracelet. She sprayed on her signature fragrance, Chloe, and put on a pair of kitten-heeled sandals that matched the dress beautifully.

Jill went downstairs and walked over to the window, which gave her a view of the road that led up to the cabin. She had hoped to see Kyle before she had to leave, but there was no sign of him. She turned and walked over to her purse and retrieved a pen and piece of paper. Sitting on the edge of the sofa, she quickly wrote him a note. Jill stood and placed the note on the hook where Kyle always hung his hat; then she grabbed her purse and left.

As she backed her Mercedes out of the garage she glanced at the clock. She had planned on running a little late, because she didn't want to be the first one to arrive at her own party. As she drove she couldn't help wondering what Tony had planned for Kyle. Though Kyle worried that she might get a little crazy, Jill hadn't let on that she had the same concerns.

She pulled into the driveway of Bebe and Tony's cabin and was thankful to see she wouldn't be the first to arrive. Many guests had already arrived and Jill wondered just how many people Bebe had invited.

Jill got out of her car and went inside where she was greeted by Bebe. The room was decorated in Jill's wedding colors, ivory and pale blue. She had chosen the colors because they reminded her of the first time she arrived at A Special Place and looked up at the amazing sky.

She looked around the room and saw the faces of women she had only known for a year but counted as friends, and some were like family members. Grace sat on a stool at the huge living room's bar and waved to her. Jill smiled and waved back. Her mother and mother-in-law-to-be had already arrived and Sharon, Monica, and Amelia, too.

Though Jill recognized the voice, a soft, sexy sound with a heavy accent, she could not find the face. Her eyes darted around the room and finally landed on Rosy Hernandez. She sat on Bebe's sofa with her legs crossed seductively, and was conversing with her mother.

Rosy was dressed as she had been every time Jill had seen her, in a manner that oozed sensuality.

"That skirt is so short I can tell the price of butter," Maddie whispered her old, familiar saying in Jill's ear with humor in her voice.

Jill smiled as her eyes widened in mock disapproval at her mother's comment. She kissed her mom's cheek and then gave her a hug and whispered in her ear, "Thank you for being here, Mommy."

"Where else would I be?" Maddie said as she looked Jill in the eye. "Come on, your sister made the seat of honor just for you."

Barbie had taken one of Bebe's chairs and decorated it with flowers that matched the rest of the decorations, and Jill sat and opened her gifts. When she was finished, the women sat and ate the wonderful meal Barbie and Bebe had made. Everyone was enjoying themselves as the hours went by.

Eventually the party started to end and people began to leave. Maddie and Regina began cleaning as the last of the guests left. Then they took all the gifts and loaded them into Jill's car. When they were finished they said their good-byes and left as well. Only Jill, Barbie, Bebe, Sharon, Monica, and Grace were left.

"What's going on?" Jill said as she noticed the suspicious exchange of glances going on between Bebe and Barbie. The two women smiled but said nothing.

Jill focused her attention on the other women who made futile attempts to look busy and seem inattentive to what was going on.

"Come on, guys, I know something is going on," Jill said again. Still, no one offered an answer.

Bebe stood and walked over to the window. She made sure that none of the guests were still lingering around and chatting outside before she started to talk.

"Jill, the night is young and so are we," Bebe said playfully.

"Besides, you need to have one night of fun and frolic before you tie the knot," Grace added, and was met by angry stares because she almost gave the secret away.

"Come on," Barbie said. "Grab your purse. We want to take you out to celebrate your final hours as a single woman."

"Barbie, I was never one to frequent the party scene in the first place, so I won't be missing much," Jill said.

"All the more reason you need to come with us," Sharon said as she stood with a delightfully wicked grin on her face. She grabbed her purse and pulled her car keys from it. "Come on, I'm driving since I'm the only one with a vehicle big enough to carry all of us."

Sharon opened the door and walked out into the night air. The other women followed laughing and giggling with the anticipation of what the evening held. Barbie continued to coax Jill along, who felt she might be headed for disaster by going out with the feisty group.

Chapter 18

As the excited group of women rode in Sharon's Excursion, they laughed and joked about the evening. Though Jill joined in, her mind was more focused on where they were going. Still no one would tell her or the destination.

Jill had never seen Sharon in such an uninhibited state. She was moving to the music in her seat, but the radio station just wasn't doing it for her. Reaching under the console, she retrieved her CD holder, and as she drove she pulled a CD out and put it on. Sharon turned the volume up and rolled her window down. She sang along as the wind whipped her hair wildly. She moved seductively in her seat, giving Jill more reason to believe that she was in for a wild night.

They had been riding for an hour when Jill realized they were on the other side of town. Sharon pulled into the parking lot of a neon-lit club. The name of the club was Sally's Hide-A-Way. On the door was another sign stating that it was ladies' night. The place obviously did a good bit of business, Jill imagined, as she observed the number of customers outside waiting to get in.

The group of women got out of the SUV and headed toward the entrance of the club. Jill knew exactly what kind of place Sally's was. She had doubts as to whether she should be here, but she felt her own sense of adventure and excitement surfacing as she continued to walk.

"I'm so glad Rosy left with her mother. I thought she might want to stay longer," Bebe said.

"Yeah, I think she was a spy," Sharon added.

"A spy, why would you think she's a spy?" Jill asked.

"Come on, Jill, who comes to a bridal shower dressed like that?" Sharon asked.

"I think Tony sent her to keep an eye on me," Bebe said, making the other women laugh.

Once inside Sally's-Hide-A-Way, the women took seats at a table large enough to accommodate their group. Waiters came to take their orders, and each of them requested their favorite drink. Jill watched with amusement as Barbie, Monica, and Bebe ogled the eye candy. Grace was more blatant with her flirtatious behavior as she boldly caressed the bare chest of one of the waiters, sending Monica into hysterical laughter.

Sharon managed to outdo them all as her skirt slid high upon her thighs; she seductively crossed her legs and twisted the end of her hair between her fingers as she gave her order. As the waiter turned to leave, she gave his backside a gentle pat.

"Ah, nice, tight and firm, just the way I like them," she said, laughing and paying no attention to the look of shock on Jill's face.

"Sharon, you're a happily married woman," Jill said.

"I know, you don't have to remind me. Come on, Jill, loosen up, it's not like I'm going to take the man home. He is just a little eye candy. And don't you think for one minute that Eric isn't enjoying himself tonight."

"I'm sure they all are and I don't mind as long as he doesn't take it too far," Bebe said. "Jill, this is your night. Anything that goes on in here stays in here."

Reluctantly Jill agreed, and her mind reasoned that at Kyle's bachelor party he would probably touch a woman or two as well. What was the point of having that kind of party if he didn't? she wondered. Bebe was right. Now was the time to get all the wildness out of your system, as long as you didn't take it too far.

Jill glanced at Barbie, whom she had always admired. She was enjoying herself and having a great time as she laughed and talked with Grace and Monica. Jill decided to stop worrying and start enjoying the night.

The waiter had returned and set their drinks on the table. As he did the lights in the room began to dim and a woman appeared on the stage with a microphone.

"Good evening, ladies. I'm Sally, and welcome to my hide-a-way. Tonight we have a real treat in store for you, and I'm told that we have several brides-to-be in the audience tonight. Well, ladies, I hope tonight the gentlemen are able to give you something you'll never forget, and remember—"

"What goes on in Sally's, stays in Sally's!" the audience cheered in unison.

With loud applause Sally left the stage and the music began to play loudly. As the lights dimmed, exotic male dancers appeared on stage. The music was fast and the men started moving provocatively as their hips gyrated powerfully. As they continued to dance they came off the stage and into the audience. In sexy playfulness the men teased and taunted the delighted women, who were happy to tuck dollar bills in their G-strings.

Jill looked over at Barbie, who seemed to have produced a stack of one-dollar bills from her purse. Her sister had a huge smile on her face as she participated in the titillating interaction.

Sharon was doing the same, and letting her fingers gently glide down the man's well-chiseled chest, before she tucked her bill neatly in his G-string. She threw back her head in laughter as she delighted herself by touching him.

Bebe and Monica laughed and applauded wildly at what was going on, and Jill found herself laughing too. These were all women that she admired for how they conducted themselves as well as their households. Barbie and Sharon had a few years of happy marriage behind them, but Bebe was a newlywed. Still, Jill couldn't help but think that she had much to learn from them about keeping a happy home, as well as a healthy sex life.

As the song ended, the men returned to the stage and, with sexy winks and smiles to their appreciative audience, disappeared behind the curtain. They left the audience charged and titillated, and before the women could catch their breath the next act began.

Jill expected another bunch of male dancers to appear and gyrate and thrust their hips again, but she was pleasantly surprised at what happened next. She sat back in her seat and took a sip of her Chambord as she watched the show.

The curtains reopened and the stage glowed with blue lighting. Glitter appeared to be falling from the ceiling, and a man sat on a sofa. Music began to play again, but this time it was low, soft, and sexy. A beautiful woman came onstage. She was dressed in a pantsuit that bared her midriff, and had slits all the way up to her hipbone. Wearing stilettos, she began to dance for him. Gently she brushed a huge fan made of feathers across her breasts. Bending down, she stood up slowly, letting the feathers rub against her bare thighs. As she danced for him, arousing his sense of pleasure, Jill watched and made mental notes.

By the evening's end Jill was happy that they had come to Sally's Hide-A-Way. Though she knew it wasn't something Sharon and Bebe did regularly, Jill had a feeling they had been here before. *Maybe that's how she keeps Eric following her around like a puppy dog,* Jill thought, smiling to herself. Jill knew from the time she saw Tony and Bebe together that Tony had it bad for her girlfriend, and Barbie always had a way of getting what she wanted from Rick. Yes, she would be wise to take a cue from these wise, married women.

"Jill, how did you like Sally's?" Sharon asked Jill as she sipped her drink.

A shy smile came across Jill's lips as she looked at the other women and then said, "I had a wonderful time. As a matter of fact I even learned a few things tonight."

"From the dancers?" Monica asked.

"A little, but I learned even more from Bebe, Sharon, and Barbie. You all seem like old pros, and I doubt this was your first time here."

"It was my first time," Barbie said in playful innocence.

"I don't think so, sis. Though you've never been here, I'm positive it wasn't your first time."

The other women chuckled at the playful banter between the two sisters. Jill sat and studied all the women for a moment. The more she thought about it she came to realize that all of them, including

Monica, had probably been to a place like this. Suddenly she felt like the virgin of the group.

"I have a gift for you, Jill," Grace said as she pulled a package from her purse. She stood and walked over and handed the gift to Jill. With a quick kiss on the cheek she added, "I hope this gift keeps Kyle's eye on you at all times."

Jill took the tiny package, and for the life of her couldn't imagine how something so small could keep Kyle's eye on her. She thanked Grace and began opening the package. Inside were three of the most beautiful thongs she had ever seen. Though she didn't own a pair because she found them uncomfortable to wear, she knew she would make good use of them on her honeymoon.

"This is for you as well," Monica said as she passed her gift to Jill.

Monica's present was just as small, but Jill knew right away that it wasn't clothing. She opened Monica's gift and was surprised to find two CDs. One was a collection of romantic songs that were designed with love-making in mind, and the other was by Petey Pablo.

"Thank you, Monica," Jill said.

Seeing the look of confusion on Jill's face, Monica quickly added with a smart wink. "I know you know what to do with the romantic songs, but the one by Petey Pablo will require some imagination."

Sharon looked around and saw that most of the patrons of Sally's were beginning to leave. The group of women decided to make a stop in the gift shop before they left. Once inside, Jill found herself surrounded by all kinds of items that would make any night a romantic one, and bring a man to his knees.

The women watched Jill as she investigated one thing after another. Sally's gift shop was filled with

nighties, feathers, lotions, boas, and beads. They
even had a small collection of stilettos and Jill quickly
decided to buy a pair. She picked several more items
that she felt would be appropriate for what she had
planned for Kyle on their honeymoon.

When she was done shopping, the group of family
and friends paid for her purchase, and told her it was
their gift to her. Jill thanked and kissed each one of
them for their kindness.

The ride home was filled with wild laughter and
even wilder conversation. The women talked and
joked about the evening and how it had made them
want to get home to their mates.

"I hope Tony doesn't try to tell me he's tired tonight,
because I'm not and I'm ready to wear him out,"
Bebe said as she ran her fingers through her hair.

"I know what you mean. Sally's had me ready for
some sweet dessert, too," Sharon added.

"You two are lucky, because I have three kids I
hope are asleep before anything goes on in my bedroom," Barbie told them.

"I don't feel bad for any of you. At least you all have
a man," Grace said loudly.

"Oh, Grace, I'm sorry. Girls, we shouldn't be talking like this in front of Grace," Bebe said giggling.

"Grace, you could have a man if you wanted to. I
know for a fact that Miguel has asked you out,"
Sharon said.

"Why don't you go out with him?" Jill asked.

"He's okay," Grace said, trying not to sound shallow. "He is just so short! I can't stand it when a man
is shorter than me."

"That shouldn't matter as long as he's good to
you, and I mean that in both ways," Sharon said, giggling, but the other women agreed wholeheartedly.

Jill knew she would be the only one not finding sexual pleasure tonight. She had made Kyle agree to wait until their wedding night as the time had almost arrived. Though she was filled with want for Kyle after visiting Sally's too, she wanted more than anything to bring Kyle to his knees with lust for her on their wedding night. Thanks to the evening spent at Sally's, she was certain she had learned what it took to do just that.

Sharon pulled up in Bebe's driveway and the women filed out of her vehicle. Saying good-bye, she pulled off and headed home. It was 3:00 a.m. and they were all exhausted. They said quick farewells to each other and got into their cars and went home.

As Jill drove in the direction of home, her head was filled with the events of the day. She was so pleased with the presents she had received at her shower, but even more so with the people who obviously loved her enough to celebrate the event with her. The small circle of tight friends had grown to include Monica. Jill found herself seeing the woman more as a younger sister, and Monica, who was initially a little frightened by Jill, now seemed to be perfectly comfortably around her.

Jill truly wasn't expecting to see Rosy Hernandez at the shower. She imagined that she had been forced to attend by her mother. Bebe and Sharon were thrilled that Rosy had left early, but it seemed to Jill that Rosy was just as happy to leave.

They had also mentioned that they felt as though Rosy was a spy. Jill knew that Bebe was more than likely teasing about Tony sending her, but still she couldn't help but think that Bebe still felt a little threatened by the beautiful, sexy bombshell.

As she pulled up into her driveway she notice the cabin was completely dark. Jill grabbed the packages from Sally's from the front seat, and decided that the ton of gifts in the backseat and trunk could wait until morning, when Kyle would be available to help her.

In the darkness she fumbled around for the door key, angry with herself for not leaving the porch light on. Finally she opened the door and walked inside. She laid the packages and her purse on the sofa while she closed and locked the door behind her. Jill went into the kitchen and got a glass of water, sipping the cold liquid as she stared out into the complete darkness of the woods. She hoped Kyle would come home soon, as she felt lonely in the huge cabin by herself.

Having finished her water, she set the glass down. She turned out the lights in the kitchen and went back into the living room. Jill turned on the porch light so Kyle would have an easier time gaining entrance than she did, and then gathered her packages and went upstairs. She put everything she had bought from Sally's in her special tote and then went to take a quick shower.

When she was finished getting ready for bed, she stood at the window and looked outside hoping to see the headlights of Kyle's Navigator, but she did not. Reluctantly she climbed into bed and glanced at the clock. It was now 4:30 a.m., and she couldn't fight the fatigue that was taking over her body. Turning out the light on the nightstand, Jill fell asleep holding Kyle's pillow.

As morning light filtered into the bedroom Jill realized that Kyle was in bed with her. She looked lovingly at his face, before she remembered that she had fallen asleep without him. She wondered what time it had been when he finally arrived home. Fighting the urge to wake him, she crept out of bed and got dressed.

Jill went downstairs and busied herself by making breakfast. As it cooked she began unloading from her car the ton of gifts she had received at her bridal shower. Temporarily she stopped putting the gifts where they belonged in order to stir the oatmeal, and then continued to work.

As she carefully put the Lenox crystal away her thoughts returned to Kyle. It had to have been well past 5:00 a.m. when he came home, since she had fallen asleep shortly before that. She wondered just how much of a good time he had, and whether he had taken his own advice not to ogle or fondle someone else.

Though she had half expected that he did, Jill didn't know to what end the fun would stop. She began thinking of the wonderful time she and the girls had at Sally's Hide-A-Way. Even though she hadn't even touched a single backside, she had done her share of ogling. In fact, watching the woman dance for the man onstage had been more fascinating than watching the male strippers. Jill smiled as she realized she had definitely learned more than she bargained for last night.

After making herself some toast and pouring herself a glass of orange juice, Jill sat down to eat her oatmeal. The phone rang and she answered it.

"Hi, Jill," Bebe said.

"Hey, I'm surprised that you are awake already."

"Well, that hot night I was hoping would continue with my husband fizzled. Eric brought Tony home at five o'clock. He was too tired to do anything."

"I guess that is the time Kyle got in, because I fell asleep just before then. He's still sleeping, and I am fighting the urge to wake him up."

"He'll be up before you know it since the wedding rehearsal is at three."

Jill glanced at the clock on the stove and saw that Bebe was right. It was already going on eleven, and they had to leave the cabin by 2:30 p.m.

"Bebe, I can't help but wonder what went on at the bachelor party."

"Jill, let me assure you that nothing went on that would jeopardize your relationship with Kyle. He loves you and knows just where to draw the line," Bebe said confidently.

"I know you're right, but I just want to hear the words from him," Jill said, still unsure of the situation.

She knew that she was pushing Kyle to the limit by backing off from sex until they were married, and could only hope he didn't find comfort in the arms of a lap dancer to ease his needs.

"Jill, I have to go. Tony just came downstairs and I want to hear about his night," Bebe said with giddy curiosity.

After saying good-bye, Jill hung up the phone and finished the last of her meal. She put the dishes in the dishwasher, and then finished putting the rest of the gifts away. She threw all the boxes away and went to get the mail.

Having found nothing interesting in the mailbox, she threw the pile of letters on the coffee table and went back upstairs. As she walked into the bedroom she stopped and looked at Kyle. His gentle snore let her know that he was still deep in slumber.

She went quietly into the walk-in closet and found an outfit to wear to the rehearsal. Jill took a shower, did her hair and makeup, and then slipped into her bra and panties. Now it was 1:30 p.m., and she decided that it was time to wake Kyle.

Jill sat on the edge of the bed and began to run the back of her fingers gently across his cheek. Kyle stirred and stretched, and then he opened his eyes and focused them on Jill. He smiled broadly as studied her face, and then let his eyes dip down to her breasts, which sat up perfectly in the sexy push-up she wore.

She leaned down to kiss him and as she did he grabbed her, making her body roll over his and into the bed. Jill laughed uncontrollably as Kyle nuzzled her neck while he tickled her sides. She begged him to stop, and after a few moments he did.

Jill lay beside him and tried to catch her breath as Kyle propped himself up on one arm and watched her breasts heave as she tried to calm down.

"You're certainly in a good mood," Jill said as her eyes held his.

"Why shouldn't I be? Tomorrow I am marrying the woman of my dreams," Kyle said as if he knew that in all the universe, there was not another woman that could match Jill. He leaned forward and kissed his treasure fully on the lips.

"Kyle, I love you," Jill said when their lips parted.

"I love you too, baby girl."

"Did you have fun last night?"

"Yes, and some of us had a little too much fun," he said as she flopped back down on his pillow.

He had piqued Jill's curiosity and she now propped herself up on a pillow in order to see his facial expression. So many times she had heard from friends what went on at bachelor parties. Now she feared that Kyle had done something terrible. Her mind reasoned that he knew better, that he loved her and wouldn't let her or their pending marriage down. All her concerns had led to this moment, and she waited to hear the worst.

"What do you mean?" she said in a voice that was strained and filled with pain.

Kyle looked at Jill and saw horrified concern on her face. He wasn't exactly sure just what had put it there, but he knew it had something to do with him. He hated seeing her face full of such an emotion. The thought of the anxiety he was obviously causing hurt his heart, and it was a pain he had to alleviate immediately.

Though Jill's eyes were filled with tears, she didn't let one leave its place. She stared at Kyle and prepared herself to hear the truth and to hopefully work out any problems from there.

Kyle sat up and gently pushed Jill back down into the pillow. He leaned over her and then kissed both her cheeks tenderly.

"Precious, tell me, what is on your mind? I know it's me, but I don't know what I did," Kyle said in a tone that was thick, yet filled with honesty.

"Kyle, I have heard so many wild and crazy stories about what goes on at bachelor parties, and I'm just afraid that you might have done something that would hurt our relationship," Jill said softly.

"Like what, have sex with another woman?"

Jill hated hearing the words, but she nodded slowly. She turned her face away from Kyle, unable to take his piercing stare any longer. She had posed the question unsure if she was ready to hear the answer, but it was an answer she needed to know before tomorrow.

Kyle placed a finger gently under Jill's trembling chin and turned her head to face him. A smile filled with amusement and love was written all over his face.

"I can only thank God that I have a lifetime to show you just how much you mean to me, baby girl.

I made a promise never to be the cause of a tear falling from your eyes, and it's a promise I intend to keep. Jill, I looked and clapped, but I never touched. Well, she did sit on my lap, but for the record I didn't enjoy it."

Jill looked up at Kyle quizzically. Giggling slightly she said, "Then tell me who did."

"Jill, suffice it to say that no one got out of hand, but a few of the fellas really did enjoy themselves. And before you ask, it wasn't Tony or Eric."

"Since you didn't enjoy the woman's attention, what did you do?"

"She took too long standing up, so I carefully pushed her away. I made sure I didn't touch any part of her that would get me in trouble later," he said. "Besides, she wasn't you, and in my eyes there isn't another woman who can compete with you."

"Oh, baby," Jill said as she pulled Kyle down and planted kisses all over his face. "I'm so sorry that I even doubted you. I think my mind is running wild from pre-wedding jitters. I know you, Kyle, and I'm sure of our love. My mind has been playing tricks on me since I knew we hadn't made love in a while. I didn't want to, but I couldn't help thinking that you might have been tempted."

"Waiting to make love to you isn't enough to push me into the arms of another woman, Jill," he said, slightly irritated. "But I can understand that the wedding has got you a little nervous. You didn't tell me how your evening went," he said, and raised an eyebrow as Jill slightly pursed her lips together and hesitated to answer.

"Well, let's just say that I learned a lot last night," she said, hoping he wouldn't press for more information.

"Oh, you're not getting out of answering that question that easy. Tell me more," Kyle insisted.

"Okay, I'll tell you," Jill said, giggling. "First of all, I didn't know that a place like Sally's Hide-A-Way existed."

"Yeah, Bebe and Sharon used to go there from time to time, but after Sharon got married, they didn't go as much."

"Eric doesn't mind that she goes there?" Jill asked in curious fascination.

"No, he doesn't. As a matter of fact, he says that Sharon seems to learn something new every time she goes there, and he is the recipient of pleasure from lessons learned well. They have a strong marriage and she would never hurt Eric that way. And just in case you haven't noticed, Eric would give his wife the world if he could, so her outings to Sally's are no big deal."

Jill thought for a moment of their first night at Roland's. She remembered how Eric and Sharon danced together. They danced as if they were making love to each other, and gave no care as to who was there. It was apparent that they loved each other deeply and had a strong marriage. Jill had learned just as much about honesty, trust, passion, and pleasure in the last several days as she had in the past year, and she was glad she had been paying attention.

"What else went on?" Kyle asked as he took note of Jill's thoughtful expression.

"Not much, baby," she said as she pulled him down on top of her.

Jill kissed Kyle on the lips softly before allowing his tongue in her mouth. She wrapped her legs around his thighs as she let her fingers run the full length of his strong, muscular back. She could feel his need for her building and slowly broke off the kiss. She released his body from her legs and inched away from him.

"Now you better hurry or we'll be late for the rehearsal," she whispered as she stood.

"One more day is all I can handle of this," Kyle said as he dragged himself out of bed and headed toward the bathroom.

Jill smiled to herself, knowing exactly what she had done to him, and considered it just a primer for all the pleasure she wanted to inflict upon Kyle once they were in Jamaica on their honeymoon.

When they arrived at A Special Place, everyone was there and waiting to get the rehearsal under way. Grace was the coordinator, and she had the wedding party practice for two hours before she was happy with the results. After the rehearsal, the dinner was held at poolside and drinks were served. Jill and Kyle stood and requested everyone's attention.

"Everyone, I know you are all worn out from the wedding rehearsal and you're ready to eat, but Jill and I wanted to say something before we eat. We just wanted to thank you all for being a part of our special day. Jill and I couldn't be happier to share the love we have found in each other with all our friends and family, and I thank each and every one of you for sharing our joy," Kyle said as he held Jill's hand.

"What Kyle just said goes for me too. I'm so thankful to have found the man of my dreams and a family that is as warm and as loving as my own. From the day I met you all, you took me into your hearts and let me know that you accepted me as one of you—as family. Now, on the eve of our wedding, two families are about to become one, and I couldn't be happier. Thank you all for making A Special Place my home too," Jill said.

The family looked on at the two people who stood before them. All of them knew in some way or another the trials and tribulations Kyle and Jill had faced personally and as a couple. But now they had weathered the storm and found the calm that would envelope their marriage. Everyone knew that whatever came their way, the couple would find strength and solace in each other, and in their family.

Kyle kissed Jill on the lips, but at the first touch of her mouth he was unable to resist the urge to take her in his arms. He did so as the family looked on, and raised their glasses to the couple and their outward display of affection.

"Aww, get a room," Tony was the first to yell out, and everyone started to laugh.

Reluctantly, Kyle released Jill, but held his lips so close to her ear that they brushed against her lobe. She could feel his warm breath on her skin as she whispered, "I'll let you go for now, but tomorrow night you'll be Mrs. Roberts, and you'll be all mine."

Jill could feel her senses tingling with anticipation over his promise, and could only hope she could keep her own. She and Kyle began to distribute the gifts they had bought for their wedding attendants. Jill had chosen for each of her bridesmaids a bagette make of heavy silk. On the front of each purse was a picture of herself and the bridesmaid the bag was intended for. Inside each bag Jill placed a special note, a gift certificate for Fashion Fair Cosmetics, and a pale blue jewelry box.

"Oh, Jill, this is beautiful!" Monica was the first to say as she pulled a lovely diamond tennis bracelet from its case.

The other women moved fast to see if their bagettes contained the same gift. None were disappointed when they opened their bags, as Jill had taken great care to express her gratitude for their love and support.

"Did you do that good a job on my gifts, babe?" Kyle asked as he scooped up a handful of presents. His comment brought out a few chuckles as the family realized he didn't know what he was giving away.

Jill hadn't expected him to announce the question out loud, and she simply shrugged her shoulders and smiled at his question. Kyle winked at her. He knew Jill's style, and was positive that Jill took care of the men as well as she had taken care of the women.

"Wow! Jill, you sure know how to show your appreciation," Tony was the first to say as he admired his gift.

The gentlemen had all received eel-skin wallets, in which Jill had placed gift certificates to Roland's. In addition, she had also given them the same pale blue jewelry box, only smaller. Inside were men's gold rings with diamonds that spelled out their individual initials. On the inside, ASP was engraved.

The thrilled wedding party thanked the couple profusely, before the waiters and waitresses began to bustle back and forth serving the hungry family. The last time the entire group had congregated here was at the grand opening of A Special Place. Now, a year later, Jill looked around and saw many of the faces that were in attendance the year before. Her family had grown and she was extremely pleased at what she saw. A Special Place now symbolized more than just the name of a resort; it also represented what she had found in her heart and in her life.

Chapter 19

It was still quite early in the morning, but Jill could tell from the commotion coming from downstairs that the cabin was jumping with excited energy. Kyle had spent the night at Tony and Bebe's place so that Jill and her entourage could prepare in private. Maddie and Barbie had spent the night, and she gathered from the amount of noise she heard that Regina, Bebe, and Monica had arrived as well. As she prepared to get dressed to go downstairs for breakfast, there was a gentle knock on the door.

"Come in," she said as she slid her robe over her shoulders.

Bebe entered the room with a huge grin on her face. Before saying a word she walked over and hugged her friend. The two women held each other for a quiet moment, and let the profound effect of the day's coming events swirl around in their heads.

"Jill, I can't believe you're getting married today," Bebe said excitedly, as their hug ended.

"Me neither. It's like a dream, Bebe, and I don't want to wake up and find out none of this is real."

"Oh, it's real, girl," Bebe said as she pinched Jill's arm.

"Ouch! Okay, I guess I am awake," Jill said, laughing. "But what if Kyle gets cold feet? What if he leaves me standing at the altar?"

"Jill, Kyle Roberts will do a lot of things, but leave you standing at the altar is not one of them," Bebe said, shaking her head in dismay. "Come on, let's get you downstairs to breakfast. Maybe seeing how excited your mom and Regina are will help you calm down." She took Jill's hand and led her downstairs.

When Jill reached the living room she saw that it was filled with her bridal party. The room was filled with gowns, shoe boxes, and accessories, and looked more like a bridal boutique than a living room. Barbie's kids, who were the only ones in the wedding, were running around, content to stay out of the way and play with each other.

Jill followed Bebe into the kitchen where she found her mother, Barbie, Regina, and Monica having breakfast. The women greeted the Jill with enthusiasm, and Maddie stood to make her a plate.

"Was she awake when you went upstairs?" Maddie asked Bebe.

"She was putting on her robe when I walked into her room."

"Jill, you have to hurry. We have to be at the beauty parlor by ten o'clock. You just have enough time to take a bath, and then we have to get ready to go," Maddie told her.

Jill grabbed a few grapes from a bowl on the table, ignoring the heaping amount of eggs, bacon, and grits her mother had placed before her. She was too nervous to eat too much of anything, and was content to nibble on grapes and drink her orange juice.

As she plopped the last grape into her mouth, Maddie ushered her back upstairs to get ready. Jill did as she was told. She quickly washed and dressed and when she was done she went back downstairs.

The women were filing out the front door, and gave Jill only enough time to grab her purse as they left the cabin.

The group rode in three cars and arrived at the Perfect Image just before ten o'clock. The shop already had several patrons, but had enough chairs and hairstylists to accommodate Jill's group. Desiree was Jill and Bebe's regular hairdresser, and would be taking care of them. Sharon saw another stylist who worked there, and was being attended by her. The rest of the wedding party was being taken care of by other stylists at the Perfect Image.

Knowing Jill's hair, Desiree worked quickly. She created a stunning up-do with tendrils framing Jill's face. When she was finished, Desiree handed Jill a mirror so that she could closely examine the style. Jill was quite pleased with her work and thanked the hairstylist by tipping her handsomely.

"You look beautiful, sweetheart," Maddie said to Jill.

"Thanks, Mom. And may I say you look quite stunning yourself?" Jill replied, as Maddie turned around in a sassy manner, allowing Jill to get a good look at her stylish do.

Jill laughed as she took note of her mother's new spirit. It seemed to Jill that Durango had a way of bringing out the best in people as well as the hidden other side of one's personality.

"Oh, Jill, your hair looks so sharp," Barbie said. "It's too bad there isn't another wedding taking place soon. I'm going to miss having all this fun with you."

"We don't have to wait for another wedding, Barbie. I was hoping to see you at Christmas."

"I hope so," Barbie answered.

As the women's hair was finished, they were moved to the other side of the salon to get manicures and pedicures. Jill enjoyed the time as she was able to laugh and talk in one place with all the women who meant so much to her. After the wedding her own family would be going back to Pittsburgh, and she would miss them terribly. But she knew that her mother and father, as well as Barbie's family, would return.

Three hours later everyone, including Lacy, was finished. Ricky and James had their hair cut and looked very handsome. The group piled back into the vehicles they had arrived in and returned home.

With only two hours before the wedding, the women busied themselves getting ready. Upstairs, Jill was being helped into her gown by her mother and mother-in-law. Maddie took great care as she placed the tiara on Jill's head, fitting it perfectly around the beautiful up-do. The dangling pear-shaped earrings shimmered, like the dress, with her every move. Maddie stepped back and admired Jill as tears rolled freely down her cheek.

"Oh, Mom, you are going to ruin your makeup," Jill said as she dabbed Maddie's tears away with a tissue.

"I don't care. It isn't every day that my daughter gets married," Maddie said. She took the tissue away from Jill and continued to pat her eyes.

"I know Regina already gave you something blue, so I want to give you something borrowed," Maddie said after Regina had stepped away.

Maddie reached inside her pocket and produced the golden, heart-shaped brooch that had belonged to her own mother, and handed it to Jill. Jill's maternal grandmother had her wedding date engraved on the back, and Jill's mother had done the same. Jill looked at the piece of jewelry and saw that Barbie's wedding date was there also, and now it was her turn to add her wedding date to the family heirloom.

"Thank you," Jill said simply.

"For what?"

"For being my mother," Jill answered as she hugged Maddie.

As they arrived at A Special Place, Jill was the first to emerge from the superstretch Escalade limousine, and was followed by the rest of her bridal entourage. She paused and gazed up at the sky, which seemed to have been created this day just for her. It was the same pale blue she had fallen in love with the first day she arrived.

The color of the sky only served to complement her attendants' dresses, which were tea-length gowns of the same shade of blue. Though Jill's dress fell full to the ground, the bridesmaid dresses were of similar style and trimmed in ivory satin.

The wedding would start in less than half an hour, so the women were quickly ushered to one of the resort's guest rooms to make final preparations. There they touched up their makeup and received their bouquets of flowers.

Jill tried to stay calm and took deep breaths, but she nervously chewed on her bottom lip expecting something to go terribly wrong.

"Jill, you have to stop chewing on your lip because you're ruining your lipstick," Barbie said as she pulled a tube from her bagette and reapplied Jill's shade.

"Barbie, do you think Kyle has arrived yet?" Jill asked nervously as she observed Barbie's reaction to her question.

"Yes, I think he's here," Barbie replied, smiling.

"I can't seem to calm down. I just know something is going to go wrong, and one of the worst possible things would be if the food wasn't ready or Jillian's staff wasn't prepared, or—"

"Jill, Kyle is here. Of all the places in the world he could be, I promise you he is right here," Barbie said calmly, trying to allay Jill's fears. She took Jill's hands into her own and gave them a reassuring squeeze. "In less than an hour you will be all his and he will be all yours. I promise you, sis."

"Oh, Barbie, I'm so glad you're here. I don't know what I would do without you," Jill said as she gave her sister a big hug.

Maddie and Regina said quick good-byes as they hurried to join the other guests who were already seated under the canopy of the resort's garden. Just as they left the room, Grace entered in a hurry.

"Okay, ladies, it's showtime," Grace said as she entered the room. "Jill, you look stunning. Kyle is going to be knocked off his feet." She paused to study the enchanting beauty. Then, as if trying to break a spell, Grace slightly shook her head and said, "Let's get going. I promised Kyle that I would have you down the aisle as fast as I could."

That last comment made by Grace had finally put Jill's single-most worry to rest. Kyle was here. She had tried to put his terrible car accident behind her, but still she feared he would leave her, that he would disappear. Jill had to remind herself of her favorite saying, that God's gift to us is today, and that's why it's called the present.

With that in mind she made a decision never to let those sad thoughts fill her head again. A content smile formed on Jill's face as she followed Grace out of the room. They walked to the side entrance of the resort, which led to the gardens. Jill could hear music filtering into the building and knew it wouldn't be long before she was standing by Kyle's side.

"You look divine, baby girl," her father said to her as he approached. "I have no doubt that Kyle will treat you like the treasure you are," Rob finished as he fought back a tear that tried to escape.

"You are right, Daddy, and I pray that my marriage is as joyful and lasts as long as yours has," Jill said as she lifted her veil to kiss his cheek.

As the wedding march began to play, each of the bridesmaids was met by a groomsman and proceeded down the aisle. Finally, it was Jill's turn. As she and Rob walked hand in arm, she could see that quite a few people were in attendance. But at this time she only had eyes for Kyle.

Jill continued to walk down the aisle stepping on the rose petals Lacy had just dropped. Her bouquet was full and long, ending almost at Jill's knees. Woven through the greenery, fragrant akito roses, orchids, and calla lilies burst from the arrangement and were framed with hosta leaves.

The sun's rays made her dress shimmer with her every step as she appeared to glide toward Kyle. This was the moment she had been waiting for, the dream that had finally come true. She had her career, a new life, and a new husband. Life was all she had hoped it would be.

White-and-pale-blue-dyed roses covered the arch where her father delivered Jill to Kyle. He took Jill's hand and placed it in Kyle's.

"Take good care of my baby," Rob whispered in a voice low enough for only Kyle to hear.

"I promise I will," Kyle whispered back as he made eye contact with Rob.

Rob took his seat next to his wife, who couldn't control the tears that formed a steady stream down her cheeks.

Jill turned to Kyle and smiled brightly up at the man who represented her world. Though she tried to focus on what the preacher was saying, her head continued to race with wonder over what was happening to her.

She trusted Kyle with all her heart and wanted her very soul to be part of his forever. Right now was all she cared about and she knew he felt the same way.

"I do," Jill said in soft honesty, in answer to the preacher asking her if she would take Kyle's hand in marriage.

Kyle reached down and took a ring from the pillow Ricky held and slipped the wedding band on Jill's finger. Then she did the same.

"I now pronounce you husband and wife. You may kiss your bride," the preacher said joyously.

Kyle's arms went around Jill's waist instinctively as her hands held his neck gently, yet naturally. All who looked on could see the passion Jill and Kyle possessed, and it made each of them reminiscent of their own romantic encounters. The videographer moved in to get a better shot of the newlyweds' first kiss. Loud applause erupted as Jill and Kyle turned to face their guests. Cutting through the well-manicured gardens, the couple walked back toward the resort to the receiving line so they could greet their guests.

As guests filed past the bridal party, Jill was thrilled to see all of her family from back East, as well as her parents' neighbors. All of the office staff from Iguana had come for the wedding, including Matt and Joan

Singletary, and Phil Harmon. But Jill's face lit up
when she saw Lois and Diane, and she was anxious to
talk to them.

"Oh, girl, I can't believe you are finally married,"
Di said as she hugged Jill. "Say a prayer for me that
I'm next," she added as she introduced Brian, her new
man, to Jill.

"I will, Di," Jill said as she kissed Diane's cheek.

"We are so happy for you, Jill," Lois said as she
and her husband, Paul, kissed Jill, too.

"Thanks, Lo. I'm so glad you came."

"You know I wouldn't miss your wedding for the
world," Lois said, smiling. "And you better remember
to pray for Di, because she has fallen head over heels
for Brian," she whispered.

"I will," Jill said with a wink.

Reverend Gregory, his wife, and their sons Matthew,
Mark, and Luke came to congratulate Jill and Kyle.
Each of them studied Jill's new husband for a second.
None of the brothers could measure up to him by any
standard, and without lingering around Jill with their
usual looks of lust, they simply said hello and followed
their parents.

Jill felt a warm, pleasant feeling when her eyes fell
upon her ex-neighbors from her New York high-rise
apartment. Darlene and Mike walked toward her,
and Helena tottered between her parents and held
their hands.

After congratulating Kyle, they turned to Jill.

"Jill, I am so happy for you!" Darlene said as she
hugged Jill.

"Thank you, Dar, and I owe it all to you."

"To me, why?"

"For telling me that somehow love would find its
way into my life when I least expected it. You were

right," Jill said, beaming as she tenderly caressed Kyle's back.

"And you deserve every ounce of joy you have found. Oh, by the way," Dar said as she leaned closer to Jill and whispered in her ear with mischievous quiet laughter, "Dre has more trouble than he can handle with his woman. He mentions you from time to time, and I don't miss an opportunity to rub his face in missing out on the best thing that could have happened to him."

"You're terrible," Jill said, laughing as well.

"I know," Dar finished as she kissed Jill's cheek and went to catch up with her husband and daughter.

Jill looked on and hoped that one day soon she would find a little more of the happiness and contentment Dar had.

The wedding party posed for pictures for over an hour before joining their guests inside Jillian's. The restaurant had been closed to the public and was open only for the wedding reception. Waiters and waitresses quickly and expertly served the guests a meal that was fit for a king. As they ate sitting at the bridal table, Kyle leaned over and softly kissed Jill every time he heard the gentle chime of silverware tapping stemware.

As the wedding song began to play, Jill and Kyle stood in the middle of the dance floor and moved to the music as if they were truly one. The song "Happily Ever After" filled the room as well as Jill's and Kyle's hearts, since it represented all that their marriage represented. Jill danced slowly and gracefully in Kyle's arms. She looked up at him with all the love any one woman could hold in her eyes.

As the song continued to play Jill danced with her father, father-in-law, and all of the groomsmen. Kyle

danced with the moms, as well as all of the females in
the bridal party. As that song ended another began to
play, and many of the other guests started dancing too.

Later the couple stood and posed as they cut their
five-tier cake, and then playfully smashed a piece in
each other's face. Jill laughed wildly before lovingly
nibbling cake from Kyle's face.

"Don't start anything you aren't prepared to finish,"
he whispered jokingly into his wife's ear.

"Oh, I want to get a lot started, and I'm prepared
to finish as well, Mr. Roberts," Jill said in a sultry
voice, making Kyle smile at her, and his eyes sparkled
at the hope of things to come.

The photographer continued to take pictures without getting in the way, but Jill couldn't remember ever
having her photograph taken so many times. Still, she
smiled happily for the camera, preferring to have as
many memories of her wedding day as possible.

It was time to toss the bouquet, and as she had
guessed, Diane caught it. It was a wild catfight between
Diane and Rosy, but in the end Diane had claimed the
prize. Jill was immediately happy that she had gotten
a throwaway bouquet, as she looked at the one Diane
had just roughed up when she lunged for it.

Though hours had gone by, Jill felt as though the
whole event had been a fleeting moment. She and
Kyle had to prepare to leave. They were spending the
night at a hotel in town, since they had a flight early
tomorrow morning to Jamaica.

As they bade farewell to their guests, Jill couldn't
help but feel a little sad at having to leave her family
and the friends she hadn't seen in a while. She made
it a point to talk to each of them and made them
promise to come out for a visit before too long.

Having said their good-byes, Jill and Kyle left the

reception. The chauffeur stood holding the door of the Escalade open, and waited until the couple was seated comfortably before closing it behind them. Kyle turned toward Jill and was captivated by the warm smile she gave him.

"Now I have you all to myself, Mrs. Roberts," Kyle said as he brushed Jill's cheek softly with the back of his hand.

Jill closed her eyes briefly at his touch and let the words she had been yearning to hear linger in her ear. She was officially married to him. She was someone's wife. Jill could feel her heart pounding wildly in her chest, and knew it had everything to do with her husband's touch. *My husband's touch,* she thought, letting the words play over and over in her head, and loving what she heard.

"It feels like heaven," Jill replied as she slowly exhaled the breath she didn't know she was holding.

As the superstretch limousine pulled off, Jill and Kyle found themselves locked in passion-filled kisses. They had a good ride in front of them and Kyle wanted to get Jill warmed up for what he had in mind later on. He gently laid her body on the seat as he continued to kiss her. He wrapped his arms around Jill's waist and pressed her body to his. His tongue felt the silky moistness of hers, and this time he didn't have to remember his promise to wait until they were married.

No, he wouldn't make love to her in the limo. Jill deserved more and he wanted to give her more. But he was happily building up to that kind of pleasure. Kyle mouth left Jill's lips and went to investigate her ears. He played with her earrings, tugging on them gently, before he let his tongue slip into her ear.

Jill caught her breath sharply as she felt her body

grow warm with pleasure. A low moan escaped her lips as she realized that Kyle had complete control of her. If he wanted to take her right now she was more than willing and quite ready.

But Kyle made no move to get Jill out of her undergarments. Instead, he continued to make love to Jill's ear, and then her neck, and descended to her cleavage. As his tongue gently sucked one nipple, his thumb played with the other.

This kind of foreplay excited Jill greatly and to the point where he had her crying for more.

"Kyle, please make love to me," she said in a breathless whisper.

They were the words he had been waiting to her, and now she was saying them to him. It had been a while since they had had sex, and Kyle had honored her request by waiting until their wedding night. He had accomplished his goal by taking Jill to a level of want that her body couldn't deny, but she would now have to wait for him.

"No, baby, not yet, but I will take care of you tonight," Kyle said in a thick, deep voice, which let Jill know that he was in as much need of her as she was of him.

He glanced out the window and saw that they were nearing the hotel. Jill sat up and reluctantly pulled herself together and fixed her hair.

They pulled up to the hotel's entrance. The chauffeur got out and held open the door for them. As Jill and Kyle entered the hotel, the bellman attended to the luggage that the chauffeur was pulling from the trunk.

When they arrived at the door of the hotel's bridal suite Kyle wasted no time in making the night a memorable one for Jill. In one quick motion he swept her off her feet and into his strong arms.

"I want to carry you through the door," Kyle said and he held her body securely as he followed the bellman.

Jill was at a loss for words and could only smile and plant kisses on Kyle's cheek. She wrapped her arms around his neck and enjoyed the security of being his.

Kyle tipped the bellman as he left, and hung the DO NOT DISTURB sign as he closed the door.

When Kyle turned around he saw Jill standing in the middle of the room. She stood before him still holding her bouquet and looking very innocent and demure. They had made love more times than he could count, but looking at her now she seemed so different. She was no longer his girlfriend, or his fiancée, but his wife. He was suddenly thankful that Jill had made them take a break from sex, because for the first time he would be making love to his wife, and it all felt new and exciting to him.

Kyle walked with even slow steps toward her until his face was only millimeters away from hers. Jill could feel the warmth of his breath on her face, and she inhaled deeply as if to consume his soul. She wasn't conscious of the music playing softly in the background, or the twinkling of streetlights from outside. At that moment, she couldn't even tell you the color of the walls, or even her own name, because the only thing that mattered to her was the nearness of the man who made her lose her mind.

Jill felt Kyle's arms around her and she instinctively closed her eyes and parted her lips as he began to kiss her. She felt his fingers undoing her gown and felt her soul begin to crave his in a way she had never craved it before.

Kyle had always been a patient lover, and tonight

would be no different. As her beautiful gown fell away to reveal an even more stunning body, Kyle kissed every inch of her skin and she trembled at his touch. He picked Jill up and her legs straddled his still-clothed body. As she kissed him he began to walk toward the bed. Kyle laid Jill down gently and started undressing himself.

Jill watched as Kyle undressed and found herself fascinated with every movement of his physically fit body. She had seen him nude so many times before, and he was an awesome image to behold. Years of working on the ranch had given him muscles cut as deep as if he lifted weights regularly. His chocolate-colored skin made Jill anxious for a taste.

As she watched Kyle, she looked at him with a different vision. Tonight she saw her husband, the only man who would make love to her body for the rest of her life. Jill knew she had married the kind of man who believed a great lover was one who let the nights change, and never the woman.

She also knew that making love tonight would be different; not just because they had been on a sexual hiatus for a while, but because they had a newly formed bond, which would be consummated shortly. With that thought, Jill lay back on the pillows and continued to watch her husband disrobe his magnificent body, and tried to wait patiently for him to pleasure her.

Kyle climbed into bed with his body already giving evidence that he was more than ready for Jill, but his first priority was to bring her to peaks of pleasure before taking her over the top.

Kyle laid his body on top of Jill's and began to kiss her lips gently while his hands caressed her sides. His lips played at the corner of her mouth but didn't touch her lips. He could feel Jill's quick short breaths and he knew she was growing impatient for the love-making to begin, but still he teased her.

He adjusted his arm and raised his hand to Jill's lips. She parted her lips and as his fingers gently brushed the side of her face his thumb sought the warmth of her mouth. She sucked it only for a moment before he slowly withdrew it. Then Kyle slid his hand down her torso until it found the warmth between her inner thighs. As his hands rubbed her thighs his wet thumb found ways to drive her crazy.

Now Jill began to ache from want of him, but Kyle still continued to enjoy the reactions of her body. Jill's legs parted willingly as soft, hushed moans escaped from her lips. She rolled her hips toward him, and Kyle knew she was in need of him.

Kyle's finger slid into her saturated opening and Jill let out a cry of delight, which was stifled by Kyle's kiss. Jill's hands went to either side of his head as she held it to hers and continued kissing him. His tongue entered her warm mouth and his head was filled with the thought of knowing that this was his woman, his wife.

"I'm all yours, baby, so please don't make me wait any longer," Jill said breathlessly in his ear.

They were the words Kyle had wanted to hear, and without any further prompting he obliged her request. He positioned himself on top of her and allowed his hardened member to enter her. The couple had always used protection, but now there was no need, because now she was his. They both wanted to feel each other's flesh and hold nothing back.

Jill wrapped her legs around him and shifted her body so it fit perfectly to his. At first his strokes were slow and soft, but as he looked into the face of the woman who was now his wife, the words Jill had just uttered filled his mind. It felt as if he had waited an eternity to hear those words, and now he had.

Jill found herself pleasurably gasping for air as her hands squeezed Kyle's shoulders. His thrusts had become more powerful and Jill's moans of passion filled the room. Kyle could feel beads of sweat forming on his face, and moments later he felt them rolling down his back. He made love to his woman as if it would be their last time together, and he held nothing back.

Kyle raised his body and lifted one of Jill's legs and crossed it over in front of him, which enabled her to roll over onto her belly. Then he placed a hand on either side of her hips and raised her up until she was on her knees. As he was still inside her, he continued with the same needful thrusts as he made love to her.

His body stiffened as he pushed all he had into Jill, and her voiced resonated loudly as she cried out in deep pleasure and a smile of utter contentment formed on her lips. Both of their bodies lowered back down to the bed in exhaustion and Kyle lay on top of her.

After resting for a moment, Kyle moved to his side of the bed and propped himself up on an elbow. He stroked Jill's hair from her still-moist face and smiled, knowing he was the reason for its dampness. Jill was completely worn out from their making love, and he waited until her breathing took on a more normal pattern before he spoke.

"Thank you," Kyle said, making Jill's eyes open momentarily.

"For what?" Jill murmured tiredly.

"For being all mine," he said simply and kissed her closed eyelids.

Kyle wrapped Jill in his thick, strong arms and held her close to him. Though she was asleep he studied her face and watched as her chest rose and fell in a steady rhythm. It had been a wonderful day with an incredibly wonderful ending. Contentedly, he drifted off to sleep holding the woman who made his world perfect.

Chapter 20

Like fine lace, morning found the two lovers'
bodies intricately entwined. Though awake, Jill lay still
and studied Kyle's face. He was handsome, rugged,
and belonged to her alone. Gazing at his closed eyes
and thick lashes, she recalled the soft brown eyes
that lay underneath. She remembered the fire they
could hold in anger, and the passion they possessed
when inflamed with lust. A smile formed on Jill's
lips as she recalled the look he gave her as they made
love last night.

Jill's eyes rested on Kyle's strong, broad chest, as it
rose and fell in breaths that were even and deep.
With her index finger she delicately traced the outline of his muscles, and resisted the urge to plant tiny
kisses all over him.

Everything was perfect, yet something still wasn't
quite right. Deep inside her heart she knew what
her spirit craved, and that was a tiny little person, who
looked just like Kyle. But the timing wasn't right.
Though Desert Star was doing well, it was still a new
company and needed to be nursed to the powerful
public relations firm she knew it could be. It was still

what she wanted, and Jill reasoned that there would be plenty of time to start a family later.

Although they hadn't used protection last night, Jill imagined that it would be a while before she would conceive. *It took both Barbie and Mom a while before either of them got pregnant. Why should I be any different?* Jill thought. A forlorn look came across Jill's face. Slowly her eyes rose to Kyle's. He was awake and lay silently looking at her.

Upon seeing the look of concern on his face, Jill tried to appear more cheerful, but it was no use.

"What's wrong, baby?" he asked as he continued to study her.

"Nothing is wrong. I was just thinking about our flight to Jamaica. We really should be getting ready to leave," Jill said, as she turned her face away from his.

"No, I don't think we are going anywhere until you tell me what's on your mind," Kyle said, now with more determination in his voice.

Knowing that Kyle wouldn't let the issue rest until she confided in him as to what was on her mind, Jill lay back on her pillow and looked up at her husband.

"Kyle, I just love you so much," she said softly and simply.

Kyle let out a little chuckle, and then said, "I love you too, baby, but I don't think that's what's bothering you."

"In a way it is. It's like I can't get enough of you."

"Well, that's a good thing, isn't it?" he said as he began to nuzzle her neck.

"Yes, it is, but I need more."

"Whoa, you are insatiable, Mrs. Roberts."

"No, Kyle. I don't mean just sex," Jill said with a little giggle. "I mean, I want to have your baby," she finished on a more serious note.

Kyle continued to look at Jill with more tenderness filling his eyes than she had ever seen. An intriguing smile was on his lips, as she listened intently for what he had to say. They had never really talked about at what point they wanted to start having kids. All he knew was that eventually they both wanted to start a family. Kyle knew that Jill wanted to get Desert Star up and running. It was her dream and her baby, and he had promised that he wasn't going to get in the way of her goal. For now, he was simply happy having made her his wife.

"Kyle, when you had your accident I felt as though my whole world was coming to an end. I knew beyond a shadow of a doubt that I couldn't live a day without you."

"Jill, that's all behind us now. We have a life together ahead of us," he said as he gently stroked her cheek.

"I know that, but there is a part of me that wants to always hold on to a part of you. The only way I can do that is to have something that is created by the two of us."

Kyle leaned down and kissed Jill tenderly on the lips and then whispered in her ear as if he were afraid someone else would hear, "Baby, I'll never leave you. And whenever you're ready to start our family I'll give you everything you need to make the most beautiful baby the world has ever seen."

Again Kyle made her look at him with stars in her eyes. He was her soul mate, and no one in the world could ever take his place. Jill believed with all her heart that what Kyle had said was true. He would never leave her, because he lived in her heart.

As Kyle moved closer to Jill, he began planting soft kisses on her mouth. His hands sought warm, soft places to play and Jill quickly realized that Kyle wanted to pleasure her body. She glanced up at the clock and saw that they had less than two hours to get to the airport.

"Honey, we don't have time to stay in bed," Jill said.

"Why not? I thought you wanted to make a baby," Kyle said as he continued to gently play with her nipples.

"Nice try, but we can't do it right now, because we'll miss our flight."

"Jill, I need you," Kyle said as he watched her leave the bed.

"If that's true, then you should be following me," Jill said as she looked over her shoulder and gave Kyle a sexy wink. With that, Kyle leaped out of bed and ran to catch up with Jill as she entered the bathroom.

Jill turned on the water and adjusted its temperature. Then the two lovers got into the tub and began bathing each other. They enjoyed the feel of each other's skin as their fingers slid through the lather. Having finished bathing, they continued their playful cleansing, which became romantic lovemaking.

Through the mist of the steam Jill could barely see her lover's face, as he pressed her body against the shower wall. Kyle's tongue played hide-and-seek in Jill's mouth, as he hoisted her leg up. He pushed his hardened member into her flesh, and moans of delight escaped from her throat.

It was what she had wanted, and he was what she seemed to always crave. Jill had thought that their being married would bring something special to their lovemaking, and it did. Now she gave her body to him with uninhibited passion. Nothing was taboo as long as she was with him.

Jill rolled her hips back and forth as she gave as much pleasure as she was receiving. She came long before he did, but continued to make Kyle feel good until he was ready to explode, and he did.

"I really wish we had taken that later flight," he said breathlessly, and he lowered her leg.

"I know, but once we're on the plane I'll let you sleep. Well, that's if you don't want to become part of the mile high club."

"Jill!" Kyle said in shocked amusement.

"I was just teasing," she said as she left the shower giggling.

Jill dried off and did her hair, and then the couple quickly dressed. They ordered breakfast from room service, but it tasted nothing like the wonderful morning meals Kyle cooked. Still the couple ate, knowing that the food on the plane would be far worse. When they finished eating they called for the bellhop. He arrived shortly and took care of their luggage. When they arrived in the lobby, they went to the registration desk and checked out of the hotel. After they finished taking care of business, they went outside and found their bags were already being placed in the limousine.

Jill had chosen the hotel because of its close proximity to the airport, a move she was happy she had maneuvered, since she and Kyle had spent more time in the shower than she had anticipated. Still, they would arrive at the airport with enough time to catch their flight.

When they arrived, the chauffeur pulled in front of their airline. He got out and retrieved their suitcases from the trunk. Jill and Kyle followed the man to the curbside check-in. Kyle thanked the man for his assistance and then tipped him.

After they were finished checking in, they walked inside the building and toward their terminal. As Jill and Kyle arrived, the passengers were beginning to board the aircraft. Once inside the plane, the couple took their seats in first class. A flight attendant had offered them a meal, but the couple declined it and instead opted for coffee.

Hours later they landed in Miami and had to change airlines. Jamaica Air would take them to their final destination. The next flight lasted almost two hours. It was late afternoon when the newlyweds arrived in Montego Bay, Jamaica. It had seemed like a never-ending day, and though they were anxious to get to their hotel, Jill was equally as anxious to go out and see some of the sights she had read about.

They retrieved their luggage and headed outside to hail a taxi. The weather was hot, which Jill was accustomed to, but the humidity took her by surprise, as she began to perspire without exertion.

A taxi stopped and Kyle opened the door for Jill to enter the vehicle. The driver quickly got out and started putting their luggage into his trunk, and then everyone got back inside the car.

"And where I be takin' you today, man?" the cab-driver said in a carefree tone, with a heavy Jamaican accent.

"Sandals Montego Bay Resort," Kyle told him.

As the taxi pulled off into the traffic, Jill sat back in her seat and enjoyed the view. With Kyle's arm around her shoulder, she looked out the window and saw beautiful, tall palm trees swaying with the breeze. The late afternoon sun gave no evidence of relinquishing its heat from the earth's surface, and Jill dabbed her forehead with a tissue. The cab's air-conditioning was obviously broken or the driver would have had it running, she imagined.

Jill silently thanked her lucky stars that the ride from

the airport to Sandals had been a relatively short one. She credited the time difference and the wedding as the reason she felt so tired, but the minute she stepped out of the cab she felt exhilaration take over her body. Jill looked around at the impressive entrance to the resort, and fell in love with its charm. She was surrounded by four huge, white columns, which supported the carport, and beautiful palm trees graced the driveway.

While their luggage was being attended to the couple went inside the resort and walked toward the registration desk. Kyle told the clerk who they were and she rapidly prepared all their documents.

"Here you are, Mr. Roberts," she said in a pleasant voice, which was just as thick with a Jamaican accent as their taxi driver's had been. "If you will follow Roscoe, he will take you to the honeymoon beachfront concierge room," she added as she handed the keys to the man standing next to Kyle.

"Thank you," Kyle replied. Then he turned and took Jill's hand as the two followed Roscoe out of the resort's lobby.

Minutes later, Roscoe was opening the door to their honeymoon suite. While Kyle was busy with Roscoe, Jill looked around and let her senses absorb the beauty of the area. Rich mahogany furniture filled the room while matching tropical-flower-printed fabric graced the bed and windows. It was a rather large room with giant white French doors that led out to a patio that gave them direct access to the beach.

Jill stopped walking momentarily to pick a bird-of-paradise up from its vase, and then she continued to walk out onto the patio. There she paused and took in the magnificent view of the white sandy beach. She let her gaze drift even farther out into the blue-green waters of the Caribbean Sea. Jill inhaled deeply and let the salt air fill her lungs, and she felt as if she had breathed in all the goodness life had to offer. When she slowly released it, it was as if she could feel a lifetime's worth of anxiety and anticipation leave her body.

It was at that moment she felt strong arms enclose her body as her back was pressed into a muscular chest. Kyle's lips lightly tickled her earlobe as he spoke in a sexy, hushed voice.

"Is this what you wanted?"

"This is exactly what I wanted. You did an excellent job on planning the honeymoon," Jill said as she continued to look out over the water.

"Oh, I've only just begun. I have a week's worth of wonderful things planned for you."

"I hope you do," Jill said as she rubbed his arm.

Turning around to face her husband, Jill tilted her head back and Kyle began to kiss her. Over the past year she had learned to read him, and right now his kisses weren't a prelude to sex, but a gesture of love. His kisses were light and soft and he pulled away and looked at Jill with all the gratitude any man could have for a woman.

"Nothing in this world gives me more pleasure than knowing that you are now my wife," he said as his eyes pierced Jill's soul to the very core.

"And nothing gives me more pleasure than knowing that I'm yours."

"Are you hungry?" he asked as his fingers gently stroked her cheek.

"You know I am. You should be too, since we haven't had lunch yet and it's almost dinnertime."

"Why don't you go and freshen up and I'll read the brochures and see what restaurants are on the property?"

"Sounds good to me," Jill said as she gave Kyle's lips a final kiss and then left the patio.

Jill quickly grabbed an outfit and her tote and went into the bathroom, which was very impressive as well. She set her tote on the stool in front of the vanity. She opened the bag and arranged her essential items on the table. Then she turned on the water to fill the large tub and poured a handful of her jasmine-scented bath salts in.

Beautiful cocoa-brown ceramic tile ran across the floor and the walls, and big, thick, fluffy white towels hung decoratively and waited to envelope her body in their softness. Jill undressed and slipped into the warm water. Instantly she felt her taut muscles begin to relax. She closed her eyes and allowed herself to enjoy the peaceful moment. Jill didn't allow thoughts of Desert Star to enter her mind; now was the time to enjoy herself as well as her husband. She had made a promise to herself that she wouldn't even call to check and see how things were going at the office. Bebe was perfectly capable of handling things alone; besides, the business would be there when she got back. However, her honeymoon was a once-in-a-lifetime thing.

Startled, Jill opened her eyes as she realized that she was drifting off to sleep. She didn't know how long she had been in the tub, but as she looked at her wrinkled fingers, she realized it must have been a long time.

Taking a thick towel, Jill got out of the tub and dried herself off. She spent the next twenty minutes primping before she entered the bedroom.

"Wow, you never cease to amaze me," Kyle said as he looked Jill over from head to toe.

Jill wore a lavender, ruffle-hem halter dress. Gold hoop earrings dangled from her ears as a matching lavender headband kept her hair in place. The black and lavender kitten-heeled sandals she wore gave her a sexy stride, as she walked over toward Kyle.

"Thank you," she said as she came to stand only millimeters away from him. He reached out for her, but she leaned away. "Oh no, you have to freshen up, so we can get out of here and get something to eat."

"Okay, I'll be ready in a few minutes," Kyle said reluctantly, but headed into the bathroom.

When Kyle had left the room, Jill went back out onto the patio and sat down in one of the chaise longues. The sun was beginning to dip low in the sky, and hues of pink and purple filled the horizon. The view almost reminded Jill of home. The sparkling waters were the only difference.

For an instant Jill toyed with the idea of calling Bebe again, but quickly changed her mind. Even if she did call home, Bebe probably wouldn't give her any information. More than anything, Bebe had wanted Jill to enjoy this time with Kyle. The workaholic in her would have to be kept at bay.

"Are you ready to go?" Kyle said as he stood in the doorway putting on his Rolex.

At the sound of his voice Jill turned and looked up at Kyle. He was dressed casually in a cream-colored cotton shirt with several buttons undone from the neck down, and dark brown slacks that reminded her of his gorgeous skin tone. The sight of him was enough to make her heart skip a beat. She could smell his cologne. He wore Curve, which always made Jill want to taste his skin. *No, not right now,* she said, smiling at the thought.

"Yes, I'm ready." She stood up and walked to where he stood. "You look good enough to eat," she said as she playfully nibbled on his lower lip.

"I'm going to hold you to that. We better get going because I'm starving."

"Okay," Jill said.

She grabbed her purse and they left the room. Kyle had decided they would have dinner at the Bayside Restaurant. When they arrived, Jill was immediately taken in by the romantic atmosphere. Square tables were adorned by light pink linen tablecloths, and candlelight illuminated each one. Jill and Kyle were seated at the waterfront.

They each ordered a blue mountain salad, before dining on the main course of jerk chicken and prime rib. The couple laughed and talked as they ate, as each realized the profoundness of the moment, which was how deeply in love and compatible they were.

"Do you think that in ten years we'll still be like this?" Jill asked.

"No, I don't," Kyle replied simply. He looked at the shocked expression on Jill's face before adding, "I think we will have gone places emotionally that will only serve to bring us closer," he added, which brought a look of relief to Jill's face.

"I think you're right," she said, smiling.

When they had finished with dinner they decided to share dessert, which was a decadent dark chocolate mousse. Using one spoon, the couple took turns feeding each other.

After they finished with their meal, the couple left and strolled around the grounds of the property. Steel drums could be heard, and Jill and Kyle stopped to dance in the courtyard. It had been a long day and they were too beat to be adventurous, so they ended up at the desk of the concierge, where they made plans for tomorrow.

Hours later, the couple found themselves back in

their bedroom. A good night's sleep was the only thing on both their minds, but they didn't miss the opportunity to enjoy one another's warm, bare skin, as they cuddled the night away.

Every day the couple spent in Jamaica was filled with fun and adventure. Jill and Kyle did everything from taking a trip to Ocho Rios to visit Dolphin Cove, to deep-sea fishing and snorkeling. They took tons of pictures as well as made a CD of their trip. They had a chance to visit Negril, and did a little shopping and dining while they took in the sights.

One afternoon, after Jill and Kyle had spent the morning in bed, feeding each other fruit-filled crepes topped with whipped cream, they finally decided to take a stroll on the beach. She dressed in a blue, asymmetrical halter top and a white sarong. Kyle had put on a pair of khaki shorts and a floral-printed shirt.

The love-struck couple exited their suite from the patio, and began to enjoy a long walk on the sun-drenched beach. They strolled hand in hand, and Jill allowed her senses to take in every pleasurable aspect the day had to offer. She felt the hot, white sand crunch under her feet with every step she took. The sun was bright and unyielding as it cast down its rays. Jill looked out into the ocean and noticed that a light, tropical breeze rocked the water into small waves, which made the liquid shimmer and sparkle as if a billion diamonds lay upon its surface.

Then she gazed into Kyle's handsome face, and Jill smiled knowing he was all hers. Feeling the strong hand that held hers, she knew it would supply all that she needed. The island overflowed with fine, tapered-waisted, broad-shouldered brothers, whose chocolate-colored skin tones were twice kissed by the sun, but they couldn't hold a candle to her Kyle.

The Jamaican accent was sensual, and would captivate and entice you into acting in ways you otherwise would not. When the men spoke a woman wanted to listen, and was enchanted with his every word. Jill let out a slight giggle as she imagined that Sharon, though faithful to her husband, would still find a way to give these men a run for their money.

"What's so funny?" Kyle said as he looked at Jill in amusement.

"Nothing, really, I'm just thinking about Sharon," she said, with laughter still in her voice.

"Don't tell me any more," Kyle said, smiling. Knowing how spoiled his sister-in-law was, he could only imagine what Jill was thinking about her.

Jill squeezed his hand as they continued to walk, assured that what they had would last forever.

On their third day in Jamaica the couple went horseback riding. After eating a quick breakfast that had been delivered by room service, they left the hotel to embark on their tour. The two-hour journey took them from the lush green mountains of the country to the edge of the coastline.

For a time they raced along the shore, and Jill laughed wildly as she passed Kyle. The horse's thunderous gallop splashed water on them, but the spontaneous couple gave no care. They were doing exactly what they wanted to do, and that was to have fun.

When they slowed their horses to a walk, Jill was able to squeeze the water from her hair. The sparkling, emerald-green water glistened as the sun cast its glow from above. She thought back to their business trip to Florida, and noticed that the water looked nothing like what she saw now.

Jill glanced over at Kyle, who seemed happy and content. She knew what he was thinking and how he was feeling, because she felt the same way. Kyle turned to see her smiling at him and decided to share his thoughts with her.

"Riding like this makes me think of Patches," he said, patting the horse as it trotted through the water.

"I know," Jill said as she rode alongside Kyle.

They rode bareback toward the thick greenery, which was thick with beautiful trees and flowering plants. At first Jill thought that Kyle would turn the horses around, but he continued into the thick forest. Several feet inside the brush Kyle dismounted and tied his reins to a nearby tree. Then he walked over to Jill's horse and helped her to dismount and tied her horse up in the same manner. He then took her hand and walked a few feet farther into the deep, tree-canopied forest.

Jill didn't say anything but let her senses absorb her surroundings. The same kind of beauty she found in Colorado existed here, but in a different manner. Mountains were mountains, but here they were coated with lush green plant life, and in Colorado, with snow. Both elements were of natural creation, and possessed beauty in their own right.

Beautiful flowers, including oleander, graced their path. Jill listened as the ground crunched softly under their feet from fallen leaves. She could hear birds overhead as they flew from one branch to another. Sunlight filtered through the trees as she looked up in order to spot several brightly colored parrots.

Kyle stopped walking and turned to face Jill. He took her in his arms and began to kiss her long and lovingly on the lips. Closing her eyes, she put her arms around his neck and returned his passionate advances. Jill felt his warm hands on her back as he pressed her body against his, but her eyes flew open when she realized what he was trying to do.

"Kyle, don't take my swimsuit off," she whispered as if someone would hear her.

"Why not? I want to make love to you," he said simply.

"But someone might see us."

"Who? We are out here all alone. Jill, you can't tell me that you have never dreamed of making love in a tropical forest near the beach? This area is filled with ebony and coconut palm trees, and they will keep what we do from prying eyes," Kyle said, and then he let his tongue softly run the length of Jill's neck.

It was a gesture that softened Jill's resolve. He was right; she had thought of making love outside in the open, and knew that the natural setting would only heighten the experience. *It would be a shame to go home and miss out on the experience,* she reasoned. Kyle resumed unfastening the back of Jill's bikini and she didn't stop him this time.

Jill's purple bikini top fell to the ground and she could feel Kyle's warm palms cupping each of her breasts. He delicately sucked one nipple and then the other, as Jill ran her fingers through his hair while he did.

Kyle kissed between each breast and then left a trail of kisses from her cleavage to well past her belly button. Jill could feel his fingers on her flesh as they slid her swimsuit bottom slowly down her thighs, and she stepped out of it.

When he was finished undressing her Jill did likewise to him. She slowly pulled the string that secured his trunks to his waist. Then she pulled them down, lowering her own body until her hands, like his trunks, rested on the soft earth. Eye level with his erect member, Jill found herself waiting in eager anticipation to begin making love in the serene setting.

When Jill stood up, Kyle began kissing her again. He French-kissed her as he guided her backward to the smooth bark of a tall tree. There he pressed her body against its trunk while allowing his hands to stimulate her body.

With Mother Nature providing all that they needed to produce an environment conducive to romance, Jill gave herself to her husband willingly and without reservation.

With powerful arms holding her up, Kyle moved between Jill's legs and penetrated her. Their lovemaking started out as it always did. Kyle gave Jill only a touch of what was to come, which was just enough to make her want more.

Her breath was halting and deep as she tried to move her body closer in order to receive more of him, but Kyle continued his game.

"Kyle, I need all of you," she finally said. Her breath caressed his cheek as she said the words.

It was all he needed to make him obey her command. The next thrust Jill received from him was strong and deep and sent pains of pleasure through her body. A gentle rain began to fall, covering the lovers' bodies. Jill felt the warm droplets as they soaked her hair. She pressed her hands against Kyle's wet back and held on to his shoulders as she moaned loud and uncontrollably. Jill's legs wrapped around Kyle as they both arrived at the point of pleasure that released their love.

Kyle lowered Jill's legs to the ground, but continued to hold her close to him. He smiled back at Jill as he realized that she had enjoyed herself just as much as he had, if not more.

"That was awesome," Jill said as she stroked his neck with delicate fingers.

"It was more than awesome, but I can't think of any other words to describe what you just did to me," Kyle said as he stepped away.

They quickly dressed and walked toward the horses holding hands. The couple mounted the horses and went back to where their excursion began.

When they returned to the resort, Jill and Kyle went to their hotel room to freshen up. When they had showered and changed, the couple went to the Oleander Restaurant. It was a sophisticated dining room with crimson-colored chairs underneath white-linen-covered tablecloths. Beautiful gold-and-floral-printed draperies hung from giant custom windows, and Jill felt like a queen as she was seated at a table with a breathtaking view of the sea.

Quiet conversations were heard coming from a room filled with mostly newlyweds. Jill enjoyed the seven-course meal, and she especially liked the Jamaican steamfish with Mahi-mahi. Jill and Kyle's conversation was low and intimate as they talked about their day and promises of tomorrow. For dessert they had Caribbean cream with banana rum and raisins, and again they used only one spoon.

It was getting late, but when they finished dinner the couple decided to go on a midnight cruise. They walked to the dock and boarded the fifty-five-foot yacht, then were off sailing under a sky that was quickly giving way to nightfall.

They sat at a table close to a rail and sipped Jamaican rum. The steel band played festive music and soon Jill and Kyle found themselves on the dance floor. It seemed as if they had been dancing for hours when they returned laughing and breathless to their table.

"I don't remember ever being this exhausted after dancing at Roland's," Kyle was the first to say.

"I know. I feel like we were doing a marathon," Jill said, laughing and taking a sip of her drink.

She looked up to see a star-filled sky. They twinkled brightly and reminded her of her nights on the patio when she first came to Durango.

"What are you thinking about?" Kyle asked after seeing the reminiscent expression on Jill's face.

"I was just thinking about the first few weeks I spent at A Special Place. Sometimes I would sit out on the patio and just look up at the stars and dream."

"Were you dreaming of me?"

"I guess in a way I was," she said, smiling.

The four-hour sailing trip was just about over and the band played one last tune. It was a slow song and Kyle stood and held out his hand. Jill placed her hand in his and stood. She followed him to the dance floor and like the gentle Jamaican breeze, floated into Kyle's arms.

As they moved slowly to the rhythm of the music, Jill rested her head on his chest. With bodies embracing and fingers entwined, the couple danced their last dance aboard the yacht.

When they returned, the boat emptied its jovial passengers onto the dock. There wasn't a guest around that wasn't a little tipsy, but no one complained. Jamaica was the place to leave all your worries and cares behind, and live the carefree life.

Kyle's arm was around Jill's waist. It was the way many of the couples departed the vessel, and as they made their way back to their room, Jill wondered how many of them were newlyweds and how many just came trying to seek out a passionate experience.

The thought reminded her of her plans for the evening with Kyle. Tonight she would make his mouth water as she made his wildest dreams come true. She would make him see her through different eyes and realize that she had what it took to keep him happy and content until they were very old and gray, and maybe beyond that.

"All that Jamaican rum has you as happy as can be," Kyle said as he looked at Jill's face, which held a mixture of mischief and excitement.

"I guess so, but I wouldn't say it's only the rum that has me this way," she said, smiling up at him.

As they arrived at the door to their room, Jill blocked Kyle's entrance and placed her palm gently on his chest. Through thick lashes she looked up coyly at him.

"Honey, I really would like another drink. Would you mind going to the bar and getting me a rum runner?"

"I wouldn't mind at all," Kyle said unsuspectingly. With a kiss on her full lips he left, leaving Jill to enter the room by herself.

As soon as Jill was inside she grabbed her tote and pulled out several candles and lit them. She placed them near the love seat, as well as on the nightstands. Then she quickly went inside the bathroom to prepare herself for the night. Jill knew it would be no time at all before Kyle returned, so she worked as quickly as possible.

There was a knock on the bathroom door and Kyle tried to turn the knob.

"Babe, are you all right?" he asked in a voice filled with concern.

"Yes, I'm fine," Jill said calmly as she continued to dry her body. "Why don't you sit on the loveseat? I'll be out in just a minute."

"Why didn't you wait for me? I wanted to take a bath with you."

"No, honey, not this time. I'll only be a few minutes more and then I'll be out."

"Okay, but don't take too long—your drink is getting warm," Kyle said reluctantly as he went to sit down.

Moments later the bathroom door opened and Jill stepped out. As soon as Kyle's eyes fell on her he sat up and was completely mesmerized by what he saw. With jaw slacked and eyes unblinking, he watched as Jill walked gracefully past him in a pair of black stilettos. The beautiful black and blue sheer chiffon fabric caught the wind as she walked and floated tantalizingly across her thighs. As Jill turned toward the entertainment center Kyle could see that the outfit was made to make him weak in the knees, and it did as he looked at the peekaboo holes cut in the side, revealing brown skin that made him want to reach out and touch it.

As Jill turned on a CD, the room was filled with the deep sexy voice of Petey Pablo. With her back facing him, Jill leaned forward and touched her toes, giving Kyle a good look at her shapely, long legs. She came back up slowly, letting her own fingers glide across her legs as she did. Doing a booty shake that made Kyle's heart quake, Jill moved closer to him, but not close enough to allow him to touch her. The bass of the music filled the room as Jill continued to dance. She gave Kyle sexy little glances over her shoulder as she continued to titillate him.

Kyle's smile was filled with awe and pleasure, as he

watched his wife dance for him. He was completely aware of all the passionate and erotic feelings she was stirring inside him as she danced to the beat and brushed her breasts with a fan made of feathers and in the same colors as her outfit. Kyle saw before him a woman who was completely in control of her sexuality and felt uninhibited when it came to pleasing her man.

When the music came to an end, Kyle found his lap filled with the mythical creature he called his wife. Jill sat straddling Kyle's thighs with her own. With eyes as slightly opened as her lips, Jill planted a small kiss on Kyle's mouth. As she sat on his lap she could tell that she had pleased him well, but still she asked the question.

"How did you like that, baby?" she said breathlessly against his lips.

"Wow! I don't know the words to express how you captivate me. Jill, thank you so much for being my woman," Kyle said as he stroked her back.

It was all she really wanted to hear, and Jill smiled as she began to kiss him full on the mouth. She silently thanked Bebe for taking her to Sally's Hide-A-Way. And she was thankful to Sharon as well, for teaching her how to make your man have eyes only for you.

Kyle's tongue found its way past her parted lips, as his hands found a way to get her out of the outfit. However, he did leave her stilettos on her feet as he made love to her, preferring to enjoy the other side of her sexual personality a little longer.

Chapter 21

Jill and Kyle had gone shopping at the straw market before their late afternoon flight. Between the two of them they had bought so many souvenirs that they had to buy three extra suitcases. They ate in town at a little restaurant that had the best Caribbean jerk chicken and rice Jill had ever tasted. The couple ate until they were stuffed, and hoped that the meal would hold them until they were halfway through their flight, since they hated the food on the plane.

Jill had their bags packed and at the door when the bellman arrived. As Kyle attended him, Jill leaned against the doorway and looked out at the sea. With her arms folded across her chest she gently hugged herself. Warm thoughts filled her head as she recalled their stay in Jamaica. Her honeymoon was filled with the stuff dreams are made of—for that matter, so was her life.

Some people dreaded going home after a wonderful vacation, but not Jill. Everything that was important was in the States, and she couldn't wait to return. As she stood admiring the sun-drenched sky, her mind returned to the romantic horseback ride she and Kyle had taken only days ago. He had been full of surprises too, and she loved his spontaneity.

"Babe, are you ready to go?" Kyle said in a love voice with his lips slightly brushing her ear. His arms went instinctively around her waist as he stood behind her and looked out at the ocean as well.

"Yes, I'm ready to go home," Jill said simply.

She turned around and kissed his lips tenderly, then took her thumb and gently rubbed away the lipstick her lips had left on his. Smiling, he took Jill by the hand and the couple left the room for the last time.

They made their way to the lobby and checked out of the hotel. The doorman got them a taxi and put the luggage in the trunk. Kyle held the car door open as Jill got inside, and then he entered as well.

The ride to the airport was quiet and the couple sat holding hands and looking out the window as they rode.

Once at the airport, Jill and Kyle checked their luggage and waited for their flight to board. The ticket agent told them it would be a few minutes, so Jill had a seat while Kyle went to get them something to drink. When he returned he had an ice-cold Coke for each of them.

Jill wiped the sweat from her brow with a napkin as she sipped the cold drink. The ride in the taxi had been hot, with only warm air blowing in the window as they rode. She was anxious to board the air-conditioned plane, sit back, and relax for a while.

Kyle was hot too, but made no mention of it either. He tried to take Jill's mind off the heat by talking about the family.

"I bet we received a lot of phone messages while we were gone, and I know most of them will be from your mom," Kyle said teasingly as he took a long drink of his soda.

"Why do you think my mom would call? She knows we only arrive home tonight."

"Yeah, but she was so excited about our trip, and I know she can't wait to hear all about it. Besides, you're her baby, and calling probably made her feel close to you."

Jill sipped her soda and thought about what Kyle had just said. He was right; her mother would probably call even though they weren't home. Knowing her mother, she would have made up reasons to leave messages. Jill made a mental note to call her mother first as soon as she got back home.

"I wonder how Bebe is doing. I hope no major problems came up while I was away. I'd hate for her to handle any mess alone."

"Jill, Bebe isn't alone, she has Monica and Amelia. You have a very capable business partner," Kyle said matter-of-factly.

"I know."

"And you two have taken the time to hire very efficient and knowledgeable staff."

"That's true too, but I—"

"I think you need to trust them, babe. You all are a team, and when one of you has something going on in her life, the others pull together and hold down the fort."

Jill smiled, knowing her husband was right. Wow. The idea of her having a husband still blew her mind. She dropped her head knowing that Kyle was right. In the revelation that she now had someone to call her own, Jill's soul felt safe and her heart secure.

She lifted her head to gaze into his soft brown

eyes. She saw there all that mattered to her, and that was love. Jill leaned forward and kissed him.

"Thank you," she said softly.

"You're welcome," he replied quietly.

It was announced that their flight was now boarding. Kyle threw their empty soda cans away, and then they gathered their carry-on bags. The couple boarded the small plane and took their seats. During their conversation in the airport, Jill had forgotten how hot she was. Now, sitting in the air-conditioned craft, she rested her head on Kyle's shoulder and fell asleep. Soon the aircraft was in the air and headed for Florida.

It wasn't a long flight, but when they arrived in Miami, it was almost 5:00 p.m. Once again they changed planes to one that would take them to Colorado. When they arrived in Colorado, they still had to catch a commuter plane. The three-hour time difference would get them to Durango before 9:00 p.m.

Jill and Kyle departed the plane and gathered their luggage from the baggage claim area. Kyle piled their suitcases on a cart and then the couple made their way out of the airport. He looked around hoping Tony would be waiting, but he couldn't spot him.

"Did Tony know what time our flight was arriving?" Jill asked in a travel-weary voice as she continued to search for Tony's vehicle.

"He should, I gave him a copy of all our flight numbers," Kyle said, letting a hint of irritation fill his voice.

"I think I see him," Jill said as she pointed to a familiar vehicle.

Kyle saw him too, and stepped out to the curb and began waving his brother down.

Tony pulled up in front of them and parked.

He got out and opened the hatch as he said, "Hey, big brother, I thought you wouldn't mind if I brought your Navigator."

"No, I don't mind. I'm just glad you're here," Kyle said, smiling as he hugged his baby brother.

"Hey, sis, how was Jamaica?" Tony asked Jill as he hugged her, too.

"It was wonderful, Tony. How have things been here?"

"Couldn't be better," he replied as he helped Kyle put the suitcases inside the SUV.

Jill's eyes fell on the now empty interior, and she noticed that Bebe hadn't come with Tony. Curiosity got the better of her as she asked, "Where is Bebe?"

"She's still at the office. She has been working on several accounts, but the Mulher Bela account is done. She and Monica worked overtime on that one," he said as he closed the hatch.

Kyle turned around to see the worried expression on Jill's face. She had been a little disappointed that she wasn't able to go to Brazil to meet with the client and had left the major account in Bebe's and Monica's laps. Though she knew both women were extremely capable, she didn't feel as though she had done her share of work on the account.

Kyle could see that she was fighting the urge to stop by the office and check on things, but this time he offered no advice. He knew that Desert Star had been Jill's dream come true. It was still her baby, and she wanted to do everything possible to help it thrive. But the reason for promoting Monica and hiring Amelia was so that they could have time for each other. Now he would have to let Jill figure out what she wanted to do; after all, he had told her he could handle her being a businesswoman.

Kyle's eyes left Jill's face, but she knew what he
was thinking. She had just arrived home from her
honeymoon. Though every fiber of her being wanted
to be at the office, she knew that her place was with
Kyle. She reasoned that Desert Star would be there
Monday morning and that was when she would go
into work. For now, she was happy to be with her new
husband, and she wanted to let Kyle know that he was
and always would be her top priority.

"Well, I'm sure they did an excellent job. I'll have
to call Bebe tomorrow," she said, letting her voice give
no evidence of care.

Kyle walked toward her and opened the door. He
assisted Jill as she got inside and sat down. "That's my
girl," he whispered in her ear before softly kissing her
cheek.

Tony climbed in the backseat and Kyle went around
and got in the driver's seat. He sat for a moment and
adjusted the position of the seat as well as the mirrors.

"Kyle, you're not that much taller than I am, man.
What are you doing?" Tony said in playful irritation.

"Oh yes, I am too," Kyle said, laughing as he pulled
out into traffic.

"Only by a couple inches."

"And a few pounds," Kyle said, continuing the playful banter. He had missed his brothers more than he
cared to say, but quickly enjoyed reconnecting with
Tony.

The three family members laughed and talked as
they drove. Tony filled them in on all that had gone
on while they were away. Jill was surprised to find out
that Grace was dating someone. It was a local guy, but
Jill didn't know him.

They pulled up in front of Tony's cabin and he got
out of the vehicle. As Jill looked around, she saw that

Bebe's car was still missing, and knew she was putting in a long, hard day at Desert Star. She would see Bebe tomorrow and get caught up on all the particulars.

"Good night, Kyle, sis. Bebe and I will be over tomorrow," Tony said as he tapped the rim of his hat.

"Good night, Tony," Jill said.

"See you tomorrow," Kyle yelled after him.

As he walked up the steps to his cabin door, Tony raised his hand in a gesture of farewell.

Kyle pulled off driving in the direction of their cabin. He looked over at Jill, who was gazing at the sky and had a contented smile on her face. Her expression caused him to smile as well.

"What's on your mind, beautiful?" he asked as he reached for her hand with his free one.

At hearing his voice, Jill turned her head to face him. She kept the gentle look on her face, but her smile broadened a little as her eyes met his.

"I was just thinking how good it is to be back home. Don't get me wrong, Jamaica was exciting and enchanting, but I'm glad to be back where I belong."

"Do you mean back in Durango, so you can get back to Desert Star?" Kyle asked, hoping that was not the case.

"No, silly. I mean that I want us to get started on our lives. Now is the time for us to settle down and really act like husband and wife, not just an engaged couple that is living together."

"Aha, well, I just hope that we don't get too complacent being with each other, because I really would like to see more of the sexy siren that enchanted her husband with her lap dance," Kyle said with more pleading in his voice than he had intended to project.

"Don't worry, she'll come out on occasion." Jill laughed as she realized that all the planning and preparing that she had done to create the tantalizing woman of Kyle's dreams had paid off.

"Jill, have you ever danced for anyone like that before?" Kyle asked, trying to sound nonchalant.

"No, I haven't."

"You certainly dance like a professional," Kyle said with a hint of relief in his tone after hearing Jill's answer.

"Thank you, but I only dance like that for my husband," she said as she picked his hand up and brought it to her lips. Planting a gentle kiss on his hand made him turn to face her again.

"I don't think I'll ever get tired of telling you how much I love you," he said in words that deeply resonated his true feelings.

"Good, let's keep it like that because I feel the same way."

For the rest of the short drive home the couple were content to ride in silence and hold each other's hand. When they arrived at the cabin it was dark outside. It had been a long day and they were exhausted. After Kyle parked they decided to bring only the necessary items inside, and save the rest of the luggage for tomorrow.

The weary couple went inside. Briefly, they stopped in the kitchen for something to drink. Jill listened to phone messages while Kyle looked through the mail that had been left on the table by Eric. As Kyle had guessed, there were several messages from her mother, but none were urgent. Maddie mostly had called to say that things were fine in Pittsburgh and that she missed Jill very much.

She missed her mother too, as well as Barbie and her family. It was wonderful having all the people she loved so close. Now they were gone, and Jill wondered when she would get to see them again.

"We are still getting tons of wedding cards," he said, breaking Jill's concentration. "Any important phone messages?" he asked as he walked over toward her.

"Not really. You were right, I did get a bunch of calls from my mom. She didn't have anything important to say, but I can tell that she already misses me."

There really wasn't anything Kyle could say or do to alleviate the sadness Jill felt over missing her mom, but he knew of one thing that might cheer her up.

Taking her hand he said, "Let's go out back and say hello to Patches."

Jill did smile as Kyle continued to hold her hand and led her to the back door. The couple went outside into the fresh mountain air. They went down the steps of the deck and walked out a bit into the yard. There Kyle gave an ear-piercing whistle, and moments later his beautiful stallion was standing before them.

Patches was almost as happy to see Kyle and Jill as they were to see him. Kyle patted the horse's head as Jill stroked his mane. It was obvious that Tony had been taking good care of the horse while they were away. Patches's coat felt as soft as silk, and Kyle checked and saw that fresh water had been supplied.

Kyle produced several carrots from his pocket and gave them to Patches. The horse pranced happily in front of them before taking his treat. After Patches had eaten, Kyle patted his side, letting the horse know he was free to leave, but the animal stood and continued to let Jill enjoy rubbing his coat.

"I did miss this," Jill finally said.

"What?"

"I missed being at home, looking out at the mountains, Patches, and our family and friends."

"You're not going to include Desert Star?" Kyle asked suspiciously.

"Yes, I did miss work, too, but didn't you notice that I didn't call to check on how things were going once?" she replied with a note of accomplishment in her voice.

"Yes, I did notice, and I'm proud of you," Kyle said, now taking Jill in his arms and looking deep into her moonlit eyes.

"Well, you should be, because it was kind of hard for me to do," Jill admitted as she let out a giggle, and Kyle laughed too.

"I thought it was."

"My career is still very important to me, but I am quickly realizing that I can have and handle being a business owner and a wife. My life with you has to take precedence because you mean the world to me," Jill said as she looked up into his warm, brown eyes.

"And you mean the world to me, babe," Kyle said as he kissed her slightly parted lips.

With his arms around her waist the couple returned to the cabin and Kyle closed the sliding glass door and locked it behind him.

Before heading upstairs, Jill got the lemonade from the refrigerator. She poured them both a glass and then handed one to Kyle.

"What do you have planned for tomorrow?" he asked.

"First of all, I'm going to sleep in, and when I do wake up I think I'll serve my handsome husband breakfast in bed."

Kyle smiled at Jill as she told him of her plans, and then he said, "After I finish eating I have to go to the ranch and check on things."

"Kyle, I thought we'd spend Sunday together," Jill said disappointedly.

"And we can, but I have to get some reports ready for the investors that are due Monday morning. The men will want to get paid on time, so I have to do payroll."

"Can't you do all of that from home?"

"Yes, I could, but I need to pick up their time sheets and get some of the statistical information from Bebe. I'm hoping she left it in her office at the resort. Jill, I am still in charge and I still have to check on things."

"Now who's the workaholic?" Jill said in playful irritation.

"Oh, no, ma'am," Kyle said as he set his empty glass down on the counter. He moved closer to her and put his arms around Jill, and began kissing the length of her neck. "I know just when to be home and give you my undivided attention."

"Yes, you do," Jill replied as she too set her glass down. "And I'm learning how to do that as well."

"When I get back from the ranch I would like to spend the rest of the day at home, just you and me enjoying each other's company. We won't even answer the phone," Kyle said hopefully, knowing that Jill would arrange to talk to Bebe while he was gone.

"That sounds good to me," she replied as she took Kyle's hand and led him upstairs to their bedroom.

Standing next to the bed, Jill began to undress Kyle, and when she was finished he did likewise to her. Though they were both tired they couldn't spend the first night in the cabin as husband and wife without christening the bed as such.

Jill sat down on the edge of the bed and slid her body back. Then she lay back and beckoned Kyle to come to her. Making love several times since getting married had been new and exciting, but it didn't hold a candle to the love they made in their own bed.

Jill's legs parted as her husband moved between

them. Kyle kissed her from her navel to her lips before allowing his body to come in full contact with hers. His tongue gently probed the inside of her mouth. Jill wrapped her legs around his in an effort to prevent his decision to force an extended round of foreplay. Tonight she wanted him to give her what she needed and as quickly as possible.

Unable to change his position and knowing of Jill's intense desire to have him inside her, Kyle gave her what her body craved. He always made sure he pleasured her in as many ways as he could before bringing her to the height of passion, but tonight he was thankful she didn't want that. Kyle's body was just as ready for hers as she was for him.

He entered her gently with strokes that enflamed her velvet softness. Before she had time to take another breath Kyle began to penetrate her with great force and urgency. Jill's moans grew louder as she arched her back to receive all of him. Her fingertips dug into his shoulders as Kyle got what he desperately needed from her.

Jill's body lay tired and motionless from receiving so much fulfillment in such a short amount of time, but it was what she needed. Inside her body she could feel the release of his seed, and it made her thankful that she was a woman—that she was his woman.

Kyle's body arched as he delivered the last drops of his love inside her, and then his body collapsed in exhaustion on top of her. Jill inhaled slowly as she tried to slow her breathing. As she stroked his damp back she kissed his moist neck, and loved the feel and scent of him.

When his own breathing had calmed down Kyle slid from on top of her. "Thank you," he said.

"For what?" Jill asked, though she already knew the answer.

"For letting me get to the real enjoyment quickly."

"You're welcome," was all she said.

Chapter 22

When Jill awoke, Kyle had already left for the ranch. After taking a shower and dressing in a pair of her own jeans, she put on one of Kyle's T-shirts. Jill liked the touch of the fabric on her skin and smiled at her reflection in the mirror. The shirt was entirely too big for her, but she needed to feel close to him, and since she hadn't planned on going anywhere, the shirt was perfect for wearing around the house.

Jill chuckled to herself as she thought of all the beautiful and expensive business suits and the exquisite, sexy dresses that filled the giant closet. She would never have been caught dead wearing such a getup just a year earlier. Now it felt not only comfortable, but right.

She went downstairs to the kitchen and made herself a simple breakfast of cereal and fat-free milk. Though Jill still fit into her jeans, they were becoming a little snug, so now was the time to cut back and lose a couple of pounds, she thought.

After she had eaten she picked up the phone and called Bebe. To Jill's surprise there was no answer. She hung up and imagined that the couple had plans of their own today. Jill decided that she would wait until tomorrow to see Bebe and the two would get caught up on the week's past events then.

For now she wanted to unpack their suitcases. Jill busied herself cleaning the cabin and then began planning a sumptuous dinner for Kyle to enjoy when he returned home. During the preparation of her meal the phone rang.

"Hello," Jill said, halfway expecting it to be Kyle, or at least Bebe.

"Hello, sweetheart, it's Mom."

"Hi, Mom," Jill said, genuinely happy to hear from Maddie.

"I'm not going to chat long, I just wanted to make sure you two made it back safely," Maddie said.

"We got in late last night. Kyle got up early this morning and went into work."

"Why would he do that? I thought he would want to say at home on Sunday to be with his new wife. You two should still want to cuddle and hug each other all day long," Maddie said pointedly.

"I don't think he'll be gone long since he only has to do paperwork and payroll," Jill replied flatly.

"Jill, don't get irritated with me. I'm just saying that I won't hear the pitter-patter of little feet at the rate you two are going."

"Mom, we've only been married a week! I thought this was going to be a pleasant conversation, and not one about me having children so soon. I'm married. Why can't you be content with that for now?" Jill shot back hotly.

Before she knew it, Jill had slammed down the phone. Her breaths were deep and her chest rose and fell quickly in her agitated state. She paced back and forth across the kitchen floor before she finally sat down at the kitchen table.

Resting her elbows on the table and her head in her hands, Jill tried to make sense of what had just happened. Her first instinct was to call Barbie, but she wanted to handle the situation on her own.

What had happened between herself and her mother was wrong. Maddie hadn't made her feel like this in over a year. Now the feelings of inadequacy Maddie had made her feel for years came back in a flash. Jill felt as though she always had to live up to her mother's dreams for her, but no more.

Jill stood and walked to the refrigerator and retrieved the pitcher of ice water and poured herself a glass. She sat down again and sipped the cold liquid slowly. She could feel herself calming down. She began to examine her relationship with her mother. Maddie had found a great deal of happiness and security in her marriage to her father. Jill knew that her mother only wanted the same thing for her daughter.

Maddie had given birth to Barbie when she was only eighteen, and then had Jill only a few years later. Her mother had never worked outside the home and was content taking care of her two young children and making a home for her family. When her father arrived home from work, her mother had dinner ready. She wore a beautiful dress and earrings every day, and greeted Rob with a passionate hug and kiss when he came home. Jill knew that her mother wanted only to be Mrs. Robert Eugene Alexander, and being anything else paled in comparison to the joy she experienced being his wife.

Jill knew she wanted the husband and kids too, but she knew she wanted a career as well. Now she had all that she wanted and was sure that in time she would have a baby of her own. But why was her mother so anxious for Jill to become pregnant? she wondered. The only thing Jill could come up with was her age. She was eleven years older than her mother had been when she had her first baby, but that still wasn't a good reason for her to push Jill so.

She finished drinking her water and then picked up the phone and dialed her parents' number.

"Hello," Maddie said quietly.

"Mom, I am so sorry for hanging up on you. You raised me to be more respectful than that, and I apologize, Mom." Jill paused as her voice became soft. "I need for you to respect me too. I have feelings and you don't seem to care about them."

"I do care about them, Jill, and you're right, I have to show you more respect. I was way out of line with my comments," Maddie said sincerely. "I don't know what I was thinking, but I didn't mean to imply that you were taking too long to have kids. You're a good girl and I am so proud of you," Maddie finished saying, and Jill smiled at her mother's comments.

"Mom, is everything all right with you?" Jill asked as the thought occurred to her that Maddie might be gravely ill. She listened to her mother's reply and tried to decipher any hint of obscure sadness.

"Oh no, I'm fine," Maddie assured her.

"You would tell me, right?" Jill asked, sounding almost childlike.

"Yes, I would tell you, but I'm fine, sweetheart."

"I love you, Mom."

"I love you too, and I won't say another word about babies."

"You won't have to because you know as soon as I find out you'll be the first to know."

"Good. Make sure you tell Kyle I said hello and give my handsome son-in-law a big hug and a kiss for me."

"I sure will, Mom," Jill said, smiling.

She hung up the phone and sat quietly for a moment. The relationship between herself and her mother had definitely changed, and for the better. Though Maddie was still able to push Jill's buttons, now they were able to talk and come to an understanding. Jill smiled as she stood and went back into the kitchen.

The next several hours Jill spent unpacking and cleaning the cabin. She did a couple of loads of laundry and then went upstairs to take a shower. Her thoughts were still on her mother. Jill knew her parents had the right formula for longevity in a marriage. Maddie had a special way of greeting her man when he came home from work. Now Jill would take a cue from her mother and do just the same.

With jasmine-scented body wash, Jill lathered the loofah and began washing her body. Then she washed her hair with the same scented shampoo and conditioner. When she was done rinsing off, she gently patted her skin dry and wrapped her hair in a towel. Quickly she moisturized her skin and then, applied a leave-in conditioner in her hair before blow-drying it. Then she used a hot curling iron and rolled her hair.

Jill left the bathroom with a towel wrapped around her, walked across the bedroom floor, and stopped at the window. She looked outside and saw the sun beaming brightly. There wasn't a cloud in the sky and the trees moved ever so slightly, making Jill believe that it would be another really hot, dry day.

She had always loved the heat, and knew exactly what she wanted to wear to welcome her husband home. Jill went into the closet and found the perfect sundress. It was a little sleeveless number that she had picked up in Jamaica. The dress was an explosion of purples, pinks, and oranges, the kind that she loved to see in Colorado sunsets.

After slipping on a black lace thong, Jill put the dress on. Just like in the dressing room of the boutique in Negril, the dress fit perfectly and made Jill feel as though she were the most beautiful creature on earth.

She went back into the bathroom and styled her hair. Jill applied makeup in earth tones that complemented her dress. When she was finished she stepped back and admired her reflection. There was still a lot more she could learn from her mother, and if she was smart, she would take notes as she went along. Kyle would definitely love seeing her in this dress, and Jill knew she owed a debt of thanks to her mother.

Once downstairs she started dinner. Tonight she wanted to prepare steak and baked potatoes. *A fresh salad would be nice too,* she thought, and began preparing that as well. Jill started to set the table, and then lifted her eyes to the sliding glass door. A smile came across her face as she realized that a romantic dinner outside would be perfect.

As the steaks continued to grill, Jill set the table on the deck for two. She had spread a bright yellow linen tablecloth on the table and had used the new Lenox china she had received as a wedding gift. The centerpiece was a vase of wildflowers she had gathered from the edge of the property. The flowers were bursting in colors of yellow, blue, and pink, and complemented the table well.

Jill stood back and observed her table, and felt as though something was still missing. She went back into the house and returned shortly with two long yellow tapered candles. She placed one on either side of her flowers and then put a glass hurricane over each in case the wind decided to pick up.

Back inside the kitchen, Jill glanced at the clock and saw that it was now 4:30 p.m. Jill imagined Kyle would be home soon. She hoped he would be home before dinner was ready, and decided to give him a call. Jill picked up the phone and dialed Kyle's cell phone number.

"Hello," he said in an anxious voice.

"Hi, honey, it's me. I hope I'm not bothering you," Jill said.

"Hey, babe, I am a little busy, but I'll make time for you. What's up?" Kyle asked. "Oh, hold on a second."

Jill could tell that Kyle was doing business and really didn't have time to talk to her. In the background she could hear a man's voice asking him questions, and Kyle replying to him. She had known he would be busy today, and immediately regretted having called him.

"I'm sorry about that, Jill. What were you saying?"

"Oh, I was going to get dinner started and was just wondering when you would be home," she lied as she looked sadly at the food that was already being cooked.

"I'm sorry, babe, I'm going to be here for a couple more hours. Is that okay?"

"Yeah," Jill said, trying to sound upbeat in an effort to disguise her disappointment.

"Are you sure, Jill?"

"Yes, I'm sure. I know you have work to do, so take your time."

"Thanks, honey. I'll be home as soon as I can," Kyle said and hung up the phone.

"So much for a romantic dinner," Jill said aloud as she too hung up.

With steaks half grilled and potatoes half baked, she turned everything on low in an effort to salvage her dinner.

Jill poured herself a glass of lemonade and walked back out onto the deck. She could see Patches in the distance. Setting her glass on the table, she walked down the steps of the deck and whistled for the horse. At hearing the piercing sound, Patches raised his head and came running at a lightning speed toward Jill. At first she thought the huge animal would run her over, but with the accuracy of a race car driver, Patches stopped next to Jill.

Jill's face glowed as she saw just how much Patches missed her. The horse threw back its head and nuzzled his nose in Jill's hand.

"Hello, Patches," Jill said as she stroked the horse's back. At the woman's touch, Patches pranced around impatiently and moved closer to her.

"I'm sorry, Patches, but we can't go for a ride today. I'm waiting for Kyle to get home."

Patches seemed to settle down as Jill continued to rub his back and talk softly and soothingly to him.

"Maybe next weekend we can go for a ride, that is, if you aren't too tired," Jill said humorously, knowing that Patches worked just as hard as she did Monday through Friday. "Wait here, I have something for you." She dashed into the kitchen and returned with a handful of sliced carrots and apples and fed them to Patches.

After he had eaten the last one, Jill patted the horse good-bye and went back into the cabin. She washed her hands and then checked on her slow-cooking meal. If Kyle didn't get home soon, the only thing that would be worth eating would be the salad.

She got her glass of lemonade from outside and refreshed her drink, and then went into the living room and turned on the television. For a while she flipped through the stations before settling on the news. Jill had only been watching for a short time when she heard Kyle's Navigator pull up.

Turning off the television, she jumped up and ran into the kitchen. Jill checked on the food and increased the temperature. Then she quickly poured him a glass of wine and returned to the living room just as Kyle was coming through the door.

The tired, weary look on his face was replaced with one of admiration and appreciation as his eyes fell on Jill.

"Wow! You look magnificent," he said as his eyes took in their fill of her beauty.

"Thank you," Jill said softly.

A sexy saunter filled her steps as she approached him. Jill kissed Kyle's lips softly, letting her breasts ever so lightly brush against his chest. Jill took a sip of wine before placing the glass in his hand.

"Tell me, Mrs. Roberts, is coming home to you going to be like this every time? I'm just asking because I don't want to get my hopes up."

Jill smiled as she realized she had achieved her goal, which was a smile on Kyle's face and a show of admiration.

"Yes, this is what you have to look forward to every time you come home to me," she whispered in his ear as she pressed her body against his and wrapped her arms around his neck.

Jill began kissing him gently on the corners of his mouth, before she let her tongue softly lick his. With his free hand he held Jill's body tightly against his, and she could tell that he was filled with want for her.

"I have dinner ready," Jill said, as she played with the hair at the nape of his neck.

"The only thing I want to eat is you," Kyle replied as he kissed her neck, leaving a trail of moist kisses behind.

"There's plenty of time for that," Jill said, smiling. She took Kyle by the hand and led him into the kitchen. "I spent all day cooking and cleaning and getting ready for my man," she said as they walked out to the deck. "I want to spend all night pampering you."

Kyle smiled as he took a seat and admired Jill's beautifully set table. He took another sip of his wine before Jill sat down on his lap. The couple kissed as if they really could devour each other. Kyle could feel the tension of his workday easing away, and Jill was happy to be the one to relieve the stress from his mind and give him something more pleasurable to focus on.

Jill placed a hand on either side of his face as she returned his eager kisses. She loved everything about him and wanted more than anything to be everything he could possibly desire. She knew in her heart that she was, and prayed that their passion would last forever.

Kyle's hand massaged her thigh, and Jill could sense herself wanting to give in to his advances.

"Dinner is ready," Jill finally said when their lips parted. She wanted to stand up, but Kyle kept his arms firmly around her waist. Jill knew exactly what Kyle wanted. Through nonverbal communication he expressed just how much he loved her. Jill knew that in Kyle's eyes she was the very essence of womanly perfection, and her heart filled with love for him in this knowledge.

"I am starving, and I'll clean my plate as long as I can have you for dessert."

"I promise," Jill said with a final kiss.

Reluctantly, Kyle released Jill and followed her into the kitchen. She began preparing their plates while he washed his hands. Then the two went out back onto the deck where Jill lit the candles and they ate dinner.

"How was work today?" Jill asked after they had blessed the meal.

"It was rough. I had to let one of the new guys go. I felt bad because he really needs the work, but he just isn't cut out to be a ranch hand," Kyle said as she began eating.

"Well, why don't you find something else for him to do?"

"We tried that. Eric gave him the job of giving guests guided horseback tours."

"How did that work out?"

"Not well. It's pretty bad when the guide gets lost and has to radio back for help. That apparently happened twice while we were away. I wanted to keep him, Jill, but there's no way I can," Kyle said, shaking his head and sounding as if he had lost a longtime friend.

"I know you would have kept him if there was any way possible," Jill assured him.

"Dinner is wonderful. Thanks, babe."

"I'm glad you like it."

The sun was beginning to set and the atmosphere Jill had created was romantic and mellow. With the candlelight dancing and a gentle breeze flowing, the couple sat and talked long after finishing their meal. The food, the wine, and the woman had definitely made Kyle forget the troubles of the day, and

Jill listened intently as he told her all the things that were going on at the ranch.

It grew dark outside and Kyle watched as Jill's face glowed in the candlelight. He stopped talking and looked at the content smile on her face as she listened to him. He pushed back his chair and motioned for Jill to come to him.

She stood and obeyed his command. When she arrived at the other side of the table, Kyle took her right hand and kissed her wedding ring.

"Thank you for being my wife," he said sincerely.

"Thank you for being my husband," she replied as she leaned down and planted a kiss on his lips.

Placing a firm hand on either side of her hips, he slid her dress up her thighs. Then Kyle pulled Jill down onto him so that her legs straddled his. As he continued to kiss her, his hands began to pull the spaghetti straps from her shoulders until the dress dropped and exposed her breasts.

First Kyle took one taut nipple into his mouth and began to suck until the action brought low squeals of delight from Jill. Then he moved his lips to the other breast and did the same. Jill's hands cradled his head in hopes he wouldn't stop any time soon.

Jill could feel the huge bulge in Kyle's pants and knew that very soon he would pleasure her in another way. She slid her hands between their legs and freed his hardened member. Then it was Kyle's turn to do the same.

He let his hands slide up her thighs until they found her thong. Mere strings and lace were all the garment was made of, and with one had Kyle tore her panties away. It was a move that titillated Jill to the highest degree. Jill found making love to Kyle out in the open sinfully erotic. But they were married, and

if her husband wanted to make love to her in the grocery store she would oblige him, *well, as long as no one
is looking,* she thought.

Kyle wrapped his powerful arms around Jill's thighs
and lifted her. His next move brought a gasp of painful
pleasure from Jill as he lowered her onto his erection.
Jill's body shuddered as each thick inch of him entered
her body. It took Jill a few moments before her body
adjusted to the size of her husband, but when it did,
she began to give him the ride of his life.

He found himself fighting to maintain control,
but Kyle knew he was fighting a losing battle. The
sweet wetness that enveloped his hardened penis
made him want to explode, but he wouldn't before
making her want to faint.

As their tongues explored each other's mouth,
Kyle's fingertips played with Jill's nipples. Then he let
his hands drop down to her backside, which he
grasped firmly as he thrust himself deep inside her.
Jill's mouth left his as she cried out in passion. She
threw her head back and opened her eyes. Stars twinkled high above and she felt as though each one of
them were exploding between her legs.

It was then that Kyle allowed himself to release
inside her. He continued to hold on to her shapely hips
as he delivered the juice that was reserved only for her.
With the final drops going inside her body, Kyle rested
his head on her chest. He rubbed her back softly and
slowly as he continued to try to catch his breath.

Finally, he lifted his head and gazed into the eyes of
the woman who represented Mother Earth to him. To
him, Jill represented all that was right, pure, and perfect. He kissed each nipple before kissing her lips.

"I am so in love with you," he said as she wiped a

bead of perspiration from her forehead. "Jill, you have no idea how crazy you make me, do you?"

"No, I don't. But if this is what it is, I hope you never gain your sanity," Jill whispered in his ear before she began to nibble it.

The temperature had dropped and Jill shivered as a breeze caressed their bodies.

"Come on, let's take this inside."

"You're not finished?" Jill asked in surprise.

"By no means," Kyle replied as he slid the straps of Jill's dress back over her shoulders.

Jill smiled at the thought of her husband's enormous sexual appetite, and wondered what he would do to inflame her again.

Kyle began walking toward the door, pulling Jill gently by the hand behind him.

"Shouldn't we at least clear the table?" Jill said.

Kyle took a few steps back to the table and blew the candles out, then proceeded to the door again.

"The cleanup can wait. I can't," he said as they entered the cabin.

He locked the door behind them, and in one quick motion lifted Jill into his arms. She giggled, finding Kyle's actions playfully romantic, and surprised herself when she realized that she was in need of him again as well.

Kyle carried her up the stairs and into the bedroom. Once there, he placed Jill on the bed and helped her out of her dress.

"I'm sorry about ripping the pretty black thong you had on," he said, as she undressed.

"It's okay. It was for a good cause."

"It was for a wonderful cause," Kyle said as he climbed in bed on top of her.

Jill's head melted into the pillows. After a few

moments of foreplay both were ready and willing to create pleasure that would make each other beg for more. Well into the night the couple caressed and fondled each other and Jill wondered how on earth she would be ready to get up and out the door by 6:00 a.m. But she really didn't care. Right now with Kyle was all that mattered.

Jill lay back and let her body be filled with him and her mind with love.

Chapter 23

Jill was the first one in the office and decided to put on a pot of coffee. As it brewed, she retrieved her mail from her desk. She walked slowly back to the front of the building as she read the letters. Most of the mail was invoices and a bill for her business credit cards. Other than that, there was nothing else that needed her immediate attention.

Jill quickly made herself a cup of coffee and headed back to her office. She read through the invoices before putting them in the bin for Amelia to take care of. Then she turned on her computer and read her e-mail. Mulher Bela had sent her a note to express their pleasure over the outcome of their promotional campaign.

A twinge of guilt fluttered through her mind as Jill once again resented not being on deck for the major account. She quickly sent a reply and thanked them for their business. A knock on the door startled her as she glanced around to see who was there.

"Welcome back," Bebe said as she stood grinning in the doorway. Bebe stepped into Jill's office, and Jill's face broke into a huge smile as she stood to hug her.

"Bebe, I can't tell you how good it feels to be back," Jill said.

"I knew you'd be the first one in today."

"You know me too well," Jill said as she returned to her seat.

"I wanted to call you when you got home, but when Tony got home he said that you guys were pretty beat, and yesterday we were pretty busy ourselves," Bebe said as she took a seat.

"We were exhausted Saturday, and Sunday we were busy, too," Jill said in a voice filled with sexy demureness.

"Oh," Bebe said in an amused tone as she arched one eyebrow.

"Yes, I was quite worn out," Jill said as she laid her head back and tried to suppress a giggle. "But I would have perked up as soon as I heard your voice."

"How was Jamaica?" Bebe asked excitedly.

"Oh, Bebe, it was wonderful. We got to do a ton of activities, but my favorite was making love every night," Jill said mischievously.

"I bet it was," Bebe said, laughing.

"Bebe, I am so sorry that I didn't help as much as I should have on the Mulher Bela account," Jill said as the lightheartedness left her voice.

"Don't be, you had more important things to do at that time."

"I still feel guilty for leaving all the work for you and Monica to do."

"Jill, you can't always change the timing of these events. Your wedding just happened to coincide with a business trip. There will be others. And you have to remember, you and Monica did most of the work on the account while I was in Hawaii," Bebe reminded her.

"That's true, but I still feel guilty."

"The only thing you should feel guilty about is missing out on a trip to Brazil. The people at Mulher were wonderful to work with, and Monica and I did an excellent job. You'll be quite proud of us when you read this brief," Bebe said as she handed Jill the file. "Rio de Janeiro is so beautiful. But enough of that, I want to hear all about Jamaica."

"Bebe, my honeymoon was more than I ever could have dreamed it would be. Jamaica was sexy, romantic, and fascinating," Jill said, beaming as she recalled her trip. Bebe looked on smiling as Jill continued, "Although we went shopping and sightseeing, we did manage to take a day trip to Ocho Rios. The rest of our time was spent making love every chance we got, and every place we could. It felt so good being with my husband that it almost felt sinful," Jill said with a girlish laugh. "I had to keep reminding myself that it was okay for me to feel this good," she finished shyly.

"I know what you mean," Bebe said with a knowing wink. "Did you take a bunch of pictures?"

"Yes, I did. I think I want to have the family over to show them the DVD we made of our trip. How does Friday the twenty-fourth sound?"

"We'll be there. Do you need me to bring anything?"

"No, I think I have everything under control."

Jill leaned back in her chair and thought about what she planned to make for dinner Friday night. Counting in her head, she realized that her family was continuing to grow. With her in-laws and Grace, Monica, and Orlando, whom she considered family as well, she had to prepare for thirteen people. A gentle smile came across her face at the revelation.

"What are you thinking about?" Bebe asked.

"Bebe, do you realize that our family has grown?"

"Yes, you and I are the newest official members."

"That's true, but did you stop to think about how quickly it has grown and how close we all are?"

Bebe smiled back at Jill, knowing how important family was to her. If it hadn't been for Jill, Bebe knew that she probably would have lost Tony for good. Instead, she was an official member of the growing population of Robertses that Jill was so proud of. Bebe even gave Jill the credit for making Regina want to move back to Durango. Regina and Jill both took the issue of family very seriously, and never missed the opportunity to make an outsider feel welcome.

Another knock on the door brought both women's attention to the entrance where Monica stood. She smiled brightly and looked at the newly wedded Jill.

"Welcome back," Monica said as she walked toward Jill and leaned forward, planting a kiss on her cheek.

"Thanks, Monica. How have things been around here?"

"Better than expected. Did Bebe fill you in on the Mulher Bela account?"

"No, not yet."

"Why don't we save filling Jill in until we get to lunch? Then she can fill us in on her honeymoon," Bebe said as she stood to leave.

"That sounds good. I'll be ready by noon," Jill said.

"Fine, but I want you to tell me everything," Monica said, sounding as if the wind had been let out of her sail.

Jill smiled as the junior executive left her office in playful disappointment. Monica seemed more like a little sister than a coworker, and acted like one too. The thought made Jill think about her own sister, and she made a mental note to call Barbie before she went to lunch.

Sitting in her chair, Jill got busy working and catching up on all the business that had been awaiting her return. After negotiating contracts, arranging promotions, and returning business calls, Jill reserved the last ten minutes before lunch to make a personal call to her sister.

She quickly dialed Barbie's number, and after six rings Jill was surprised to get no answer. Reluctantly she hung up the phone and then dialed her mother's number.

"Hello."

"Hi, Mom, it's Jill."

"Hi, sweetheart, I've been waiting to hear from you. I wanted to call you over the weekend, but your father wouldn't let me. He thought you two would be worn out from traveling."

"We were exhausted, Mom," Jill replied, and was secretly thankful for her father's insight.

"How are you?"

"I'm fine. Today is my first day back to work. I had a ton of stuff to catch up on, but I put quite a dent into it this morning. Things should be back to normal by the end of the week." Jill said hopefully.

"That's good. By the way, today was your sister's first day of class."

"Oh, I didn't know that," Jill said, surprised.

"She didn't want to tell you because she wanted you to concentrate on your wedding."

"But, Mom, Barbie tells me everything. She never keeps anything from me. I would have been happy for her. I could have at least congratulated her or sent her a card."

"I know, sweetheart, but Barbie wanted all eyes on you. You were so excited and you had so much on your mind with your wedding and your in-laws. Barbie knows how elated you were over your bridal shower and the honeymoon, and she didn't want to steal your thunder. Barbie made me promise not to say anything until after you got back from your trip."

"Do you know what time she'll get home today?"

"She should be home by six p.m."

"I'll give her a call them. How is Daddy?"

"He's fine, but he's not home right now. He's helping the reverend out at the church. But I expect him home before three."

Monica stuck her head in Jill's office and pointed at her watch. Jill nodded to her and signaled that she would be ready to go in just a minute.

"Mom, I have to go. Bebe and Monica are waiting for me to go to lunch. Give Dad a kiss for me and tell him I'll call again later. I love you."

"I love you too, sweetheart, and give the girls a hug and a kiss for me, and tell them I said hello as well," Maddie finished as she hung up the phone.

As Jill returned the phone to the receiver she stood and gathered her purse. Leaving her office she walked quickly down the hall to catch up with Bebe and Monica, who were already waiting at the door to leave.

"I'm sorry I made you wait, but I was talking on the phone to Mom. She says hello and sends hugs and kisses. Is Amelia coming with us?"

"No, she said she has a few errands to run, but she'll join us tomorrow. How's Mom?" Bebe asked as the three women left the building.

"She's fine, but I just found out that today was Barbie's first day back to school."

"Oh, why didn't she tell you?" Monica asked.

"My mom seems to think that Barbie wanted to keep the family's attention on me," Jill said regretfully as she got into Bebe's car. "I appreciate what she did, but now I feel like Barbie's joy had to take a backseat to my happiness. It shouldn't be that way, and I don't want her to feel like it has to be that way either."

"Whoa, I think the sisters are going to have a few words tonight," Bebe said playfully.

She pulled off and headed in the direction of A Special Place. "But don't be too hard on her, Jill. Barbie only had your happiness in mind by keeping her news away from you."

"I know, I just wish she hadn't kept it a secret. She even swore Mom to secrecy."

"If you ask me, it sounds like she loves you an awful lot," Monica added.

"I know she does, but the feeling is mutual," Jill replied, as she thought about what she would say to her sister tonight on the phone.

Bebe pulled into a parking spot at the resort and the three women got out and walked toward the Ranch House. The weather was warm and dry, and there wasn't a cloud in the sky. Jill looked around and noticed that not a tree in sight gave evidence to a breeze that would offer relief to the heat. But once she was inside the Ranch House, the cool air-conditioned room offered pleasing comfort to her skin.

The Ranch House had become a familiar sight to Jill. She looked around and saw many of the restaurant's regulars sitting at the bar. As the women made their way to a table, Jill waved to Grace, who signaled that she would be right with them.

"Oh, it feels so good in here," Bebe was the first to say as she set her purse down.

"Yes, it does. It's so hot that I feel like I'm melting," Monica agreed. She took a napkin from her purse and dabbed the beads of perspiration from her forehead.

"Well, is it hot enough for you?" Grace said as she approached their table.

"Grace, it's too hot," Jill told her, and Grace chuckled.

"Welcome back, Jill."

"Thank you. Are you and Monica free Friday the twenty-fourth?" Jill asked.

"I'm free every night," Grace replied.

"I don't think I have anything going on," Monica added.

"Good, come out to the cabin then. I'm going to have a little dinner party and show the honeymoon pictures and movie."

"It's not X-rated, is it?" Grace asked smartly.

"No. Well, at least the part I'm showing you isn't," Jill replied, making the women burst into laughter.

"I'll be there," Grace finally said.

"Me too," added Monica.

Grace quickly took the women's orders and hurried away to fill them, as she knew that they all had to return to work.

Just as Grace left, Kyle, Tony, and Eric arrived. Tony and Bebe seemed more like an old married couple than newlyweds to Jill. Bebe tilted her head backward and Tony leaned forward and kissed her on the lips. The simple yet romantic gesture was something their lives had been building up to ever since they had met. Jill knew the comfort zone between them was very natural given the length of time they had known each other.

A smile formed on Jill's lips as well as she felt the gentle touch of Kyle's mouth on her neck. Now wasn't the time or place to do what she instantly thought of doing, but tonight she would make him pay passionately for instilling the erotic thoughts in her head.

"What you want isn't on the menu, Jill," Kyle whispered in her ear.

"How do you know what I'm thinking?" she asked with a slight blush.

"I know. Unfortunately, we can't stay for lunch. I saw Bebe parking, and I just wanted to come see you for a second. Tony has to help round up some horses for an owner, and I have to help Eric."

"Okay, but you have to promise to make it up to me tonight," Jill whispered coyly, as she looked up at Kyle with mesmerizing brown eyes that held hope for pleasures to come.

Kyle stood silently for a moment, as he was captivated by her charm once again. He was completely aware of how this woman, who was now his wife, could make his manhood stand at attention without even touching him. Struggling to get his emotions in check, he continued to lean close to Jill. Though it was the wrong thing to do, he had no choice. To stand up straight would allow everyone to see how enflamed with passion he was for her. So he tried to change the subject.

"What are you ladies up to today?" he asked, hoping someone else would answer besides Jill.

"We are planning to come over to your place to see your honeymoon pictures and movie on the twenty-fourth," Bebe answered. "We don't have anything else planned, do we, babe?" she asked Tony.

"It's a few weeks away, but I think we're free. What time should we arrive?"

"Seven o'clock, and bring your appetite," Jill said, smiling.

"Oh, you know you don't have to tell Tony that," Bebe said, laughing as well as she rubbed her husband's taut abdomen.

"Well, we better get back to work," Kyle said as he finally stood. With a quick kiss on Jill's cheek he turned and left.

Jill sensed a change in Kyle's mood and excused herself from the table. As she left the table to catch up with him, she was thankful that Tony was still inside the Ranch House saying good-bye to Bebe.

"Kyle," she called out.

He stopped in midstride and turned around to see Jill walking quickly toward him.

"Honey, is everything all right?" she asked as she looked deep into his eyes again. Jill ran her hand slowly down his arm, and he could see that she was filled with concern for him.

"I'm fine, babe. Why?" he asked, a little confused.

"You just didn't seem yourself inside the restaurant."

Kyle smiled broadly as he took Jill in his arms. He pressed her body firmly against his own as he began kissing her as if no one else in the world mattered. Jill allowed her mind to be filled with all the erotic desires that she had entertained earlier. If he wanted her now, she knew that she would be more than happy to rid him of any sexual tension he needed to release.

Finally, when their lips parted, they continued to stay locked in an embrace. Neither wanted to let the other go, but each knew that they had to make a decision.

"So do you want to blow off work and go home for a few hours or what, Mr. Roberts? You know, I'll make it worth your while," she said as she lovingly wrapped her arms around his waist.

"I'd love to but I can't. I have too much work to do, babe," Kyle said. Mischief filled his voice, and Jill knew that he really wanted to, but work just wouldn't allow it.

"You didn't answer my question. Is everything okay?"

"Yes, things couldn't be better. I'm surprised that you still don't know what you do to me. Just a look and I'm putty in your hands. You make every sleeping desire and thought come to life in an instant, and suddenly I have no control over who I am or what I want. The only thing I know is you, and how much I need to have all of you. I know it sounds crazy, but—"

"No buts, it's what I want too. I know what you're talking about and my heart is filled with the same kind of passion for you. I just don't get hard when you look at me," Jill said, making them both laugh.

"Oh, you noticed that, did you?"

"Yeah, I noticed, and it surprises me that you don't know that you get me hot and bothered that same way. Women just don't show it in the same way as men do, but when you're so totally in love with someone you can't help but fill with intense desire," Jill said as she let her tongue gently lick his bottom lip.

"Thank you."

"For what?"

"For knowing just what I needed and offering to let me make love to you in the middle of the day."

"The offer is still on the table, cowboy."

"I'll wait till tonight. I'm going to show you that I can exercise some control where you're concerned."

"Are you ready to get started, big brother?" Tony said as he came out of the Ranch House.

Reluctantly, Kyle released Jill and she stepped away puckering her lips to form a kiss. She turned and walked back into the Ranch House, and Kyle stood and watched until her form disappeared.

"Are you okay, man?" Tony asked.

"Yeah, I'm fine," Kyle replied as the two started back toward the corral.

Inside the Ranch House Bebe and Monica sat enjoying their lunch. Jill walked over to the table and sat down. There was a steak, a salad, and a glass of iced tea waiting for her. She smiled as she placed the cloth napkin on her lap and began to eat.

"Is everything okay?" Bebe asked sincerely, and Monica looked on with concern filling her eyes.

"Yes, everything is more than fine," Jill said as she began to eat.

The conversation during lunch centered on going to Jill's the night of the twenty-fourth. The family loved any excuse to get together and have fun. The women discussed what they would have for dinner, and Jill made a mental note to call Regina and let her know of the plans. Bebe said that she would make sure Eric and Sharon knew.

After lunch the women piled back into Bebe's car and headed back to Desert Star. Though Bebe and Monica chatted continuously, Jill was lost in her own thoughts. She and Kyle were both business owners, and that fact left little time for them to concentrate on each other. She had wanted to work part-time after Monica was fully trained, and hoped that soon she would be.

Now more than ever, Jill wanted to be there for Kyle. She was his wife, his everything, and she didn't want to let him down. There was nothing she could do about his job. Kyle was the eldest son, and with that came a lot of responsibility, especially as far as the ranch and resort were concerned. Samuel Roberts had other properties around the country, and Jill was just thankful that Kyle didn't have to travel.

"Jill, did you hear me?" Monica said.

"Oh, I'm sorry. No, I didn't. What were you saying,

Monica?" Jill said as she pulled herself away from her thoughts.

"I said that I want to come over and cook with you on the twenty-fourth, is that okay?"

"Sure, I think that will be great."

They arrived at Desert Star to find Amelia had already returned. The woman greeted them with a smile and messages. Though her own workload was mounting, Amelia continued to prove she was capable of handling it all with proficiency.

Jill asked Amelia if she would be able to make it to her get-together, and she said she would come.

They all started back to work, thankful for each other and for Desert Star.

The evening found Jill at home before Kyle, and she was happy for the opportunity to make herself presentable for her husband before he arrived. She went upstairs and took a shower and then changed into something comfortable. Kyle loved to see her in sundresses, so she slipped one.

Once downstairs she began making dinner. She began chopping fresh vegetables to make stir-fry, and diced chicken to add to the pan. As she cooked, she looked up and saw that it was already time for Barbie to be home. Jill wiped off her hands and picked up the phone. She dialed Barbie's number and placed the phone to her ear and kept it in place with her shoulder. As Barbie's line rang, Jill continued to prepare her meal.

"Hello."

"Hi, Barbie."

"Jill, I'm so glad to hear your voice. How is everything?"

"Things are good. I made it home before Kyle and I'm trying to get dinner ready before he arrives."

"Well, aren't you quite the little housewife?" Barbie said playfully.

"I'm trying to be. I don't know how you do it all, sis."

"Oh, don't worry, you'll get the hang of it. It's called balance, and it can take years to achieve."

"I hope you're right," Jill replied prayerfully. "Barbie," she added, her voice now more serious.

"Yes."

"Why didn't you tell me you were starting school?"

"Jill, I just didn't want to steal your thunder. It was your time to shine, and I wanted everyone to focus on you."

"But you're my sister. I wouldn't mind sharing the spotlight with you."

"That's not how it's supposed to be. The bride shares the spotlight with no one. Besides, going back to school is not a big deal. I'll be finished before you know it, and then it's my turn to have a party."

The words made Jill laugh. Instantly she remembered why she adored Barbie so much. It wasn't in her nature to rob anyone of their moment. Barbie was the one person who would always take a backseat for the ones she loved.

"Have I told you lately that I want to be just like you when I grow up?" Jill said in a voice filled with admiration.

"No, Jill, it is I who wants to be just like you when I grow up," Barbie said softly. "Suffice it to say that we are both two incredible women."

"Agreed," Jill said as she wiped a tear from her eye with the back of her hand.

Though Jill didn't know it, Barbie was drying a tear

as well. The same amount of love, admiration, and hope filled her heart for her younger sister as well.

For the rest of the phone call Jill listened as Barbie went on and on about school, and what she was learning. Barbie seemed to be thrilled to be attending college again, and Rick was living up to his part of the bargain by helping out with the house and kids. Jill was happy for her sister.

As her phone call ended, Jill heard the front door open. She turned around to see Kyle entering. With a shirt tucked into sung-fitting jeans, and his dark brown cowboy hat sitting so low on his head that his sexy dark brown eyes sparkled from just underneath, her heart skipped a beat when she saw him.

Jill hung up the phone and wiped her hands off on the towel. She walked slowly toward Kyle. The gentle night breeze that flowed from the sliding glass door caught her dress and made the hem caress her thighs gently.

"Dinner will be ready shortly, cowboy."

She stopped just in front of him and he inhaled deeply, letting her perfume fill his nostrils. Kyle rested a hand on each of her shoulders before letting his hands slide down her arms and rest on her wrists. He folded her arms gently behind her back as he started kissing her.

"I've been waiting all day for dessert. I'll have dinner later," he replied in a deep and needful voice.

Kyle led Jill to the sofa where he sat down, and Jill climbed onto his lap and straddled his thighs. She took off his hat and placed it on the coffee table, and then she began kissing his neck as she gently massaged his shoulders. Kyle's hands found better things to do as they left her waist and slid down to her hips, and then ever farther down to fondle her backside. He could feel his passion mounting and moments later his hands glided underneath her dress to remove her panties. To his delight she wasn't wearing any.

"Oh, Jill," he said, letting the words fall out of his mouth in intoxicated disbelief.

With that, she worked quickly to free him of his pants. Jill undid his buckle and slid the belt from around his waist, and then she unbuttoned and unzipped his pants. She reached inside and pulled out the part of him that needed her so very much.

Jill raised her body high enough so that when she came back down, his gaining entrance inside her made her moan with deep, pleasurable cries. At first she rode him slowly, making sure that they had both achieved as much delight from what she was doing as they possibly could. Then she began to speed up the pace, each time letting her silky wetness completely cover his massive shaft.

As she rolled her hips Kyle held on to her tightly. He could feel himself giving in to her demands, which were to make him lose his mind, and have him begging for more. Jill expertly did just that as Kyle pressed himself back inside her. Her back arched as he delivered powerful thrusts in unison with hers.

Jill couldn't help but cry out in passion as she felt all the love Kyle had to give. Moments later Kyle exploded inside her. When they were finished, Jill rested her head on Kyle's shoulder and tried to catch her breath.

When their bodies had calmed down, Jill reluctantly left Kyle on the sofa. She walked into the kitchen, and was immediately thankful she had turned the wok on low and that her dinner hadn't burned. She turned the wok off and left the kitchen.

When she went back into the living room she took Kyle by the hand and led him upstairs.

"Come on, baby, I want to finish feeding you some more dessert," she told him.

That night she pleasured Kyle's body in more ways than one. As they made love well into the night, the only dinner they had was each other, but both were satisfied.

Chapter 24

The evening air was still warm and stars were beginning to fill the sky. Jill and Monica had finished preparing the meal for the family. Jill was thankful for Monica's help, since she hadn't been feeling well for the last several days.

Jill seemed not to have as much energy as she usually did, and often went right to bed after dinner. Kyle had suggested that she start taking vitamins and cut back on the amount of work she was doing at Desert Star.

The firm continued to grow, but Jill hadn't given Monica as much of the workload as she could have. Though Monica was doing very well with all her assigned clients, Jill and Bebe still handled the bulk of the business, since Monica was still technically a junior partner.

Jill had been thinking of hiring another junior partner, but she didn't know where to look. Finding Monica had been a fluke, since she had already been working with them when they needed someone. Amelia wasn't the partner type. The woman was happy being the secretary and really didn't want to dabble in public relations, nor did she have what it took.

Monica was busy setting the table, and Jill lit a few candles around the living room. The place looked great and the food smelled marvelous, but Jill couldn't help feeling nauseated.

Eric, Sharon, and Ally arrived and shortly after, Samuel and Regina walked through the door. Jill gave her in-laws a big hug and asked them if they wanted something to drink. As usual Samuel requested Hennesey, and Regina wanted a rum and Coke. Jill always made sure she had a bottle of each on the shelf for them.

When she returned with their drinks she saw that Amelia had arrived, as well as Tony and Bebe.

"Where is Kyle?" Regina asked.

"He should be here any minute. He went to the store to pick up some blueberries for your cheesecake, Dad."

"That's my boy," Samuel said proudly, thankful that his favorite dessert was on the menu.

"He loves you too much," Regina said in a voice filled with pride. Then her eyes fell on Jill and a look of concern filled her face. "Jill, are you feeling well?"

"Honestly, I haven't been feeling too good the last couple days. Either I'm working too much or I'm coming down with the flu."

"Darling, you have to slow down. I thought Monica was going to help ease the amount of time you and Bebe had to put in at the office," Regina said.

"Yes, and she is, but Desert Star just keeps growing. I'm afraid that we're going to need another junior partner soon."

"Well, you better make it quick. I don't like to see

my daughter looking so run-down," her father-in-law said.

"She doesn't look run-down," Regina said as she gently swatted her husband's arm. "She just looks a little tired."

Jill didn't know if they were just observant or overly blunt, but the truth did hurt. She didn't let on that what they had said had offended her. She stood quietly for a moment and wondered why she had taken the comment to heart at all.

The door opened again and this time Kyle walked in. His smile broadened as he looked around the room and saw that everyone had arrived. As was always his way, he quickly walked over and greeted his parents, hugging his mother warmly and kissing her on the cheek before shaking his father's hand, halfway giving him a manly hug as well.

Before her in-laws could start talking about how bad she looked again, Jill made her way to the kitchen. Monica was there checking on her jambalaya, which seemed to be turning Jill's stomach.

"Would you like to sample some?" she asked as she extended the spoon toward Jill.

"Not right now, Monica. Do you need any help?"

"No, I have everything under control," Monica replied as she turned her back and continued to get dinner ready. "I'm just going to warm a loaf of this delicious, crusty bread, and we'll be ready to eat. Oh, by the way, your mom called while you were in the shower. She said to tell you that she got the pictures and it looks like you and Kyle had a great time in Jamaica. She also said that she's sorry that she can't be here tonight—Jill—Jill?" Monica looked around the kitchen, but Jill wasn't in sight.

Taking the stairs two at a time and running into the

master bedroom, Jill ran into the bathroom and pushed the door closed behind her. Collapsing to her knees over the toilet, she began to vomit. Jill's stomach tightened as she heaved several times into the commode.

Lifting her head, she brushed her hair back from her face. Jill breathed deeply as she realized that she was coming down with the flu. It had been several years since she had even had a cold. Her system was completely run down. What she probably needed was a few days off from work to rest, but there just was no way she could leave the heavy workload for Bebe and Monica to attend to.

Though she did feel better, she sat for a few minutes more to make sure nothing else was coming up. When she was positive that she was finished, she stood and flushed the toilet. There was a knock on the door, and the sound startled Jill.

"Yes," she said, hoping that whoever was on the other side had not heard her hurling.

"Babe, are you okay?" Kyle said.

The question alone let Jill know that he had heard her. She struggled with finding the right words to say so as not to alarm him, but she could find none.

"I'll be out in a minute, honey," she said, trying to sound upbeat.

Quickly she washed her face and hands. She caught her reflection in the mirror and saw just what Regina and Samuel were talking about. Jill looked pale and washed out, and she knew she had to get some much-needed rest. She applied a little makeup before she opened the door. As she did, she found Kyle sitting on the bed.

"Hey," she said softly.

He held out his arms for her to come to him. Jill

walked toward him with a smile on her face, but Kyle could see right through it. She sat on his lap as if she were a little girl. His arms went around her waist, and his eyes sought to seek the truth in hers.

"Are you not feeling well?" he asked.

"No, I haven't been feeling well for a few days. I think I'm coming down with the flu," she said quietly.

"Why didn't you say something? We could have postponed tonight. Everyone would have understood."

Jill smiled at the care and concern Kyle was showing her. She caressed his temples before planting a kiss there.

"All I need is a few days of rest and plenty of orange juice. Before you know it I'll be as good as new."

Through the makeup and the smiles, and even through her words, Kyle could see that Jill was putting on a brave face. She was more exhausted than she was willing to let on, and wouldn't have ruined anybody's evening with her own problems.

"You are going to stay in bed all weekend. I don't want you to lift a finger, because I'll be here to take care of you."

"Kyle, you don't have to stay with me. Remember, you have plans to go fishing with your brothers and your dad this weekend. I'll be just fine," Jill said, trying to reassure him.

"I know you will be, because I'll be here to make sure you are," he said as he entwined his fingers through hers. "There are plenty of fish in the river, but there's only one Jill Roberts, and it's my job to take the best care of her that I can." He raised her fingers to his lips and kissed each one. And then he said, "Why don't you stay up here and rest? I'll let the family know that you're not feeling well," caressing her back.

"No! I feel much better," Jill said as her eyes

widened. After what Samuel and Regina had just said she knew she had to put her best foot forward. And Kyle's announcement of her not feeling well would surely bring everyone to her bedroom as if she were in grave condition.

"Okay, but I don't want you running around downstairs. Let me do everything, all right?"

"All right," Jill agreed.

She stood up and they went back downstairs. It was as if she hadn't missed a beat as the family continued to laugh and converse. No one had realized she was gone, and she noticed that Orlando had arrived and was sitting with Monica. Grace had come as well, and was locked in what seemed to be an interesting conversation with Regina. Kyle gave Jill a knowing look. She nodded, then reluctantly went and found a seat on the sofa.

Kyle began passing out some of the pictures of their honeymoon. Jill was happy to narrate. The pictures didn't do Jamaica justice; still, everyone was talking about going on a trip to see the beautiful island.

Kyle put the DVD of their trip on and then dimmed the lights. As the family watched the television, beautiful scenes of Jamaica appeared on the screen. Kyle had filmed their beautiful honeymoon suite, as well as the picturesque view of the Caribbean Sea from their patio. A shot of Jill hamming it up for the camera was next. She acted silly and sexy for a moment, which brought laughter from the family. Then they began laughing even harder when she started making silly faces.

Ocho Rios was next, and there was more footage of Jill, but this time she was yelling for Kyle to come save her in the dolphin cove. She sat perched on a rock, and refused to walk toward him. Though Kyle

tried to coax her into walking over, she was telling him
that she wanted him to come and get her. The family
was filled with amusement, and Kyle finally walked
over and picked her up. Though you could no longer
see Jill's face, you could hear her voice, as Kyle kept
the camera going. Jill was playfully agitated by the fact
that Kyle hadn't rescued her sooner.

After watching the rest of the DVD, which contained the couple deep-sea fishing and snorkeling,
and footage of some of the tours they had taken of
the banana plantation. The movie ended and Kyle
turned on the lights. With the help of Monica, he ushered the family into the dining room for dinner.

Samuel said grace for the family and then they
began to feast on Monica's delicious meal. Her jambalaya sat in the center of the table, and was accompanied by a platter of crusty bread and salad.

As everyone ate, the conversation centered on Jill
and Kyle's trip to Jamaica. Amelia was full of questions,
as was Sharon, who complained loudly that she hadn't
been on a vacation since before Ally was born. Eric was
quick to tell her that he would take her somewhere
special soon.

Though everyone had filled their plates and began
to eat heartily, Jill only had a piece of bread on hers,
and she nibbled slowly on it.

"Jill, is something the matter?" Regina asked, noticing that Jill hadn't gotten any of the jambalaya.

"I'm fine," Jill murmured.

"Well, you should try to eat a little more than that,
or you won't keep up your strength," Kyle said.

"I'm fine, honey," Jill whispered, trying not to draw
any more attention to herself.

"He's right, darling. You had a long, hard day at
work, and you really need to eat."

"I know," Jill replied politely with a forced smile.

"We should have just canceled tonight," Kyle whispered to Jill.

"No, that wasn't necessary."

Trying to put on a good show, Jill used the serving spoon and put some of the jambalaya on her plate. Though she stirred it around on her plate, she didn't eat any of it, but continued to pick at the piece of bread.

When the meal had ended the men all went to play a few games of pool. Jill got up and started to clean the kitchen. As she set a stack of dishes in the sink, Regina approached her with a glass of water in one hand and took Jill by the other.

"Darling, I want you to sit down and take it easy," Regina said as she led Jill to a chair and made her sit down. "You cleaned before we arrived, I'm sure, so now let us take a turn. We'll have this place together in no time," Regina finished as she placed the glass of ice water in Jill's hand and with a loving wink turned and went to help the other women.

Under Regina's orders the women worked fast. Jill watched as Regina delegated chores. None of them, including Sharon, who didn't take kindly to anyone ordering her around, complained. In fact, they all seemed to look to Regina for leadership. Jill once again found herself admiring the way Regina carried herself. She seemed to command their love and respect, rather than demand it because of her status. She smiled as she took another sip of her water, and prayed that one day she would be just like her.

After the women had cleaned, they all went into the living room. Regina was the first one to grab her purse, and then she walked toward the den.

"Samuel, I think it's time that we left," Regina said.

"Right now, Regina? I need a little more time to win some of my money back from Orlando," he complained jokingly.

"That's what you say all the time. Come on, I think we need to let Jill and Kyle get some rest."

"Okay, baby doll," he said, putting his pool stick down, and vowing to win his money back next time.

Orlando waved good-bye, obviously thankful for his winnings. But it was only moments later that Monica said that they should be on their way as well, since they had to make a stop before they went home. When the game ended Eric, Sharon, and Ally left, and Amelia and Grace did too. Tony sat in the den and talked for a few minutes more, which gave Jill and Bebe a chance to talk alone.

"Jill, are you feeling well?" Bebe finally asked.

"No, I haven't been feeling too good for the past few days. My stomach has been a little upset, and I think I have a virus. More fluids and plenty of rest and I'll be good as new," Jill said.

"We should start on that right away then. I'm going to get you another glass of water," Bebe said. She went into the kitchen and returned moments later. "Why don't you go on upstairs to bed, Jill? You look exhausted. Tony shouldn't be much longer."

"Thanks, Bebe. I'd give you a hug, but I'm afraid that I might give you whatever it is that I have."

"Never mind the hug, it's the thought that counts," Bebe said, laughing.

"Good night," Jill said as she started up the stairs.

"I'll call you tomorrow and see how you're doing," Bebe called out after her.

"Okay."

Once in her bedroom Jill quickly undressed and changed into her nightgown. She washed her face and brushed her teeth and then got into bed. With a final sip of her water she turned out the lights and fell asleep.

The next morning when Jill awoke, Kyle lay next to her. He protectively cradled her close to his body, and she could feel his chest rise in deep, even breaths. She looked up into his handsome face and smiled as she remembered how blessed she was to have him as her husband.

But as she lay there, she became acutely aware of the nauseated feeling that began to come over her again. She gently crept out of bed and went into the bathroom. Jill threw several handfuls of cold water on her face and enjoyed the refreshing liquid on her skin, but still her stomach threatened to do somersaults.

She left the bathroom and walked back into the bedroom, where she slid on her robe and slippers and tiptoed out the door. She went downstairs and got herself a glass of orange juice from the kitchen and drank it, but soon after she was once again in the bathroom paying homage to the porcelain bowl. She stood up and looked at her weary reflection in the mirror, and as she turned around from washing her face she saw Kyle in the doorway.

They went into the living room and Kyle sat down with Jill.

"Hey, beautiful." He kissed her cheek. "Today I just want you to rest, and if you don't feel any better by Monday, I'm taking you in to see Dr. Tomlinson," he said sternly.

"Okay," Jill replied. "I'm really tired, honey. I thing I'll go back to bed."

"Sure." Kyle stood and helped Jill off the sofa and

walked her to the bottom of the stairs. "I'll make you a pot of chicken noodle soup later."

"Thanks," Jill said in a tired voice and started to climb the stairs. "If Bebe calls tell her I might not be in the office on Monday."

"Oh, believe me, I'll give her the message."

Jill climbed back into bed and fell asleep again. Several hours passed and Kyle checked on her a few times. She rested peacefully and Kyle didn't disturb her. But as five o'clock drew near, Jill awoke on her own. She came downstairs and found Kyle sitting quietly on the sofa watching television. From behind she slid her arms over his shoulders and across his chest, and then kissed his neck.

"Someone must be feeling better," he said as he turned his head and nuzzled her cheek.

"I don't know about all that, but I sure got plenty of rest. Why did you let me sleep so long?"

"Because you needed it. Are you hungry?"

"Yes."

"Sit down," he said as he stood and gently pulled her around the sofa. "I made your soup. I'll go and get you a bowl," he said and disappeared into the kitchen only to return shortly with a bowl.

Kyle sat back down next to Jill and she put her legs across his lap. He scooped up a spoonful of the soup and blew it until it cooled, and then he placed a spoonful in her mouth.

"Mmm, that's delicious," Jill said.

Kyle smiled. It was the first relaxed smile she had seen on him since he knew she wasn't feeling good.

In truth, Kyle was quite worried. He had had a stomach virus before, and it had only lasted a day. He could only hope that she would feel better today, and that nothing more serious was going on with her.

Jill had finished every last drop of the soup and was now rubbing her tummy thankfully.

"I feel much better," she told him.

"I thought you would," he said as he put the empty bowl on the coffee table.

"Do you think everyone enjoyed themselves last night?" she asked.

"I didn't hear any complaints, not that any of them would."

"Good, I didn't want to spoil anyone's evening."

"Babe, you didn't. The most important thing is your health. I still think we should have postponed the event."

"Kyle, I'm fine. I just need a little rest and some TLC," she said, stroking his arm.

The words brought a smile to Kyle's face. Jill moved her legs as Kyle grabbed the empty bowl from the table.

"You'll get plenty of that because I'm going to take care of you all weekend," Kyle said as he stood and walked into the kitchen.

He was gone only a few minutes, and when he returned Jill was asleep. He sat down on the sofa, and Jill's body was magnetically drawn to his. She snuggled against him and continued to sleep. Kyle wrapped an arm around her and then picked up the remote.

"I think you might have narcolepsy in addition to that virus, Jill," he said, smiling. He planted a tender kiss on her forehead and watched television.

As the weekend went on, Jill's condition didn't improve. Sunday only brought more of the same, as Jill continued to feel tired and ill. Kyle had told Bebe that Jill was sick, and that she wouldn't be in the office on Monday. Bebe understood, and told Kyle to tell Jill not to worry about a thing.

Monday morning found Jill and Kyle in the office of their family physician. The couple sat in the waiting room holding hands. Kyle kept the conversation upbeat, though he truly was fearing the worst. What exactly was the worst he didn't know, preferring not to give it a name. He prayed silently that God would give them the strength to handle whatever lay ahead; that he would bless him with the strength to see Jill through what was to come.

"Jillian Roberts," the nurse called out.

Though her voice was of normal volume, it seemed to shatter the serenity of the room. Jill stood and before Kyle released her hand, he kissed it.

"I'll be right here when you come out," he said softly.

Jill gave him a slight smile and turned to follow the nurse back to the exam rooms. She too was afraid, but refused to give in to the fear. She didn't know what was wrong with her but wouldn't let herself become a nervous wreck and make Kyle worry even more as well.

Kyle watched her until the door closed. Finally, he exhaled deeply. Rubbing his hand over his forehead, he stood and began to pace the waiting room. He eventually went outside and continued his pacing, but returned to the waiting room for fear Jill might come out soon. He watched *Accent Health* on television until he grew bored of the show. Kyle drank two cups of coffee and tried to read a magazine. Just when he thought he would jump out of his skin, the door leading back to the exam rooms opened, and the nurse asked him to follow her.

Kyle had expected Jill to return, and not for the nurse to ask him to come back. Everything told him that something was wrong, but his heart and mind refused to believe it. Squaring his shoulders, he resolved himself to be strong and supportive. He had to show Jill that nothing was going to happen that they couldn't handle together. Even though his own heart was trembling, he made up his mind that Jill wouldn't see his fear.

The nurse led him into Dr. Tomlinson's office where he found Jill sitting quietly in a chair. She wore a slight smile on her face, which Kyle had difficulty reading. At best, whatever was happening couldn't be too bad. Dr. Tomlinson stood and walked over to Kyle.

"Hey, Kyle, it's good to see you again," he said as she shook Kyle's hand.

"I don't know if I can say the same, Steve," Kyle replied nervously.

"I'm going to leave you two alone. I think your wife has something she wants to tell you," Dr. Tomlinson said and exited his office, closing the door behind him.

"Babe, what's going on?" Kyle asked as he sat down in the chair next to Jill's.

His eyes were filled with concern, and Jill couldn't help but smile. She did have something to tell him, and the news would change both of their lives forever. They had only begun their married lives together, and hadn't really had a chance to enjoy one another well. Now she was about to tell Kyle that he was going to be a father. Her heart told her that he would be as happy as she was, but her mind said that he would have wished they could put off having children for a while.

Kyle was so busy with the ranch. She too hadn't factored in children this early in their marriage. Desert Star had been taking so much of her time that she and

Bebe had to make Monica a junior partner, which forced them to hire a new secretary. What had started out as a two-woman operation had grown into four. With their firm's clientele growing at such a rapid pace, Jill didn't know how they would manage without her in the office. Now she feared having to leave for even a longer period of time than her wedding and honeymoon had required. Still she was happy and had to believe that everything would fall into place, since life really had no choice.

"Jill," Kyle said, breaking her train of thought, "tell me what Dr. Tomlinson had to say. Whatever it is we will handle it together."

Kyle's words were low and sincere, and he took Jill's hands in his own. She felt the warmth of his touch, and the strength of his hands made her realize that everything would be okay for them.

"I'm glad you feel that way because . . ." she started saying with a small smile and a trembling voice. "Because you're going to be a father," she finished.

For a moment Kyle sat in stunned silence. His eyes never left Jill's, but it took time for the information she had just delivered to register. Slowly a broad smile formed on his gorgeous face and his eyes twinkled like she'd never seen before.

"Whoa, babe, please tell me you're not kidding?" Kyle said, obviously thrilled with the news.

"No, I'm not kidding," Jill told him as a tear escaped.

Kyle stood, pulling Jill up to stand as well. He took her in his arms and held her as if he never wanted to let her go. Kyle kissed her tears away, and Jill smiled at his joy.

"I though you might be a little upset over the timing," she said.

"How could I be upset? We haven't been exactly

using protection on a regular basis. Besides, I can't think of anything that would make me happier than the news you just gave me." As his smile faded, the look of concern that he had worn since Saturday reappeared. "Jill, I was so scared that whatever was going on with you was something bad. I can't imagine a life without you."

"And you won't have to," she told him as she gently put a finger against his lips to silence him.

"So, what you've been experiencing is morning sickness, huh?" Kyle said as the smile returned.

"Yes, that's all it is."

"Well, do you know how long it will last? Because I don't know how long I can handle it," he said playfully.

"Oh, now, mister, you said that whatever was going on with me, we would handle it together, and I'm going to hold you to that."

"Okay, okay, as long as the end result is a little girl who looks just like her mama," Kyle said as he lovingly rubbed Jill's abdomen.

Jill didn't make a request verbally, but wished that the child would be just as handsome, smart, and charming as its father.

The couple finally left the doctor's office and headed home. There would be plenty of time to tell all their family and friends their good news. Tonight was a private celebration. Kyle toasted Jill with champagne, and in between trips to the bathroom, she sipped her water.

Grand Arrival

Outside on the deck Jill reclined on a lounge chair. With her feet propped up on a pillow and a tall glass of lemonade next to her on the table, she relaxed and looked up at the cloudless blue sky. In the distance she could see the trees dancing in the breeze. Her smile was one of contentment as all was well with her and Kyle. Desert Star was in the excellent hands of Bebe and Monica, and the baby inside her was due any day now.

A trip to the hospital a couple of days ago proved to be a false alarm. The contractions she had been experiencing were only Braxton-Hicks, and now her abdomen tightened again and relaxed a few moments later. Believing that nothing much was going on now either, she rubbed her swollen abdomen and continued to think about her life. Just a few short years ago she was lonely and looking for love. Now she had a husband, a new home, a thriving business, and a baby on the way.

Though she and Kyle knew the sex of the baby, they didn't share their secret with anyone, preferring to let it be a surprise. Not knowing if the baby was a boy or a girl almost drove Maddie and Regina insane. Both women already had grandchildren, but still treated this birth as if they were expecting their first.

Jill had gotten the baby's nursery ready, and was thankful for all the wonderful gifts she had received at her baby shower. She knew that her mom and Barbie would be in attendance, but Jill was truly surprised to see Diane and Lois.

Her old coworkers had stayed for the whole week, and the three had a wonderful time during their visit. They had gone sightseeing and to dinner almost every night, which made Jill reminisce about their days together in New York. When Diane and Lois left for home, Jill was sorry to see them go, but they promised to come and visit again soon.

Having finished her drink, Jill stood to go inside the kitchen and get herself some water. Just as she did the phone rang and she went to answer it.

"Hello."

"Hi, Jill, how are you feeling?" Bebe asked.

"Fat. No, change that, very fat," she said, holding her belly.

"You know you've been eating for two."

"Don't remind me," Jill said, laughing. "How are things there?"

"We're doing fine, but you shouldn't be thinking about work. You have to concentrate on bringing my healthy niece into the world."

"And what makes you so sure it's a girl?"

"Women know these things. I just feel like you're carrying a girl. Besides, Mom thinks so too. She says that women who are carrying a female usually eat a lot of spicy foods during the last month of their pregnancy."

"How would she know? She had all boys," Jill said, laughing.

"I don't know, but that's what she said."

"Okay," Jill said wryly.

"Hey, are you up for some company tonight?"

"Sure, what time will you be here?"

"About six. Is that okay?"

"That's fine. Hey, why don't you stop and pick us up a pizza with extra jalapeño peppers?"

"Sure, I will," Bebe said slowly, noting Jill's request for something spicy to eat.

"I'll see you later, Bebe," Jill said, giggling.

Jill's appetite had grown just as much as her girth. Kyle loving teased her about having to protect his plate. The joke had stemmed from her finishing her meal but still being hungry and helping him with his.

She hung up the phone and walked over to the refrigerator. She poured herself a glass of cold water and grabbed the bag of potato chips as she headed back outside. Before she even got through the doorway she quickly set the glass down but dropped the bag of chips. The contraction she was having was strong and painful and seemed to last longer than the one before. Bent over slightly, she held on to the wall and waited for the pain to pass.

When it did, a thin film of perspiration coated her forehead. Still holding on to the wall, she walked slowly to the kitchen table and sat down. Jill waited for a while but didn't have another one. She picked up her glass and took a sip. Feeling better she began to head outside again, but the next contraction came and was just as powerful as the first. She dropped the glass and it shattered at her feet. Jill leaned against the wall holding her hard stomach. This was different and Jill decided that she should time the contractions just like the nurse had shown her.

Stepping around the broken glass carefully, she

picked up the phone and carried it with her into the living room. Jill lay down on the sofa and before closing her eyes noted the time. She had only had them closed for a little while when her belly started to tighten again. She looked at the clock and saw that ten minutes had passed. She timed herself again and in ten minutes time she had another painful contraction.

Jill picked up the phone and dialed Kyle's cell phone number. On the first ring he answered, and she was glad to hear his voice.

"Hey, babe, what's going on?" he said, giving her only half of his attention.

"Hi, honey, I think it's time," Jill said.

"Jill, are you sure? I mean we were just at the hospital three days ago and it was a false alarm," Kyle said as he continued to work.

"I know, but I think this is the real thing. The contractions are more frequent and regular."

"Do you want me to come home right now?"

"Y-E-S!" Jill said as the next contraction peaked.

"Okay, I'm on my way," Kyle said after recovering his cell phone that he almost dropped. "Hold on, babe, I'll be home in a few minutes."

Jill hung up and tried to relax and breathe. She continued to time her contractions, and they were still coming with regularity. She felt an intense urge to go to the bathroom, but was afraid to move from the sofa. After the next contraction, she felt a gush of water between her legs and instantly knew that this time when she arrived at the hospital she would be leaving with a baby in her arms.

When Kyle arrived he saw that Jill's water had broken and that he had to get her to the hospital as quickly as possible. Though he had helped bring many horses into the world, he really didn't think he could do the job of delivering a baby. He grabbed her hospital bag from the hall closet and then helped Jill into the vehicle.

"How do you feel, baby?" Kyle asked sympathetically.

"How do you think I feel?" Jill said in agitation.

"I know this is rough, but I'll have you at the hospital in no time. Just sit back and try to relax," he said as he put Jill's seat belt on.

Irritated and anxious, Jill didn't answer, but continued to concentrate on the breathing technique she had learned in birthing class. She focused on herself and blocked out everything and everyone else.

Kyle didn't take offense at Jill's behavior. He had accompanied her to all the classes, and knew just what to expect. He knew his job was to be supportive in any way possible, and right now he was doing just that.

When they arrived at the hospital Kyle pulled in front of the door of the maternity wing. After putting the vehicle in park he jumped out and ran inside. He returned shortly with a wheelchair and assisted Jill into it. Then he pushed her inside where a nurse took over.

"I'll see you in a few minutes, babe," Kyle said as he kissed her.

The nurse rolled Jill back to a labor room and Kyle was told it would be a bit before he could see her. He used the time to call the family. He reached his mother on her cell phone. She had been out with friends and probably would arrive as fast as her lead foot could get her here.

Next he called Maddie, who had been in town for the past two weeks, but opted to stay at A Special Place. The original plans had been for her to stay at the cabin, but Maddie wanted to give Jill and Kyle some privacy. She did come out to visit them every day, and was probably getting ready to go over to the cabin right now. Kyle was glad that he had caught her before she had left her room, since he had left Maddie's cell phone number on the refrigerator.

Maddie was excited, and Kyle told her that he would make arrangements to have Tony bring her to the hospital. He called his brother, and Tony said he would have her there shortly.

"Mr. Roberts, we're ready for you now," the nurse said.

Kyle took a deep breath and followed the nurse. He was ushered into Jill's room and quickly went to her side. He stood quietly for a second and held her hand, and was careful not to bump her IV. The monitors were beeping as they read the mother's and baby's heartbeats. Another machine recorded Jill's contractions. Kyle couldn't remember their names, though he had been told them when they took a tour of the hospital. But names didn't matter now as long as Jill and the baby were fine.

He looked down and saw before him the most beautiful women he had ever laid eyes on. Though she complained about being fat, and was quite unhappy about not being able to fit into her tiny size 6 clothes anymore, he only saw beauty with every pound she gained. Jill was strong, smart, and funny—everything he needed and wanted in a woman.

"I love you." He mouthed the words inaudibly.

"I love you, too," she replied.

Regina and Maddie arrived at the hospital. Both women had wanted to be in the delivery room for the birth of their grandbaby, but though Kyle and Jill wanted them near, they wanted to share the delivery of their first child only with each other.

Jill pushed and panted for another hour, and Kyle stood by coaching every step of the way. He took a towel and dampened it with cool water, and then placed it on her forehead. He cheered her on as her strength ebbed. Most of Jill's labor had taken place at home, but she had two more hours of hard labor.

Dr. Bryant, Jill's obstetrician, summoned Kyle to the foot of the bed where he could see the head of the baby coming out. Kyle continued to encourage Jill to push, and with a few more tries the baby's head was out. The doctor quickly suctioned its mouth. Jill moaned and panted as she labored, and with the next couple of pushes she finally brought a precious new baby into the world.

"Oh, Jill, I've never seen anything more incredible in all my life. He's perfect," Kyle said in a voice mixed with pride and awe.

Dr. Bryant let Kyle cut the umbilical cord, and then the nurse whisked the baby away. As the doctor continued to work on Jill, Kyle returned to the head of the bed, where Jill was smiling brightly. He leaned over and kissed her tenderly.

"Thank you," he whispered in her ear.

"You're welcome," she replied as she reached up and placed her hand behind his head. Jill pulled Kyle toward her until his lips touched hers. She gave him a tender kiss before releasing him.

"And thank you," she said.

"For what?"

"For making all my dreams come true."

The nurse returned and handed the baby to Jill and for the first time she looked into the face of the person who was responsible for making her have late-night cravings for chocolate cake and pizza with extra jalapeño peppers.

"Hello, handsome," she said as she kissed her baby tenderly on the cheek. He's gorgeous, isn't he, Kyle?

"Yes, you do good work," Kyle said admiringly.

"You gave birth to a big boy, Mrs. Roberts," the nurse said. "He weighs nine pounds and eight ounces."

"No wonder you ate so much, you had to," Kyle said in astonishment.

"I guess I did," Jill replied.

"Mr. Roberts, would you like to take the baby out to see your family? You have two very anxious grandmothers in the waiting room," the nurse said, smiling.

"Of course. Jill, do you want me to tell them the name we picked, or do you want to have the honors?"

"I think you better. We already kept them in suspense long enough over the sex. If they don't get a name they'll explode."

"I'll be right back," Kyle said, and with a final kiss on Jill's forehead he left the labor and delivery room.

As soon as he appeared in the waiting room, Kyle was immediately surrounded by Regina and Maddie. Both women stood and admired their newest grandchild. Kyle told them how much the baby weighed, and at what time he came into the world.

"Does he have a name?" Regina asked.

"Yes, Mom, he does. Which one of you would like to hold Kyle Alonzo Roberts Jr.?" he said proudly.

"Oh, Regina, it's a boy!" Maddie exclaimed.

Maddie held out her arms and took the baby. With the nurse standing close by, Kyle left the two grandmothers to admire Kyle Jr. as he went back to see Jill.

Dr. Bryant had finished working on Jill, and though the IV still remained, the monitors that had been attached to her abdomen had been removed.

"Need I ask what they thought of him?" Jill asked, beaming.

"I think it's safe to say that they fell in love with him

the moment they saw him," Kyle told her. "How do you feel?" he asked as he rubbed her shoulder.

"I feel skinny?" Jill joked as she rested her hand on her tummy.

Kyle stayed at the hospital for the day, and through the course of it, many of their other family members and friends came to see Jill and the baby. All admired the handsome newborn, who looked just like his father.

Two days later Jill was home and enjoying her son. Her mother had gone back to Pittsburgh, but promised to come back in a couple of months. Maddie called every night to see how Jill was doing, as well as inquire about the newest love in her life.

Kyle was at work, but as soon as he returned home his evenings were filled with getting to know his son. He delighted in changing the baby, and watched in awe as Jill breast-fed their growing son.

Jill had been sitting on the patio enjoying the warmth of the sun on her skin. She kept the baby near her yet out of the sunlight and covered. He was a lot like his mother and seemed to enjoy being outside under the unyielding Colorado sky.

Kyle came home and went out to the patio to see his family. He greeted Jill warmly with a kiss on the lips, and gave her a single white rose. Jill smiled as she remembered the roses he had sent her at her mother's house a few years before. She put the fragrant flower to her nose and inhaled, letting the aromatic scent fill her lungs.

"Hey, beautiful," he said.

"Hello, handsome," she replied.

Kyle walked over to his son and smiled at the

slumbering baby. He wanted so much to pick up the
infant, but decided to let the child rest undisturbed.

"I'm going to go upstairs and take a shower. Can I
get you anything, babe?"

"Oh, ask me that question in six weeks. There will
be plenty you can give me them," Jill said saucily.

"Be careful, Mrs. Roberts. I'm already struggling
with keeping myself in check every time I'm near
you," Kyle said as he stroked her hair. He kissed her
again and then went inside.

Jill smiled to herself and was thankful for all the
blessings she had received. She stood up when Kyle
Jr. started to cry. She picked up the baby and went
back into the house. Jill went upstairs and into the
bedroom. The sun cast a golden glow on walls, which
made the room feel warm and cozy.

She propped herself up in bed and undid her
gown. The baby quickly turned its head toward the
offered breast and began to nurse. Jill had never felt
so complete, so whole. As she continued to nurse, Kyle
finished his shower and entered the bedroom. He
smiled at seeing his wife and child.

"Are you happy?" he asked.

"Of course I am. Why do you ask?"

"I just thought you might miss being at Desert Star,"
he said as he sat down on the other side of the bed.

"I do, but I wouldn't have changed a thing. I love
being your wife, and I love our son. Don't you see,
baby? God led me to you. I have a husband, a child,
and Desert Star. I have nothing to regret, and I have
everything I ever dreamed of."

"I love, you," he whispered.

Then the couple sat quietly and watched as their son
nursed. Finally, all the things Jill's heart had longed
for belonged to her. She had a growing business, a

beautiful baby boy, and the handsome cowboy who made it all possible. And just like the beautiful desert flower she had named her business after, her strong sturdy little family would support each other and thrive in the face of adversity, just like the Desert Star.

Dear Reader,

Wow! What a wonderful and exciting literary ride we've taken together! I would like to express my gratitude to all the fans of my work who have kept in touch via e-mail and at my book signings. I am so thrilled that you all enjoyed my debut novel, *A Special Place*, so much that you asked for another story that revolved around the original characters. *Desert Star* is for you.

It's my belief that if you are going to write to entertain, you have a responsibility to your readers to evoke a laugh, a tear, a remembrance, or just simply make the reader stop and think about love and life. My goal was to make you feel as though you are living the moment with my characters, that you have traveled through time and arrived in another place. I wanted to whisk you away, if only for a day, to where your dreams take form in the shape of your heart's desires.

Most of you who keep in touch with me via e-mail already know that I'm almost finished working on my third novel, which is titled *The Journal*. This story takes place in Florida, and the characters are filled with hope for love, desire, and commitment. I'm sure you will enjoy *The Journal* just as much as my other books.

Please stay in touch as I love hearing from you. My e-mail is: carringtonbooks@yahoo.com.

Happy reading,

Kim Carrington

SIZZLING ROMANCE BY
Rochelle Alers

__HIDEAWAY	1-58314-179-0	$5.99US/$7.99CAN
__PRIVATE PASSIONS	1-58314-151-0	$5.99US/$7.99CAN
__JUST BEFORE DAWN	1-58314-103-0	$5.99US/$7.99CAN
__HARVEST MOON	1-58314-056-5	$4.99US/$6.99CAN
__SUMMER MAGIC	1-58314-012-3	$4.99US/$6.50CAN
__HAPPILY EVER AFTER	0-7860-0064-3	$4.99US/$6.99CAN
__HEAVEN SENT	0-7860-0530-0	$4.99US/$6.50CAN
__HOMECOMING	1-58314-271-1	$6.99US/$9.99CAN
__RENEGADE	1-58314-272-X	$6.99US/$9.99CAN
__NO COMPROMISE	1-58314-270-3	$6.99US/$9.99CAN
__VOWS	0-7860-0463-0	$4.99US/$6.50CAN

Available Wherever Books Are Sold!

Visit our website at **www.arabesque.com**.